I0561088

Copyright 2018 Meg Castro

ISBN 9780998651811

Published by: Bohlander House Press, Dover, NJ, USA

Www.bohlanderhousepress.com

This book is dedicated: To my family, especially my son, who has to deal with an author as a mom. Sorry, Mr. Dude.

Chapter One

Kelly was going to kill her roommate if she survived the living hell she walked into earlier tonight.

Pausing to catch her breath behind a hay bale, Kelly listened for her attacker. He too had stopped listening to where she had run off too. She tried to quiet her breathing so not to give her location away. Kelly was a were-tiger and with the full moon just a few nights ago her heightened senses allowed her to make out the large farmhouse a few hundred yards away. She just had to get through the corn field without alerting her attacker. This is why she did not go to parties; you never knew what whack jobs you'd meet.

Kelly brushed a sweaty blonde strand out of her face, scanning the field she picked out a path that she could take. She couldn't risk transforming; she had yet to master the art of transforming while running. She never thought she would need to learn that skill, oh irony. Kelly picked up on movement, he had started to go off to the left, and she took some handfuls of dirt and threw them in three different directions, then bolted for another section of the corn field. The farmhouse was getting closer as she sprinted with the speed of a tiger, then an arm grabbed her waist and pulled her into a hard chest.

Light colored eyes looked down at her, taking in the sweaty and dirty face in front of him. Her outfit was ripped and at some point she had kicked off her sandals. When she went to scream, he picked her up by the throat and shook his head, then threw her into a pile of logs. He was counting on her reflexes; she landed in a crouch position and took off. She started to summon up her strength and tried to call forth her animal.

Kelly felt the initial pull of fur pushing through; suddenly she felt a fire go through her shoulder. She smelled silver in the air as she crashed down to the ground. He stood over her laughing quietly. Kelly closed her eyes and began praying to whatever deity she could think of. And then it all went black.

She awoke some time later chained to a stone wall. After testing the restraints she realized they too were made of silver. Fuckers knew she was a were-animal. Trying to look around she saw a bandage had been placed on her arm. There was talking in the hallway.

Two men walked in, one was the bald man she had met up with at the party. Then there was a new guy she didn't recognize, he had dirty blonde hair and deep blue eyes. He also had a black bag hanging on his shoulder. He set it down on the floor and began searching through its contents.

"I see you are up," her captor said to her. "My associate tells me that he had some difficulty acquiring you."

Kelly didn't respond. She would not give him the satisfaction or pleasure of hearing her beg for her life or hear her scream. She knew she was going to die, so she would do it her way and not give him any satisfaction.

"Ah the strong silent type," he observed. "I prefer those, they're more fun to break." He ran a hand down her face which she turned away.

Both men pulled on their black leather gloves, as not to leave any prints or get any silver on their skin. The one who had abducted her slowly pierced the vial with the needle and began to pull the slivery liquid into the needle. When he was done, he took a towel and wiped the tip of the needle.

Carefully he handed it to the blonde man. It dawned on her as to what the contents of the bottle were and fear began to spread through her. Silver in general was not fatal to a were-animal; it made the wound difficult to treat and took a long time to heal. But if liquid silver was directly injected into the blood- stream or organ then that's what made it lethal.

The leader of the two prepared the needle and looked at Kelly while he did. "I have been told that this is rather pain- less," he informed her.

Kelly had heard otherwise, she refused to show fear so she just stared at him with no expression. He slapped her across the face, when not even a tear sparkled in her eyes he let out a frustrated scream. With one hand he tore her shirt down the middle and ripped her bra off. Testing the needle, he smiled at her. Kelly realized he was going for the heart, she began to struggle. With one hand he made her still. He jabbed the needle into her and injected the silver. Her scream bounced throughout the cavern.

"I guessed they're wrong," he said when the body stopped convulsing.

****

Joe Arnold woke up before the sun rose on the Fourth of July. He wanted to get an earlier start than usual; it was his year to host the annual Farmers Fourth of July Party. The weatherman predicted it was going to be a hot day in New Jersey. His daughter's boyfriend had texted him late last night letting him know the local teens had a party at one of the overgrown fields down the road. Usually, when there was a party the drinks and the druggies liked to pass out in his field at the end of the night. When this happened he would wake them up, bring them back to the house get food and water into them, and arrange for them to get home.

Being quiet so he did not wake his wife, he left their bedroom and walked downstairs. He ate a quick breakfast and filled his thermos with iced coffee then left the house for the day. One of the dogs was awake and decided to come with him. They began their stroll along the fence that lined his property on the old dirt road. No beer cans or passed out bodies yet, he thought, which was a good sign his fields were empty. His dog tensed up and let out a low growl. Joe looked around; he saw it, the naked body laid out in an odd angle. For a moment he stood frozen in his tracts.

He had fought in the first Iraq war and seen his share of death. But something about the way the woman laid sent chills up his spine. He approached closer and his dog growled. Joe saw the body was that of a young woman who was very much dead. Wanting to get away from the body he hurried back the house and called the cops.

Within an hour the area was swarming with activity. Captain Anthony White got out of the car, coffee in hand. Tony, as he was known, was around 5'10 and still in shape. He was heading close to sixty and was determined to be in as good a shape as he was when he was thirty. His blue eyes still sparkled but his brown hair was now gray and silver. He had lived in Grabenberg, NJ all his life; his two kids went to school in the town and his wife worked at the local elementary school. He met one of the officers who were first on the scene.

Chris Washington had gone soft around the middle and had an attitude that was infamous. He had once been a varsity football star but never made it through college, a fact he was still bitter about. He stood about the same height as Tony, but kept his hair in a crew cut. Tony was not a fan of his, for Chris was narrow-minded, opinionated, and short tempered.

"Hey Chris what do we have?" Tony asked sipping his coffee. He stepped under the yellow tape.

"Farmer was checking on the fields, there had been a party at one of the abandoned fields down the road. He got around the bend and saw the body lying in the grass. Ran to the house and called us." Chris told him as they walked to the crime scene. Part of him wanted to laugh over the fact that a war veteran run running like a school girl at the sight of the body. He also knew that action would get him written up by Tony.

"She was in her early 20's. There's a bullet wound in the shoulder, evidence that body has been beaten and cleaned," Chris continued telling him.

Tony nodded and walked to where the forensic team had started to set up. They had been called in from the Sheriff 's office in Morris County. Tony looked at the body and felt his stomach turn. The woman had been brutalized. Her head laid at odd an angle indicating her neck was broken. There was a wound in her right shoulder that had produced a lot of blood. A cross was carved into the stomach of the victim. Sara Cliver, the medical examiner, walked over to him.

"What can you tell me kiddo?" Tony asked her.

"Broken neck occurred after death, bullet wound before death," Sara began as she rolled her shoulders. "As for time and cause I need to get her back to my lab."

"We can arrange that," Tony replied. "Anything else?"

"You're going to want to call Al," she told Tony.

She had been in court earlier in the day, her coveralls covered her suit. Her heals were replaced with converse. And to deal with the heat, Sara pulled her hair up. When Tony called her she had been able to leave the court house not having to stay for further questioning.

"Why is that?"

"One, she's from my pack and two, I think it's linked to the others since a note was left."

There had been other murders in the area, each one a different type of paranormal, each death more gruesome. "My intern found it when they went to throw up," she replied handing him the envelope. He recognized the handwriting.

He stared at the envelope. "I'll give him a ring when I get a better idea of what's going on."

Tony spent an hour with Sara going over the state of the body and the different wounds. When done with that he walked over to where a pile of women's clothes lay. The clothes showed there was a struggle, there was dirt on the jeans, the shirt and bra both had been ripped open. Sara's intern was taking fiber samples from the clothes and soil samples. There were reddish colored stains on the clothes, but that was it. There was no blood anywhere, if there were any foot prints and tire prints they were brushed away.

After taking a look around the scene he talked to the Sheriff's office to fill them in on the body. The body count was now up to five. Ending the call he scrolled through the limited numbers in his cell and hit call when he found the right one.

"Hi Al, its Tony," Tony responded when his old buddy Al answered.

Alfred Moore was head of OPIA, Occult and Paranormal Investigation Agency, which also had him running the northeast branch currently out of NYC.

"What's up Captain?" Al asked his buddy. He was in the middle of working in one of

OPIA's many labs that were stretched out across New York City.

The Occult and Paranormal Investigation Agency had branches throughout Europe and North America. The UN wanted to create international laws that would protect and also establish a judicial process dealing with all things that went bump in the night.   It then expected each country that was a member of the UN to create their own laws at home that went along with the international set. In doing so they created an agency that held the same power as the FBI, CIA, Scotland Yard, and Interpol. Their sole purpose was to deal with things that went bump in the night and included those who hunted those protected by the Occult and Paranormal Laws.

"We got another one up here. I need an expert now."

Al motioned to one of the agents in the room that he would be outside. Al ran a hand over his bald head. "Why? We're running a little thin at the moment."

"Yeah well things are getting worse here," Tony replied impatiently.

"Another body?" Al asked holding back the groan. The amount of cases that got dropped on him recently was staggering.

"Yes, can you send anyone?"

"I'm got to be honest with you," Al started. "I got a delegation of vampires missing in the Midwest, which we are working with the Vampire Council on, we have the UN summit, plus moving to our new location in Newark. All my experts are out."

"Al, another note was left."

There was silence at the other end. Then Al let out a long sigh, "You know I'm going to have to call her and talk her into this?"

"I know."

"Which means calling Dietrich for the fifth time today to inform him that I will be getting his surrogate daughter involved in this."

"I know, Al," Tony repeated. "I can call him if you want."

"The way today is going I might as well do it," Al replied. They said good bye and hung up. What was going on in Grabenberg, NJ could be connected to the other issues that had been arising over the last few months. Al had one choice in who to send and Tony knew that. The only problem was not just convincing her but convincing the Vampire Council she would not be in danger. Some days he really hated his job.

Chapter Two

It was about two in the morning in
Germany. In the northern Rhine valley about
an hour north of Köln sat a small walled town,
it was one of the last walled towns in Germany.
Rarely did tourist venture to the small
mountain village. The villagers liked their
solitude, their peace and qui- et. Their secrets
could be kept and protected here.

Kirsa Heinrich stood on the old battlements
of the wall and looked into the dense forest
before her. On three sides of the walls were
fields that were farmed, two faced the woods
and the other was the main entrance forming a
pentagon. The walls completely encircled the
main town of about 1500 people; there were

farmers that lived outside of the wall.

The castle was found on the forest end of the town where it stood between the two forest gates. From the castle you could get on to the battlements through archways that could be closed if there was war. The castle and village had belonged to her family since the 700's. Her family was unique; it was one of the few mortal line's that was under full protection of the Vampire Council. It had been since the death of an ancestor in 1000 C.E. Because of the protection, her family housed and kept safe priceless artifacts and documents that belonged to the six lines.

In the 1700's her family left for the New World, leaving the estate in the hands of a family friend named Wyrm. He watched the estate until Kirsa returned to live in solitude for the last two years. What had hunted her family in Germany had found them in the New World, instead of fleeing again her ancestor chose to stay.

Now Kirsa and her cousin were back living in the manor. Adam, her cousin, and she had both lost their parents about five years prior. A year ago, Adam and his wife relocated to Germany with their son Matthew. Six months after their arrival her niece, Adala, was born. Kirsa and Adam sought refuge and protection here in the village of Geheimestadt.

To keep both of them occupied they had begun modernizing the estate while leaving its history intact. They had made the first floor to look like it would have during the medieval era. There was the ballroom, banquet hall, throne room, library, parlor and then an example of the lord and la- dies room, even a servant's quarter. They had installed a commercial kitchen on the first floor. In the basement they redid the wine cellar, dungeon and armory.

They were thinking of opening it up for tours and local functions. The upper floors were strictly for the family. The second floor housed the family kitchen and dining room, a living room, small library, and game room. The third and fourth floors were the family suites with the fifth floor being strictly for guests. Renovations were still a long way from being done, but it was livable with modern conveniences.

Godsmack played through her iPod as Kirsa leaned against the old smooth stone, tarot cards laid on the small wooden outdoor table next to her. She had pulled her unruly curly hair into a short pony tail. The hood of her sweatshirt was up protecting her from the cool wind, she wore flannel pajama pants and flip flops showcasing her black toenails. Curled up next to her was her black greyhound Zero, who was snoring in his sleep.

Kirsa turned her head when she heard a noise behind her. Adam, who had the same pale skin and dark hair as her, walked out holding his daughter whom was bundled in a pink blanket. He walked over to join her by the wall of the battements. She paused her music and took the ear phones out of her ears.

"The angel couldn't sleep?" Kirsa asked Adam. For the past few nights, Adala had been fussy. Kirsa helped with staying up with her so that Adam and Anne could get sleep.

"Nope. She woke up an hour ago. I gave up on rocking her. When I saw you out here, I figured I would interrupt your brooding."

Adam yawned and wondered if he would ever get a full night sleep. If Adala wasn't awake then it was Matthew who would come into their chambers to sleep with them.

Kirsa slanted her almost black eyes at him. "I am not brooding I am thinking deeply."

"Uh huh," Adam replied resting his back against the stone wall. He noticed the tarot cards, "I take it the reading didn't help with the mood?"

"The gods are laughing at me is what I have decided," Kirsa rested her chin on her arms.

His bright blue eyes narrowed as he studied her face. They were both only children and were close in age. Often they were mistaken for siblings rather than cousins, since they had the same coloring. Being both only children, they were the closest thing each other had to siblings.

"What were you thinking so deeply about?" he asked repositioning his daughter in his arms.

"I'm thinking of going back home," she said.

She saw the surprise flash in his eyes. For the past few years she had been trying to find her place. With Adam and his family here, she saw that this was where they belonged. She had yet to find hers.

"To New Jersey?" he asked. She had also lived in Georgetown and New York City prior to coming to Germany.

"Grabenberg, the family estate."

Adam adjusted Adala in his arms. "That's surprising, what brought this on?"

"Redoing the estate here has me wanting to rebuild back in Jersey," Kirsa said. "There is nothing left of my home there, except for the guesthouse."

"What are you going to do while there?"

She took a deep breath. "See if maybe I could work on a case here and there."

Adam said nothing just raised an eyebrow and studied her. Kirsa had been a top OPIA agent; she was one of the few that held an international license. What was even more amazing was she had done this by the age of twenty-three. Then shortly before her twenty-sixth birthday, she walked away from it all.

"I miss the work, I miss the thrill of solving the case," she held up a hand so he couldn't cut in. "I also remember the negatives that came with it. And by going back to the states I would lose the privacy I have here."

"It would also act as a statement that you are not hiding, but going back to face the past," Adam finished. He understood her and her reasons. That didn't mean he had to like them.

"Exactly."

Before Adam could say anything else, Kirsa's cell phone went off. When she saw the number she raised an eyebrow.

"Who is it?" Adam asked.

"OPIA," Kirsa said as she flipped open her phone. "Yes Alfred," Kirsa said, as she answered the phone.

"I can tell I didn't wake you," her former

boss said on the other line. "I was worried you would be asleep."

"You know me, I'm a night owl. So to what do I owe the pleasure of this call?"

It had been a few months since she had last talked to Alfred. He and Kirsa were the only two east coast agents that were also international agents. About a month ago he had stopped pleading with her to come back to work, which some part of her thought was odd.

Al never gave up when he wanted something; he was relentless and waited for the other person to cave. When she had submit- ted the paper work to take a permanent leave of absence she thought he was going to have a coronary. At the same time he understood why. Three years prior to her leaving she had lost her parents, then her Aunt and Uncle.

"I need to pick your brain," Al told her.

Kirsa leaned against the wall as Adam walked up and down the walkway, "Then pick away. What's up?"

"I need someone to help connect the dots," he explained. "A group of radicals has been targeting the northeast United States for about the past six months. We have been following the cases closely. I got a call today about another one, yet the some of the information has me scratching my head."

"What about?" Kirsa asked. Radical religious groups always piqued her interest, a weakness that Al was well aware of.

"Well to begin with the previous bodies have all been posed, where this last body was found by a farmer dumped in his fields. I'm thinking the killer ran out of time or wanted to throw us off."

"Al, how many bodies are there?" Kirsa asked raising an eyebrow. Out of the corner of her eyes she saw Adam stop and turn to watch her.

"This one makes five, the bodies have all been connected to the same group."

"How can you tell?"

"Similar clues found at all the scenes."

"What about this one that has you confused?" Kirsa wish she had a pen and paper so she could be taking notes. Al- ready her brain was starting to formulate ideas.

"Two things, really. The first is, unlike the other four bodies, this one has a set of bite marks that are not near any major artery."

"Clean or messy?" Kirsa asked examining the paint behind her nails. They had finished painting the main dining hall earlier in the day and even after a long soak in the shower she was still finding spots on her that had paint on.

"Clean." Alfred said as he turned in his chair at his office in New York City.

"Not a vampire bite. Come on Al, really? You needed my advice on that?" Kirsa asked him.

"No I could figure that one out on my own. It's the second part, notes have been left and this one was different."

Kirsa tensed up. "How and what kind of notes?"

Adam shot her a look. He knew what or who could be behind the killing just by hearing the word 'note'. It was one of the reasons they both had fled to Germany to live in their family ancestral home. Here they could hide, back in the states they were tabloid stories.

"The other four have been more on a biblical side. This one is more of a mission statement." Alfred told her. He knew the less he told her the more she would want to know.

Kirsa was silent. Then she inquired "Were there any markings on them?"

"A sun and cross."

"Where?" Kirsa asked closing her eyes.

"They have been centered on the east coast, the northern part this time."

"You said that already, damn it. Which state? Massachusetts, Vermont, Maine?" Kirsa asked impatiently. He was avoiding answering her question, which was never a good sign.

There was a long sigh. Al knew at some point during the conversation he was going to have to tell Kirsa the location. That was the part he feared. Even though he knew he needed her on the case he also wanted her safe and protected from all this.

Al spoke "Grabenberg, New Jersey."

Kirsa hung up on Alfred. Adam stared at her when he saw her close the phone.

"What's wrong?" he asked, following her back into their home.

"They're in Grabenberg," she said heading towards her room. The fear was clear in her voice. "In the morning talk to Wyrm about increasing security here. I will call you when I land."

"Kirs, you're not seriously thinking about going back there?" he asked as he watched her grab her suitcases out of a giant wardrobe.

She looked at her cousin who was more like a brother to her. "What else can I do?"

Kirsa began to fill the suitcase with her clothes. Adam watched her and then laid Adala down on the bed. He walked over to Kirsa and laid a hand on her shoulder, she looked up at him.

"I'll make the calls to get you ready to leave a.s.a.p.," he told her. He kissed her cheek and picked up Adala again.

Kirsa watched her only remaining family leave the room. She would be leaving him and his family behind to face her past alone. Sighing she grabbed her cell phone and made two phone calls.

Chapter Three

Tony had spent most of the morning on the phone with OPIA, the Morris County Sheriff's department and whoever else thought they needed to be involved. In the end it was decided that Tony can keep the case as long as he was aided by OPIA, which was the plan anyway. The Sheriff Department had been furious with Al's decision that Tony could still have the case. Especially when they found out that Tony had more people on his force that were certified to investigate the paranormal than the Sheriff did. It was going to make the Labor Day baseball game even more interesting this year.

When he arrived at the farm, Tony got

reports back from the teams that he made up. Last night he had the leader of the local pride, Phil, track the trail that the victim had taken. Phil, a were-lion, was a certified tracker and could be brought in police and federal cases. He trained many of the were's in his pride to be trackers, making him one of the best. Today, Tony had his men focusing on the spots that Phil had indicated.

Tony was talking to some of men when he noticed a red Durango coming down the dirt driveway. The media that had arrived in the morning and had been sequestered to another area away from where the police were working, he also kept them away from Joe and his family. Tony had the DA, Tessa Morgan, fielding the questions so far.

This was the fifth body found within a thirty mile radius of Grabenberg; some reporters were starting to make connections that the murders were occurring around a town that had always welcomed the unwanted. Tessa was attempting to convince reporters that to connect the cases at this time was inappropriate.

The SUV was stopped by an officer, instead of being directed toward the reporters they were directed to where the investigators had parked their vehicles. Tony watched as the driver side door opened and the driver got out looking around. Her dark violet eyes were covered by sunglasses and she pulled her short curly hair back into a stubby pony tail.

Kirsa took a long sip from her Dunkin Donuts cup; she had changed while en route to Jersey. Instead of jeans and a t-shirt, she wore brown dress capris and a purple short sleeve blouse. On her feet she wore canvas sneakers to deal with terrain. Around her neck was a pendant of the goddess. She played with it as she walked to the front of the car. Closing her eyes, her senses picked up. Kirsa could smell the blood, the fear, the hunger.

When she opened them Tony was standing before her. He was her godfather and had been her father's childhood best friend. She smiled at him and took in the scenery around her. The field was filled with corn stalks; in the distance she saw the barn and a silo. The farmer was a few feet away talking to a police officer while the other officers were gathering evidence and looking around, dazed.

"When did you get here?" Tony asked as he hugged her tightly.

"I got in early this morning. Alfred called me last night," Kirsa said. "Hence the coffee."

"You should have called and let me know, we would have picked you up." He could tell by her calling Al by his full name she was pissed.

"Don't worry about it, I didn't really call anyone to tell them I was back."

Tony looked at her, "I didn't want to have to bring you to this, but we had no choice."

"It's okay, I'm not mad at you. A little annoyed at Al, but hey he's my boss, I'm supposed to be pissed at him."

"I take it then you are an acting agent again?"

With her coffee cup she motioned to the badge that was hooked to her capris. While on the plane, Al worked on getting her reinstated as well as getting all the authorization to carry a concealed weapon.

"Thanks Kirsa." Tony dropped his hand from her back as they walked. He could only imagine what she must be going through being back in New Jersey.

"No problem," she replied as they moved past the officers. She felt the stares and heard the whispers as she walked with Tony. After her family's death, half of the town thought of her as being cursed and avoided her like the plague. It was one of the reason she liked the small village in Germany.

Kirsa took it all in and followed Tony into

the field. The scent of blood grew stronger making her teeth feel tight. She saw where a white tent had been put up to shield the techs from the hot sun. Kirsa brushed a curl out of her face and stopped for a second. Her vision blurred and she began to see what had happened, Tony grabbed her to steady her. The rest of the scenery became fuzzy on the edges as the scene played out before her.

The young woman was running through the field and kept looking back over her shoulder. Her blonde hair was sticking to her face. She ignored the rocks digging into her bare feet. She felt her ankle turn as she stepped in a hole. She quickly struggled to get back up and continued to run ignoring the new pain in her ankle. If she survived, she would cry about it later. As her lungs screamed for air and her heart felt as though it would explode she prayed to any deity that would hear her. She felt something hot pierce her shoulder and then was being tackled.

Kirsa snapped out of it. Tony looked at her knowing she had seen a vision. Kirsa was a medium, she hated being titled as one. This gift alone had sparked an interest in the occult which led to her being an OPIA agent.

"What did you see?" he asked her.

"Young woman, possibly nineteen or twenty, I would bet she went to the university. I got the feeling she knew the attacker, though not well," Kirsa relayed what she saw. "She might have met him at the party down the road. He hated her for what she was. I get the feel- ing that he knew about her much longer. He terrorized her. He let her think she could get away as he chased her through the corn. She was not killed here. He chased her here, and then brought her to another spot like a cave or something along those lines."

"What do you mean he knew her longer?" Tony asked as he wrote it down in his notebook.

"I get the sense that he was aware of her being a were-tiger, when she had not told many people. The only people that knew about her were her family and the local pride," Kirsa explained. "Would Sara know who she was?"

Tony shook his head, "She recognized her as member of the pack, but couldn't remember her name. Phil is coming in to see if he can identify her, Sara think's she is one of the college students that the pack adopt while they are at the University."

"If he had been watching her you have to figure he had been around for a month," Kirsa continued. Tony looked at her in surprise. "He would be following her around the time of the full moon to make sure".

"Why not target a leader?" Tony pondered.

"It would cause more turmoil within the pack."

"Think about it: a young were-animal is going to be easier then dealing with the head. They aren't as in control of their powers as an Alpha would be." Kirsa pointed out to him. "Seriously would you want to try and take down Phil?"

"Point taken,"Tony said. Phil was a sweet guy but he was huge.

She walked to where the body had been. "So how does someone randomly kill a were-animal?"

"Silver bullets?" a voice said behind them. "I see our resident freak has returned."

Kirsa turned and saw Chris Washington standing there. She silently cursed to herself, and then asked the goddess for strength and patience with this man. Chris was as closed-minded as they came; he believed in every old wives' tale there was. He probably had a clove of garlic on him right now.

"Good afternoon officer," she greeted with a cheerful smile, ignoring his second comment.

"Agent," he replied. He had never liked Kirsa, they would have been in the same class if she had not skipped high school completely and went onto college. It was one of the many reasons he listed as to why he hated her.

"Were there any bullet wounds on the body?" she asked.

"One up by the shoulder," Chris told her.

"Was there silver residue at the entry site?"
"Don't know, didn't look closely."

"Then how do you know it was a silver bullet? Silver bullets are restricted; one needs a special permit to be able to have them," Kirsa replied politely.

"Don't get why the general public can't hunt them," he sneered.

"Enough, Washington. Go help bag up evidence or keep the media away," Tony told him.

Tony then turned and looked at Kirsa, "I take it you would like to see the body?"

"Does Sara have her?" Kirsa asked.

"Who else would I trust with a body?"

It took about thirty minutes to get to the coroner's office. After getting checked through security they walked to the office of Sara Cliver. Sara was one of the few certified Paranormal Coroners in the US. She went through train- ing courses with OPIA, the FBI and the CIA. Because of her certification, she had become head coroner for Morris County by twenty seven. She chose to keep her office in Grabenberg since she was from there and her career started from. About once a week she would head to Morristown to the prosecutor's office to filter through paper work and whatever else needed her eyes.

It seemed like a lifetime had passed since she had been here. They walked to the Coroner's office and Kirsa knocked on the open door. Sara jumped up and hugged Kirsa when she saw her walk into her office. It took a few minutes of girly gibberish before Sara realized why Kirsa was here.

"You're my expert?" Sara asked holding Kirsa at arm's length.

"That would be me," Kirsa replied and laughed as she was hugged again.

"I want to be selfish and be thrilled you're here. At the same time I know it's going to be rough being back home," Sara said with understanding on her face.

Her mother had been raped and murdered on a business trip in L.A. when Sara was only ten. Sara, her brother, nor her father never got over it. They moved on but that was it. If anyone understands what it was like to deal with tragedy and horror, it would be Sara.

"It's okay. I was thinking of coming back here anyway when I got the phone call to come help," Kirsa told her.

Kirsa and Sara had been friends for most of their lives. When Sara's mother was killed her father moved her broth- er and her to Grabenberg, NJ so they could live with their maternal grandparents. Their father spent three days a week working in Hartford, Connecticut, where they were originally from. The problem was that Sara was a were-tiger and needed a safe room for the full moon. When Kirsa's father heard this, he offered the use of the safe room in the basement of the Heinrich estate. It caused an instant bond between the two families and a tight friendship between Sara and Kirsa.

Sara nodded and grabbed a file. "I have her ready; barely touched her since we brought her in late yesterday. The pictures I took should be ready later today, when I get them I will make a set for you."

They put on the exam robes and gloves. Kirsa pulled her hair into a blue cap and put the goggles on. Kirsa went through Sara's initial report, circling areas that need furthered study before they moved onto the body. When they were done with the pictures Sara unzipped the body bag revealing the victim.

The victim would have been beautiful alive. Her hair was blonde like corn silk, and skin was clear. Kirsa began to ex- amine the body closely. There were no signs of sexual assault, but there were signs that the girl put up a fight.

"I took a bunch of physical evidence from under the finger nails," Sara told her when she saw Kirsa examine the hand. "Unfortunately he cleaned the insides so I don't know if the swabs I took will come back with anything."

Kirsa nodded and walked over to the table and began with examining the face. She opened the eyelids to see the pupils.

"She was beginning to transform," Kirsa said. "Her pupils had begun to turn into a cat's eye."

"I noticed that yesterday when I did a preliminary exam," Sara told her. She handed Kirsa a magnifying glass. "Take a close look at her pores."

Taking the magnifying glass, Kirsa focused on the arm and began to notice faint orange hair beginning to push through. "How do you kill a were-animal in mid-transformation?"

Sara set her clip board aside and leaned against a cabinet. "I talked to Phil about it last night," Sara informed Kirsa. "His theory is that she could have been in middle of transforming when shot with the bullet. The shock to her body, being young, would have caused her to stop but not necessarily reverse, especially if she didn't have full control of her powers."

"Did she have full control?"

"Phil said one of the guys was working with her on controlling it and how to unleash it at will," Sara explained. "She's a made were-tiger, was attacked when she was thirteen so it's a little trickier teaching them how to control it then if they were born a were-animal."

"So I take it he was able to ID her?"

"Yeah," Sara sipped her water bottle. "He is with her parents now. Tony thought it would be best if they heard it from Phil."

"It's got to be rough for him," Kirsa said.

Phil Michaels was leader of the local pack, or pride as he referred to it. He was a rare were-lion, his father had been the leader but died two years ago from prostate cancer leaving Phil the new leader at thirty-one. n his two years as leader he had already to proven to be a strong one.

Changing topics Kirsa asked about the bite mark. "I've heard there's a bizarre bight mark."

"Yes I have been having fun with my intern over it," Sara confessed. "He is completely stumped, that was after he threw up. Yesterday was not a good day."

"I take it this was his first paranormal body?"

Sara nodded handing her the magnifying goggles, "He recovered quickly and has been studying the picture and his text books."

Kirsa took the magnifying goggles from Sara and put them on. She studied the wound, taking swabs from the bite. Using her gloved hand she examined the wound more closely. There was not much bruising around the punctured marks and blood had dried around the area. There was no other tear in the skin except for the two tiny holes. Kirsa motioned for Sara to take a picture. She continued to make mental notes as she looked around the body.

"These are not vampire fang marks," Kirsa finally said.

"You're sure?" Sara asked her, she had come to the same conclusion. Then laughed at the look Kirsa shot her. "I'm joking, I had already ruled out vampire bite."

"If you hand't I was going to tell Tony to have you go for training again," Kirsa said.

"Can you explain in the recorder for the intern?" Sara asked. "You're better at breaking it down."

"What we refer to as the fang of a vampire is the Canine tooth," Kirsa began. "When a vampire is hungry, angry and, well, horny the canine extends itself. It is used similarly to how we use it; it needs to tear apart food just like our own canines. However, it needs to be sharp enough to pierce the skin initially, and then when it sinks deeper it rips the skin. They don't actually suck blood through the fangs; the fangs are more for tearing the skin to get to the blood. Most damage is done when taking the fang out of the skin. If that had been a vampire there would have been a nasty gouge on her thigh instead of two neat, tiny holes." Kirsa took a sip of water.

"So there would have been a lot more bruising then?" Sara asked as she looked at the wound.

"Yes," Kirsa replied. "He also would have bitten closer to a major vein like the Femoral; this bite is nowhere near one. There is no way a vamp would have done this."

"What about a newly risen?" Sara asked. She knew the answer to this but wanted Kirsa to explain it to her intern.

"She would have been drained completely if it was a newly risen vamp and the damage far worse. I'll dig up some photos for the intern to look at."

Kirsa looked up as something caught her eye. "Have you done any body fluids test?"

"I took the general swabs and rape kit samples. Why?" Sara inquired.

"There is an injection site on her breast; it has gray matter around it." Kirsa pointed to the mark. Sara snapped some photos, wiped the area with a swab, and measured the incision mark.

Sara got a syringe out of a bag and got it ready. She handed it to Kirsa. Kirsa slid the needle into the skin near the heart. As she pressed on the lever, they both gasped. Red blood came out along with a silver liquid.

Kirsa pulled the syringe out when it was filled and placed it in the evidence bag. She looked at Sara as she marked the bag.

"It's going to be liquid silver." Kirsa informed her, she saw the moment flash of fear in Sara's eyes before they went back to clear.

She left Sara to finish the exam. Tony got up from the chair when she came out of the room. "It was not a vampire bite, but I'm not ruling out that one was not involved. On top of that, the victim was killed during transformation. Her pupils are a cat's and fur can be seen coming out of the pores," she told him. "She was also most likely killed from the liquid silver they injected into her heart."

"Did you say liquid silver?" Tony asked his blood turning cold. He made a mental note to make sure when Sara was working there guards on duty.

"It's hard to get your hands on, you have to have certain certifications to be able to order the silver needed to be melted down. It's highly toxic to were-animals and vampires, especially if injected into the blood stream or vital organs, like the heart. The person doing it will have to be able to afford to get it off the black market," Kirsa explained.

Tony made notes of it. "What do you think?"

"Let's see, that would be the second were-animal killed in a month: a witch was killed three weeks ago: and there have been two vampires killed." She stopped and stared at him through her sunglasses. "I say you have a killer who does not like people who are either different or protected under the occult laws," Kirsa replied.

"Where does the witch fit in?"Tony asked raising an eye- brow.

"The witch's practice a religion most people still do not get or understand. Paganism or witchcraft is still considered to be classified as part of the occult. When the laws were created, they decided to group pagans and those practicing witchcraft in with the vamps, were animals, the fae, and necromancers. Many pagans are fine with that since being under the occult laws gives them extra protection."

Pausing, she looked at the pictures on the walls. "This was done to make a statement; I want to see this cryptic note that was left." Tony nodded. "This was left with the body." He handed her the note.

Kirsa slipped on the gloves that Tony gave her and took the envelope. She recognized the symbol on the front of the envelope. It was a cross inside a beam of light. Carefully, she took the note out of the envelope and read what it had to say.

"We are not evil. We are good. We are of the True Light. We search to destroy evil and to destroy the one that will kill them all. We cannot be stopped and will destroy those who get in our way."

She slid the note back into the envelope and looked up at Tony. "This isn't the first one is it?"

"We have five notes in total. There was one at each killing," he told her. "With the exception of this one, each pertains to the bible."

"I am going to need copies of all of them if you want my help," Kirsa told him as she handed the note back to him.

"Who are they referring to in the note, the one's death will kill then all?" Tony asked.

"It's an old rumor, that if you kill a member of what is referred to as the sixth blood line then all the vampires in the entire world will die at the exact instant the one dies."

Tony knew of the legend. It was believed that six vampires were born of one of the first women as punishment. The six went off to form the six main blood lines that were still around today. However the sixth line had vanished about a thousand years ago. It was said to be the most pure of the six lines because the head of line never turned anyone making the vampire virus in him pure to the original one. Tony stared at her, the fear he felt earlier about her being on the case began to rise again.

"It always comes back to that doesn't it?" he asked. "Yeah, pretty much," Kirsa told him. "By the way, I'm sure you already figured this out, but the group is most likely the same one that I dealt with three years ago in South Carolina."

"You sure you want to do this?" Tony asked. He needed her, but the god-father in him also wanted to protect her and keep her safe.

"Yes. Stop by tomorrow and I will show you some of their earlier work," Kirsa told him.

"Are you going to be safe working on this case?" Tony asked.

Kirsa sighed and looked past him. "I am going to call Dietrich when I get back and let him know what's going on. If he doesn't already know, he will find out eventually and the Council has done some extensive research on the group. I am sure I will get an additional guard until I am done working the case."

"Is Zero with you?" Tony asked.

"Of course, I couldn't let him be spoiled by Adam and Wyrm," Kirsa replied referring to her greyhound. "He'd be fat and even lazier if I left him with them."

Tony nodded. "Are you back in the city?"

Kirsa had lived in New York City for three years. She sold her apartment there and had everything put into storage when she left for Europe two years prior. Europe was her salvation. She shook her head no and he raised an eyebrow.

"The guesthouse," she told him. She kissed his cheek then turned and climbed in her car.

"Honey, you can stay with Donna and me. Steph is at a summer program; you can use her room." Tony told her.

She smiled weakly. "I need to do this Tony."

Chapter Four

The sun was setting by the time Kirsa headed for home. She drove through the main part of town taking note that very little had changed in the few years she had been gone. Grabenberg was a small town nestled away in the mountains making it a peaceful place to live. During the summer the town was fairly quiet because Grabenberg University was out. In September about two thousand college kids made their way into the town. For the most part the town was open minded and accepting. It was one of the first places where a were-animal could own property, or a vampire could walk down the street and not be staked.

After her parent's death, those that

disapproved with her family's connection to vampires began to voice their opinion as opposed to keeping silent. The talk became too much and Kirsa left hoping to find some peace after her whole world had been turned upside down. Making a decision, Kirsa packed up and left her home for Germany where her family had an ancestral home. Being in Europe she took the opportunity to an extensive amount of traveling.

Her childhood friend, Sabrina still lived in Grabenberg along with Lars, a vampire who sometimes acted as Kirsa's bodyguard. Yet there was no Adam to share tea with at two in the morning and there would be no drop in from Ayden O'Brian.

She pulled the SUV through the back entrance to her family's estate. The guesthouse had once been the original house. It dated back to the 1700's. After the large manor was built the original house had been converted into a guest- house. When Kirsa was growing up, their housekeeper Ava Lyon and her family had lived there.

It had its own private driveway and its own fenced in back yard complete with rusted swing set. She got out, grabbing the groceries from the back. She knew within moments her cell phone would be going off, there was no hiding the stunned looks on the faces at the grocery store that a Heinrich was back in Grabenberg. Sighing she walked to the old center hall colonial. After walking into the kitchen, she put the groceries away then put Zeros leash on him for a quick walk.

Kirsa walked out of the garage and down the over grown stone path. Once she would have come up the main drive. Once, she would have been greeted by a beautiful stoned manor that looked like it belonged in old Europe with ivy sprawling up the stone façade. She would have walked through the dark wood doors and smelled her mother's cooking and heard her father working. They both would have stopped to see how her day was. Now what greeted her was blown out remains of the house. Her parents were now buried at the family crypt in Germany, leaving her alone. It was why she had not come back here for two years.

The house looked like a building somewhere in Europe that had been bombed out during WWII. Stone had turned black and nature had begun to grow over what remained of her childhood home. She walked to where the front door once stood and set the flowers down on the threshold. There were no words to be said, no tears to be cried, for her grief was deeper than that. This was where her parents, Hagan and Anne Heinrich, had perished. They had not been killed in a car accident, or even a simple house fire. No, her parents were killed in a far more horrible way.

It had been five years ago. Kirsa was finishing her doctorate at Georgetown, she was moving from her townhouse there into her apartment in NYC. Her roommate, Emma Anderson, was getting ready to leave for class when there was knock on the door. Emma had just popped her head into Kirsa's office telling her she had a date after her class so she would not be home until late and to remind her to set the alarm.

Kirsa had just broken up with her fiancée and they were worried he would arrive unannounced; they had become diligent in setting the alarm in the old row house even when they were home. She knew that Kirsa was trying to finish her dissertation before she headed home for the weekend.

****

Emma brushed a strand of red hair out of her eyes as she answered the front door. She was startled when she sawDietrich Nacht standing there. Dietrich was the current head of the Vampire Council and lived in Salzburg, Austria.

"Hi, Kirs didn't say you were coming," Emma said letting him in.

"She doesn't know. Is she here?" Dietrich asked

kissing Emma's cheek.

Emma nodded. She had met Dietrich enough time to know that something was not right. "What's wrong?"

"Everything," he laid a hand on her shoulder and took a deep breath. "Is she here?"

Emma nodded. "She is in the den. Dietrich, should I not go to class?"

"She is going to need you." With that he made his way down the hall of the row house to the back. Kirsa was in her office working at her laptop. A stack of notes were on one side and an open book lay on the other.

Dietrich knocked on the door frame and watched as surprise flashed onto Kirsa's face. She got up and gave him a hug. She wore her hair long back then. Kirsa was planning on cutting it when she went home as a celebration of her new found freedom.

"Hey! What a surprise?" she exclaimed as she sat back down. He sat on the ottoman in front of her. Kirsa studied his face.

"What's wrong?" She had known Dietrich all of her life and had never seen him look this upset.

He was not sure where to begin or how to start. It had been decided that he should be the one to tell her. The call had come earlier in the day; thankfully he was already in the States for a meeting in NYC.

The meeting had been canceled, he had to drive to DC to see Kirsa immediately. He ran a hand through his graying black hair. His pale blue eyes glistened.

"I don't even know where to begin," he told her, taking hold of one of her hands.

"At the beginning sounds good," Kirsa replied, the horror that was reflected in his eyes was getting her nervous. "You're scaring me, Dietrich."

He took a deep breath and began. "There was an explosion at the house."

"Your house?" she asked, thinking of his beautiful home in Austria.

He shook his head. "No. Yours."

She jumped up, ready to run for the door. "My parents?"

He watched the color begin to drain from her already pale face as she began to understand why he was now here. "Your parents were in the house at the time."

Kirsa stared at him, fear made her speechless. She sank back down in the chair and closed her eyes hoping for some ray of sunshine. However, as an agent for OPIA she knew what the chances were to survive an explosion.

"I'm so sorry liebling," the tears were in his

eyes, he pulled her into him.

"Both?" she whispered against his sweater.

He nodded and pulled her into his arms and just held onto her as the shock was absorbed.

****

There was little memory of the days that followed. With the help of Dietrich and her friend Ayden O'Brian she made arrangements for her parent's remains to be flown to Germany. What little family she had at the time met her at the old family estate in Germany. The Council came to mourn and with that came her old bodyguard Lars. Ayden, who was a Shadow for the Inner Council, had come for security and comfort.

Ayden and she had been friends when she was a teenager; their friendship became strained when she was dating Anton. Yet he was her rock during the funerals and aftermath. She wanted no medication or anything that people were trying to give her. She only accepted the tea Ayden made to help her sleep at night.

The funerals were held in Germany at the family estate. Like so many other Heinrich's before her parents, they were placed in the family crypt long before they should have been. She remembered the whispers and condolences. She remembered feeling numb as her parents were laid in their tombs.

Kirsa laid two roses where the threshold of what was once her home had been. Kirsa was now one of the last two Heinrich's, her family had been hunted for centuries. Her cousin, Adam was the only child of her dads' sister. About two months after her parent's death they were back in Germany for another double funeral. Adam's parents were killed in two separate car bombings. After the death of his parents, his wife and he were placed under Council guard. It also meant that both Adam and Kirsa inherited the mass fortune, estate in Germany and the contents of the vampire vaults their families had help guard.

"I promise to end it all and to rebuild. I miss you both," Kirsa whispered. She hoped her parent's spirits would not be here but instead be in peace.

Kirsa turned slowly from what remained of the old home and walked back toward the guesthouse. One day, she would rebuild just to show them that she would keep living and that she would rebuild on what they destroyed. The property itself was still breathtaking; all 800 acres were in use. There was the orchard, the organic farming section she rented out to farmers, the horse ranch that was shared with the family's old friends the Black's. Her best friend, Sabrina ran the ranch now with her younger brother Brian.

The original structure of the guesthouse was built in the 1700's and had been added onto through the centuries. There was an open stair case in the center that led up to the second floor; the kitchen ran along the back. The front of the house contained the formal dining room and living room. Off the kitchen were the TV room and a small half bath. Upstairs was four bedrooms, and then an additional bedroom and rec room up in the attic. The basement was still contained the original root cellar and kitchen from when the house was first built.

Kirsa had always liked the home, when she was growing up and up until her parents death their house keeper had lived here. Ava Lyon had been the housekeeper for as long as Kirsa could remember. She lived in the guesthouse with her husband Mark, who was the vet for the Black's ranch, and their three boys.

Daniel, Collin and Thomas were around the ages of Kirsa and Sabrina and Brian Black making them a gang for most of their lives. She had run through the front door with her friends so many times. Anton, Sabrina and Brian's older brother, always thought their games were childish and often kept to himself no matter how hard they tried to get him to join them. It felt odd that for the time being, this was going to be her home.

After taking a quick shower and changing into more comfortable clothes, Kirsa decided the only way to calm her mind was to cook. Soon, pasta sauce was simmering on the stove inside the kitchen. Kirsa stood on the deck off of the kitchen; she kept the French doors open so that she could keep an eye on dinner. At her feet lay her black Greyhound named Zero. He was snoring away, tired after already eating dinner and running about in the fenced-in back yard. The trip across the ocean probably had thrown his entire system off. She took a sip of the white wine she was drinking.

Kirsa had called Adam when she returned from the main house. She wanted him to know she was ok. He was worried for her; Matthew got on the phone and told her about his adventures with Uncle Wyrm. After hanging up with them she had retreated outside where she was making mental list of things to do. The kitchen with its white countertops needed to be updated, but she was thinking that would be the last things to do.

The upper floors needed to be updated and furnished. Which meant the first thing to do was to get her furniture and stuff out of storage, then put a fresh coat of paint on the walls, and finally begin redoing kitchens and bathrooms. She also needed to contact contractors about rebuilding the Heinrich estate.

After seeing what was left of the estate this afternoon she realized it was not just her that needed it rebuilt, but the town as well. Her family had always been key members of the community. Not only were they one of the founding families, but they opened their home up for town functions and events. Kirsa would like that to happen again.

Kirsa picked up the scents of three people even before she heard them talking. They walked through the kitchen and stopped in the doorway that led outside. It was as if they were unsure she was really standing there. Kirsa turned and smiled, she set her wine glass down on the deck railing. Elaine and Sabrina Black stood there,Lars hung back busying himself with opening the wine he brought. The two rushed over and hugged her.

The three women just stayed that way for a few moments. Elaine was in her early 60's, she was slightly plump but it fit her perfectly. Her auburn hair was cut in a cute bob style and her hazel eyes were filled with love. Sabrina stood at 5'8, was trim and skinny, with flaming red hair and blue eyes like her father.

Elaine pulled away and just looked at Kirsa. "You look wonderful," she finally said after they all stopped crying.

"Thank you," Kirsa replied. Sabrina leaned next her. "No, you look like you are at peace and steady again,"

Elaine told her.

"I'm almost there. Close but not yet. Where are Uncle Aaron and Brian?" she asked, referring to Sabrina's father and her younger brother.

"Oh, they will be by tomorrow. They did not want to take part in the tear fest," Sabrina told her.

"Men," Kirsa rolled her eyes as they walked inside.

Lars was opening a bottle of red wine, "We heard a rumor you were back in town, we had to come check if it were true," he said in his thick Norwegian accent.

He had dyed his hair electric blue, making his blue eyes pop out even more.

"And bring wine just in case?" Kirsa asked as she went to the fridge pulling out a vial. They watched as she took its contents then a sip of her wine.

"How many are you up too?" Elaine asked her accepting a glass of red wine. The liquid in the vials was part of the treatment for a disorder that Kirsa suffered from.

"Four a day," Kirsa said sitting down at the table. "I can take it straight now. A few months ago everyone was hiding it in whatever I was drinking."

"How are you feeling?"

"Fine, mom," Kirsa laughed causing Sabrina to chuckle. "Are you guys staying for dinner?"

"I will. Mom and Dad have a dinner event," Sabrina replied.

Elaine stayed for about a half hour before she forced herself to leave. She and Aaron were hosting a fund raiser for families devastated by crime and violence. Elaine also knew that what Kirsa needed was a friend not a nagging mother.

Chapter 5

After the pizza had been eaten and wine glasses had been refilled, Sabrina and Kirsa went for a walk around the yard. The sun was just finishing it's descent from the sky making it a deep purple with hints of red. Stars had begun to appear while Zero danced around them as he ran back and forth. Heading back to the old back porch, they sat on the stairs and just watched the night sky in silence as Zero curled up next to Kirsa.

"So who told you I was back in town?" Kirsa asked. "I was going to call after dinner."

"Lars actually, though Sara called me after

you left her office," Sabrina told her.

She understood that Kirsa needed time to get settled and use to the idea of being home. She was going to give Kirsa until tomorrow but the moment Eliane heard that Kirsa was back her mother had to come see her. Sabrina knew this was not going to be easy on Kirsa.

"How are you holding up so far?" Sabrina asked.

"Better than I thought," Kirsa said. "I stopped by the house earlier."

Sabrina did not need to ask which house Kirsa was referring too. She knew that Kirsa meant she had gone to where her parents lived and died. Saying nothing, she laid a hand on Kirsa's leg, to let her know she was there.

"I had to get it over with," Kirsa continued, "I knew that if I waited it would just be looming over me."

"How long are you planning on staying? Lars seemed unsure," Sabrina asked. Dietrich had called Lars to let him know that Kirsa could be coming back to Grabenberg and that if she did he would be doing body guard detail.

"At least until the case is over, but most likely longer than that," Kirsa answered.

"What do you mean by most likely longer?"

"Before Al called, I had been thinking about coming back here," Kirsa admitted to her closest friend. "Not to just visit, but to rebuild. While we were rebuilding the estate in Germany made me think that I should rebuild my parent's home here. I figure I could update the guest house, make it my home base until the main house is ready."

"What would you do with it?" Sabrina was curious. She hadn't heard about any plans to come back and live. She also knew that Kirsa was not the type to live in a large palatial home.

"Open the house up for public and private functions. Most likely I would live in the guest house, and have the main house fixed up to what it looked like when it was first built," Kirsa explained.

"I like the ideas. What about Ayden though?" Sabrina asked, referring to the sexy Irish vampire that had become a constant companion with Kirsa while she was in Europe.

"He supports me with the ideas," Kirsa said with a shrug. She caught the look from Sabrina. "We've been talking about them. Right now he is really busy with the Inner Council.

They have him working on a case, he can't even tell me about it. When he's done with that we'll talk and figure out what is going on with us."

Sabrina nodded. She had seen them together when she joined them in Switzerland for a week. They were comfort- able with each other, and they glowed in each other presence. But Ayden was part of the O'Brian bloodline. If Kirsa was a regular human it would not be an issue. If the legends were accurate, then there would have to be a lot political moving around to allow them to be together.

"Have you two slept together yet?" A month ago the answer was no, Sabrina was wondering if it had changed.

Kirsa snorted at the question. Leave it to Sabrina to jump to that question. "No."

"You have to be the only person I know that is dating a vamp and has been able to ignore their sexy vampire charm." Sabrina pointed out. "I'm shocked he hasn't burst into flames from sexual frustration!"

Kirsa laughed. "I know. But at the same time, I don't have a good track record," Kirsa reminded Sabrina. "The one person I have been with turned out to be psychotic. Not that I'm saying that will happen with Ayden but I'm just scared."

Sabrina nodded. She knew all about her first love and what occurred after the break up. Kirsa's first lover was Sabrina's older brother Anton. They talked for a little bit more, before jet lag hit hard. They made their way back to the house. Lars stood on the deck waiting for Sabrina to finish. When she was done, Lars approached Kirsa.

"The Inner Council has reinstated me as your body guard," Lars informed her.

"I kind of figured they would," Kirsa replied.

"I'm going to head back with Sabrina, but call or text if anything happens. I'll be over first thing in the morning."

"I am planning on spending the day here, if that changes I will call," Kirsa assured him.

She watched as her best friend and her body guard left, Kirsa retreated upstairs with Zero. Zero followed her and plopped down on his doggie bed that was already in the master bedroom. Kirsa turned the c.d. player on that was sitting on an old maple desk that Lars had dug up for her and sat down.

She put on yoga pants and a t-shirt and sat before a crate that, for the time being, would be her alter. Before she could phone anyone, she needed to relax. Whenever she saw death or a spirit talked to her it opened up her senses too much. Lighting the candles and saying a prayer to Freyja she closed her eyes and let herself unwind.

Freyja was a Goddess of the Norse Pantheon. She was one of the few Goddesses that Kirsa felt comfortable praying to; she was considered to be a protection Goddess along with love, witchcraft, wisdom and a list of other attributes. After a few minutes, Kirsa felt better, she closed her circle and blew the candles out.

She picked up her cell and called Alfred, head of OPIA. He picked up on the first ring.

"Yes?" Al answered.

"It's Kirsa," she responded.

"So what did you think of the case?" Al asked her.

"I'm on it." She informed him.

There was a pause. Then he spoke. "You're going to work on the case?"

"Honestly, did you think I wouldn't?" She asked him as she stared out the window

In his office in New York City, Alfred stared out at the nighttime scene. "No, I knew you would."

"I can't sit back and let the Church of Light take over my town," Kirsa told him.

"You absolutely sure it's them?" he asked. Hearing her confirm made him excited and fearful for her.

"They copyrighted their insignia about four years ago, and that's the one found on the notes. They are using similar wording, leaving bodies to be found," Kirsa told him.

"You have Lars with you right?" he asked. Since the murder of her parents, whenever she attended an event or worked on case, Kirsa usually had a bodyguard assigned to her by the Vampire Council.

"Yes, I'm also going to be calling Dietrich when I get off the phone with you," She informed stepping out on to the balcony. There was a nice cool breeze, and she could hear the crickets in the background.

"OK. You have your badge and equipment right?" Al inquired.

"Never leave home without them," she replied.

"Ha ha. I am going to want updates. Encrypt them for level 4, my eyes only."

"Ok."

She hung up with Alfred and looked at the clock. She calculated the time difference and then dialed her phone for Austria.

"*Guten Tag,*" a familiar voice said on the other end.

Kirsa responded in German, letting the house keeper know she needed to talk to Dietrich.

"Ah Kirsa, what can I do for you?" Dietrich greeted her as he came to the phone.

"I don't know," Kirsa replied. "I am helping Tony White out with a case here in Jersey. There have been a series of murders."

"Yes I know. You have been brought in why?" Dietrich asked as he leaned back in his chair.

It was after midnight in Austria. He had a Council meeting in an hour to get to and this would be brought up. They had been watching the murders carefully, yet the fact that Kirsa was brought in almost solidified their worst fears.

"The murders appear to be connected by notes that are being left at the scene. The insignia on the envelopes make it seem like it's the Church of Light."

Dietrich sat silent for a few seconds, not

sure what to think. He was also trying to ignore the concerned look from the man sitting across from him. "I see. So, you are being asked on to help because it deals with a cult and also the occult?"

"Yes. Tony and Al are both worried about my safety. They know that Lars is here and will watch over me, but Tony wants you to know what is going on," Kirsa explained.

"That he would," Dietrich replied. He liked Tony. Tony had been best man at Kirsa's parents wedding and had grown up with her father. He knew the family secrets. Dietrich did not let Kirsa know that both had already called him to voice those concerns.

"I am going to need to talk to the Inner Council about this," he informed her.

"Also do you think you can send me some of the information you have on the church?" Kirsa asked.

"That I can do," Dietrich told her. "How are we doing besides all this?"

"I'm staying in the guesthouse," Kirsa replied.

There was silence and understanding. "I wish I could take it all away and make it better. What happened should never have happened."

"Part of me wanted the house to be there and them to be waiting for me to come home. But it finally became real in a way. What is left of the house is charred black, her gardens are gone. They're gone," Kirsa said staring out into the night.

"There is a part of me that keeps waiting for your father to call me and tell me a joke or something. We all miss them," Dietrich agreed. "But I know that gives you little comfort."

"I'm going to rebuild it. Exactly how it was. I want to shove it in their faces that I will not hide anymore."

Dietrich opened his mouth then closed it. "Your father and mother would be honored and proud of you for doing that."

After a few more minutes they hung up the phone. Dietrich looked across his desk where a young man was sitting. He leaned back in his chair tapping his fingers on the desk, studying the young man.

"Ayden I have an assignment for you after all," Dietrich began. "That was Kirsa."

"I picked up on that, what's going on?" Ayden O'Brian asked.

He knew she was back in Jersey she called him when she had landed and had quickly filled him in on what was going on.

"The case that she is now working on I believe ties nicely with the one you have been working on for the Council," Dietrich told him sliding a large case file over to him. "I want you to go to Grabenberg, you will be Miss Heinrich's Shadow and another set of eyes on the case." Ayden nodded. "How long I am her Shadow for?"

Dietrich raised an eyebrow and smiled. He could make things easier for them, cut through the politics. "You let me know what is going on when the case ends and that will determine if you become her permanent Shadow. Do you understand what I am telling you?"

Ayden smiled. "Thank you, sir. I will let you know what is going on once I get there."

"Ayden one more thing," Dietrich said before Ayden left. "She is my joy, my daughter in ways, keep her safe."

"I promise," Ayden assured him.

Dietrich nodded and watched the young man leave his office. He hoped he was doing the right thing. Ayden was the best Shadow. With the potential threat of a spy within the General or Inner Council, they could use him in Europe. At the same time, Dietrich did not want Kirsa facing the horrors that awaited her without the one person she trusted most.

Chapter Six

Kirsa was finishing her coffee, it was ten thirty in the morning and she had been up for about two hours already. Zero woke her up around eight for breakfast, she tried to get him to go back to sleep after he ate but he was not having it. So by nine, she had showered, dressed in jean shorts and a black tank top. Her hair was drying into curls, and her feet were bare. The cell phone that sat on the railing began to vibrate.

"Hello," Kirsa answered.

"Hey kiddo, did I wake you?" Tony asked. He wasn't sure if she would still be asleep from the time difference.

"No, Zero had me up at eight."

Tony chuckled on the other end. "Is it alright if I swing over and we can talk about the case some more?

"Sure, just bring coffee with you and possibly a Taylor Ham, egg and cheese," Kirsa instructed.

"Give me about twenty minutes," Tony replied.

She hung up the phone as Zero bounded up the stairs. He leaned against her, with his tail thumping against her thigh. Kirsa scratched his ears then walked over to the old lawn chairs that were set up on the deck with the old plastic side table. She set her coffee down and Zero plopped down on the old blanket she had laid out for him.

Thankfully, she had gotten a hold of the storage place that had her furniture and they were going to start packing up her things for her. The first truckload was due to show up tomorrow morning.

Twenty minutes later Kirsa heard a car pulling into the long driveway; it pulled up around the house and stopped just before the garage doors. Kirsa opened her eyes and watched Tony get out of the car carrying two Dunkin Donut coffees and a brown bag. She sat up in her chair and took a coffee and the bag from Tony.

"Good morning," he said kissing her on the forehead. Tony sat down in the other chair and pet Zero who was dancing about in excitement.

"Good morning and thanks," Kirsa replied as she bit into the breakfast sandwich.

Tony eyed the white binder that lay on the small table. He put the folders that he had been carrying under his arms on top of it.

"What would you like to know, Tony?" Kirsa asked taking a sip of her coffee.

"Everything," he responded.

Kirsa chuckled. "Then I will start from the beginning." She took another bite of her sandwich and a sip of her coffee before beginning. "The group you are looking at is called the *Ecclesia de Luminis*, or Church of Light, which I believe you knew that already."

"Yes, I recognized the symbols from the South Carolina reports," he let her know. South Carolina was a case Kirsa had worked on several years ago that first brought the Church of Light into the national spot light.

"Why the Latin name?"

"The original premise of the church started roughly in the 1300's," Kirsa explained.

Tony stopped her. "Did you say 1300's?"

"I said they were old. Anyway, there were a lot of religious groups that develop during this time period as a result of the plague. Many people thought that it was the end of the world and that God was punishing them. However, unlike the other groups that targeted different religions this group went after the darker stuff. They preached about how the plague would only end if all the vampires and were-animals were killed. They got a huge following, and eventually the plague begins to subside. The group kept a following; it was smaller though, only in the hundreds."

"Obviously that didn't end their existence, if they are still around today," Tony observed.

"Fear is a powerful motivator. The only information we have on the founder is that it was a man and was referred to as the Father. Since then all the leaders have all taken that title. During the Inquisition and the Witch Hunts, they became popular adding to the furor of killing those deemed evil. During the Age of Enlightenment they decided to not be as public as they were once. They maintained a following by word of mouth. Then with the invention of the Horror Films they begin to address how vampires and were-wolves are real and need to be killed." Kirsa stopped and finished her sandwich.

"I bet they go insane when the vampires and were-animals and the other supernatural's get rights?" Tony assumed.

"Not only that, but their numbers rise dramatically. People begin to think the Church of Light is right in killing the supernatural's that are allowed to live side by side with humans. The church begins to preach that the only way for the second coming to happen is if all of the supernatural are killed. Many are fine with this," Kirsa told him. "No other Christian religion claims any connection to them."

"I don't blame the others groups for staying far away from them. Though I bet they took a hit with what happened in South Carolina?"

"Yes. When word got out that the head of the East Coast Branch, not only killed but tortured non-supernatural's, their numbers took a dive. The church tried to redeem itself by saying they killed those who were helping the supernatural community. For many that was not a good enough explanation but for some it was enough.   Their numbers are on a slow rise again."

"I'm taking it though that South Carolina is

not the first time this decade they killed. You were only able to get them because Anton got cocky and messy toward the end."

Kirsa nodded. She got the binder out and handed it to him. "These are pictures and police reports that pertain to killings the Church of Light are believed to be responsible for just in the last five years. This covers just North, Central and South America. I have four black binders that cover Europe and most of Asia if you want to see those as well."

Tony took the three inch binder and just stared at it. This was bigger than he could possibly imagine. Tony prepared himself. He knew when he opened the binder he would be faced with gruesome images. Nothing could prepare for what he was about to see.

The pictures showed what had been a large home of stone and brick demolished, furniture turned to ashes, parts of bodies strewn throughout the wreckage. There were pictures showing where the front door should have been but now the view looked all the way to the backyard. This meant that all the rooms between were gone. Wires were dangling from the ceiling and walls. He knew these pictures. He knew this scene; they were pictures of her parent's house after the explosion. Tony looked up at Kirsa.

"Did they know?" he asked, his blood turning cold from fear.

If the cult knew anything about Kirsa's family, then it could very well mean that she was a target herself. For centuries, her family had been hunted because of its ties to the Vampire Council. When a committee was formed to establish laws pertaining to the supernatural, her father was one of the one's that had been called in to help draft the legislation. It had only added more fuel to the fire.

"Honestly, we don't know what they knew before or what Anton told them," Kirsa explained. "From what we gathered they killed my parents, Aunt and Uncle more for their connection to vampires and other supernatural communities than anything else."

"Anton told them nothing?"Tony asked looking up from some of the photos.

"Thankfully, all he really knew was about the protection order written by the Council. I never really trusted him with any of the medical information," Kirsa said sipping her coffee.

"You couldn't have hid your disorder from him?"

"He knew I had a blood disorder of some

sort, I tried to let him think it was hemophilia."

Tony continued and saw how these pictures went into more detail. They showed the contents of the hidden vault that had survived the explosion. Each item was identified. He flipped to the next section. The pictures were more disturbing in away. These were of a dungeon one would see active in medieval Europe. There were bodies chained to the wall; one was on a rusty old table partially cut opened. Different torture devices were placed throughout the room and showed use. A trunk was opened, inside were silver bullets, holy water, stakes and garlic.

"Garlic?" he asked raising an eyebrow.

"Apparently not all their information is correct. These were taken in South Carolina. Only one person was caught and he refuses to admit it was the work of the cult. He is currently serving five life sentences at the Paranormal Prison in upstate New York."

Tony looked at her and knew she was talking about Anton Black. "They start killing again five years ago. Why?"

Kirsa leaned back in the chair crossing her ankles as she sipped her coffee. "There are a few theories on why. Twenty years ago with the passing of the laws their numbers jump astronomically high. But then about ten years ago, the numbers begin to drop and have continued to drop to the point where only the most radical stay."

"But not all radical groups kill," Tony pointed out as he continued to go through the binder.

"No not all," Kirsa agreed. ""About ten years ago they get a new leader. The one before died under mysterious circumstances. This new one, is a bit more radical, blames society for what has become of the world, that our acceptance of evil has led us down a path of darkness."

"So because society is more accepting, the group sees this as sin spreading and evil gaining more power," Tony concluded.

"Basically," Kirsa agreed.

"And you are sure they know nothing about your family?" Tony asked again.

"Does anyone know anything about my family? The Council does not know why they are to protect my family bloodline. The blood oath was written a thousand years ago. Not even Wyrm can remember," Kirsa assured him. "I have a journal they believed to have been written by a descendent. It was found when the vault was cleared out. Dietrich wants me to read it and see what I find."

Tony stood up. "Kirsa, this is bad." "I know."

"Sara put a rush on the toxicology report; it should be in by tomorrow. I will send you a copy," he told her.

"Ok."

"By the way where is Lars?"

"He is staying with Sabrina until a threat is posed," Kirsa replied draining what remained of her coffee.

"Is he your bodyguard?" Tony asked.

"Loosely. If I'm at the house he thinks I'm safe. But, if I am going out alone and not meeting up with someone I know then he has to come with me."

Tony nodded as he stood up. "I know you can't copy the entire binder; but can I have copies of whichever ones may help us with this case?"

"Yeah. I have my lap top, so I will send them to you via email."

"Alright, I'm going to head back to the station and type up what you told me; then brief some of my guys." Tony told her.

"Sounds good, call me if you need any recaps.' Kirsa said kissing him good bye.

She watched him get into the car and drive away. Why she let herself get dragged into these cases she had no clue. But here she was again dealing with death when she had already seen enough. Kirsa walked to the end of the deck and leaned on the railing. It was a beautiful day out. Zero had woken up when Tony left and was now running in circles having the time of his life.

Yet still it was hard not to allow her mind to wander back to five years ago when her life had begun to change.

Chapter Seven

Five years ago she had been a shell of a person. She had been Dating Anton Black, Sabrina's older brother, for a few years by then. They had become serious talking about marriage. The day it ended they had spent the day shopping for rings in Georgetown. At this point she was also living in New York City for part of the week while finishing her dissertation at Georgetown. After ring shopping and dinner they went back to her town home. Her roommate was away for the weekend so they were alone.

Back then she was carefree, no body-guards unless she was attending a formal event. No fear that someone was out to get her. No looking over her shoulder at a strange noise, no being paranoid that someone was watch- ing her, or at what lurked in the shadows.

Anton had been trying to get her to agree to come to one of his church meetings. He had yet to reach the rank of East Coast head of the Church of Light back then, but he was still a key member. For most of the day she was able to ignore it and act like she was busy window shopping. Now sitting just the two of them out on the back porch with their wine there was no distractions for her to use as an excuse.

"Will you at least come to one of the meetings?" Anton asked her as they sipped their wine.

It was hard to look at herself during that time period; she was just a shell of herself. Her hair was long and she wore baggy clothes as if she was trying to be invisible. She had very little self-confidence or belief in herself. Most of the time she allowed Anton to win arguments, it was easier to deal with him when he got what he wanted. Even if it made her miserable.

Not looking at him she answered. "No."

She sipped her wine in the silence and watched the stars come out. Part of her did not want the old fight to start up again, but another part of her was ready for the fight this time. A phone call from an old friend a few days prior had begun to chisel away at the meek person she had become.

"Why?" he asked.

"For one, the night you want me to go I have plans that I can't break. Second, why would I go someplace where I would be deemed evil because of my beliefs?"

This was the same argument they had been having for the last few months. In the beginning he was alright with their different views on religion. Lately he was pressing the issue more and more, wanting her to join his church. A group she knew to be on the watch list for Cult like activities. It was also a group that both she and Ayden had been researching for the Vampire Council and OPIA for the past two years.

"First, what is so important that you cannot go to a church meeting?" Anton asked.

"I am defending my dissertation that night," Kirsa replied simply. It was the truth, and she could not reschedule it.

"Ok, fine. But they don't think you're evil for your beliefs," he told her. Kirsa turned and raised an eyebrow at him. "You have just been led astray."

"Anton, no," Kirsa told him getting up. "I'm not going to your meetings so stop asking. I don't ask you to come to coven meetings or pagan events."

"Kirsa it would mean a lot to me if you went," he pleaded getting up and laying a hand on her shoulder. He knew what worked to get her to cave.

"Well it would mean a lot to me if you stopped going," she replied. She was almost as surprised as he was by her statement.

"That's not going to happen," he informed her. His voice was cold as ice.

She looked at him. The part of her that had been researching his church wanted to scream and yell at him. Then there was the part of her that wanted to cave in and just give him what he wanted. The problem was she was finding it hard to recognize herself when she looked in the mirror.

"Then accept me for who I am and get over it," she suggested. "Anton, I'm tired of this fight."

He kissed her forehead. "Then it's settled. You will come to the next meeting."

"Wait. What? How does being tired of fighting with you about this lead you to thinking I'm going with you to a meeting?" she asked flabbergasted.

"Because that will end us fighting," he told her getting up.

He wanted to take her in his arms and let her know how happy he was that she would attend a meeting with him. In his mind her wanting to end the fight meant her succumbing to his wishes once again. After all he always knew what was best for her. It took how many months for that Irish monster called Ayden to finally back off. He never liked how that one in particular, he didn't like how he watched her or how he would talk to Kirsa. Lars wasn't so bad; he stayed out of Anton's way when he was around.

"Why do you want me to go to a place where they will see me as the enemy and have to save me?" Kirsa asked the frustration evident in her voice.

"You're not the enemy. The lies your family has told you are the enemy."

"What does my family have to do with this?" Kirsa demanded, her voice rising slightly.

"You can end the protection of those animals. The church will protect you if you turn from Satan's creatures." Kirsa rested her head on a hand and took a deep breath. A migraine was forming. In a very quiet voice she asked "You have told them about my family?"

He stared at her dumbfounded he was not sure why they were still discussing this. "Kirsa, I had too. Don't you see? I had to ask for forgiveness for loving you."

She felt her heart rip and tear. The emotional drain she had been feeling for the last few months had finally hit. Kirsa looked up at the sky and gathered what little energy she had. She thought of a silent prayer of protection from the gods then took the foolish promise ring off of her finger and handed it to him.

"Leave, Anton," she whispered. Her voice did not waiver nor did it hint of tears.

"I know you're not serious," he replied.

"This time, I am," she said looking at him. "This time no amount of begging or pleading will make me take you back."

"Who else will put up with what you are?" he asked her.

"I don't know. But I'd rather be alone then with someone who cannot love me for who I am. Now leave, or I will call the cops."

He turned and said nothing. When she

heard his car door shut and pull out of its spot she sank to the ground. She picked up her cell phone and called Sabrina. It went to voice mail.

"I finally did it. It's over. I told him to leave."

She hung up, curled into a ball on the stairs and wept away all her dreams and wishes.

****

Kirsa stared out the window onto her family's property. Five years ago she was broken emotionally and psychologically. She had let someone control her in every way possible. It was hard to look back and see why she let someone do that to her. In five years, she rebuilt her life. She was not counting on finding someone. If she did, then it was a bonus. Instead, she was determined to find out the history of her family, to rebuild her home and to live. Twirling a curl with her finger she sighed and walked back inside.

Chapter Eight

Sara found Kirsa by the rubble of the main house. She had tried calling her to go over the autopsy results and to see how she was doing. When she couldn't find Kirsa at the guest house she had a feeling she would find her here.

"They were my rock, my support system," Kirsa spoke as Sara approached.

"They were," Sara agreed. The Heinrich's had opened their home to Sara and her father. She had a safe place to transform those first few full moons.

"I was such a mess," Kirsa sighed as she stared at the charred remains of her home. "I'm still a mess."

"Your entire foundation had been wiped out from under you," Sara countered. "You were allowed to be a mess. You were allowed to just get away from it all to figure out a new path."

Kirsa turned to look at her best friend. "In Germany, I found peace restoring the manor," Kirsa admitted. "Researching with Wyrm on my family history. Ayden visiting in-between cases."

"Is that what you are hoping for here? By rebuilding?"

"Even if I chose to sell it once it's done, or use it as something other than a home, they deserve to have it rebuilt," Kirsa answered.

In the last few months she had begun to feel as if it was time to return to her home in New Jersey and finishing rebuilding. And in order to rebuild, it meant finally coming to terms with everything that had happened. It meant saying goodbye to the past so that the future could come.

Pulling herself out of the funk she was in she turned to Sara. "What brings you here?"

"The case," Sara admitted. "We can postpone."

"No I need the break from brooding," Kirsa told her.

They headed back to the house. Kirsa poured them both fresh coffee then they headed into the living. Her case files were already spread out on an old desk that she had found in the attic.

"The first body that had been found near was that of a vampire named Ivan," Kirsa stated.

"He was found by hikers who stumbled across his body hiking in the woods outside of Grabenberg," Sara told her. "The body had been decapitated but the head was found in a sports bag next to the body. There was no serious mutilation to the body. If anything, it looked like Ivan had fought back but was over powered."

Kirsa stared at the information, not even a were-animal could over power a vampire enough to do the damage that was done to Ivan. She had been through all the folders already but something about Ivan was bothering her.

"You would know better than me," Kirsa began.

"The answer is no," Sara said before Kirsa could ask the question. "Even Phil said that he wouldn't have been able to take down Ivan in that manner. If it was a were it would be a lot more bloody and grotesque. You would see claw marks, teeth marks."

Kirsa nodded in agreement. Sara saw the perplexed look on her friends face. "What is it?"

"This doesn't leave this room," Kirsa warned. Sara nodded. "Ivan was part of what the Councils had nicknamed the next generation. He was being trained to take a seat on the General Council of Vampires."

"That's a big target," Sara stated.

"There were rumors that he might become the Russians Line head when their current one stepped down."

Sara let out a whistle. "Did you ever meet him.

Kirsa had met him, he was deathly pale for those of his line could not step foot in the sun; even with protection, for any ray that hit them would burn severely. Before she had left Germany she caught some whispering between Wyrm and Adam about the prospect of a spy in the Council that was leaking information to some unknown people.

"I have, he was sociable, polite," Kirsa commented. "Did you finish Kelly?"

"Just got permission to release her body to her parents," Sara sighed. "But the liquid silver is the cause of death."

"They're not sticking to a m.o," Kirsa noted.

"Your thinking multiple killers," Sara replied.

"I am," Kirsa agreed.

"Tony and Al both are not going to like that," Sara noted.

"I know."

"Then lets pour over what we have to give them pause to realize it's a possibility," Sara suggested.

They worked for four hours pouring over the crime scene photos and case notes of each of the victims they had so far. They noted the differences between each case, how they were connected, but how it could be a different player at the same time. When Sara left they were both mentally exhausted. Between them, they were both troubled about Ivan being killed. Neither ready to voice their opinion on how it could be done.

Kirsa opened up her email on her lap top and began the encryption process for the email she was going to send Al.His encryption was fool proof. The only way to get it was if he told you willingly, so even if one was held against their will they would not be able to give the code. That was the magick of Al. Kirsa also could not go and tell anyone the encryption because it would come out wrong.

Boss man,

I began looking through the files that Tony gave me. Something does not make sense. I need you to look over the first kill, and I am also going to need the files on the three vampires that were murdered in Chicago about five months ago. Ivan was part of that group. Something is bothering me about this. How could a mortal take down a vampire and not just one but possibly four at one time. Hearing rumors about a spy in a certain council, this could be a link.

KH

Kirsa looked over the email again and attached the encrypted file on Ivan. She hit send just as she heard the doorbell ring. She closed her laptop and placed the files in a locked drawer. Taking her notebook with her she walked to the front door. Sabrina stood there smiling holding pizza. Kirsa looked at her watch and saw it was noon.

"Figured you haven't had enough real pizza yet," Sabrina said kissing Kirsa on the cheek and entering the house. Zero bounded into the room and greeted Sabrina by running around her and wagging his tail a mile a minute.

"Come on into the kitchen. I was working in the office," Kirsa told her as they made their way to the back of the house. "You missed Sara. She was here earlier."

"Did I interrupt?" Sabrina asked. Sara had texted her about where she found Kirsa. So she thought coming over and checking in on her seemed like a good idea. And pizza was the perfect excuse.

"No I need the break and this is the perfect distraction." Kirsa got out some paper plates and felt the stare from Sabrina. "Sara and I were working the case so my mind is all fuddled."

Sabrina opened up the pizza box and folded it over. "Half cheese and half pepperoni."

"I love you," Kirsa replied sitting down at the table. Zero plopped down on the kitchen rug and gazed wistfully at the pizza box.

"I take it you started working on the case?' Sabrina asked taking a sip of water from the glass that Kirsa had poured her.

"Yeah, Tony dropped the files off yesterday so I was just going over them. Some things don't add up, but then they never do."

"Think Lars could be of help?" Sabrina asked.

"He's not high enough to have the answers I need, but thanks."

"I take it that work is not what you needed to be distracted from?"

Kirsa bit into her plain cheese pizza and savored in the deliciousness. Nowhere outside of the New York area got pizza right. She had been too exhausted the other night to fully appreciate the taste. Now that Jet Lag was over she could.

"No, if anything work was my distraction," Kirsa sighed as she put her slice down to take a drink.

Sabrina studied her friends face and knew something was wrong, which she was not really surprised about.

"You wanna talk about it?"

"It's not just my parents but Anton also."

Sabrina leaned back in her chair and looked at her friend. "I figured your parents but Anton?"

"Think about it, we all hung out; it was Anton, you, Brian and me," Kirsa said reminding them both of their childhood. "Then you added Daniel, Collin and Thomas and we were our own gang. I know Anton didn't spend a lot of time with us but he was there. I guess that's the hard part. Looking back and trying not to feel hurt and betrayed."

"Brian and I went through it. Actually so did the Lyon's," Sabrina told her. "Danny never wanted you to know but I thought he was going to kill Anton when it came out what all happened. At the same time we all felt hurt and betrayed."

Kirsa stared at her. "I never knew."

"Kirs, you buried your parents and Aunt and Uncle within months of each other than found out that Anton was involved. I think the five of us were in constant contact for a while. None of us really knew how to come to terms with any of it. Then Collin finally came up with something."

"Leave it to the lawyer," Kirsa laughed. "What did he come up with?"

"That the Anton in our childhood memories is not the same Anton that betrayed us. I think that kind of helped us come to terms with what he did," Sabrina told her.

"How about your parents?" Kirsa asked.

"Oh my God, they figured that out as soon as everything came out. It's why they were able to move on so much faster because to them he was not the son they raised." Sabrina studied Kirsa. "You're not still in love with him?"

Kirsa almost choked on her pizza. "No. Definitely not. I think I was in love with the idea of us."

Sabrina looked into the living room from the kitchen table. "You need furniture."

"The storage place brought the necessities first. Now they're going to bring everything else so I can go through what I want to keep or donate," Kirsa informed her. "Way to change topics by the way."

"No problem. So you really are planning on settling here?" Sabrina asked.

"Yeah," Kirsa replied. "Let's move outside."

They had killed most of the pie, leaving only two pieces left. Kirsa wrapped them in foil and put them in the fridge. Grabbing their waters, they walked outside to sit on the chairs that were on the deck. Kirsa wanted to enjoy the sun on the skin while she could.

"When do your parents go back to South Carolina?" Kirsa asked.

"Another day or two," Sabrina told her. "Was it business or pleasure?"

"Both, they got to annoy Brian and me. But they also had to some work with the foundation they set up in memory of your parents."

Kirsa nodded, not saying anything. It still pulled at her heart that they had done that. The foundation gave out aid to those who were victims of violence. She sat on the board of directors but was an absent member which the other eleven members totally understood.

"Do you remember when we were teenagers and would talk about Lars growing up? We use to daydream about him and all the others that came to visit," Kirsa said to Sabrina.

"What about Ayden? You compared every boyfriend and crush to him," Sabrina reminder her.

"Ayden," Kirsa replied. She smiled remembering the almost year and a half she spent traveling with him.

"Kirs, I swore when you came back from Europe he was going to be with you," Sabrina told her.

Kirsa sighed. "That situation is complicated. However touring Europe with him was the first real vacation I ever had. A year spent touring Ireland, Norway, and Iceland all with the very sexy Ayden."

"You had to have kissed?" Sabrina asked. Kirsa very rarely talked about her year off.

"There might have been a few but somehow we were always interrupted. Besides it was a childhood crush I had on him."

"Had?" Sabrina asked turning to face her. "If he showed up you would jump his bones in a heartbeat."

"There are two reasons that won't happen. One, that only happens in my fantasy and two, it's complicated."

"May I remind you of Italy in the neighborhood bar where you two were a wee bit tipsy?" Sabrina reminded her with a smirk.

When she had been able to schedule time off from the ranch she met up with Kirsa in Europe. On this particular night, Ayden and Kirsa were so into each other that Isabella and Sabrina actually left the bar to give them space. Of course they laughed all the way to the next bar about the two of them.

"We both slept alone that night," Sabrina shot her a look. "Alright look we did not have sex. We came close but it would have been a mistake and we both knew it."

Sabrina raised an eyebrow and took a sip of her water. There was more to the story then Kirsa was sharing. So she stared at her friend waiting for her to cave.

Kirsa sighed, twirling a curl with her finger.

"You are a pain in the ass, we are somewhat together." Before Sabrina could rejoice Kirsa put her hand up to stop her. "The problem is for him to move here or to Germany he would have to petition the Council as well as the head over here or be assigned as my permanent Shadow. Besides that he knows I have trust issues still."

"So you have talked."

"We still have not slept together and I still have major trust issues," Kirsa repeated.

"That might be, but that journey did you well," Sabrina informed her then chuckled at the surprised look on her friends face. "When you told me you were leaving to go to Germany and possibly travel I thought 'thank you God.' Because I knew you needed to get away, you needed to find yourself again and learn to put the pain aside. It will never go away but you learned how to live with it.

"When I saw you in Italy with him and then when you settled back in Germany, you had become a more grown up version of yourself. Most importantly, you lost the wounded look. I think spending time with Ayden made you realize something that you lost with Anton."

Kirsa went to speak but found no voice. It was the first time Sabrina had ever expressed her concern and her pleasure in the journey Kirsa had embarked on. Hearing it come from her best friend solidified some of her own thoughts.

"Thank you," Kirsa said.

"So is he a good kisser?" Sabrina was answered with a pillow thrown at her.

"I am not answering that question," Kirsa glanced at her watch. "I have a doctor's appointment; do you want to join me?"

****

While Sabrina and Kirsa made their way to Morristown for a doctor's appointment, Tony stood with Lars and another man at the murder scene of Kelly. Joe and one of his sons were off to the side with another officer answering some more questions. Lars had a baseball cap on, a hooded sweatshirt on with the hood up and sunglasses.

He was not what one would call a day walker, meaning a vampire that could walk uncovered in the sunlight. He looked over at the man currently crouched, examining where the body had been found. Ayden was a day walker, but he was still pale as anything. Just because he could walk around in the day did not mean he could tan.

Ayden O'Brian was one of the best

Shadows of the Vampire Council. The Shadows were an elite group that was part body guards and part spies. They were able to kill whoever endangered the person they were assigned too. To become one, one had to be nominated and have full approval of the Inner Council. You had to be the best fighter and hunter, your senses had to be fine-tuned, you had to be able to leave no trace and move around unnoticed.

They were like undead assassins with a license to kill. He was now here to help with Kirsa and the case. Lars had just picked him up from the airport and at Tony's request and brought him to the scene. He prowled around the area of the field where the crime had happened.

"There was a vampire here," Ayden began. "He has to be ancient; he knows how to hide his scent which is why it's hard to pick up on it. But Phil's right, there was one that chased her."

Tony wrote down what Ayden told him as they moved to the dump site, he watched as Ayden crouched down to the ground and sniffed the air around it. With all the searches he knew Ayden was trying to decipher the scents.

"There are two vampire scents here, though the one is really odd almost familiar in away and distorted at the same time," Ayden confirmed what Phil had reported.

"So we have two vamps involved with the cult?" Lars asked pulling his hood father down his face.

Before Ayden could answer one of the officers walked over. He had a pained expression on his face.

"Captain, Washington just pulled up and he looks pissed," Anthony Sousa told them.

"Shit."Tony replied. It was Washington's day off. "Alright, Lars can you go with Sousa. If he sees both of you here he will explode and I would rather not have to deal with that."

The two men nodded and walked away. Tony and Ayden stood watching the crew cut blonde storm their way. They exchanged looks with each other as he approached.

"What the fuck is this asshole doing here?" Chris demanded pointing a finger at Ayden.

"I have asked Mr. O'Brian to come here and help out," Tony explained his voice perfectly neutral.

"What authority does he have here?" Chris wanted to know as he clenched his fists.

"By being a Shadow, I am a qualified international OPIA liaison. I was told to come and help out with the case here," Ayden explained trying not to be smug.

What he said was true. When the Occult and Paranormal Laws were created, the UN allowed the Vampire Council to select certain Shadows to be trained by OPIA. This would allow the Shadows to work side by side other agents when they were needed.

"And why is that?" Chris asked.

"That would be between me and the agency," Ayden replied folding his arms across his chest.

Chris turned his fury on to Tony. "He is only here because that whore is here…"

Tony stopped him with a look. "You are lucky this is your day off because otherwise I would be hauling your ass to the station for holding up an investigation. And by whore you better not be referring to Kirsa Heinrich, because if you are then we are going to need to have a conversation on how to treat superior officers," Tony told him. "Now will you kindly get off my crime scene before I have you escorted?"

"You're sticking up for this fucking bloodsucker?" Chris asked.

"This 'fucking blood sucker' saved my life and for that he will always have my respect and friendship,"Tony responded. He then motioned to two officers who had been paying attention in case they needed to break up a fight.

"I can leave on my own," Chris replied picking up on the signal. He stormed away with the two cops following him just to make sure that he did in fact leave.

Lars returned and stood with the two men. They stood in silence for a few minutes.

"How does he know I am connected to Kirsa?" Ayden asked.

Tony looked at him. "With the exception of South Carolina, you and Kirsa have never worked a case together,"Tony said. "I'll look into it."

"And there were three other Shadows working down in South Carolina," Lars added. "He's a ticking time bomb, Tony."

"I know, so does everyone else in the department," Tony replied. "Before we were interrupted you said something about two vampires?"

"I can't be certain because of all the different scents," Ayden told him. "But there is definitely a scent of a vampire, and an old one, lurking around."

"Some of the farmers have been complaining about animals missing," Joe told them as he approached them, his son following behind. "I'm sorry about Chris. This is my property and I want people to feel comfortable."

"Joe, it's not your problem that one of my officers runs his mouth," Tony said.

"That may be, but I am sorry for it."

"Thanks Joe," Tony told him. "Do you know which farmers they are?"

"Sure I can write the names down for you," Joe said. "Do you know if anything was left behind?" Ayden asked. "From what they said, there were no noises coming from the barn to show the animals were spooked. They would arrive in the barn in the morning and an animal would be gone. They ranged from a chicken to a calf. No footprints, no blood, nothing," Joe explained.

"It would have to be an old one to not leave any trace, more so because he did not disturb the other animals. If a newer vampire was to approach a barn the animals would have become agitated," Lars said. "You got any were-animals working for you?"

"No," Joe said then thought for a moment. "My oldest girl is dating a were-lion."

Ayden jerked around. "Really? A were-lion?"

"Is that bad?" Joe asked concerned all of a sudden.

"No they are unbelievably rare," Ayden said. Phil was the only one he had ever met that was one. "They are some of the best trackers too. Your daughter is a lucky one to be dating one. He will protect her and your family with his life."

"He's part of Phil's pack," Tony told Ayden. "He's been training him to be a tracker. He's the only other were-lion on the east coast."

"Do you want me to have him stand guard?" Joe asked trying not to blush.

"Not exactly. When he is here though, have him walk around and see what he picks up."

"Ok."

They started walking back to the farm house. Ayden was taking in the scene. He was ignoring the glares from Lars. Lars had always been a little jealous that he could walk about in the day light and not burn. He was not his strongest during the day but he did not have to deal with the nasty burning that went with the sun.

"Tell me about the case that you think

might be linked?" Tony asked as they stood at their cars. Lars had already gotten in the car and shut the door so that he could escape the sun.

"About three months ago a delegation of what is labeled the next generation for the Vampire Council was to come to America and meet with the heads here. However, they never go to their final destination. Some were killed instantly others were left and the rest were taken. No word has been heard from those taken. No ransom, nothing. The vampire you found a few months ago was one of the members that been taken," Ayden explained.

Tony let out a whistle. "Damn. Alright we will be in touch."

Ayden watched as Lars drove through the country side, then into the town center. They were heading toward the mountains.

"Have you told her that I am coming?" Ayden asked Lars.

"No. Thought you could surprise her. It would perk her up a bit," Lars replied.

Chapter Twelve

Going to the doctors was not a simple endeavor for Kirsa. For her it meant blood being taking, results being studied. And bad news always following.

Her doctors, Allan Finn, walked in. He was in his late 40's and been her hematologist for about ten years now. He had worked under her father's doctor. His blonde hair was starting to go grey around the edges, but his brown eyes still twinkled when he smiled.

"How have you actually been feeling?" he asked her as he sat down at his desk.

"Rundown, my energy starts to drain sooner. I have sometimes have issues remembering what I am supposed to be doing. The circles under my eyes are not fading anymore when I do get more sleep,"Kirsa told him. It was pointless lying to him; he always managed to get the truth out of her.

"And upping your dosage and amount of times a day is not helping?" he asked making notes. A few months prior, he had been in Germany for a conference. While there he paid a visit to Kirsa and had upped her dosage.

"It does but it wears off after a while. I really don't want to keep vials with me all the time." Kirsa told him.

There were practicality issues with carrying vials of blood around with her. Something about being on a crime scene and having to take one out did not sound like a good idea.

Dr. Finn looked over her records and then pulled out three pieces of paper that contained different data on them. He looked at Kirsa not sure where to start.

"We need to talk seriously about your future," he began.

"I feel like I am going to be getting the college lecture from a guidance counselor."

He chuckled. "This coming from the girl who skipped high school, we do need to talk seriously."

Dr. Finn pulled out a sheet labeled "Living Vampire." It showed the body functions, the different cell counts and blood levels. A living vamp was a rare occurrence. One parent needed to be a vampire and the other parent would be one step away from the becoming a vampire. Even then it was only a twenty five percent chance they would survive and become a living vampire. The living vamp was mortal but had heightened senses.

For them to become a full blood vampire, it would only have to take blood from a vampire and go through the actual death, whereas a regular mortal would have to go through a series of "kisses" before the final one. Or on the rare occasion be drained of blood until they were almost dead and forced to drink their makers blood. That was the most violent way of turning. Until a living vampire became a vampire they were still mortal, they could die or be killed just like anyone else.

Dr. Finn then pulled out the same type of data on vampires. Kirsa compared the two pieces of paper. Kirsa was not sure where he was going with this but she already didn't like it.

"Many of us thought that you would end up being closer to that of a living vampire. We thought that the disorder that runs in your family was an early form of it. "

"I'm hearing a very disturbing 'but' coming on," she said not sure what to think.

"Here is your data." He pulled out the sheet of paper. "You can see that your body stats are not like the living vampire at all."

"So what are you telling me?" she asked him as she looked over the three different read outs compared to her own. Staring at the three charts, she could see where this could possibly be heading. It was heading in a direction no one had considered.

"The disorder that runs only in your family is truly one of a kind," Allan confessed. "Leaving out the medical jargon, your body is dying and at the same time preparing for the turn. You are already getting known vampire traits. Heightened senses, your pupils no longer dilate like they should. Remember we once thought that in order to keep you alive you might have to go through the turn by feeding from a vamp?"

"Uh huh," she said. "We talked about this a year ago. That I would have to go through the normal procedures of a person willing to change or that of a living vamp waiting for the 'last kiss' as they call it. Why?"

"From what the information your body is now telling us, you are not going to have to do that," he watched the shock and confusion wash over her face.

He wished Hagan was there to comfort his daughter. Four months before his death he had been told the same news. However, Hagan had not passed the information onto his daughter when he died.

"Ok, so I will, what, wake up one day and be a vamp?" Kirsa asked a little bit confused. This was different from what they had always assumed.

Dr. Finn sat back in his chair. "No. You are in away going to slowly turn into a vampire."

"You're joking right?" Kirsa asked, not sure if she wanted to believe him.

"I'm afraid not. You are going to experience your own death. Unlike those wanting the change, you will not need blood. However just like a person who wants to become a vamp it could kill you at the same time. Your body could go into shock about experiencing its own death or change, and you could die from the shock."

"And my chances are?" she asked,

"Fifty?fifty," he told her. "That's just a guess though because no one in your family that we have researched had your advanced stage."

Kirsa stared at him. Never had anyone

thought that the disorder that ran through her family would be fatal. The ones who had it, had been killed or died long before the disorder advanced enough. She knew that she was of the few where the disorder advanced at a quicker rate. Her father had only started the vials in his thirties. If he ever went to the bags she hadn't been told.

****

During the ride from Morristown back to Grabenberg, Kirsa told Sabrina what Finn had told her. Sabrina, knowing there was nothing she could say, squeezed her hand. She then called the ranch to tell them she would be out for the rest of the day but would have her cell if she was needed. When they returned home Sabrina suggested beginning to go through the boxes that had been delivered and sorting them into keep, donate, or for the manor. Sabrina knew that it would keep Kirsa's mind from dwelling on what had happened at the doctors.

They were sitting in the center of the living room with boxes all around them. They were laughing over some of the pictures that they were unwrapping. Sabrina found the one of her, Lars and Kirsa on the beach. Both Kirsa and she were in two pieces and Lars was completely covered.

"Do you remember that?" Sabrina laughed pointing to the picture.

Kirsa stopped wrapping a family vase for the manor box and looked at it laughing. "Yes and the little boy who asked him why he had all those clothes on at the beach, Lars bent down and explained why, the kid wanted his autograph."

One of the cons about dating a vampire was they tended to burn up in the sun. Unless they were a day walker then it didn't matter. Unfortunately Lars was not a day walker so no walking hand in hand on the beach when the sun was out. However to be loved the way she was and to love back that way was worth the sacrifice.

"Where is your pale other half?" Kirsa asked as she added more to the manor box.

Sabrina continued sorting kitchen stuff, "I don't know. I know he has been doing some things for the Council. He was up around the same time I was this morning, said he had a meeting."

"There is a lot going on right now within the Council," Kirsa explained. "From what I got out of Wyrm, someone with in the council is passing information to some of their enemies."

Sabrina looked at her for a moment and let out a whistle. "Wow. I take it the General Council is being looked at?"

Kirsa nodded, "Ayden and three other Shadows had to investigate each member without them knowing."

The Vampire Council was comprised of two Councils, the Inner Council and the General Council. The Inner Council was made up of the five heads of the five blood lines. There was a sixth seat but it remained vacant. The General Council was made up the elected heads of each of the sub or family lines that were within the five lines.

The Councils appointed bodyguards to watch over the general members or any vampire that might need extra help. The Shadows were more than body guards. They were appointed by the Inner Council and acted as: body guards, assassins, warriors, diplomats, and where OPIA was present they were liaisons.

"I take it that's why Ayden has been so busy lately," Sabrina realized.

"He wanted to come with me but is so tied up with the case that he couldn't."

"That had to kill him."

Kirsa nodded as they continued to go

through the boxes. After they emptied about half of the boxes Kirsa rolled her shoulders. "You wanna beer?" Kirsa asked.

Sabrina looked at her watch and saw it was close to 6pm. "Sure why not."

Kirsa checked on the London broil that was marinating on the counter before opening the fridge to pull out two beers. She heard a car pull into the driveway and called into Sabrina that Lars was back.

"Hey Lars you want a beer?" she asked grabbing two DAB's, a nice German beer, as the back door opened.

Kirsa froze a little when the scent hit her. Kirsa had noticed that within the last month her sense of smell had increased and became more refined. This scent did not belong to Lars, but the answer seemed impossible.

"I would love one but I'm not Lars," a thick Irish accent replied.

Kirsa stood up closing her eyes and was convinced that she was hearing things. A hand came and grabbed the beers out of her hands then set them down on the counter. Kirsa turned and stared up into amazing clear blue eyes. Light brown wavy hair was falling into them and cascading in curls down past broad muscular shoulders.

"Tell me I am dreaming." she whispered. No way was he here in her kitchen. Not when he was supposed to be away on a case.

"If you are then so must I," Ayden whispered back as he stared at her for a moment. "I have missed you."

He picked her up into a hug holding her as close to him as possible. She laughed as she wrapped her arms around him. Pressing their foreheads, Ayden stared into her eyes before he kissed her. It had been about two months since they had seen each other. They lingered over the kiss trying to make up for two months. When they finally broke apart Kirsa laughed and stared at him. He set her down he kissed her forehead.

"What are you doing here?" she asked. Neither paid any attention to Lars standing in the doorway.

"Dietrich asked me," he informed her. "I'm your Shadow."

Kirsa blinked. "What?" It was almost unheard for a human to have a shadow assigned to them.

"I was in his office when you called and now here I am," he explained to her.

Kirsa looked at Lars. "He is what you had to go and do and you didn't tell me."

Lars shrugged his shoulders and took one of the beers that were on the counter. "It was worth it to see the look on your face."

Kirsa walked over and hugged him. Lars sat his beer down and hugged her back.

"Hey Kirsa where's my beer?" Sabrina asked coming in from outside. "Holy shit, Ayden!"

Ayden smiled as Sabrina hugged him. "I believe this beer is yours," he said handing her the beer.

Sabrina laughed and took it. "I can't believe it; we were just talking about you."

Kirsa shot her a dirty look. Ayden caught the look and laughed. Within minutes he and Lars were ushered out of the kitchen so that Kirsa could prepare a celebration dinner for him coming to America. Vampires could eat food; they tended to take small bites here and there.

Their body broke food down much the way that it did with blood, yet if they ate too much it could take a while to completely break down in their system. Some food, though, could take months to completely break down leaving a vampire feeling bloated or feeling full. Red meat was one of the foods their body had no issues breaking down.

Kirsa relaxed during dinner, they laughed about their travels, about things happening at the ranch. It was nice to have this again, this normalcy of friends.

As the sun set, Zero laid down next to Kirsa as they all lingered over their wine. Lars studied Ayden over his glass of wine.

"So where you staying, Irish?" Lars asked finishing the wine in his glass.

Before he could answer, Kirsa spoke. "Here."

Lars raised an eyebrow at the look Ayden gave her. "You think that's a good idea?" Lars inquired, ignoring the protective feeling that arose.

"There's plenty of rooms here for him to stay in," Kirsa pointed out. "Why? I'm a big girl, Lars. I can have co-ed sleepovers."

Lars narrowed his eyes, Sabrina just laughed and took his hand. "Come on protective big brother let's get you home. I will talk to you tomorrow, Kirsa."

Kirsa nodded as she sipped her wine, Ayden rose as Sabrina got up. When she and Lars left he sat back down, Kirsa smiled at him. Silence fell between them but there was no awkwardness to it.

"I can stay at the Council safe house in Morristown," Ayden pointed out.

"How will you be my Shadow if you stay somewhere else?" Kirsa asked with a smile. "It would be hard to be a bodyguard that far away."

"Keep up with lines like that, and I will find ways to silence you," Ayden warned with a smile. He got up and kissed her lightly, "Go take a bath. I will talk care of the dishes."

Kirsa walked up the back stairs that led to the master suite. It would be nice to soak in the bath tub and read more of the journal that Dietrich had given her. When her par- ents, Aunt and Uncle had been killed, Kirsa and her cousin Adam cleared out the Vaults that contained the histories of the vampires.

They handed countless of untranslated documents over to Wyrm telling him to translate and copy. The old Council had decreed that human families tied to the Council should keep safe the history of the vampires. The Heinrich family had been chosen. In the twentieth century Adam's parents were chosen to hold the other half of the contents.

Adam and Kirsa decided the contents should be brought to the Heinrich estate and be cataloged and researched. At first the Inner

Council was reluctant, later decided they were right in copying the contents considering how close they had come to half the vaults being wiped out. It was a four year process, Kirsa photographed every object: book, journal, jewels, weapons, and anything else that they had contained.

A few months ago Wyrm handed Adam and Kirsa the translated version of the family journals and documents that had also been in the vault. The Inner Council did not have the copies yet because Wyrm thought the heirs should be the ones read them first.

The journal she was about to read came from the around the time period the blood oath had been made between the First Council and her family. Walking into the bathroom, she turned the bathtub water on and began lighting the candles that she had set around the room. She poured scented bubble bath into the water.

Stripping down to nothing she walked into her bedroom and grabbed the journal and then stepped into the hot bath. Sighing, she felt her muscles relax and her body begin to unwind. Maybe Sabrina was right. She needed to do this. She thought it was cute how Wyrm had it printed in old fashion handwriting instead of a normal font. Opening to the first page of the journal she began to read.

****

The lord has died. According to father, they do not know who the heir is, for the lord of the land had no children. No one is mourning his death for he was a horrible man who treated everyone like we were worthless. Which in his eyes, I guess we were. He would not allow anyone but aristocrats into the castle; he once turned the Prince away because the Prince did not like how the lord treated his people. The Prince felt that the lord was mistreating his people and said so.

We are waiting for some of the laws he imposed to be done away with but they cannot be done until a new lord is found…

A stranger rode into town today. He was breathtaking, black hair and deep brown eyes, high cheek bones, pale skin, and tall. My brother and I were walking to the market when the man rode up on us. He got down from the horse and introduced himself as Hagan. We introduced ourselves. He asked us for directions to the castles for he was a relative of the late lord. We gave them to him…

"Do you care to show me?" Hagan asked from under the hood of his cloak, his dark hair was pulled back and blended in with the black cloak.

Charles and Kirsa looked at each other. Kirsa spoke as her brother stood behind her. "We would my lord, but we can go no further than the bridge before the castle road."

Hagan stared at her not understanding. "Why is that?"

"The late lord passed a law twenty years before stating that only nobility was allowed to travel the castle road," She informed him. Self-consciously she smoothed out the front of her deep brown dress.

"What if you had a complaint or an emergency?" Hagan asked dumbfounded. He had never heard of a lord being that arrogant that he would not allow his own people to come on the grounds.

"We were instructed that three times a week his secretary would come in to town to hear any complaints or cases."

Hagan closed his eyes, silently cursing the man who had come from his blood. "Then let us break this law."

He lifted Kirsa up on the horse so that she may ride as he walked with her brother. The stranger had been careful as to not let the hood fall from his face shielding himself from the sun. He then let her ten year old brother lead, they made their way to the castle.

At dinner that night father told us that the council met and found the document showed by Lord Hagan was in order and that after the burial tomorrow he will be our new lord. My father seems to like him and says he will be good for our town. He also told me that the new lord asked if he could *pay a call tomorrow early evening and take me on a walk. My father told him that it was fine with him if I wanted to go. I cannot believe that this man has taken an interest in me. Tomorrow night I need to collect herbs for one of the women in town is near ready to birth, so I will take him with me.*

****

Kirsa closed the journal and leaned back into the bath tub. She had once been told that she had been named for an ancestor like her father had been. She knew the town her ancestors came from was an odd town. It had always been a sanctuary for people who did not belong. For centuries, vampires worked right next to a regular human. A were-wolf was not looked upon as a freak but instead would be a guardsman. It rarely had interference from the government; for even the government knew that the town was overseen by the Vampire Council.

The Vampire Council was in its fourth Council since it began in the 500's, every new head marked a new Council. The Council that had made the blood oath to Kirsa's family in 1000 C.E. was long deceased and had chosen not to pass the information on when the new members were selected by the elders at the time. There were rumors, speculations but the truth was clouded in a mystery.

Slowly she blew the candles out and got of the tub. After drying off, she put on boxer shorts and a black tank top. She walked to her bay window and curled up on the window seat. The moon was in the sky and the stars were out. She smelled him before he entered her room.

Ayden knocked on the opened door and then entered her room. It was not big, but not small. The walls were a pale yellow; the furniture in the bedroom was made of a rose wood. Kirsa sat curled on the window seat, her hair was damp from the bath. Scents from the candle and bubble bath still lingered in the air. Ayden walked up to the window and stared out on to the night sky.

"It's so clear out," Kirsa said breaking the silence.

"It is, reminds me of home," he handed her a glass of wine.

Kirsa smiled. "You wanna sit down?"

He nodded and sat on the other side of the seat resting his wine glass on the window sill next to hers.

"So Dietrich sent you?" she asked.

"Yes and no," Ayden replied turning to look at her. He saw the surprise flash into her eyes.

"Yes and no?" Kirsa repeated. "Meaning what?"

"I also told you I wanted to talk to you," he reminded her. "I had been in Dietrich's office the night when you called."

"Why?" Kirsa asked unsure of what to think. Dietrich had made no notion that there was someone else in the room when she had called.

"I was telling him that I was taking a leave of absence. I had purchased a ticket to New Jersey to see you. I gave him the information I found out about the cult and then was going to leave to take the flight which I still wound up taking."

"Why?" She hated to repeat herself but it seemed necessary.

"Simple, I missed you and didn't want you going through this alone. The past year spending time with you, traveling all around Europe with you filled me with memories and feeling. I could not get them out of my head. I missed you, just being around you." He twirled one of her curls around his finger.

"Shamus got sick of me moping about the farm and told me I either had to come here and see you or quit moping about, so I chose the first option," Ayden said simply. "I was at

Dietrich's because I had finished work on my case and I wanted him to know I was going to New Jersey, I didn't know how long, but that I needed to see you. He told me ok and then you called. When I heard about the case, I volunteered to be your Shadow, Dietrich could trust no other to protect you. I came here because I wanted too, no one sent me."

Kirsa turned and stared out at the night sky. She was not sure what to think or feel. What was real or what was child hood fantasy.

"You missed me?" she asked with a smile.

He chuckled. "All I know is that I needed to see you and be here with you. I don't know what might happen I just know I missed you. It was like a part of me was gone."

"Ayden…" she began.

He put a finger to her lips. "I don't know what we are and I know you have trust issues. All I am asking is to let's just see what happens."

She gently kissed him then curled into his arms as they sat and watched the stars come out. It was time to start moving forward and putting the past behind her.

****

On one of the service roads that ran

through the Heinrich property a car was pulled over with all it lights off. He had spent a better part of the night watching what had been going on at what was deemed the guest house. It was his job to find out information on the Grabenberg cases. Picking up his cell phone he scrolled down to Nick Cullen. Nick was Second in Command for what had been named the Salvation Project. He reported to the head of the East Coast Branch of the Church of Light.

On the second ring Nick picked up.

"Hey we got a problem here," he told Nick.

"What sort of problem?" Nick asked. He had been working on wiring in the headquarters in Grabenberg, NJ.

"Let's just say Miss Adam's worst nightmare has come out of hiding."

"The good doctor?" Nick asked taking the pen out of his mouth.

"Yes and not only does she have one blood sucker hanging around her but another arrived this afternoon and is staying at the house with her."

"Damn," Nick said on the other end. "Alright keep doing what you are doing. I will pass the information on. Let me know if anything else pops up."

With that they hung up. He deleted the call and then started his car up, it was late and his wife would start wondering where he was since he didn't often work the night shift.

Chapter Thirteen

*He*r home office was starting to come together. With her furniture delivered the pace was starting to feel more like home. What Kirsa didn't fit into the shelves she piled along the wall of the room. Zero, of course, had a bed in this room as well, which he was currently snoring on. With her office set up temporarily she could focus on the case files. Sara had dropped off some pictures of the bodies from all the involved cases earlier in the morning; she also wanted to check on how Kirsa was settling in.

After she left, Kirsa sat in her office and began to go through the pictures, even as a veteran to gruesome things her stomach still turned at some of the pictures. On a large white board she started to tape up the important information.

The first victim had been a vampire. They had not used a stake to kill him because that would be too easy. Instead they slowly dropped holy water on him, exposed small parts of him to sun and deprived him of any form of blood. The pure agony was etched in his face even after he died. His body was burned from the water and exposure to sun but he died from starvation.

The note that was left with him was blunt. It read: Nowhere in the seven days did God create creatures of the night. Therefore they are the work of the devil and must be destroyed.

Kirsa placed the note on her desk and ran a hand through her hair sending curls every which way.

She looked around her office trying to reorganize her thoughts. The house was now unpacked and furnished, making it feel more like her home as oppose to a guest. There was a knock on the French doors, a second later they opened and Lars walked in yawning. Each morning he made it routine to come over and check in on how she was doing and if anything happened. It didn't matter that Ayden was now in the house. He handed her a mug and plopped down on the overstuffed leather chair that sat across from her desk. She asked what was up.

"Well, Doctor, I think my problem is I have this crazy thirst for blood," Lars said smiling.

Kirsa almost spit the contents back into the mug from laughing. She shook her head smiling as she swallowed.

"What brings you here so early?" she asked as she looked at the clock, it was only 10 am. This meant if he was up, every blind was pulled down and curtains closed.

"Sabrina was up and out early this morning. She had to teach a lesson at 11 and had paper work to do." Lars replied. He took a sip from his mug. "Brian dropped her parents off at the airport."

"I'm sure you guys will be happy to have the place back to yourselves," Kirsa replied watching him drink his mug. Its contents were steaming.

"What?" he asked noticing her staring at his mug.

"How can you drink it warm?" Kirsa asked then held up a hand at his slow smile forming. "Wait, I don't want to know."

"Brie also told me that you are needed at

the Ranch at some point to discuss some business stuff." Lars then focused on the closed letter on her desk and raised both eyebrows. "What are you reading so early in the morning?"

"Letters from the other murder scenes." Kirsa told him.

He let out a whistle. "Fun, nothing like a little light reading in the morning."

"You really came in here to annoy me?" she asked closing the folder before he could see the pictures and notes.

"Actually I have a question for you?" he asked her.

"What?" she asked, raising an eyebrow.

"Where are the vials?" he asked. Lars knew that in her coffee each morning was at least three vials of blood. He had dropped some bags off for Ayden in the fridge and didn't see any of her vials.

"Oh, I don't need the vials anymore." she told him. Part of her hoped that she could fool a vampire even though she knew that was highly unlikely.

"What are you on now?"

She stared at him; she really did not want to

get into this. "With everything going on you want to discuss my blood dosage?"

He sipped his mug and stared at her. There was no point in trying to glamour her, her condition made it hard for that to work. So if he stared at her long enough she would eventually cave and tell him.

Rolling her eyes, Kirsa caved. "Ok fine. The vials were no longer doing their thing. So he has me on synthetic for the time being."

"Uh huh, how much? Vial, injection, 8oz bottle or IV bag?"

"You're impossible, you know that," Kirsa replied. "I'm on the bags."

"Do you want to talk about the doctors?" he asked.

"No," she said simply.

"Where's Irish?" Lars asked. "Shouldn't he be hovering in the shadows ready to pounce?"

"Dietrich called and needed to talk to him about something," Kirsa told him. "What's your issue with him again?"

"Issue? I have no issue with the Irish Rover," Lars said. "So why the serious look?"

Kirsa leaned back in her chair. "I think we need to take a trip upstate."

"No, absolutely not," he exclaimed. "No way in hell am I letting you near that monster," Lars said standing up, he knew exactly what she was talking about. "Are you insane?"

She was not surprised at all by his reaction she knew he was going to react this way. It was not like she was suggestion they go on vacation. She was pretty sure Tony would hit the roof when she ran her idea by him also.

"It is perfectly safe.The Paranormal Prison is the most secure prison on the continent.That's why it has prisoners from Canada, Mexico, and the rest of Latin America," She pointed out.

"It's not that I'm afraid something is going to physically hurt you. I'm worried about you emotionally," Lars said sitting down. "You're going there to talk to him aren't you?"

"Yes, he is the only link we have to the church," she retorted.

"So what, that makes him fucking available for questioning?"

"Yes, look I'm not asking for permission on this. I'm asking if you want to come with me. Either way I'm going."

"Why?"

"Because until I have probable cause to talk

to Veronica Adams, he is the only access I have to the higher up workings of the Church of Light without having to get a warrant."

"And you think you'll be able to walk in there and not get upset?" Lars laid a hand on top of hers. "Honey, I was there, I watched you go through all the levels of hell. I have also watched you pull yourself out of them and start anew. Seeing him again will bring it all back."

Kirsa stared at him, "Are you kidding me?" Kirsa asked exasperated, she was getting tired of people tiptoeing around the issues. "The person I knew never existed. The person I'm going to see killed my family and tried to kill me. I'm going there to try and get answers."

"Why is it so important?"

"Because more people are going to die by the hands of this cult and he is the only access I have to them!!"

"Damn it, this is crazy," Lars told her. "You think Ayden or I are going to let you go waltzing in and facing him."

"Who is she facing?" Ayden asked standing in the door way.

"Anton," Kirsa told him. She watched his eyes go dark then clear up. Ayden despised Anton, more so than almost everyone else. He was one of the few people that knew about what really went on when she was with Anton.

"Why?" Ayden asked simply.

"Too see if we can get any more information out of him on the church and what has occurred since his fall from grace," she told him.

He stood there for a moment thinking it over. Ayden took a sip from his mug and looked at Kirsa, reading her face and her eyes.

"Ok. I don't like it but he is the only access we have to the cult and if they are active again, which it seems they are, then trying to get information out of him might not be a bad idea."

Lars threw his hands up in disgust. "Am I the only one who sees an issue here?"

"No," Ayden replied. "I think we all go, including Tony. If you want to be in the room with him then bring Tony with you, but the two of us are outside that door at all times. So help me, if he hurts you, he's dead."

"Agreed," Kirsa replied.

"Oh and I am allowed to go in fully armed," Ayden added as he drank his mug.

"I will let Tony know, now out of my office

both of you." Kirsa waited for them to leave before she called Sabrina.

"Hey," Sabrina replied on the other end.

"I have to run something by you before I call Tony," Kirsa told her.

"Sure, what?" Sabrina asked putting her feet up on her desk in her office.

"I think Tony and I need to talk to Anton. I just want to double check with you that it's okay before we run up there."

"I don't see an issue. I will talk to mom and dad and see if they need him to sign off on anything. I know they were redoing their will and some of the business agreements. Which, speaking of, we have business stuff to discuss."

"Lars told me," Kirsa told her.

"Sure, let me know when you are headed up to see him. Did Lars hit the roof when you told him?"

"Hell yeah," Kirsa replied. "What about Ayden?"

She smiled at his reaction. "That it is up to me, if I go he wants to be there."

"Good man."

"We need a gossip session at some point,"

Kirsa replied. She saw her cell phone ringing, it was Tony. "I gotta go, Tony is calling me."

"Sure."

****

Ayden drove with Kirsa as they made their way to the summer camp. All Tony would tell them on the phone was that something had been found in the old boat shed. They pulled into the parking lot and climbed out of the car. Campers and parents were gathered on the other side of the parking lot watching. Tony ducked under the crime scene tape and met them.

"I called you as soon as I got the call," he told her as he lifted the tape out of her way.

"What happened?" she asked as they walked past the soccer field.

"The back part of the camp is rarely being used because a new building was built closer to the main grounds last fall. The older buildings are mostly used for storage now. Every morning the senior counselors check the older buildings just to make sure no one decided to camp out there and have a private party. What they found this morning was far worse," Tony explained as they walked.

"Don't finish. I can figure it out," she told him.

Chapter Fourteen

They were walking into the woods and toward the edge of the lake. There was an old wooden structure that looked like the roof was going to cave in at any moment. Tape was up around the building some of the cops looked green around the edges. She felt fear trickling through her spine, which she was picking up from the cops on the scene and the two counselors that were being interviewed. The emotions were so strong it was hard for her to filter them away or ignore them.

"Tony how bad?" she asked him.

He looked down at her. "One of the worst I've seen."

Two officers raised the rope for them to

pass, Kirsa took the gloves from Tony. "Ayden stay here with Tony," she told him.

"Sara will be here in a moment," Tony told her as he let her into the old boat house.

The emotions that she picked up were contradictory, on one hand Kirsa picked up a strong sense of fear and yet she also picked up a sense of relief for a job well done. She ventured further into the building. Part of her wondered if the building was going to fall down around her as she walked. There were holes in the wall and floor. Old broken boats were piled looking as though they would tip over with the faintest of breeze. As she cautiously made her way around one of the piles she saw it on the far back wall almost hidden from a pile of oars.

It was nailed to the wooden walls. The body was positioned with its arms stretched out, one nail through each of the palms; the feet were also spread apart with a nail through each ankle. A knife pierced the abdomen and continued into the wall. The body had sagged to the hilt of the knife. As were a few of the other bodies, this one was also naked. From where she stood, she could see that there was little bruising on the body meaning most of the damage was done post-mortem.

Kirsa got up closer to the body before she

realized that it was a female. This time the person took a page from Jack the Ripper and sliced her breasts off.The body was spotless just like all the others had been. Her blonde hair had been braided and violets had been placed in a wreath around her head.

The victim's mouth had been stitched shut, her eyes had been closed and gold coins were taped over them. The skin had been removed skillfully from the face revealing the muscles under the skin. The eyelids and lips were the only parts left on the face. Kirsa felt around the body and felt something odd where the organs were supposed to be. Hearing a noise she looked and Sara coming towards her with her forensic kit.

"Do you have a camera and a knife?" Kirsa asked.

"Yes why?" Sara asked putting her bag down. She got out the knife then got her camera ready.

"Take a picture of the mouth stitched shut then I want to open it. They don't want us to see what's in the mouth," Kirsa told her as Sara handed her a scalpel.

Sara nodded; she began to snap pictures of the mouth and then a close up of the stitching. She nodded to Kirsa to let her know it was ok for her to open the mouth. Slowly, Kirsa moved the scalpel across the stitching until the last one was done. With two sets of tweezers they carefully pulled out each strand and placed them into baggies then took a picture of the mouth again closed. Slowly Kirsa opened the mouth and saw what she had feared. Fangs.

"They killed a vamp," Kirsa whispered. "Fuck."

"But how?" Sara asked. Nothing about this case was making any sense.

"I don't know? How did they kill Kelly or the others before this?"

The two searched the front of the body then very carefully they began to examine the back of the body with mirrors. They did not want to remove the body from the wall yet. The mirrors would help show what the back of the body was without messing up any evidence that might be found on the nails before they took the body down. Kirsa saw it on the left shoulder blade, a small purple fleur de lis. The room spun around her, Sara quickly was at her side helping her sit on the floor with her head between her legs. When the world stopped spinning she sat up.

Kirsa stared at the body and for the first time in her career, she could not separate her work from her personal life. It was staring at her in the face, she closed her eyes and tried to steady her breathe. She knew that Sara was next to her, yet she could not feel her touch for her body was numb. Part of her wanted to wake up from this nightmare and the other part of her knew that this was no night mare but her life.

"You knew her didn't you?" Sara assumed, rubbing her back. She had seen the recognition flash in Kirsa's eyes as she had located something on the back. She had gone through similar emotions when she first saw Kelly, but what was done to this person was far worse.

Kirsa looked away from the body as Sara sat beside her and put an arm around her. She was fighting back nausea and tears. It was harder to block out emotions when you knew the person.

"Yeah," Kirsa whispered.

Sara leaned her head against Kirsa's. "Who is she?"

"They just killed a two hundred year old vamp. And not just any vamp, she's the daughter of Sebastian."

"Head of the French Blood line, Sebastian?" Sara asked just to be clear. From being friends with Kirsa, she had a basic understanding of vampire politics. Then it sunk in as to who the victim was. "Oh my god, Isabella."

Kirsa nodded and stood up, "I need to get air. Can you get a picture of the tattoo on her left shoulder blade?"

"Sure," Sara replied and watched her walk out of the building, still trembling.

Ayden stood up as Kirsa came out from the cabin. He could smell anguish and fear coming from her. Her face was blank and body slightly shaking. Lars, who had arrived a few minutes ago, stood behind him covered from the sun.

Kirsa was met by Tony, Lars and Ayden who were both watching her closely. She took the bottle of red water that Ayden handed her and looked at Tony.

"Call the Paranormal Prison, set up an appointment for either later today or tomorrow. We want to question prisoner 20601," Kirsa instructed her voice void of emotion.

Tony stared at her. "Why?"

He knew who the prisoner was, once a week he got updates on him. Tony wanted to know everything that he did in the prison, when he pissed, when he ate, when he got the shit beat out of him.

"They figured out how to kill a vamp that is over two hundred years old without placing a visible mark on her, that's why," Kirsa snapped, trying to focus for the world was still spinning. She noticed that all noise seemed to stop at her statement. "No burns, the damage to the outside of the body was done after they killed her."

Tony saw the look of grief in her eyes. "You knew her?"

Ayden looked at Kirsa and laid a hand on her cheek. His cold hand felt good against her skin. She closed her eyes at the touch and took a deep breath. "Yeah I did."

"How did you identify her?" Tony asked. He had seen the body and knew that identification was going to be difficult if it was possible at all.

"Tattoo on one of her shoulders. Her name is Isabella. Not only is she a vamp Tony, but her dad is Sebastian." Kirsa told him. She knew that Tony was aware of who Sebastian was.

"Are you sure?" Ayden asked as all the information began to sink in.

For being young, Isabella had always been a strong vampire. To think that someone got her was almost unbelievable. She was also one of the vampires that had gone missing in the midwest.

Lars stared at her not sure what to think, the news was not sitting well. "Honey, you are sure it's her?"

Kirsa just nodded. "Tony, make the appointment, because when the vampire world finds out they are going to want blood."

Tony nodded. "Ayden, Lars, take her home," Tony told them. "I'll call if we need anything else."

"I'll call Sebastian," Ayden told Tony. "He'll handle it better from one of us."

"Thank you," Tony said.

Tony watched as they walked toward the cars. Ayden walked next to Kirsa with Lars following. A casual observer would never know these two men were trained killers. That while they were looked unassuming, they were taking in every smell and every sight. They were cataloguing every person at the crime scene. The father in him wanted to protect her and guard from all of this and at the same time he knew she was their only hope at solving this case.

Chris came up to Tony. "I found some evidence. Did Kirsa leave already? I take it she couldn't handle what's inside."

"Where is the evidence you found?" Tony asked not answering any other questions that were being thrown at him.

****

Ayden was sitting on the couch; Kirsa was curled up in his arms. It had been decided that they would inform Dietrich who would then tell Sebastian. In German, Lars was explaining everything that was going on and what they had found out from the crime scene. Kirsa was translating for Ayden, some of the color had returned to her face. Lars hung up the phone and collapsed on the couch next to Ayden.

"He is floored; he does not like this one bit," Lars began as he ran a hand through his hair. "However, Dietrich agrees with you about seeing Anton tomorrow. He wants you to call him with information about when the body can be released. He would have Ayden or me escort it too France but he does not want either of us to leave," Lars told her.

"I'm under 24 hour protection, aren't I?" she asked.

"Yep, one or both go with you any and everywhere," he told her. "Ayden, tomorrow your certificate will arrive that gives you legal right to shoot to kill."

Being Kirsa's Shadow meant Ayden had authorization to be wherever she was. Even if that meant a crime scene. It also meant that if his person was threatened he could shoot to kill. Federal agency and police force would know he was protecting someone working on the case and therefore he was armed.

"Ok," Ayden replied. He went back to just comforting Kirsa.

It was night by the time Sabrina made it over to the house. She found Kirsa sipping wine on the edge of the dock that was part of her property. Inside, Tony, Ayden and Lars were going over the plan for tomorrow at the prison. Sabrina sat down next to Kirsa and looked at the night sky's reflection in the lake.

"I saw architect plans in your den," Sabrina said.

Kirsa took a sip of white wine and leaned back against an over turned boat on the dock.

"Yeah," Kirsa replied. "I was able to find the original blue prints to the house and had an architect go over them and see if he could make any improvements and what it would cost."

"You're really going to rebuild?" Sabrina asked looking at her.

Kirsa let out a sigh. "If he falls within my price range I will."

Sabrina nodded. "Will you live there?"

"I don't know. I might at first to see how it

is," she said with a shrug. "Otherwise I just completely redo this place maybe run the house as a Bed and Breakfast or a town function place, who knows."

They sat in silence for a while, letting the crickets and other night noises become louder.

"If it was someone who was a loner, a rogue, it would be easier," Kirsa finally said. "I could put up the wall that blocks me from personalizing the crime. Brie, I barely recognized her."

Sabrina had been at the morgue when her father had to make the ID's on Kirsa's parents. She had seen parts of the bodies that had not been blocked by her father or the blankets. It was a fact that she had never spoken of before.

"Kirs, believe me when I say I understand," Sabrina said putting her arm around Kirsa.

Sabrina had gotten off the phone with Sara a few minutes prior. Sara, who could not officially tell her anything about the body, had told her it was as bad as when Kirsa's parents were killed.

"I only identified her by the tattoo." Kirsa said staring out at the lake. "I toured parts of Europe with her."

"Dad identified your father by a scar behind the ear," Sabrina told her.

Kirsa turned and looked at her friend. It was the first time Sabrina talked about the night in the morgue.

"He was ashen when he came out of the room. Mom had to get sleeping pills for him later."

"How did he ID my mom?" She did not want to know but she did.

Sabrina took a sip of Kirsa's wine. "Her bracelet that she always wore, the one you gave her when you were 10, it was burned into her skin."

Kirsa nodded. "I know Dietrich was with him, but he would not tell me."

"Yeah, well what neither knows is that I also saw from the doorway," she took a sip of her wine. "They wanted me not to enter the morgue so I stayed outside but when dad dropped to a knee, I saw. I figure between what you saw with Isabella and what I saw with your parents, we could relate and help each other out."

Kirsa leaned her head against Sabrina's. And there they sat for the remainder of the evening.

****

Lars joined Ayden outside on the back

deck. Sabrina and Kirsa had retreated to Kirsa's bedroom. Ayden was leaning on the banister staring out into the wooded area of the property.

"I just checked on the girls. Kirsa is a sleep and Sabrina is reading a book." Lars told him.

Ayden nodded not saying a word. There was some- thing out there in the dark of the woods. It had been out there for most of the night, watching and just waiting. *He's out there.* Ayden told Lars in his mind.

What do you mean he?

The rogue we were talking about earlier. I can sense him. Though, he does not know I can.

"How do you think Sebastian is going to react to the death of his youngest child?" Lars asked out loud.

"When reality hits he will be out for blood," Ayden said going along with Lars with the conversation.

"It should be interesting when they get the DNA they found on the body back."

"That it should and when we tell Sebastian who it was, I hate to be the one responsible," Ayden added.

They walked into the house Ayden had the

satisfaction of knowing they rattled whoever it was that was out there. He saw Sabrina come down stairs. She walked over to him.

"She wants you," Sabrina told him. "I'll deal with the old grouch."

Ayden nodded and walked up the back staircases to the second floor. He found the door to her room open. Ayden closed it as he walked in; the lights were on low. He walked toward the bed in the center of the room. Kirsa was curled in the middle of it. She looked up at him when he walked into the bedroom. He sat on the edge of the bed. Her hand reached out and fingers curled around his.

"Is it horrible of me to want them all to die painful deaths?" she asked him.

Ayden laughed in a pained way. "Not when I want to suck each and every one of them dry."

"Will you lie next to me?" Kirsa asked. She did not want to be alone.

Ayden nodded and changed his position so that he was lying on his back; he pulled her close to his side.

He kissed her forehead, "Kirsa I should tell you something," Ayden sighed. "Isabella and I had a thing a few decades ago."

Kirsa felt a pull of jealousy. "Really?"

"We were serious during the twenties, and then would occasionally meet up from time to time."

Kirsa nodded. "Europe?" She didn't want to think that anything had occurred between the former vampire lovers while things were happening between Ayden and her.

Ayden turned her face so that she was looking into his eyes. "I ended that part of our friendship after I saw you on your twenty first birthday."

Kirsa went to say something but he silenced her, gently kissing her.

"You need to go to sleep," he told her as he pulled her against his side again. He stroked her hair and hummed. She nestled closer to him, and slowly felt sleep come over her.

Chapter Fifteen

The following day Kirsa was headed to the Prison in upstate New York. Kirsa sat in the back seat with Lars while Ayden drove. Tony sat up front with Ayden going over the case notes from South Carolina. No one was happy about this trip. Going to visit the prisoner, her ex, was not on the top of anyone's list of things they wanted to do. But at the moment Anton Black was a necessary evil.

"Did Dietrich call in our guns and weapons?" Lars asked Ayden from the back.

"Yes, I got copy of the approval," Ayden told him.

"What is the document that Sabrina gave you?" Lars asked turning to face Kirsa.

"A document that says he signs the rest of his trust fund, stocks and bonds, and share of the ranch back over to the estate so that it may be redistributed," Kirsa explained to him.

"Ahh. His lawyer ok'd it?"

"Yep," Kirsa replied.

Truthfully Anton's lawyer disliked him. But he worked for the Church of Light and had represented Anton at his trial and usually represented the church when need be. He was not thrilled with the deal and was sworn to client-counsel privileges.

Kirsa looked out as they drove through Northern New Jersey and into New York. The ride was beautiful and perfect for a Sunday if they were not going to a prison. Her family and Sabrina's used to come here to go apple picking.

Maybe this fall they could do it again. She flipped through the autopsy report and shook her head. The cause of death had been an injection of holy water into the veins which caused the organs to melt. What had been placed into the cavities of the body were baggies filled with rolls of film. They were currently being developed and then Kirsa was going to help go through them. Right now she was mentally preparing herself for the meeting with Anton.

The Paranormal Prison was located about 45 minutes past Warwick, NY. It housed anyone who broke the "occult laws" as they were nicknamed. The inhabitants of the prison were a wide range and mixed together. Very few windows were in the place because of those vampires that worked there or were prisoners.

Most of the employees were supernatural because of the wide range of inmates. All bars were coated with silver and the week of the full moon special doors would go down to protect the rest of the prison from the were-animals. When they were transformed they got a special place in the yard to run about. There were regular humans in the prison and they were usually the most hated of all the prisoners. It meant that if they were there they brought harm to someone protected under the occult laws.

The prison itself was made of brick with narrow slits of windows placed throughout. Those windows were coated with a special tint that allowed no UV rays into the prison.

The building looked like an enormous red fortress that loomed out of old farm land.

There were 200 acres that belonged to the prison. The yard around the prison was gated with barb wire, 50 ft. out from the fence were guns that were stationed to fire if the motion sensor went off, and another fifty feet was another barbwire fence with a small river that had been dug around the outer fence as a deterrent to prisoners and those who wanted a closer look.

There was one road that entered into the prison, to get to the prison you had to stop at the first gate at the beginning of the road; there you got clearance to make it pass the bridge. Then the bridge was lowered for you to cross over the river. Once across the bridge was raised, and you were checked in by a computer scan of your eyes, finger print, and body. If you passed through there you could enter the building and hopefully you made it to the visitors list. Otherwise you had to leave and go through the entire process again to get out.

****

Anton Black stood just less than six feet. His hair was black had once hung past his shoulders. His eyes were an ice blue and he once had the build of a boxer. Now his hair had been cut to that of a crew cut, and his once sparkling blue eyes were hollow now. His tan skin had paled to a pasty color and his muscles were gone yet his strength had somehow remained. He had been told there would be someone coming in to see him.

It was probably another head doctor to pick at his brain so he could write a paper on a sociopath. Anton heard a noise and figured his new neighbor was waking up. A rogue vampire had been placed in the cell across from him. The vampire knew who he was and would periodically bare his fangs at him. Anton tried to tell the guard about the vampire but the guard just laughed and told him he was no one. Which was bullshit, he was still somebody. Three armed guard's approached the door and slowly opened the door to his cell.

"Prisoner 20601, get up and approach the door backwards," The guard announced.

Life prisoners were addressed by their number, never by name. The prison tried to wipe out sense of identity.

Anton got up and turned around walking backwards to the door of his cell. He felt the metal slap of the hand cuffs go on. Then the ankle bands went on and last he was strapped into a chair. He was considered high risk because he tried to kill a guard, had tried to escape twice all in the first six months he had been in the prison. The three armed guard's moved down the hall pushing Anton with them. The warden met them at the meeting room.

"You are being met by a detective and an agent. They bring documents from the Black family for you to sign."

"My family has sent something for me?" Anton asked. He was wondering what his family wanted. They did not visit, nor did they write him. They had made it clear that the son they raised was dead, and not the monster they saw standing in his place.

The warden stared at him. "You have no family."

The warden motioned to the guard's and they wheeled him into the room. They removed Anton from the chair and placed him into a steel chair and belted him into that. The guard's left leaving him there alone. He wondered what his family would be making him sign. Obviously the scum lawyer had approved the document because it was being brought to him. The church needed to get away from this lawyer; he was weak and did not agree with their policies. The door opened and Anton started laughing when he saw Captain White walk into the room.

Tony sat down and looked at Anton. Anton heard a voice saying something outside and then he felt his heart falter. She wore a black suit with faint red pin striping. Underneath was a red silk blouse that accentuated her pure white skin. Her hair had been cut into a bob sending her hair into a mass of curls. He never liked women with short hair, but on her it framed her angelic face.

Kirsa sat down next to Tony and took a folder out of her black leather brief case. Anton searched her eyes for some type of warmth but he saw nothing.

"Mr. Black we have questions for you regarding several murders that have occurred around Grabenberg, New Jersey," Tony began.

"Obviously I couldn't have done them since I'm locked in this hell hole," Anton replied. He kept searching Kirsa for something. All he was finding was a blank wall of emotions, no hint of recognition,   nothing.

"We are not saying you did. We would like to see if you could provide us some information about the killings," Tony told him.

Anton leaned back as much as he could in the chair. "What do I get out of this?"

"The vamp that was moved in across from you, the one that scares you," Kirsa began catching his attention, "We will have him moved away from you."

Anton stared at her. How she knew he was

afraid o the vamp he had no clue but then she always knew too much. She had always been able to pick up on others thoughts here and there.

"I will see what I can do," Anton told them.

Kirsa slid the pictures of the first few victims. The last victim she showed him was the one found in the corn field. Anton looked at each of them.

"Notes were left with them?" he asked as he studied each picture. They were going with a different tactic, a bit more violent and theatrical then when he was in charge.

"Of course," Kirsa replied. "They are worded so elegantly too. There must be a woman doing the writing this time."

Kirsa saw the flash in Anton's eyes meaning she was correct about her hunch of a female being involved.

"We have started our work again," Anton replied simply. "What do you want from me?"

"Why?" Kirsa asked simply.

"To rid the world of evil. Our reason has never changed," Anton told her.

Tony handed the envelope to Kirsa who took the pictures out and slid them on the table. There were seven pictures of Isabella there. Anton looked at each one of them and it was when he got to the picture of the tattoo that he froze.

Anton looked up at Kirsa looking for conformation on what he feared was right.

"You are absolutely certain of the identity?" he asked.

Even though Kirsa had not included him in much of the vampire politics, he knew who the heads were and their children.

"Your people killed Isabella, one of the heirs to the French blood line," Kirsa informed him. "Holy water was injected into her to melt her organs. As you can see the skin on her face was peeled back and her mouth had been sewed shut."

Anton could barely stomach the pictures. These had been the most violent and brutal murder the church had done. It was unlike the church to desecrate a body like this. For the body to be not whole, the person would not be able to enter Heaven.

He shook his head. To violate a body in such a way, and not just anyone but the daughter of one of the strongest vampires was stupid.

"Sebastian knows of his daughters' death.

We had to do all we could to keep him from coming to you," Kirsa told him.

Anton stared at her and shook his head. Just like before, he would not help her or anyone. He would not betray his faith or his people.

"I cannot betray my faith," he whispered. Carefully he slipped the metal pick out of his sleeve and began to cautiously work on his handcuffs.

She saw the internal war in him. "What has this faith given you? What have you had to hide from all your life?"

He looked into her eyes. "You."

Knowing that he was going to say nothing, Kirsa took the other folder out of her case and took out a plastic pen that contained no metal pieces and slid the document to Anton.

"Aaron and Elaine Black ask that you sign over your trust fund, stocks and your third of the ranch back over to the family," Tony told Anton.

Anton closed his eyes. He opened them and looked at the document. He took the pen and signed his name. He slid the paper to Kirsa; she grabbed the paper as he grabbed her hand and pulled her across the table. Tony went to grabbed her but Anton took a blade out and placed it to her neck.

"How can you come here with no emotion?" he whispered. "How can you walk through that door like you do not know who I am?"

"Because I don't know who you are," Kirsa told him. "Now take your fucking hands off of me."

She knew that behind the two way mirror the guards and Ayden were waiting for a clear shot. Anton gripped his arm around her tighter so that she was pressed against him. So that no shot could be made.

"I am hard for you," he growled in her ears. "How about nailing you right here on the table in front of them?" Kirsa smiled.

She could feel her fangs grow, they had started to appear a few months ago and usually when she felt threatened. Kirsa had yet to use them. Looking into the eyes of Ayden she smiled sweetly showing just a bit of fang even if they weren't large yet, and bit down on Anton's hand drawing blood. The metallic taste filled her mouth; it was not sweet but tasted anemic and sick. She then flipped him on to the metal table with a crash, denting the table.

"I said get your fucking hands off me," she

whispered, she began to shake from adrenaline as she walked out of the room.

Anton leaned up and before the tranquilizer gun was fired at him he threw the small blade at her. Kirsa caught it before it hit her. She had seen it leave his hands and reacted faster than a normal human. The guards came in and grabbed Anton who was now drugged.

As they dragged him out of the room he howled, "It's all about your blood!"

Lars helped restrain him back into his stretcher as he continued to howl about her blood and curse. As Anton continued, Lars punched him across the face to get him to shut up something the guards pretended not to notice. Tony walked over to Kirsa and hugged her, he held onto her for a few seconds to let himself know that she was ok. Ayden came in and Tony let go leaving the room.

Ayden brushed a strand of hair out of her face and wiped some blood away from her lip. He pulled her close to him and just held her and breathed in her scent. Kirsa held on to him and felt secure there.

Chapter Sixteen

*I still do not know what first drew me to Hagan.
Yes, he was very handsome which drew him much
attention from the women. But there was
intelligence behind his eyes, his was well traveled. I
found that I looked forward to our walks at night
when he would tell me of the sights he had seen. I
found it endearing that each night he would ask my
father's permission to walk with me. He did not use
his title to get his way. On our walks the only
notion to his title was the guard that walked behind
us.*

Often, I forgot about that poor guard who was

forced to listen to our conversations as we talked late into the evenings. The question of why this man of power would want to spend time with me vanished as well. For I began to think of him as a man and not a title.

****

Kirsa was sitting on the edge of the dock; Zero had his head rested in her lap as they watched the stars come out in the sky. The pond on her parents property was calm and had the night sky mirrored in it. Behind her was the guesthouse, she could still smell dinner. Kirsa sipped her beer and enjoyed the quietness of the night. The journal of her ancestor lay next to her.

The words still fresh in her mind, as she reflected on the events of the day. Lars had yelled about what occurred in the prison. Sabrina had managed to calm him down enough that she dragged him away to her home so that Kirsa did not have to deal with him at the moment. So it left her alone with Ayden. Ayden knew she needed time to herself so after dinner she came out here to wallow in her misery.

Looking back she was not sure what attracted her to Anton. She had been working in NYC for a few months when he appeared at her apartment there. Growing up she had always thought of him as a brother. Anton knew how to romance and how to flatter. He used them both living in the city as a reason to get together. Within three months she lost her virginity to him. Every weekend he spent in NY with her. It was about a year into the relationship that he started to chip away at her self-esteem. He would make comments about her outfits or hair style.

Anton never hit her, never physically abused her. He used his words. He would tell her she was lucky that she had him, that no one else would deal with her and all her disorders. It took tragedy to make her see what was going on. But ending it did not heal her. It left her emotionally exhausted. Unsure if she could ever be in a relationship again. In the past six months Kirsa began to find her footing. Began to see what her worth was, became confident in who she was as a person. When she could look at herself in a mirror and not cringe.

The visit confirmed to her that whatever Anton had once meant to her he stirred no emotions at all. She also had not expected him to try and harm her; it just proved how much she did not know him. He had given away one bit of information. The new head of the East Coast Branch was a woman. Kirsa had a few ideas as too who it could be. She heard noise from behind her. Zero's tail began to thump against the deck. Ayden sat down next to her and took a sip from his beer. They sat there for a while not talking and just listening to the noises.

"So when did the whole canines getting longer thing start?" Ayden inquired putting his arm around her.

She looked at him surprised, that's not what she thought he was going to start with. "I guess about a month or two ago. I never have used them as defense before."

"I'm glad you had them," Ayden admitted. He glanced at her for a moment. "How is the disorder going?"

"I don't know," Kirsa sighed. "It's frustrating, another scenario has come up and I don't even want to think of what that could mean."

"Are the journals helping?"

"Nothing of it is mentioned yet, but I just started reading them."

"Does it scare you?" Ayden asked her. She didn't really talk about the disorder, what her thoughts on it were.

"Sometimes. Sometimes I just think of some of the positives that it has brought me." Kirsa admitted, staring out across the pond. "Being able to bite that asshole was a nice plus."

"Do you still love him?" Ayden asked brushing a curl out of her face.

Kirsa turned and looked at him. It was hard not to smile when she was around him. Leaning forward she kissed him lightly on the lips and laid a hand against his cheek.

"The person who I loved never existed," Kirsa admitted. "I wanted to believe in what we have but it was a dream. So no I don't think I ever truly loved him. Now, there are no feelings with him, just disgust at what he has become."

"Good," Ayden replied.

Before she could say anything Ayden leaned forward and kissed her. It shouldn't have surprised her because they had kissed a few times since he had returned. But this was different, almost as if he had to claim her. To assure himself that she was here, that she was his.

They broke apart and Ayden kissed her nose and just stared down at her. Kirsa leaned her head against his chest.

"I have been told that my placement as your Shadow could become a permanent situation if we want," Ayden said as he kissed the top of her.

She stared at him not sure what to say or think. He kissed her forehead and pulled her closer.

"I don't have a good track record," Kirsa began. "I don't want to ruin anything with you."

He kissed her lightly again. "You are in control."

Kirsa smiled. "Thank you."

She rested her head on his shoulder and they watched the stars come out together with the dog snoring behind them.

****

At dawn, Kirsa was lying awake despite Ayden's best efforts sleep had evaded her for most of the night. Tony was firm last night that he only wanted her at the station if it was absolutely necessary. After showering and getting dressed she made her way down into the kitchen. Kirsa ground coffee beans and placed them in the filter before turning the pot on. While the coffee brewed she got out an IV bag and poured its contents into a glass, walking out onto the back porch she sipped from her glass.

Zero came out and rubbed against her to let her know he was awake then ran into his yard to do his morning business. Finishing the contents of the glass she walked inside and poured a cup of coffee. As she took the first sip she heard a car pull into the drive way and then a door shut. Kirsa walked to the front door and watched Al Moore walk up the front path. He looked startled when he saw her waiting for him.

"Good morning," he greeted. "How did you know I was here?"

"I heard your car," Kirsa responded. She moved to the side so he could enter. "Plus I could smell you."

Al stopped and went to check then realized that she had picked up on his scent. Al shook his head as he bent to pet Zero. He was about 5'10, he kept his dirty blonde hair close cropped from going bald at an early age, it was his bright blue eyes that Kirsa found his best feature. They were always alert and taking in his surroundings.

Like usual, he wore what everyone at OPIA deemed his uniform, a tweed sports coat with leather pads at the elbows, brown corduroy pants and a white polo shirt. It didn't matter how hot or cold it was that was what he always wore in a variety of ways. His Irish brogue was beginning to fade but came out full force when he was angry. He had been head of OPIA for the last ten years. Everyone liked him unless you got on his bad side. His temper was rare but was legendary.

"Where are Ayden and Lars?" he asked noticing how quiet the house was.

Kirsa give him a pointed look, "It's eight in the morning, you expect two vampires to be up at the moment?"

"Good point."

"Want any coffee?" Kirsa asked.

"Sure, I also need to talk to you," he told her.

"I figured that," she said.

She went into the kitchen and fixed them their coffee the she led him to her office where she could shut the door. If it had been night she would have suggested they go some- where else because of the vampires super hearing. But, since it was daytime their hearing would not pick up words only that there was talking going on.

Al looked around and saw paint swatches taped to the faded wall; he saw that she was settling in despite the storm that was raging around her. He sat in the chocolate brown chair and set his briefcase down next to him.

Kirsa took a seat at her desk and looked at

him; he had his serious face on. "What's up Al?"

"Dietrich and I were talking early, very early this morning," Al began. "With everything that has been going on in the last few days he has decided it is time to let you in on a few issues that have arose in the past few months."

"This is a lot deeper than just the murders aren't they?" Kirsa was picking up on what was not being said. A skill that Dietrich called a gift and a curse, for often enough she knew more then she cared too.

"Yes, some of what I am going to tell had to be approved by both Councils. Until Isabella was found and then yesterday at the prison, we thought and hoped that none of this was related."

Al opened his briefcase and pulled out several folders and placed them on the redwood desk. Several contained the seal of the Inner Council. Kirsa just watched him; she did not want to know what was in the files.

"You were correct in your email when you hinted at a possible spy," Al told her. "Shamus was the first to become suspicious a few years ago. Some information about the Council was reaching some of the more conservative religious groups."

"I know that at a few events that were supposed to be Council only there were protests, and no one knew how the groups found out," Kirsa took a sip from of coffee. "Adam and I also noticed that it seemed as though Wyrm was being more insistent on knowing where we were at all times. "

"From what Ayden was able to find out, is that for the last several years someone connected to the Councils has been giving information to the Church of Light," Al informed her. "The night you called Dietrich about taking the case on here, Ayden had just given him his findings."

Kirsa looked at the folders on the desk and knew that within the folders was the work that Ayden had been work- ing on. She was not quite sure she wanted to know. She looked at some of them. One caught her completely off guard.

"Sebastian and Dietrich have been researching your family and the rumors since the death of your parents," Al explained. "Ayden found out about six months ago that the full rumor had been told to the church. The folder with your name on it contains what they found out, however Dietrich has asked me to ask you not to read it until you are done with the journals," Al explained.

"Ok so not only do they know the workings of the Council they also apparently know some of the rumors about my family? Is that what Anton meant when he said it's about my blood?" Kirsa asked him.

"From what Ayden has gathered the church has a two part strike plan. The first part is to do away with the heirs to the blood lines. By doing away with them, and they have got- ten rid of two now, they will weaken the future of the Council. Now, by this we know the spy's knowledge is limited."

"Because if he or she has more access they would know that there is a list of potentials that are all treated the same," Kirsa said.

It was safe to say it in front of Al because in his vault was the list of succession not only for the vampires but for each of the were groups, the fae and other supernatural groups so that way if anything happened, an outside party would have the crucial information. It was one of the rulings that came out of the Paranormal Laws, and who better but the head of OPIA.

"Exactly, so we are letting them think that information is correct. Only a handful of people outside of the Inner Council know about the succession list."

"I'm afraid to ask what the second part of their plan is," Kirsa sighed. She had a hunch and knew she was not going to like it if she was right.

"The second part is that if you are indeed the heir to the sixth line then you have the pure vampire gene, so by killing you would eliminate all vampires that walk the earth, or at least weaken them greatly," Al told her.

"This again is full of shit, because even if I was the heir, killing me would not eliminate the entire vampire population. Which shows that they are getting incomplete information. I guess that's positive in some way."

"Correct. Right away we can eliminate the Inner Council, and Shadows. If it was a Shadow, they are privy to most of the information of the Inner Council," Al agreed.

"It also rules the heads of the sub-lines and most General Council members. The heads of sub-lines know that there are multiple candidates for succession and so do most General Council members," Kirsa added.

Al looked at his watch and got up. "The folders are yours, they are under lock and key when you are not in the same room with them. I have a press conference in two hours."

After, locking the files in the top drawer of her desk, Kirsa got up to walk him out, "Oooo about what?"

"Rumors of a changeling in one of the nurseries in a NYC hospital," Al laughed. "Anyway there is no evidence supporting it what so ever. But I have to do damage control."

"This is why I will never ever want your job," Kirsa told him before she kissed him good bye on the cheek.

"I will talk to you soon, keep sending the emails." Al turned and walked toward his car.

Kirsa shut the door then jumped a mile when she saw Lars standing in the kitchen doorway watching her. She must have been distracted by Al to not notice that Lars was up and about. And that was the problem when one was around Al, but that was Al for you.

"What was Al doing here?" Lars asked casually sipping from his mug.

Kirsa walked toward the kitchen to pour herself a new mug of coffee. "He obviously heard about Isabella and Tony filled him in on parts of what happened yesterday."

"So he was just checking up to make sure you were ok?" Lars inquired. There was something about the director that set Lars on edge and it wasn't because he was part fae.

"Yes, he wanted to make sure that I still wanted to be on the case."

"What did you tell him?"

Sipping her coffee, she eyed Lars cautiously over her mug. "I told him I still wanted to be on it. What's with the twenty questions?"

Lars shrugged. "With everything going on the last two days, I guess I'm just waiting for something else to go on."

Kirsa walked over to him and patted his cheek. "Why don't you go back to bed. Tony told me not to show up at all today, so take a break and go down into your dwelling and veg."

"That sounds like a plan, what are you going to do?" Lars wondered.

"Look at paint samples," Kirsa replied, walking back to her office.

After she heard him descend the stairs, she turned on her iPod player and unlocked her desk drawer. Carefully laying the folders on her desk, she took a deep breath and opened the first one.

Chapter Seventeen

Hagan was called away to deal with an issue in a neighboring town. I did not hear it all, nor could I ask because they were whispering. When they finished talking Hagan took me to the side. He told me to be careful when I went out to pray or gather herbs. He was leaving a guard with us, he kissed me and left. I found out from the guard that a healer had been brutally murdered a few towns away. This could be why my lord was anxious for my safety. It is well known that I am a healer and know the lore's of herbs.

****

Kirsa closed the journal when the alarm on the phone went off. Sighing, Kirsa looked at her watch and figured Sabrina would be at the ranch. Ayden was still asleep and it would be dangerous to take Lars out during the day. Grabbing Zero's lead, she grabbed her keys and purse and motioned for the dog to follow. Wagging his tail, he jumped in to the back of the Durango. Kirsa climbed in and put the window down so he could enjoy the breeze.

The driveway before her parents she turned in, it forked halfway down. One way went to the house and the other way went to the ranch, Kirsa drove under the arch that welcomed her to the Black Rose Ranch. She pulled to the original barn that was now the offices and show ring. Kirsa parked in a spot and climbed out. She put Zero on his leash and walked him over to the fenced in area where Sabrina and Brian left their dogs. She opened the fence and let Zero in who quickly ran to the three other dogs. After making sure he would be ok, she walked to the entrance into the barn and entered.

The receptionist looked like she was in high school; she wore the summer uniform for the ranch. White colored shirt and khaki shorts.

"Welcome to the Black Rose Ranch, how may I help you?" The perky teenager asked Kirsa.

"Can you let Miss Black know that Kirsa

Heinrich is here," Kirsa asked.

"You can go right up to her office, Ms. Heinrich," the girl replied motioning to the stairs to the right. Sabrina had left instructions that if Kirsa showed up to send her right up.

"Thanks," Kirsa replied as she climbed the steps. The door to Sabrina's office was opened.

Kirsa poked her head in and saw Sabrina was on the phone. Quietly she entered the room and sat on the couch. After a few minutes, Sabrina hung up the phone.

"New client?" Kirsa asked.

"A bridezilla who wants to get married here and does not understand why she can't use your land without your permission for the reception tents," Sabrina asked her.

"Tell her $100 a head, and she can put the tents up but they cannot go out of designated area or use the main driveway or go near the main house," Kirsa replied. "No photographs at the main house either."

Sabrina was writing it all down. "I will let her know, if she has any questions for you I will play mediator." Sipping from her water bottle she studied her friend. "So to what do I owe this visit?"

"Al dropped some files off that deal with

everything," Kirsa sighed.

Sabrina leaned back in her chair. "What did they contain?"

"Old cases, my family, rumored reports. The list goes on," Kirsa got up and walked to the window.

"Do they confirm what you've told me?"

"Yes, that's what is bothering me."

Sabrina raised an eyebrow not sure she followed any- more. "I thought you wanted answers about your family? I'm confused."

Kirsa ran a hand threw her hair sending curls every which way. She wasn't sure how she could explain how she was feel- ing. But if there was anyone she could explain it to, Sabrina was it. Sabrina knew more about her research into her family than anyone else did.

"When its legend or rumor, there is this chance that it might not be true. When you find out that one of those leg- ends is truth then it just throws open all these doors that you weren't expecting," Kirsa explained.

"It doesn't make you a different person," Sabrina assured her. She didn't even have to ask she knew which legend Kirsa was referring to, she knew they were discussing the legend of the sixth blood line.

"I figured that out at four this morning," Kirsa admitted.

"Kirs, all this means is at some point people are going to know the truth and that unknown scares me."

"Have you told anyone but me about it?" Kirsa let out a breath, "No."

"Ahh, you're afraid that if Ayden realizes the truth you might never know how he truly feels about you?"

Kirsa looked at her and nodded. "What if it scares him and he doesn't want to be with me? What if he thinks it is enticing and stays because of it?"

Sabrina smiled at her friend, "And what if he loves you so much that it doesn't matter to him whether you are or aren't the heir to the sixth line?"

****

On the edge of Soho, in New York City was a brown- stone that had been converted into offices. Intricate iron bars were woven on the first and second floor windows. The building itself had an old Victorian charm to it. The first floor held law offices; the second floor was empty at the moment. On the third floor of the office building was the East Coast office for the Church of Light. It had moved into New York

City about three months ago with hopes that by being centered in the Big Apple it would increase awareness of their cause and improve numbers of new members.

The office for the church consisted of four rooms off of the main reception area. The main reception room had been painted in a pale yellow with a navy blue rug. A welcome mat rested on the inside of the door. There were overstuffed floral and plaid chairs grouped in threes with a country style coffee table in the center. The reading material on the table was about what the church had to offer you. The room screamed welcome. Pictures of church picnics and other events lined the walls showing smiling and happy people.

One of the doors from the reception area was that of a church counselor who was there to help members and those wanting to be members. Another led into a small library filled with approved reading material. The third room was a small kitchen so that the workers could eat and set out refreshments. The fourth room was the office of the person in charge of the East Coast Branch. Most did not enter this room.

While the other rooms had been done in warm welcoming colors, the office had not been. The walls of the office had been painted to be a stark white. The rug was black with grey specks. There was a large glass top desk in front of the windows. The room gave off a cold and sterile feel, one was not welcomed in this room. The book cases were more glass and metal, the filing cabinets were black. There were no pictures to be found in the room, not even a vase with flowers in it. The room fit the person who occupied it.

Veronica Adams was thirty years old. She had a MBA from Boston University and had been a devoted Catholic for twenty two years of her life. But after she turned twenty two, she attended an interfaith conference where a member of the Church of Light presented. He was tall, dark and hand- some. Something about him pulled her to listen. Her friends laughed and left the seminar while she stayed and clung to every word he said. It was as if he was talking to her, talk- ing about how she felt and what she had been through. She stayed for the question and answer part then found herself having coffee with him at a nearby coffee shop.

Within a year of that meeting, she cut her self off from her family, who told her not to join the group, they feared for her safety. Six years later she now ran the East Coast Branch of the church. It was still smaller then some had hoped it would be by now. But, there was bad press five years ago so that surely affected people wanting to join. To her, Anton sacrificed his life to show the true darkness and what needed to be done. But people were not ready to hear what he or the church had to say.

Brushing a strand of platinum blonde hair out of her ice-blue eyes she read through the quarterly budget and compared it to last month. She kept her hair long, it intrigued men and Anton liked it long. There was a knock on her door, she was startled by it. The person entered upon her command.

Nick Cullen, a senior counselor entered. He was part of the inner group and helped carry out the plans of the Head of the church. His dirty blonde hair was crew cut short and he had dark blue eyes. He was also second in command of the Salvation Project. Nick walked toward the desks and saw Veronica looking at him. Her pale ice blue eyes showed little warmth.

"I am sorry to disturb you," he apologized.

"Then it must be important," Veronica replied. She motioned for him to sit. "What can I do for you?"

"It deals with New Jersey," Nick told her.

Nick was one of the few that knew the plans that were being implemented in Northern New Jersey.

Veronica closed the file and pushed it aside.

He had her attention, which was hard to do when she was working with money.

"What about New Jersey?"

"Grabenberg in particular," he watched her eyes flutter with surprise. "I got news from one of our men."

"Good or bad?" she asked.

"A mixture," he told her. "I am sure you are aware that word has made it to the Vampire Council about the death of one of their own. Like the animals they are, they're crawling over each other for revenge."

"Good," Veronica replied. "We wanted to show them they were not invincible."

He nodded in agreement. "One of our men was on scene when the body was being examined. There could be a problem here."

"What kind of problem?"

Nick new she was not going to like this at all. "OPIA has made an appearance and one that is not going to go away until the case is solved."

Veronica did not like this. When OPIA showed up, they usually made things more difficult for her. Thankfully the agent she feared most had resigned. She should double check just to make sure that the person had not come back to work.

"Did they say who the agent was?" she asked.

"That's the part you won't like. It's the good doctor."

Veronica stared at him not sure what to think. "She resigned, I thought."

"I had our buddy look her up at the station," Nick informed her."He has access to the list of active agents. She was reinstated a few days ago, the day the body of cat girl was found."

Veronica got up and walked to the windows where she watched the streets below. "Has anyone else been informed of this?"

"No, I wanted to go by the chain of commands. You are my superior, and friend."

Veronica nodded. "There is a meeting tomorrow night for the region heads, I will be attending. The Father will either be phoning in or coming in person, I will inform him of what is going on."

Chapter Eighteen

*A*yden walked into Kirsa's office and paused as he scratched Zero's ear. He went to say something but stopped as he sniffed around the room. An odd scent lingered in the air, one he had not smelled before.

"Who was in here yesterday?" Ayden asked her. He hadn't been in her office at all the day before.

"Al stopped over for a bit, why?" Kirsa wondered as she stopped typing on her computer.

"What is he?" Ayden inquired. "He smells more than human but unlike anything I have encountered before."

"Really?" Kirsa laughed raising an

eyebrow. "I can't tell you."

"You don't know?"

"I know what he is it's just unless he tells me I can, I actually can't tell you what he is. It has something to do with what he is, like a natural silent clause."

"That's odd," Ayden replied as he thought about it for a moment. "So what's on the agenda for today?"

"I am waiting to hear from Tony, he was told the pictures would be dropped off at some point this afternoon."

"That should be fun, what are you working on now?"

She motioned for him to close the French doors. When he did he sat in one of the chairs. "Al dropped off the Council files about the spy and other pieces of the puzzle that fit with this case."

"I've been telling them for months that this was part of a bigger picture and to bring you in," Ayden said relieved. "I think part of them wanted to protect you from it all and the other part didn't want to accept the whole traitor amongst us idea."

"Yeah well between Ivan and Isabella I think they finally agree with your recommendations because I know have all the folders under lock and key."

"What about the journals that you have been reading, will they help with any of this?"

Kirsa leaned back in her chair, "Right now I am really just in the beginning of the journal of my namesake where she meets Lord Hagan and the start of their courtship. There isn't any mention yet about the Council or the blood oath that had been made."

Ayden looked at her oddly, "When is the journal written?"

"Roughly around 1000, why?"

"And Hagan is the name of the lord," Ayden repeated. "I need to look into some ancient lore that Shamus once told me, it involved that name around the same time."

Before Kirsa could ask the theme to *Police Academy* went off, she picked up her cell phone. "Hi Tony, what's up?"

Ayden had to laughed at the ring tone for Tony then listened to her side of the conversation. He gathers that the pictures were in and they could head over whenever they were ready. When she hung up, she wrote a quick note for Lars then locked up all her files and lap top in the bottom desk drawer. His laughter faded when he saw her expression.

"We need to go to the police station," Kirsa told him as she stood up.

"Everything okay?" Ayden asked as he headed out of the room behind her.

"No," was all she said.

****

Tony had one of the conference rooms in the back of the police station set up for them. He made sure the coffee pot was going and that there was plenty of water. When Sara finished with preparing Isabella's body to be sent to France, she was going to join them. Twenty envelopes of pictures were stacked on the table. Each had thirty six pictures in them. A pile of legal pads and pens were piled next to the packs.

"As I explained to Kirsa on the phone," Tony began. "Inside of Isabella were rolls of film. Each wrapped carefully in plastic so not to be ruined. What lays in front of us are the photo's from those rolls."

"Do we want to grab a few envelopes each and just start taking notes on each pack?" Ayden asked.

"That would be the fastest, I would say don't stop unless you find something interesting." Tony sat down and handed out a few packs to each of them. "Each envelope is marked with a number; write the number on the page then a description of the pack. I want a new page for each package of photo."

Kirsa opened her first envelope and at once knew the pictures came out of South Carolina. She began to jot down some of the locations of the pictures, the university campus, some tourist spots, as well as roads leading into and out of Charleston.

"There are pictures of them staking out Charleston so far," she told them when she finished with the first pack. Ayden had a similar pack as well that showed them in South Carolina.

As she continued going through the next pack, the pictures began with various females and locations that later would be used to dump the bodies around the Charleston area. There were also pictures of the house that they used as a headquarters. It had been boarded up and had graffiti sprayed all over it.

She continued to flip through the South Carolina pictures. There was a college student strapped to a table. She was obviously crying, there were three men surrounding her all laughing and drinking beers. One of the men was An- ton. Another showed Anton kissing a blonde woman, Kirsa stopped and put the picture down. She wrote a name down on the notepad and circled it.

Ayden looked over at her. "What's up?"

He felt her tense up all of a sudden, and knew it had something to do with the pictures she was looking through. He knew this could not be easy for her, having to relive what this cult had done.

"Veronica Adams," Kirsa replied sliding the picture across the table.

They all knew the name. Veronica had never been charged with any crimes in South Carolina because she appeared to be only an accountant for the church and a member. There had been no evidence found that pointed towards her being involved with what went on in Charleston.

Tony looked at the picture and then at Kirsa. "We will need to copy the envelope of pictures and give it to the DA and let her handle the rest."

Kirsa made some more notes before she went through the rest of the envelope. The next few envelopes dealt with South Carolina; it looked as though they had scouted out other places before settling on Charleston as their spot.

She was on her sixth envelope and second cup of coffee when everything inside her went cold. There was a picture of her at Blarney Castle kissing the stone, another of her and Ayden walking hand in hand down the Seine in Paris. Another was of her, Isabella and Ayden skiing in Iceland, one of her and Ayden kissing outside a small bar in Italy, another of them on her balcony in Switzerland.

There was a picture of her at her parent's funeral. She was dressed in black and sunglasses on, Ayden had an arm around her waist and Elaine Black held her other hand. Her hand froze on the last picture which was of her and Ayden embracing in the woods behind the estate in Germany.

She grabbed her cell phone and soon was on the phone talking in German to whoever was on the other end. Ayden and Tony knew whatever she had just seen was horrific. When she hung up she looked at both of them with fear in her eyes.

"We got a problem," she said feeling her hands tremble.

"What's wrong?" Tony asked.

"I'm being watched." She laid the pictures down on the table for them to see. It shouldn't surprise her but it did.

They all stopped what they were doing and began to focus on the envelopes that chronicled her life. The packs that dealt with the murders were placed into another pile. Right now they needed to know how long she was being watched for. There was a picture of her and Lars playing with Zero by the lake, another of her and Dietrich hugging at her par- ent's funeral. There were even pictures from when she was living in Georgetown, which meant she needed to let Emma, her old roommate know what was going on. Three envelopes seem too chronicle her life for the last five years.

They sat back and looked at each other not sure what to think at all. She was protected by vampires and yet someone had gotten close enough to take pictures.

"It has to be an old vampire to get that close to not trigger detection," Ayden stated.

Tony looked at him; he had made that comment a few days earlier. "But how can he get past Dietrich?"

"Easy," Kirsa started. "The picture's that Dietrich is in have numerous other people in them. No one is going to pay attention to the scent of another vamp."

"I am going to see if we can set up a patrol in your neighborhood," Tony said, "If they see anything I will have them call into the house to let you know."

"I take it that was Wyrm you were talking too?" Ayden asked. "Yes, he's going to notify the village about it."

Chris knocked on the door to the room then walked in. "Dispatch got a call from some teens out at one of the abandoned farms. They said they found something there."

Chapter Nineteen

Towards the edge of town were old farms that had been forgotten about. Like many towns in the area, Grabenberg had once relied on the mines in the mountains and the crops from the field to survive. While the mines were sealed up and barricaded from trespassers, the farms were a different story. The buildings that were still intact, were often frequented by teens.

Kirsa looked out the windows as Ayden followed the directions that Tony gave him. Tony was telling him about the area and how this was the teen hang-out spot. Kirsa was remembering her own teenage memories. Even though she had tested out of high school at sixteen, when she was home from college she would join Sabrina at the parties. She was glad for the distraction from the pictures. Seeing her life unfold before an unknown person was chilling.

Ayden pulled into a long dirt driveway overgrown with weeds. The house had once been painted a bright yellow but years of neglect and weather had caused it to be almost a dull cream. Windows were boarded up and a screen door dangled from a hinge. Part of the porch ceiling was caving in.

They climbed out of the car taking in the scenery around them. Kirsa pulled her sunglasses down and looked at the house. Two other cars pulled up behind them.

"I feel like I am in some twisted horror movie," she replied breaking the silence.

Tony turned and looked at with a smile. "How many times did I save your ass by making sure you got put into my car?"

"Ha ha," Kirsa replied walking towards the house.

"Was our Kirsa a trouble maker?" Ayden asked walking with Tony toward the house.

"No more than the next kid. She just had

the benefit of her god father being me."

Kirsa turned to face them from the porch steps. "I hate to burst your bubble, but what my charming god father is failing to tell you is that though I went to the parties, I rarely drank. I was also smarter than many of my peers to get wasted here knowing the cops would show up at some part."

"But not smart enough to just not go to them," Tony pointed out.

Kirsa rolled her eyes at him as she grabbed a pair of gloves from her bag. She turned putting the gloves on as she walked into the house. The smell was one of the first things that hit her. Animal waste. Decaying animal bodies. Stale beer and rotting food. Graffiti covered the walls making it hard to tell what the wallpaper had once been.

Kirsa walked into what had once been a living room which was now filled with old beer cans. Tony had instructed the three officers to begin looking around the house before more people showed up and ruined any evidence there might be in the ground.

"Wow, you could do a history of beer," Ayden replied from behind her. He had always been fascinated with how the beer can had evolved.

"According to Chris, the kids were upstairs," Tony told them. He radioed to have another squad car meet them to help go through all the garbage.

Kirsa shook her head. She started to get an odd feeling like they were going to find something.

Ayden laid a hand on her shoulder. "You ok?"

"Just a weird feeling," she told him. There was so much history in the home; she was feeling like she was listening to a radio transmission that could not get a clear signal.

"It's going to be hard to smell out anyone in here," he told her.

Even though during daylight hours his sense were still better than most humans, they were not as good as they were at night. With all the other smells going on in the house it was going to be hard to differentiate between a new smell and old ones.

"I know."

"Good, just be on your toes."

"You too," she replied walking out of the room.

She could pick feelings left in the house,

there was bits and pieces here and there. Screams were mixed in with voices of drunken high school students. There were emotions that went from drunken passion to absolute terror. The terror was recent, it was easier to hold unto.

Tony was looking through the former dining room, kicking over sleeping bags that were strewn on the floor. There were condom wrappers littering the floor. Kirsa walked toward the back of the house where the kitchen was. The cabinets were hanging off the walls or had already fallen and lay broken on the faded tile floor. The appliances were gone leaving barren spaces where they had been. Old animal nests were nestled in the corners and broken cabinets.

A quote from the bible was spray painted on one of the cabinets:

"The wrath of God is indeed being revealed against every impiety and wickedness of those who suppress the truth by their wickedness..." Romans 1:18

Kirsa read the passage and felt a chill run through her body. "We got a message." she said into the two way radio.

Ayden came in first followed by Tony. They both read the quote. Tony took out a camera and took a picture of it.

"You think its coincidence?" Ayden asked.

"I think they wanted us to know they were here. I don't get the feeling that this is the main hide out," Kirsa replied. "The teenagers use this house too much."

Kirsa noticed that there were stairs that led up to the second floor. Something was pulling her to go up them. "Hey I'm going to check out upstairs," she told them.

"I'll be up in a minute," Ayden told her.

She nodded and started up the stairs. They creaked and some sagged as she climbed up them, part of her was waiting to fall through a stair. Stepping onto the landing she was greeting with a horrendous smell. Kirsa laid a hand on the gun holster she had put on before leaving the house.

Kirsa noticed that the doors had been replaced with boards nailed across the door way. Unlike the rest of the house, the board and nails looked relatively new, as if some- one had recently boarded off the rooms. She peered into the room closest to her and saw women's clothing piled up. Kirsa pulled the gun out of its holster, the feeling from before was getting stronger. Trying not to gag from the smell that was emanating from one of the rooms, Kirsa cautiously moved down the hall way.

She heard someone coming upstairs and smelled Ayden, she continued toward the only room with a door. Testing the door knob she slowly opened the door and heard a mumble.

Then she saw the image in her head before it happened. Before she could react she was being pulled to the other side and shielded by Ayden as the door burst open and the man hiding in the room began to shoot. Ayden fried off three shots before the guy jumped out the window. There were sirens in the background. Tony came running up the stairs with gun drawn, and saw the two on the floor.

"He jumped out the window," Kirsa told Tony, as Ayden got up off of her.

Tony nodded, turning and running back down the stairs to see if the shooter got away. Kirsa sat up and brushed herself off. She noticed blood and looked up at Ayden.

"I scratched myself when we hit the ground," he assured her.

Kirsa nodded, after they finished brushing each other off they both carefully entered the room. The smell was sickening, there were jars of body parts, and others filled with yellow and red liquid. Both of them couldn't help but gag over the smells. Kirsa radioed to Tony what they found in the room. Tony informed her that the shooter was dead. The man that jumped out the window managed to break his neck in the fall. He had stopped short when he entered the room.

"Dispatch, I need Sara and her team," Tony said urgently into the radio.

****

Ayden and Kirsa returned to the station to give statements and fill out paper work for discharging weapons. While Ayden filled out the form, Tony sat next to Kirsa in his office and handed her coffee.

Tony sipped his own. "Did you get one of your visions?" She nodded.

Kirsa turned and watched Ayden finish and walk toward them. "I saw this man and he was going to come out the door and shoot to kill."

Tony laid a hand on her shoulder; there were some that saw her ability to see ghosts and to see glimpses of the future as a gift. Tony saw it as a curse for he got to witness firsthand what it did to her.

"If you had not seen it, you or Ayden might be the one laying in the morgue," Tony told her plainly.

She looked up at him with coffee in hand, "That's what keeps sticking in my mind the 'what if '."

"Kirsa, if one focused on the 'what ifs' instead of what is they could miss the world before them," Tony advised her. "When Ayden is done, go home, relax and don't work on the case for the rest of the day. You need to decompress after a day like today."

They did not talk about the incident when they drove home. When they arrived home there was a message from Sabrina she had heard what happened. When Kirsa called Sabrina to tell her that they were both fine, Sabrina asked about Lars. Kirsa informed her friend that she had not seen or heard from him all day. Which when she thought about it was rather odd, but she kept that part to herself. They talked for a few more minutes before hanging up.

Kirsa walked up to her room, she dropped her badge on the nightstand. Her gun was locked away in its lock box in the garage. She could feel the grime and dirtiness of the house. Stripping off her clothes she threw them into the garbage bin, she did not want to see them ever again. Turning her iPod player on, Kirsa set the shower for blistering hot.

Kirsa let the hot water pound down on her body washing away her fears, in the shower she was able to finally break down and cry.

There was no one there to hush her or try to soothe her. After an hour she climbed out of the shower and put on a sleep short and a tank top.

Scrunching her hair she took the back staircase down into the kitchen and saw Ayden standing over the stove making food. She raised her eyebrow at him and walked to the fridge. She pulled out a bag of blood and poured some of it into the red wine that Ayden had poured her. Leaning against the counter she watched him at the stove.

"I didn't know you could cook," Kirsa said after a moment. Watching a vampire was interesting and entertaining, she was not sure if she ever saw one do it before. She sipped her wine and blood mixture.

He smiled and looked at her. "I don't, it's one of the prepackaged skillet dinners. Even I can't screw them up," he replied taking a sip from his wine glass.

"Are you eating also or is this feeding the human?" she asked walking to the cabinet where the plates were.

"I will probably pick off of yours, so just set one for you," Ayden told her. "I fed Zero while you were in the shower and tried to get a hold of Lars."

"Sabrina was having a problem getting a hold of him earlier," Kirsa told him. "I'm sure he is with her by now." She got a plate and fork for herself then sat down at the table.

Ayden brought the skillet over and placed some of the pasta meal on her plate. He then slid in next to her and watched her eat for a minute.

"I have a random question for you," Ayden said breaking the silence.

"Should I be worried?" Kirsa asked sipping her wine.

"No," he replied with a laugh.

"Ask away then."

"Why OPIA? Why the paranormal?" Ayden asked her. She looked at him and leaned back against the wall cushion.

"No one has asked me that before. They probably all figure they know the answer," Kirsa answered.

"What is the answer?"

Kirsa ate some more and thought about the question. One of the things she liked about vampires is that they let you take your time to think about a question. There was no rush; they had all the time in the world. Of course when you were the one asking the question, they took all the time in the world to answer a question which was quite aggravating at times.

"When I was five, I was playing in the playroom on the second floor of the main house. Mom and dad were down- stairs, it was around bedtime. I remember because I would always hope they would forget and let me play all night long."

Ayden laughed, she continued. "Anyway, I was playing with my Barbie's and realized I was being watch. When I looked up Nana was standing there. She was in this white hospital like gown. I thought it was odd because she was always in a skirt and blouse. She kneeled down next to me, like she would, then she put a cold hand on mine and told me that she loved me and no matter what she would always be proud of her munchkin. Then she was gone. Dad came up five minutes later; I was so excited that I told him. He gave me this odd look, then told me that Nana must have come to say goodbye because Pop Pop just called and Nana had died."

"He didn't freak out?" Ayden asked. Even amongst vampires, seeing and communicating with the actual dead was rare.

"He told me that it was a special talent and that I should not be afraid. They bought me a journal so that if I saw a ghost I could write it down. As I got older I realized how unique I was and how what I can do can scare others. It forced me to research things and that really sparked my interest in the paranormal."

"Not hanging around vampires?" Ayden sipped his glass and played with one of her curls.

"No, actually. I think most people think that's the reason. But to me, it's part of my life, hanging with vamps."

Ayden laughed and took a bite off her plate. In Kirsa's world, hanging with vampires was normal and if people didn't like it that was their problem not hers. He shook his head smiling.

Kirsa pushed her plate aside and looked at Ayden. "I have to call Emma and let her know what we found today."

"Kirs," Ayden began. Kirsa placed a finger on his lips.

"Ayden, she needs to know that they know she was living with me," she kissed him lightly. "I'll be upstairs in a little bit."

Kirsa slid out from the table and put her plate by the dishwasher. She headed toward her office so that she could talk to Emma in private. All around her office were pictures of her life. There was her parents wedding picture, Tony had given her a copy, they were so happy and blissfully in love. After she hung up with Emma she couldn't help but replay what happened over and over in her head. If she or Ayden had been a moment slower one of them could have ended up in the hospital or dead.

Sighing to herself, Kirsa left the room and walked up the front staircase. Ayden's room was the first door on the right. She knocked on the door frame. The radio was on low and he was pacing. She knocked on the door. He said to come in.

She opened the door but stayed in the doorway. Ayden stopped pacing and looked at her. He could not read what was on her face at all.

"Hey," he said as he walked towards her. "How's Emma?"

"Her same old bubbly self, telling me I'm being overly paranoid."

"You are," he told her.

"I keep running what happened over and over in my head," she told him.

"Tony told you not to," Ayden reminded her, brushing a curl out of her face.

"I know, but it got me thinking," Kirsa told him still stay- ing in the doorway. That way she could retreat if she wanted to.

"About what?" he asked.

Ayden heard his cell phone go off. He went to pick it up. Before he could move she was kissing him. He had not seen her cross the threshold or place a hand on his cheek. Yet she was now kissing him in his room, his arms encircled her pulling her closer. Kirsa moved her hands from his face to around his neck entwining her fingers in his hair.

Ayden pulled away for a second, staring down into her violet eyes. "I am asking this once, are you sure?"

"Yes," the next thing she knew he swept her up and dropped her in the center of his bed.

****

Later Ayden was stretched out on his back with Kirsa curled against him. If he could breathe he would be trying to get it back right now. He turned his head and smiled down at Kirsa who looked like a cat that had a bowl of cream to herself. She was flushed and ruffled.

She looked up at him and smiled. "So that's what I was thinking about."

He laughed and kissed her lightly on the

lips. "Fine with me."

He pulled her closer listening to her heart. Her head rested on his shoulder and she draped a leg over his stomach.

"I wanted to go slow the first time," he told her. "You kind of caught me off guard."

"I have to say, first time with a vamp. Not bad," she said with a smile.

He raised an eyebrow. "Not bad?"

She laughed and then groaned when he rolled her over and entered her again.

It was much later when he had her tucked against him under the covers. Sleep would be coming soon they both felt.

"No one else but you," he whispered into her ear.

She turned and looked up at him. "No one else but you."

****

We walled to my favorite spot where I pick wild herbs and flowers. He had come to accompany me often on my nightly walks. Hagan did not like to be out in day light; he explained that he had a rare disorder. It was fine with me, I often slept late because of the hours I kept tending to the sick and being a midwife.

I knew something was troubling him and asked him if anything was wrong. In the moon light he turned and looked at me. I saw it there in his eyes and knew what he was about to say. "I love you," was what he said. When I told him I loved him also he made a choked noise. Then he pulled me close and kissed me like no other has or will. That night in the moonlight we sealed our love.

Chapter Twenty

The phone had woken both Kirsa and Ayden up. She knew the ringtone and groaned as she reached for the phone that had fallen to the floor during the night. It was a little after eight in the morning. If Tony was calling this early something was up.

"Yes," Kirsa answered.

"We should work on your phone etiquette at some point," Tony stated.

"Hello darling godfather, to what do I owe this wonderful call for?" Kirsa asked. Ayden was chuckling next to her in the bed.

"According to our overnight cleaning guy, someone was in my office last night," Tony informed her.

"What do you mean someone was in your office?" Kirsa asked as she stretched.

"I think they were looking for the pictures," Tony said.

Kirsa felt Ayden move from the bed as she focused on what Tony was telling her. They were still in Ayden's room and she found it hard to focus as she watched him get dressed.

"Ok, where did you put the pictures after we left last night?" she asked.

"I brought them home, I signed them out, the DA knows I took them home," Tony told her. "We all agreed they would be safer there."

"That was a good idea,"Kirsa agreed.

"The other reason I'm calling is Sara is picking up an odd scent around her house and woods."

"How odd?"

"Enough to rattle her and call me," Tony stated.

"Do you want me to have Ayden call her?"

"She was open to him coming to help," Tony answered.

"Alright, I'll have him call her," Kirsa promised.

She clicked the phone shut and plopped back on the bed. Ayden sat next to her.

"So what's going on?" he asked.

"According to Tony: Ryan, who cleans his office, someone had been snooping around in it last night. Tony is going to have Ryan look through some of the personnel photos because Ryan told him there was a cop there who usually isn't."

"You mentioned something about me calling Sara," Ayden replied.

"She's picking up a weird scent around her place and wants your take on it."

"Hmmm," Ayden said.

She raised her eyebrows and grabbed a belt loop on his jeans pulling him back down as he was about to get up. He rolled over and looked at her.

"What theory Ayden?"

"I did not want to freak you out," he said brushing a curl out of her face.

"What theory Ayden?" she repeated. She didn't want things to be hidden from her because it might protect her.

He took a deep breath. "I think that the Church of Light might have a very old vampire working for them. Which would explain why we cannot pick up on them?"

Kirsa was quiet for a minute. "You mean older then Wyrm, old?"

"Could possibly make him look young," he watched her face. He figured that she would have flipped out or said it was impossible. "You're thinking about something?"

"You know how Wyrm translated the journals?" she asked him

"Yeah he split them up between you and Adam. Why?"

She sat up and looked down at him. "I have been reading them, trying to get at least one entry in a day since there are like ten journals that I have."

"Where are you going with this?"

She looked away for a minute. "Let's get dressed and call Tony. I think what I have read fits into all of this."

He leaned over and kissed her. "OK. Kirsa, last night I was serious about no one else."

She kissed him back. "Same here."

With that she climbed off the bed naked and walked out of his room. He stayed on the bed and smiled for a minute. Then his brain began to wonder what she was about to reveal to him.

Ayden walked down into the kitchen and put the coffee on. He heard Lars coming through the back door. Taking a package of blood out of the fridge he poured it into two mugs. With Kirsa now using bags, they kept them all in the vegetable drawer. He prepared for the lecture he was going to receive.

Lars opened the door and walked into the kitchen. He stopped short and sniffed the air. It was not his normal sniff of air to see if coffee was being made. This was one that was noticing scents.

In a flash Lars was next to him sniffing. Ayden pushed him away. "Knock it off."

"You slept with her?" Lars stated.

"I don't ask you about your sex life before coffee," Ayden replied reaching for the coffee.

He did not have the time because Lars had him up against the fridge. "Hurt her..."

"Hurt me and what Lars?" Kirsa asked walking into the kitchen. "Drop the bullshit and drink your coffee."

Lars let go of Ayden and watched Kirsa. She walked up to Ayden kissed him lightly on the lips then went to grab a package from the fridge before she realized that Ayden had done that already.

Kirsa turned and looked at them. "Look, either play nice or leave because shit is going to be hitting the fan and I need both of you right now. Oh and Tony should be here any minute."

Lars took his coffee and left the room and that was it.

****

After the phone calls and drama over coffee, Kirsa settled into her office. There were some information that she wanted to gather before she talked to Tony and Ayden. Lars had vanished from the house which at the moment was fine with her. Most likely he was over at Sabrina's. In truth she hoped he stayed there because part of her didn't want him hearing what she was going to say. She had been getting a weird vibe from Lars lately. He seemed distracted and often met them places instead of going with them.

"Tony's car just pulled onto the road. Where do you want to set up?" he asked her.

Kirsa looked around the office; it would be cramped to have the conversation in here. "How about in the living room, that way if I need anything from in here I'm right in the next room."

"Ok," Ayden went to retreat but stopped and turned around. "I went to check on Lars, he's gone along with his car."

"Good. If he is going to be in one of his moods then I don't want him to be around at this moment."

"I agree, but haven't you noticed that he's been distant?" Ayden asked.

"Yeah, I keep figuring he's with Sabrina but some of the times are when she is at work," Kirsa told him. "I'll ask her about it later."

There was a knock on the front door, Kirsa heard Zero running to the door. She walked with Ayden to the door and opened it. Tony stood there; he took one look at them and knew. He gave Ayden a stern look and Ayden nodded, then he entered the house.

"We have coffee going in the kitchen. Do you want a mug?" Ayden asked.

"That would be great," Tony told him.

Kirsa led Tony into the living room that was off of the entrance hallway. He saw the files on the coffee table. He sat down on the old threadbare chair and took out the folders he head. Ayden walked in with a mug for Tony and sat down.

"How much do you know about Vampire Lore?" Kirsa inquired.

"Like what people think is vampire lore or actually Lore?" Tony asked.

He knew there were two separate thoughts on the topic. It was something that Hagan had worked hard to help educate the general public about what was myth and what was fact.

"The later," Kirsa replied. She sipped her coffee as she flipped through one of the journals.

"Depends on the lore you're talking about," Ayden replied as he sat in the brown leather love seat.

"Do you know the lore regarding the original six?" Kirsa asked. The original six was one of the oldest tales and often caused arguments when brought up.

"I've heard reference to it but never the actual tale," Tony told her.

"The original six," Ayden began before Kirsa could, "is essentially what some think as the vampire's origin story. The short version is the first vampire, a woman we call Eve, gives birth to six children. Each of the six children is given the gift of never ending life, super human strength, and so on."

"Those are some gifts," Tony commented.

"They are," Ayden agreed. He then continued with what he knew. "It also said the each one could transform into an animal. This is where the original six tie their lines too. Dietrich is head of one of them and the lines that come from him. His flag is that of the bear, because it is said that the first of his line could transform into one."

"Those that trace their line to one of the six hold a seat in the Inner Council. All the other bloodlines that branch off make up the General Council," Kirsa added. "Each head is voted by their line."

"What does this have to do with the case?" Tony asked. He was not sure how vampire lore or politics played in with the case.

"This morning, Ayden told me the theory about the old vamp, it reminded me of something I read about in one of the journals," Kirsa told them. That had their attention. She took a sip of coffee.

"Kirsa, my namesake, goes into quite a bit of the old vampire lore and history. She is writing after the establishment of the First Council."

"The Vampire Wars," Ayden said. It was one of the bloodiest parts of the vampire history when vampires turned against each other.

"What vampire wars?" Tony asked, he sipped his coffee then set it down on the coffee table.

While Hagan was all about educating the people about the paranormal and how they were regular people. He was not about exposing all their secrets and history. Being friends with Hagan meant that Tony tended to know more than most but when it came to their histories that was out of his territory.

"Around 500 C.E., there was an uprising within the vampire community," Kirsa began. "At this point there was no real Council. No real set of laws for them, no way form of government."

"Make it easy for someone to take advantage," Tony stated getting an idea where this was going.

"Raymond," Ayden said. Kirsa and Tony looked at him. "Dietrich told me that Wyrm found some documents that indicate the vampire responsible was named Raymond. He was this vampire that had amazing mind control abilities. He knew how to speak to an audience, to get people to listen to him."

"We have a few of those in our history too

though without the extra power," Tony commented.

Kirsa picked up from Ayden. "While Raymond was building his following, the elders at first thought nothing of him until his following started getting a little too large. When the following reached close to a thousand, the heads of the five lines decided it was time to work together."

"What about the sixth line?" Tony asked, he had forgotten his coffee by this point.

"The sixth line has already vanished by this point," Kirsa answered. She sipped her water and continued. "Raymond was vicious, cold blooded, and brilliant. He knew how to strategize, how to move an army without leaving a trace. He killed anyone who opposed him, his followers, not quite as blood thirsty, would imprison those deemed useful and fed off the others. The five houses were having a difficult time keeping control of the situation. The leader of the rebels claimed that he was heir to the sixth bloodline."

"I take it there was no proof nor did it matter at this point," Tony replied.

"The sixth line has always been an enigma," Ayden added.

"So what happens?" Tony asked Kirsa.

"The five heads join forces which outnumbers Raymond's tenfold," Kirsa answered. "Under pressure of losing control, Raymond makes a critical mistake by ordering his followers to attack a village. In the village was a monastery that ran an orphanage. He ordered the killing of the orphans; while he expected his followers to listen he went and killed all but one of the monks that had been harboring him. It is said that he turned the last monk against his will."

"Might as well break a few more laws if you're going down," Tony said. "The orphans?"

"Many of his followers didn't listen, they saw the writing on the wall," Ayden assured Tony. "They gathered the orphans and got them out of the building turning them over to the council forces for safe keeping."

"And Raymond and the monk?"

"For Raymond, he emerged from the building to be faced by not just his followers but the five elders," Kirsa answered. "They brought him to the closest safe location where he was put on trial. His crimes were bloodlust and killing of the innocent, both were always established rules. He had no regard for what he did, he was sentenced to burn by the sun and if that did not kill him then a stake through the heart. His followers forced to watch. His followers were tried individually after that."

"I've heard the monk story before," Ayden said taking over. "It is still told in some of the rural parts of Germany. Part of the story I heard is the villagers that survived buried the bodies of the monks, except for one. There was one body not accounted for, and he was the most devoted and pious of the group."

"Why did Raymond claim to be the heir?" Tony asked. He never understood the fascination with the mystery line.

"He wasn't the first to claim he was," Kirsa responded. "To be the heir means spot on the inner council, your own bloodline. It is also said that the youngest of the six was the most cherished of all."

"And how does all of this tie into what is going on now?" Tony asked remembering his coffee.

"In the journal that I have been reading I've come across an interesting entry," Kirsa continued finishing her coffee. "She has been married for four years at this point to Lord Hagan Adulwulf. She tells of an evening walk with her husband where he is troubled. An old monk had paid a visit to the village earlier in the day to have counsel with Hagan. The monk explained who he was, then told Hagan he knew what he was and that he has hunted him for five hundred years. In the monks mind if Hagan had stepped up then there would not have been a war and the monk would be at peace with the Lord."

"Besides your father, the name has been mentioned from time to time. What does the journal say?" Ayden asked. He did not add that, when it was mentioned it was tied to the sixth line.

"Hagan was lord of the village that belonged to my family," Kirsa explained. "His family had been rulers of it since it had been formed by its founder. Rumors arose shortly after he arrived to the village that he bore the name of the founder and fit the description. But that would have been impossible because he have to have been well over 1000 years old. His wife, Kirsa, knew the truth, for he explained who he was before he proposed. Who and what he was did   not change how she felt for him."

"What would this truth be?' Tony asked. He almost feared what she was going to say.

"That he was a vampire, and was the only member of the sixth line," Kirsa continued before either could stop. 'Before this monks arrival, Kirsa and Hagan had experience the birth of their second child, a son."

"Wait, if let say this Hagan was the sixth, he was able to sire two children with a pure mortal woman?" Ayden asked dumbfounded. In order for a child to be sired usually the mother would have to be going through the process of changing.

"Yes they had two children," "Kirsa verified. "And no she didn't have a lover. Their minds were linked. He would have smelled another on her. He had been her first as well."

"Alright so no chance of it being an affair," Tony said understanding why Ayden had to ask the question. It was rare for a vampire and a mortal to be able to sire a child.

"Anyway," Kirsa said continuing. "Hagan explains that he had written the Council for he feared that harm may come to his family. He wanted the Council to verify the monk's story and that if he had taken claim would it have ended the war. Several weeks past and he gets word that nothing he would have done would have changed the course of history. Towards the end of the war Raymond claimed he was all six bloodlines mixed into one being."

"Talk about being full of themselves," Tony replied almost snorting at the thought. "Sorry, I know there are vampires out there with superiority complexes but knowing the one's I do I find it amusing that one would claim to be all six. Could you imagine Dietrich standing before the Council saying he was the heir to all six?"

They all chuckled. It broke the tension that had been hanging in the air since earlier in the morning. It also gave them a moment to take a breath before they continued.

Kirsa sipped some water and looked at her notes to see what they had covered before she continued. "Apparently, Hagan went and explained this to the Monk. The Monk was furious that no one would take blame for his eternal damnation; he kills Hagan by beheading him. He then vows to hunt the line until its extinction in order to make amends for what was done to him."

"Well shit," Ayden said not seeing that coming.

"I second that," Tony agreed.

Ignoring them Kirsa went on. "It was with that threat that Kirsa, the first mortal to be summoned to a Council meeting, meets with the Inner Council. They inform her of the threat and that she, her children and all that come from them would be protected by the Council. When she asked them why, they told her that running through the veins of her children was the purest, oldest and most sacred blood. Hagan had never created a vampire, he never allowed another to feed off of him."

Kirsa finished and sat in her chair letting all she said absorb into their brains. She had not wanted to tell them this all at once but it seemed that it could play a part in what they were dealing with now.

Ayden looked at her. This was going to be an enormous announcement if it was ever made. "Have you checked with other sources?"

"Yes. Adam has a journal belonging to a Council member at the time of Hagan's murder and it confirms the story." Kirsa told them.

"Have you told anyone else?" Tony asked, if this got out before the case was over all hell would break loose.

"Oh yeah I have been telling anyone who would listen," Kirsa said sarcastically. "Of course I haven't told anyone about this."

"Is it possible that since that time the Monk has been secretly behind the Church of Light?" Tony asked.

"No, he could have become a member after it had been formed. But it's not formed until one of the plague epidemics in the 1300's," Kirsa explained to him. "The group didn't start targeting my family until the sixteen hundreds."

"He's not their leader," Ayden said as it all clicked. "They most likely have told him that his salvation would be to destroy the last of your line. When he does that his soul will be forgiven."

"That was what I was thinking," Kirsa said. "He is also being more careless now because he doesn't like taking orders from a woman. Which, Anton pretty much confirmed that a female was running the show when we paid a visit to him."

"How do we trap a 1,500 year old vampire?" Tony asked.

"My thought is we capture him and get him to talk," Kirsa commented.

"How are you going to get him to talk?" Ayden inquired. Getting someone like a devoted monk to give up seeking eternal salvation to talk might be a bit tricky.

"Tony's uncle is a Priest who has met with vampires before so they can make confession," Kirsa answered.

"I can give him a call just to let him know we are going to need him. Now how do we go about capturing a vampire this old?" Tony wondered.

Ayden looked into Kirsa's eyes and saw the trust and the answer in them. "We offer what he wants as bait."

Chapter Twenty One

Jockey Hollow is a National Park located in Morristown, New Jersey. It had once served as headquarters for George Washington and his army during the Revolutionary war. One could visit it during the warmer months, taking in the beauty of nature, the history of the placed. It was also a spot one could go if they wanted to go unnoticed.

He was dressed in black slacks, black dress shirt, black leather gloves, He wore a black fedora on his shaved head and on his eyes were dark sunglasses. He stood in the shadows of a tree as he watched a young family walk by him. In all the black he wore, his marble white skin stood out. Some thought him to be albino, most of the time he made it so that no one would remember him.

Out of the corner of his eyes he saw her approach. She wore a deep blue short-sleeve blouse and Jean capri's that looked to be tailored made for her. On her feet were running shoes. Her long blonde hair was loose and the wind was blowing strands of it around. She would be a worthy prey but she was his boss, or he let her think that.

"Miss. Adams," he said softly. It had the effect of a blast of ice cold air.

Veronica forced herself not to shiver. "Good afternoon, Louis."

"Why this place?" he asked

She looked around. "I thought you would appreciate being around something with history to it."

He let it go. "You wished to discuss what is going on in Grabenberg?"

Veronica nodded and motioned to a bench in a shaded section of the park. He followed her, careful to not step in the sunlight for long. They sat down on the bench, each on opposite sides for they both freaked each other out.

"I have lost faith in the others that are part of this," she told him. "So has our Father."

"As have I," he agreed. It was true the others were being reckless and had visions of seeing only themselves as the victors.

"Yet you, I trust for I know your purpose is pure and honorable," Veronica told him. She might be vain and goal oriented but her beliefs were true. "Which is why I wanted to meet you here and not at my office or the safe house."

"I understand."

She looked at a passing couple and thought of the man she loved in jail. The rage boiled up but she took a deep breath and centered herself again.

"Kirsa Heinrich," Veronica said simply. "I believe you are right about her family's importance to the Vampire Council. From the Intel we gathered, the security around her and her cousin has greatly increased. They have given her what you call a Shadow."

"Yes I have seen him. He is their best; to get around him will not be easy if one can get around him."

"Would you be able to?" she asked. Veronica did not care to understand vampire politics or what they were; she wanted to know what was possible.

"I am not sure. For being a young one, he has very powerful abilities. I believe he has picked up on my presence when no other has in the past. To get around him directly will be near impossible."

"How about with a distraction?" Veronica asked him.

He thought about it for a moment: tapping a finger on his thigh. "That could work."

"I also want Kirsa to know we are watching her. I know of the picture blunder," she said catching his raised eyebrow. "I know you had no knowledge of what the rolls contained, that you were given the bags loaded. I know she is aware we have been watching but I want her to know."

"I have taken care of that, Madame," he said.

She turned and looked at him. One part wanted to be annoyed that he did something without her direct order. The other part of her was intrigued though.

"May I ask how you did this?" she asked him.

Louis looked at his watch. "At any moment she will be called to a crime scene in which a message will be there waiting only for her."

****

Lake Hopatcong was a large lake in north-western New Jersey. It went from Jefferson Township, to Hopatcong and incorporated other towns around its borders. During the early 1900's it had been summer spot for the rich and famous. Now the once fishing and summer cabins were turned into year round residences. The Hollywood glamour had left. On one of the forgotten trails Kirsa made her way with Tony and the Jefferson Township Chief of Police down the path. Ayden followed behind her taking in everything around him.

Along the way Kirsa picked up flashes of what the victim had seen and felt. It caused her to shiver despite being close to 100 degrees out. They came to a power boat in which the three got in. For along Lake Hopatcong were tiny islands that one could get to by boat or swimming if one had the energy. It took only a few minutes for them to arrive.

Stepping off the boat Kirsa could see the scene that lay before them, for the island was only a few hundred feet wide. Before she could step any farther the girl appeared out of nowhere. Her red hair was cut short and layered around her face. She had light brown eyes and a peaches and cream complexion. She wore a white t shirt and khaki shorts. Around her neck was a simple gold cross.

****

"I told him I wasn't evil," the girl told Kirsa. "I told him I follow my faith and have committed no sins. Yet he dragged me by the hair down the path. He gagged me as he threw me in the boat."

"What's your name?" Kirsa asked. For everything else blurred out of focus, it was just her and the victim.

"Heather. I was going to be a junior at Grabenberg University," she explained. She turned and looked to where her body was. "But he ruined that."

"What did he look like?" Kirsa asked.

"Tall, but not as tall as the long haired detective behind you, he had a shaved head. His eyes were the coldest brown eyes I have ever seen. When I looked into them I knew I was going to die."

"Did he tell you why he picked you?" Kirsa asked.

A tear trickled down the girls face. "Because I work with were-children and help counsel them. He said I was sinning because I was helping Lucifer spill his hate."

Heather continued before Kirsa could ask another question. "I told him I was Catholic and that I could not die like this. It was then he softened and said *that he once was a Catholic, that he had taken an oath long ago. He gave me the last rites."*

"Are you sure?" Kirsa asked.

Heather nodded. "Can you do me a favor?"

"Yes."

"Lie, and tell my mother I felt no pain. Then tell her I am at peace and will be with her always."

****

Kirsa had not realized she had been crying until Ayden brushed a tear away. She looked around and saw that everything was in focus and that Heather was gone. Closing her eyes she took a deep breath. The encounter had left her drained and she had yet to see the scene.

Tony looked at her. "Are you ok?" he asked her.

"Yes. I'll explain after," Kirsa told him. "Please let's get this over with."

The chief nodded and motioned for them to follow as they made their way quickly to the other side.

Horror. It was the only word that Kirsa's brain could think of. What had been to done to Isabella had been brutal and filled with hate. The scene stretched out before her was one of pure horror. A boat was tied to a tree stump. In the seat facing them was a headless female, her clothes were tattered.

Her left foot was where her right foot should be, left hand where her right should and so on. He had cut her apart then stitched her back together. Kirsa got the horrible feeling that he began the process while she was alive. The only thing he did not attach was the head. The head was resting on the seat across from the body as if it was looking at its own body.

"A note was found in a plastic bag that was stitched to the mouth. A cross necklace was also in the bag," The chief told them.

"The necklace belongs to the girl," Kirsa whispered. "Do you have the letter?"

"That's the thing we did not open it because it was ad- dressed to you," he told her handing over the evidence bag.

****

It was around four in the afternoon when they had re- turned to station, Tony had the letter photocopied and scanned before he handed it to Kirsa. She folded it and put it in a pocket. She had to write up everything she saw, Kirsa then told Sara that the girl wanted her parents to think she did not suffer. Sara nodded than gave her a hug and kiss on the head. Before Tony could say anything Ayden had her in his arms and buckled in the car within seconds.

They drove in silence. Kirsa watched the town go by, she wondered how much more suffering the town could take. It seemed with each murder, the scene was getting more horrific and the manner of death more painful. Now they were going after those who helped the supernatural.

Zero met them at the back door as they came in; Kirsa dropped to her knees and rested her cheek on top of the dog's head. Ayden walked in and got Zero's food ready and put the tea kettle on. Kirsa stood up and got out one of her herbal tisanes for when she dealt with ghosts. It was a lavender base, which helped calm her down. When the tea was ready she left him in the kitchen and went up to her room. There she shut the door and walked to her alter. After lighting the candles she cast her circle and began an incantation.

Ayden was sipping his wine glass and looked up to the ceiling when he felt the ripple of power. He knew she was upstairs casting a protection circle for all who dwell in the house. She would find a way for it to protect Sabrina as well. Lars walked in the back door; he wore black dress pants and a black shirt.

"A little formal for you," Ayden replied.

Like him, Lars preferred jeans and t-shirts.

"I had to run out somewhere. What's up?" Lars asked going to the fridge.

"Where have you been?"

"Out. Why?"

"You didn't answer my phone calls, and since when do you go out during the day?" Ayden asked.

"I told you I had to run out. Why?"

Ayden leaned against the counter studying Lars as he did. He took another sip of his glass. "There was another murder; this one was far worst then what they did to Isabella."

Lars raised his eyebrows. "Really what did they do?"

"First she was a normal person, an innocent," Ayden explained. "Her only crime was that she was a summer counselor to a camp that worked with were-children. That was why they killed her. It wasn't just how they killed her. They decapitated her and rearranged all her body parts."

"That sucks, is Kirsa upset?" Lars asked sipping a beer.

"Yes, they left a note addressed to her," Ayden replied not sure what to make of Lars not reacting to what he told him.

"Is that why you're upset? Because they sent a letter to Kirsa?"

"They killed an innocent! That alone is enough to be upsetting."

Lars snickered almost. He caught himself with a cough. "So the cult killed a human."

Ayden just stared at him for a moment. "What has gotten into you?"

"Wait. Are you actually upset over the fact they killed a girl?" Lars asked him. "If she was a vampire then yes it would be horrible, but she was an average run of the mill human."

Taking a deep breath Ayden steadied his anger, "She was an innocent. Even we do not kill the innocent, those who do are punished."

"We did though, before we became 'civilized.' Look I'm not saying she deserved to die but she was a human. She would have died eventually anyway."

"And so will I, Lars. Does that mean I too deserve to die a horrible death, because eventually I will die?" Kirsa asked leaning against the doorjamb.

Lars looked at her and then turned away and gulped his beer. He had not meant for her to hear him say that.

"Does Sabrina deserve to die in such a manner also, because she is also a mere mortal and will as you say eventually die. Are we just fair game them?"

"Kirsa stop," Lars said quietly.

"If this is how you feel then I relinquish you from your duties as my body guard." With that, Kirsa turned and walked back up the stairs.

Ayden looked at Lars and then followed after her. Lars threw the beer bottle against the stove and it shattered leaving a dent in the white metal. Cursing, he stormed out of the room.

Kirsa knew he was in the room, she had smelled him just as he entered the doorway. Ayden joined her on the balcony. Kirsa turned and looked away from him. He turned her face back to him and kissed a tear away. Kirsa leaned her head on his and let the tears fell. Yet for the first time in a long time the tears were not because of frustration or feeling trapped.

She was crying because a beautiful human being had been killed. She wiped her tears away.

"He made a mistake," she said trying to keep her voice from cracking.

"How is that?" Ayden asked holding her. He knew she wasn't talking about Lars.

"He was hoping that by making this personal I would be scared, that I would walk away," Kirsa said looking up at Ayden. "Instead he has given me a reason to finish this. So that others like Heather don't end up in his path."

Ayden kissed her lightly. "You are one of a kind."

She smiled up at him. "Will you help me forget what happened today?"

"Of course," he told her.

Chapter Twenty Two

We walked in the moonlight. I knew something was on his mind for he had been more silent than normal. Even in these woods that had become our private refuge, he was quiet. We approached the field where I often picked my herbs, he found a large rock and leaned against it. Taking my hand in his he pulled me toward. I thought he was to kiss me instead he placed his hands gently on either side of my face and looked into my eyes.

"I love you," he told me. "You are my light in the darkness."

I felt my heart skip a beat; before I said anything he placed a finger against my lips to silence me.

"Before we continue I must tell you who I am," he said. " You are Hagan the man I love," I told him.

He smiled in an odd way. "I am not a man. You

have heard rumors of things that stalk the innocent in the night. They drain the blood of their victims?"

I nodded unsure of what he was going to tell me. I was certain that no matter what he said to me, it would not change what I felt.

"The legend is that a woman, Eve we have named her, walked this earth and gave birth to some of the first mortals. When she became vain and proud God condemned her, she would have six children who were unlike any that had walked this earth. They were called the children of the night for they could not stand the light of day. Each child possessed an ability and each child craved the thirst for blood."

I had never heard this tale before, I stood there transfixed and listened while he told it to me. He watched me with his eyes as if he was waiting for me to draw back in fear.

"From these children of the night the vampire emerged," he paused for a moment. "Five of the six craved blood and began to turn others but the sixth was different. He did not crave blood as much, or the blood of Humans as much. While he did drink from humans he was always careful to not turn them into a monster. He became an outcast from his siblings.

So he wandered the earth alone, until one day he met a woman he fell in love with. He feared that if she truly knew who or what he was he would lose her, yet to bind her to marriage and not know what he was seemed cruel. So he bared himself to her and waited for her to fear him."

I looked at him when he finished his tale. I knew what he was telling me, I had heard the rumors about his family. I was not a silly maiden who was seeking an adventure.

I laid a hand on his cool cheek and looked into his eyes so that he could see into my soul. " You are the man I love; there is no monster in there."

Before he could say a word I pulled him to me and kissed him with all the love and passion that I had for him.

****

It was ten in the morning, Kirsa found herself leaning on the railing of her deck. It had been a little over a week since she came back to Grabenberg and yet it felt like she had never left. So much had happened in that week, one of them being a sexy Irishmen lying naked in her bed. She knew Ayden pretended to be asleep. He had given her a night where she forgot about reality. They ordered in pizza, which was cold when they go to it. He sat through a chick flick without complaining. He kept her mind and body occupied until the early hours of morning.

But today was a new day, and reality returned with the sun rising. She read more of her ancestor's journal looking for clues. Yet while reading it the thought of the letter downstairs nagged at her. If Ayden had known she left the room he did not show it, but she had gone down and retrieved the copy of the letter that had been left with the body addressed to her. The photocopy of the letter was in her hand. Taking a breath she opened and began to read.

My Dear Kirsa,

I once wrote the same opening to an ancestor of yours

with the same name. That letter was to tell her why I killed her husband. I did not want her to think there was no reason to it.

I digress. I should introduce myself to you. I go by Louis. It is name I chose when my life had been taken from me in an unjust way. I have been on this earth for many centuries now.

I have watched your family grow and prosper. I have watched as they have died either natural or unnatural deaths. I can not take credit for the deaths. I should tell you that I did not play a part in the death of your parents or Aunt and Uncle. It was much too impersonal I thought.

If I am charged with killing a person I want

to be involved with their death.

The young girl she almost got away. She was such a devout Catholic that I did think for a moment to let her be Free. I was not worried about being identified. But what made me go through with it was the fact that she wasted herself on the wicked. I did cry as I killed her, I cried as I chopped her to pieces. I once was a man of God, and men of God do not commit the atrocities I have. Yet I stopped being a man when I was turned into a monster.

Yet I am beginning to wish for salvation, a chance to repent my sins. I feel old. I have been told that your death will be my salvation. I am not sure I agree, but Miss Adams assures me that you are the wickedest of all. I do grow tired of the killing. Though I know I will kill again, most likely before we even meet. I have my current victim in view. She is beautiful however she is a little furry for my taste.

Until we meet,

Louis.

Kirsa folded the letter up and stared ahead. She let the words begin to digest in her brain as she began to pull things from the letter. The letter did not say much but it explained a lot.

Ayden came up behind her, pulled her close and kissed the back of her neck. She turned her head up for a kiss.

"How did you sleep?" he asked kissing her again.

"Well. Thanks to you," she told him.

Ayden in the day was always amazing, his skin was the palest of white, you could see his veins, and it seemed different hues of color depending on how the sun hit him. This could become her in the future she thought.

"What is going through your head?" he asked kissing the top of her head

She looked up at him and knew that there was absolute trust, a fact that was more important to her then how they felt about each other. That trust, she had never had before with anyone.

"What would you think about taking a trip into the City with me?" Kirsa asked him. She watched his eyes narrow as he looked at her not sure what quite to think of her question. His eyes narrowed on the letter.

"Are we going to be going to SoHo?" he asked.

"That we are," she told him.

"Their lawyer is going to throw a fit if we show up there," he told her.

Kirsa handed him the letter. "Not when we have a cause to go in and ask questions."

He stared at the letter in his hand. "He mentions the cult in the letter?"

"Not only the cult, but a Miss Adams also," she told him.

"Alright I am going to let Lars know. Why don't you call Tony," Ayden said. He kissed her quickly and left the room.

Kirsa dialed Tony's work number and was surprised when Sara answered. "Hello Sara."

"Hey, I am manning Tony's phone. Chris is off today so we had Ryan come in to look at the photos again," she explained.

"Ah. Will you let him know that I read the letter and that Ayden I are taking a trip to the city to have a theological discussion," Kirsa told her.

"I am writing this down word for word. And just to cover my ass, do we have cause for this discussion?" Sara asked. She knew about the case and what was going on as she had helped down in South Carolina due to the sheer volume of bodies.

"Tell him that the letter points to certain people. So yes we have enough to go talk to them," Kirsa told her.

"Awesome, hey since you're on the phone. I picked up the smell again."

"When are you off shift?" Kirsa asked as she perused her closet.

"I can be off for six, even if something comes in I can take a dinner break," Sara explained to her.

"Ok, Ayden and I will come by the house."

They hung up and Kirsa decided she should call one more person. She dialed the coded number and waited for Dietrich to pick up.

"Did I wake you?" she asked when he picked up the phone. It would be around 6pm in Austria.

"I have been up for a bit," he assured her as he sipped his evening blood. "What is going on my dear?"

"I'm going to be sending you a letter I received from a killer; one I believe to be an ancient vampire. Dietrich, I think he also might tie into my ancestry. I will send a brief explanation with it."

"And this is why you are calling me?"

"I'm calling because Ayden and I are taking a trip to SoHo," she paused and heard silence. "He mentions the cult and Veronica in the letter. So we are going to ask some questions."

"Be careful."

They hung up and Kirsa quickly got everything together to send to Dietrich. After encrypting everything she sent him the email with the attachments. She also sent a copy to Al to catch him up on what was going on. She did not reveal everything about her families past but enough so that he understood her urgency.

Kirsa went to her closet and began the tedious task of putting together a conservative outfit that would not piss off the ultra-religious. She pulled out a pale blue short-sleeve silk blouse and black trouser with baby blue pin stripe. It took her about forty five minutes to finish getting ready. Ayden knocked on the bathroom door as she finished with makeup. She let out a whistle. It was not often that Ayden dressed up but when he did he cleaned up well. He wore charcoal gray trousers, a red dress shirt with a black tie. He pulled his long hair back into a pony tail.

"You look amazing," he told her.

He was always stunned by her transformations from everyday, to meeting, to formal occasions. She was a classic beauty and knew how to play up her looks.

"I can say the same about you," she replied, sliding on her black heels. They added about two inches on to her height. They were comfortable and she knew she could run down a criminal in them, because she had a few years ago.

They took the PATH from Hoboken into Greenwich Village, it was only a few blocks from there to their destination in SoHo. Ayden walked holding Kirsa's hand. On the trip to the City they had talked about how they were going to do this. The decision had been Kirsa going in to talk to Veronica and he would stay in the waiting area. If there was a female secretary he would flirt, a male he would try a different approach which still involved flirting. They walked in silence; he smiled as men tended to take a second glance at Kirsa. He did not think that she realized how beautiful she was.

They approached the building and Kirsa looked up. She saw the blinds were drawn on the third floor as they often were. Taking a huge breathe she looked at Ayden, he squeezed her hand. He opened the door and they took the steps. Kirsa had a thing about elevators and avoided them at all cost. He still remembered her arguing with the elevator operator at the Eiffel tower about having to take it up.

They came to the third floor landing and saw the door that in gold letters said "The Church of Light welcomes all."

"If I burst into flames when we enter I will haunt you forever," Ayden whispered in her ear.

"I promise to buy a marble urn to put you in," she joked. They opened the door and saw a young woman about 19 years old. She had red hair and was wearing a white t-shirt that had the churches logo on it. She looked up and smiled at Ayden and Kirsa when they entered.

"Hello, I'm Erin how may I help you today?" she asked smiling.

"I am here to speak to Miss Adams," Kirsa informed her. The girl, keeping the smile plastered on, looked at a calendar. "I'm sorry but Miss. Adams does not have any scheduled appointments for today. She also does not take walk-in's. I can schedule you in for next Wednesday."

"Wow, she has a busy schedule huh?" Ayden said smiling.

Erin blushed. "Actually she is handling some issues within the church and asked to keep her book open. I am sorry for any inconvenience."

Kirsa smiled and took out her badge. "That's fine, however there is urgent matter that I must discuss with her."

The girl went to say something but instead her eyes bulged when she saw the OPIA badge that Kirsa showed her. The girl did a double take trying to process the information.

"Um, yes Miss. Adams is in today. Her door is the second one on the right. She might be a bit grumpy, she does not like being interrupted," Erin warned Kirsa.

"Thank you," Kirsa said she looked at Ayden.

"You know, I think if it's ok with Erin, I am going to stay here," Ayden said smiling again at the young woman.

She blushed. "That's fine sir."

Kirsa wanted to shake her head but instead nodded, though she knew that Ayden picked up the laughter in her eyes.

Kirsa walked to the door and debated for a second to knock on the door or just go in. Smiling she turned the stainless steel handle and walked into the office.

"Good afternoon Miss. Adams," Kirsa greeted Veronica, appreciating the surprise on her face when she turned around from her computer to stare at Kirsa.

It took a second for the initial shock of the intrusion to wear off. The woman had just barged into her office unannounced when she had told the child outside she was not be disturbed.

"Hello, I'm sorry but I have no appointments for today," Veronica replied, standing up blocking her computer screen from view. She had made that fact perfectly clear to the girl outside.

"I know Erin told us out front," Kirsa said crossing the room.

"You were not invited in," Veronica told her playing with her cross necklace.

Kirsa smiled slowly. "I do not need to be," she told her. "I am not here for a conversation, Veronica. You can drop the act that you don't know me. Though, it has been about three years since we last saw each other in person."

Outrage boiled up, Veronica fought to remain calm. "Then why are you here?"

Kirsa pulled out her badge. "I am here to ask you some questions that deal with an investigation that I am working on."

Trying to keep her anger under control, Veronica took a deep breath and sat back down in her seat. She motioned to Kirsa to do the same.

Kirsa pulled out a tape recorder and set it on the desk. "Thank you Miss. Adams. Are you ok with me taping our conversation?"

"That is fine," she said politely.

"It recently came to my attention and a local Police Departments that the Church of Light might somehow be involved with a serious of crimes in Northern Jersey," Kirsa told her.

Veronica crossed her arms. "I see, crimes occur that appear spooky, you get called in and immediately think of us."

Kirsa smiled coldly. "No, several envelopes and letters were found with the letterhead of the church."

"How do you know that the letterhead belongs to the church?" Veronica asked swiveling in her chair.

"Since the church was wise enough to copy right the symbol we were able to match them to the church," Kirsa informed her.

Veronica stared at her. She had not been expecting that. Hadn't she told the morons to use blank paper?

"That is rather odd," Veronica said. She turned and got a water bottle out of her mini-fridge. "Would you like some water as well?"

"No thank you, I'm fine" Kirsa told her. She would not trust anything that came from Veronica.

"I am confused, why come to me with these questions?" Veronica asked hoping to sound innocent.

"You are head of the East Coast Branch of the church. Congratulations on the appointment by the way," Kirsa told her. "I hope you do better than the last one."

"Thank you. However, we do have people around that could answer these questions I am sure."

"We did pay a visit to one, but we will just say he was rather uncooperative." Kirsa saw the surprise flash into Veronica's cold blue eyes. "Oh, you were not told that we paid a visit?"

"What makes you think I will cooperate?" Veronica asked. She tried not to dwell on why Anton had not told her about the visit.

"Honestly, I don't. I wasn't planning on even coming here," Kirsa told her.

"Then may I ask why you are?" Veronica asked already getting annoyed at the situation she was placed in.

"I received a letter that pointed at not only the church's involvement in the crimes but your name was implicated," Kirsa said.

Veronica felt the blood drain from her body. The rage rose higher, she took a deep breath and counted to five.

"Why would I be named?" Veronica asked.

"That's why I am here," Kirsa told her. "I must say though, I have had my suspicion that this time around it was a woman running the show."

"Why is that?" Veronica asked angling her head.

"The wordings of the notes left at each scene have a female touch them," Kirsa told her.

"Why would I be involved with the murders?" Veronica asked not yet realizing her mistake.

Kirsa cocked her head, her face went serious and her eyes darkened as she looked at Veronica. "I did not mention the type of crime."

Veronica stared at her. "Well I am sure I have heard about them on the news and that's why I assumed murders."

Kirsa shook her head. "Only the first few were on the news, and there was no connection then. We have asked the media to keep the rest quiet until there is a lead in the case. Miss Adams what do you know about the murders?"

The accusation is what caused her to snap. She forgot about dignity or even the tape recorder that was going. "You bitch. You come into my office and dare ask me questions as if you know everything? Who cares about a bunch of wicked people that were murdered? Is the world going to care that there are a few less vampires, were-wolves or witches in the world? No, we are doing what God tells us to do."

Kirsa stood up. "Then I am glad we worship different Gods. I will advise you of your legal right to counsel. You are not to leave New York City; if you do you will be held with- out bail until a trial date has been set."

Veronica looked smugly at her, "If you think your laws mean anything to me then you are clearly mistaken."

Kirsa went to say something but caught a slight movement out of the corner of eye.

Veronica was grabbing something from under her desk. Kirsa quickly dialed the emergency code that would alert Al. She had called him earlier to let him know what they would be doing.

"Then I will take you into custody now," Kirsa said standing up and unclipping the handcuffs from her belt.

"Touch me and die," Veronica snarled. She aimed her gun and fired. Kirsa saw the bullet and moved with inhuman speed, the bullet flew past her and plowed into the wall behind her.

Veronica cocked the gun again; Kirsa had her gun out in a blink of the eye and pointed at Veronica. The door to the office flew open; Ayden came in without making a noise. What Veronica did not know, was that by firing on Kirsa, Ayden now had the right to kill.

Veronica looked at the two agents, her eyes were wide and wild. She was surrounded there was nowhere for her to go. Grabbing the pendant she wore, she tore it off the necklace and through it at Ayden. He fired a shot which caught her in the knee. Veronica stumbled backwards, she hit a sconce on the wall causing the wall to fling open and she disappeared.

Kirsa was ready to follow but Ayden was holding his chest. He looked at her before he went down on his knees. Kirsa rushed towards him, kneeling down she picked up the pendant. She dropped it quickly when it burned her fingers. Ayden looked at her with surprise.

"It was filled with Holy Water," he told her.

"Ma'am, can I get you anything?" a small voice asked. Kirsa turned and saw that Erin was standing hunched in the doorway.

"Do you have a first aid kit?" Kirsa asked her. "Yes, in the bathroom."

"I'm going to need that, also any moment OPIA agents will be coming through the door."

The girl nodded and went to get it. Moments later Al rushed through the door with back up; he saw the blood and Ayden down. He knelt next to Kirsa.

"It's all on tape," Kirsa said motioning to the tape recorder that was still on the desk. "There was a hidden door behind her desk that wasn't on the blue prints."

Al nodded. "I want two of you going through the door. Let me know where it leads out," Al instructed two agents. Two men in SWAT gear nodded. One took out a note pad and pencil so they could draw out a rough path of the route.

Erin walked in with the kit and held back her surprise at the eight men in full SWAT gear that were now looking over the scene.

"Here you go ma'am?" Erin said.

"Thank you," Kirsa said. She looked at Ayden who had said nothing. The pain was evident in his eyes.

Erin saw the blood seeping through Ayden's shirt. "What happened to him?"

"The pendant Miss. Adams wore apparently contained Holy Water. It is poison to vampires," Kirsa explained. "Can you help me while I examine the wound?"

"I'm really sorry, I had no idea she had a gun or would do any of this," Erin said as she knelt down on the other side of Ayden.

"None of this is your fault, Erin," Kirsa assured her.   Erin nodded. "Is there anything I can do to help?"

Kirsa looked at Ayden. "Would you be willing to talk to someone at OPIA about what you know and have seen?"

"Yes," Erin asked. She finished taping up the wound. "Al can you take her outside?" Kirsa asked. He nodded and escorted the young girl outside.

"You need blood," Kirsa whispered to Ayden, brushing his hair out of his face. He caught a hold of it and gave a weak squeeze.

"I know," he said weakly. The pain was ferocious. He felt his skin melt and blood boil as the blessed water hit him. He could feel it spreading and the pain was mind numbing in a way.

Al poked his head in. "The ambulance is held up by an accident. They are taking an alternate route. Will be here in five minutes."

Kirsa looked at Ayden. Holy Water, or blessed water, was lethal. Once it mixed with the blood it would continue to filter through the body boiling the blood and melting organs. Ayden did not have five minutes.

Kirsa took the knife from one of the officers by her. Taking the blade she sliced her upper arm. The officer saw what she was doing; he helped Ayden sit him up so that it would be easier for him to drink.

The fresh blood hurt at first, it rushed into him and began to take over the poisoned blood. Strength began to return so that he was able to prop himself up. He kept drinking almost forgetting that it was Kirsa he was drinking from. He heard her in his mind saying stop. But he saw that her lips had not moved. Ayden pulled back and with help sat up.

Someone handed Kirsa orange juice and bandaged her wound for her. Ayden reached over and brushed a curl out of her face.

"Thanks," he said kissing her, with blood still on his lips.

Chapter Twenty Three

Al made both of them go to the hospital. Ayden was working on his second pint of blood when Lars made an appearance. Ayden knew he looked bad, his chest was bandaged, and there was blood all over him, the look on Lars face only confirmed it. IV's were hooked up to him. Lars let out a whistle and shook his head.

"You are a mess," Lars said as he walked to the bed side.

"Tell me about it," Ayden replied. He tried to move but it still hurt to do so.

"So what happened?" Lars asked. "Al was unclear about details."

"I'm unclear about details," Ayden stared up at the ceiling replaying what happened earlier. "Is Kirsa still talking to Al and Tony?"

"They were in one of those consultation rooms still," Lars informed him. "It looks like one of the doctors cleaned up where you took blood. No stitches needed," he saw the relief wash over Ayden's face. "Al is posting guard's at your door until you are released, which they are aiming for tomorrow."

"Lars it was bad," Ayden said. "I was out in the waiting room talking to Erin. You can hear the murmurs of them talking. Then it all happened at once. Veronica starts screaming, I hear something getting thrown. I am running in the room as Kirsa dodges a bullet. We all fire a round and then I am getting hit with Holy water. The rest is just noises."

"Erin is talking by the way. Her mom is with her, " Lars told him. "Erin has not seen her in two years because of the cult. Al told Tony that they have filled two tapes. She does not know exactly what is going on but she is filling in pieces. Al is waiting until Kirsa is released to do the press conference with Tony about what is going on." Lars said filling him in.

"How is the girl holding up?" Ayden asked. He remembered the look of horror on her face when she heard the gun.

"Good. She asked about both of you. Al told her about you and she said that you didn't deserve what you got. I think she was willing to donate blood."

Ayden blushed, which was hard to do considering the loss of blood and not being alive. Sabrina entered the room. Ayden could see strain and hurt behind Sabrina's eyes. She looked at him and tried to plaster on the best smile she could fake.

"I saw Kirsa briefly," Sabrina told them both. "Since when does holy water affect her?"

"What do you mean?" Lars asked.

"Apparently when she handled the pendant that was filled with holy water it burned her fingers."

Fear flashed through Ayden and he placed a hand to where the water had burned him. Holy water should have had no effect on Kirsa at all. It meant only one thing, her disorder was advancing.

"Dr. Finn is here running some blood work to see if the Holy Water has entered her blood stream," Sabrina told him.

Ayden turned and looked at Lars. Lars had not moved closer to the bed when Sabrina had come in. Lars glanced down at his watch. He pushed away from the window sill and walked over to Ayden's bed.

"Keep me posted. I have to run an errand," he told him. Lars left the room and Sabrina followed his exit with her eyes.

Ayden watched for a moment before he said anything. He could tell that something was wrong; Sabrina usually never had a hair out of place or left the house without make- up on. At the moment, her hair was pulled into pony tail; she wore no makeup and wore baggy shirt and jeans.

"I can smell heart break," Ayden said. "What happened?"

"We had an argument today," she answered him trying to fight back the tears.

"Do you want to talk about it?" Ayden asked. It would keep his mind somewhat preoccupied.

"He brought up our future," Sabrina sighed. "I told him I would be willing to take the chance of being changed. I know that there is no guarantee that I would survive it. I explained that I knew what the process entailed."

"It's not like in the movies or books," Ayden warned her. Movies and novels tended to make turning into a vampire a passionate affair and that it was a guarantee it would work. In reality it was painful, ugly and there was no guarantee that you would survive the process.

"Kirsa explained it once to me," Sabrina told him. "In one of the journals it details how the process is done, the risks, and what the person goes through.I told him I just had one condition. I want to be a mother."

"Brie…," Ayden started but she held up a hand so he stopped.

"I know that the percentage of being able to sire a child lessens with the age and since Mr. Secrecy tells no one his age the likelihood is slim. I told him I didn't have to physically have a child. Adoption agencies tend to be more willing to approve an adoption if one parent is at least mortal. It gets trickier if both are vampires."

"Ok so where is the problem?" Ayden asked pulling a hand through his tangle curls. It was obvious that Sabrina had done her homework on all of it.

"He doesn't know if he wants to have children at all, even if they are adopted," she told Ayden. Her voice wavered as she said it. "I told him that I can give up my mortality for him but that I was not sure if I could give up being a mother."

Ayden held a hand out for her and pulled her toward the bed. She laid her head down on the sheets. He stroked her hair as she sobbed.

****

Sara was sitting on the steps of a porch. Tony had called her about fifteen minutes ago telling her that he would be sending someone out there to take a sniff out the smell. He also gave her an update on Kirsa and Ayden. They were keeping both over night as precaution because of the Holy Water. Even though Kirsa's exposure was minimal the fact that she had a reaction concerned Dr. Finn.

Jeff was at the police station helping go through the evidence found in SoHo. OPIA was in charge of that particular case but Jeff had worked with them before and had gone to some of their training seminars so they called him in to help out. In an hour her pack was coming over to prepare for the upcoming full moon. She heard the car slowing down on the street and then the engine turn off.

Sara got up and walked down the stairs and smiled at who got out of the car. He came over and gave her a hug.

"Hey I just got off the phone with Tony," she told him. "I guess I will show you where I am picking up the scent."

She went to turn around but the hair on her arm bristled as if to alert her of danger. The hood came down over her head, and she felt the syringe slide into her skin. All hope of fighting back soon vanished as she felt her body go limp.

Chapter Twenty Four

The Cliver's house was quiet. The porch light was off, there was no sign of a struggle. But Sara's car was there. Lars looked around the pathway and saw some scuff marks in the dirt. Once again he took his cell phone from his pocket, scrolling down to Tony's name he pushed the button and waited for Tony to answer.

"Hey Tony, its Lars," he said as he leaned against the car.

"What's up? I'm still at the hospital," Tony told him.

"I'm at Sara's house. She's not here," Lars told him. "What do you mean she's not there?"Tony asked. He had talked to her about twenty minutes ago.

"Lights are on in the house, her car is here, but there is no Sara," Lars said.

"Alright, stay there. I am going to call Jeff."

Lars hung up and slid the phone in his pocket. He leaned against the car thinking of the other phone call he was going to be making in a minute.

****

In the mountains of Grabenberg were numerous old mining caves, many had tons of caverns in them from mining minerals. However, they were shut down decades ago. The old mining homes in the area were boarded up and forgotten about. Along with some of the tunnels, the old houses were left to be forgotten about.

It was in one of these dilapidated houses that Church of Light had made their headquarters for the Grabenberg project.They picked a house further from the rest that did not see the signs of much graffiti; of course this house was rumored to be haunted by the last manager of the mines. The first floor had been left as it was, upstairs was   left the same.

The attic had been converted into three bedrooms and the basement had a kitchen, a meeting room, a bath room and a small holding cell. There was an old storm cellar on the property which they had converted into more cells and a torture chamber.

In the basement kitchen, Veronica sat on a chair, her hair was pulled into a ponytail she was in a men's black shirt and boxer shorts. Nick Cullen knelt before her working on the bullet wound. She had called him when she was in the secret chamber back in SOHO. He made arrangements to get her from there and into Grabenberg unnoticed. Nick had to call some of their contacts to get her to the hide out safely; he thought it was worth it. The bullet, thankfully, had a clean entry and exit route. It missed the   bones in her knee.

"I have some antibiotics that I want you to take to ward off infection," he explained as he finished bandaging her knee.

She nodded as he got a prescription bottle out of a bag and opened it for her. Nick handed her a pill. She took and swallowed it with the vodka she had been drinking to numb the pain.

Nick looked at her and shook his head. "Ronnie, I wish I had been there instead of here."

She laid a hand on his leg. "Nick, don't beat yourself up. How were we to know they were going to show up?"

He walked over to the faucet and washed the blood off his hands. Veronica leaned against the back of the chair and sighed. She thought about what happened today and felt a tear fall down her cheek. If it had been anyone other than Nick she wouldn't have allowed herself to show weakness.

Nick walked over to the chair she sat in and kneeled in front of her. He brushed the tear away and looked at her.

"Kiddo, it's ok," he told her.

"I know they are evil, but I physically hurt people. I let my temper take over," she said trying to choke back a sob. "Nick I have never hurt anyone before."

Nick pulled her to him and let her cry. In South Carolina, she was being trained for her current position. She had seen what went on, but never took part in any of the beatings, abductions, or killings. Her training was in the orchestration of the operation. There was going to be no reasoning with her at the moment. So he held her and let her cry out all the horrors of the day. They heard her cell phone ring. Veronica pulled back and looked at the caller ID. She swore under her breath.   Taking several deep breaths before she answered she calmed herself down.

"Hello, Father," she answered.

"Veronica. I heard about what occurred today in SOHO," the voice said on the other end.

"I know. I let my temper win, I am so sorry if I put our mission in danger," she explained to him.

"Veronica, you felt threatened. How can I blame you for what you did? They were never to have gotten that close to you," the head of the church told her. "Instead of quivering in fear you showed them you were not afraid. I am proud of how you reacted."

Veronica tried not to take a huge sigh of relief. "Thank you Father."

"Do not thank me, my dear child," he assured her. "Now, a new arrival will be joining you and Nick at the house. She is not to be killed right away, but placed in one of the cells we made in the storm cellar."

"We will begin preparations. Who is bringing her?"

"Washington," the voice said.

"Sir is that wise? He believes in our cause

but not in our faith," Veronica reminded him.

"That is why she has been covered up so that he cannot see who it is. Nick is to meet him at the usual spot." He coughed. "I will be joining you at the caves within the next day or two."

Veronica could not find a voice. She tried again. "Father, you are coming here?"

"Yes," he answered. "Make sure there is a bed available. I understand the primitive conditions. But I think it is time that I help out with this mission."

Veronica went to say something but was greeted by a dial tone. She stared at Nick who was staring at her. "He's coming here," Veronica said to Nick looking dumb- founded.

"I heard," Nick told her. "What about Washington?" "He is dropping a victim off at the usual location," Veronica explained to him.

Nick stood up and grabbed his keys.
"Will you be ok here alone?"

"You'll lock me in?" she asked.

"Yes," he told her. She nodded. "I will be back soon."

Chapter Twenty Five

Kirsa looked out her hospital window which had an amazing view of the courtyard. She watched at they set up for the press conference that would be happening soon. The media had already begun to show up and were taking their seats. Al and Tony both agreed it was time to hold one, to lay the cars out on the table.

Al had called for a press conference to go over the case and what had happened. Sabrina has snuck into the hospital in the morning to bring a suit and make up for Kirsa to change into, along with a suit for Ayden. Al had just left the room with Ayden to go over security protocol leaving Kirsa alone with Sabrina.

Looking at her friend, Kirsa knew something was wrong. "Sabrina, is everything ok?"

"No, when this conference is over can we just go back to your house and do nothing?" Sabrina asked. She didn't want to   talk about the case, or anything.

Kirsa nodded as she walked over and gave Sabrina a hug. Sabrina rested her head on her friends shoulder. There was a knock on the door and Ayden hesitated before walking in. The two separated and watched as he entered the room. He had pulled his hair back into a braid, even in a black suit he looked rugged.

"Kirsa, the press conference is going to start in a moment," he told her reaching for her hand.

"You going to be ok up here?" Kirsa asked Sabrina.

"Jeff is going to stand with me," Sabrina informed her. "Tony figured it will keep him occupied."

Tony was in Grabenberg heading the search for Sara, he had sent Jeff to the hospital to act as additional security. Kirsa nodded and left with Ayden as Jeff walked into the room. Kirsa gave him a quick hug before heading to the elevators with Ayden. They met Al there who was holding the elevator for them.

When the doors had shut Al filled Kirsa on what was going to happen at the Conference. "We are only discussing the case, and what has occurred. If questions about South Carolina we have been given the green light to discuss since it is linked to this case," Al informed Kirsa. "Now there is a chance the rumors about your family are going to get brought up, our line for that is 'We are not discussing that at this time'. Any questions?"

"I think I'm good. Is Ayden going to be up there?" Kirsa asked.

Ayden answered, "Yes I'm going to be up there but will not be answering questions. I am strictly there as your Shadow."

The doors to the elevator opened and three OPIA agents joined them who would be added security on stage. There would be other agents hidden throughout the crowd. Kirsa was surrounded by men, which wasn't such a bad thing. One just had to ignore that they were all packing guns and knives, and numerous other weapons that could be concealed. They made their way to their way outside, Kirsa heard the flashes of cameras going off as they strode to the podium.

Al waited a few seconds before he called for everyone to have their seats. "Everyone please have your seats. As many of you know there have been numerous hate crimes targeted in an area in North Western New Jersey. Due to recent events we have decided to pass information onto public and ask for their help."

"Director Moore, can you explain what has been going on, victims, motives, suspects?" A reporter asked from the front row.

"I'm going to pass that question to Agent Heinrich," Al replied motioning Kirsa to the podium.

"The victims have been: three vampires, two were animals, a witch and what we call an innocent," Kirsa listed.

"What is an 'innocent?'" The same reporter asked.

"An 'innocent' is a term that we give to a person who is not classified under the Paranormal Laws but has been killed because of their association with someone who is. The innocent was the latest victim," Kirsa explained. "There have been messages left at each of the dump sites explaining the motive behind the murders. The people behind these murders believe they are doing the work of their God, that by killing what they define as monsters they are in fact bettering this world."

"That seems a bit contradictory on their part," a reporter from the back. "Can you tell us the group?"

"I agree with your statement," Kirsa approved. "Before I give you a name, know that not all members are involved in this. We are looking only at those members who are in the upper workings of the church. We can disclose one of the names because this person attempted to shoot me and in the process shot another agent as well."

Reporters were whispering to each other as hands were going up to ask questions. Kirsa raised a hand for them to lower theirs. "To answer the last question the group responsible is the Church of Light, and the person of interest that we are looking for is Veronica Adams. She is head of the East Coast Branch. She fled custody yesterday and is currently on the loose."

Al took a cover off an 8x10 colored glossy photo on an easel of Veronica. Her name and information ran along the bottom of it.

"Miss Adams is not the sole person behind the crimes, she is working with a group of people who are from this church," Kirsa added.

"How do you know there is more than one person involved?" someone called out.

"We have numerous sources and other evidence that have shown other people involved," Al answered. "Miss Ad- ams is just one person in a large circle of people involved in these crimes."

****

It was five o'clock but still light out, Kirsa was getting beers out of the fridge for her and Sabrina. She had traded her suit for denim shorts and tank. Ayden was up in their room working on something for Dietrich. He was going through the personnel files of the Council members. The thought was if the spy could be tracked down then possibly bringing down the cult would be possible.

On top of that Sara was gone, vanished without a trace. She would be up there helping him; she should be helping with the search for Sara. But at the moment she was putting all that aside, Sabrina needed her at the moment and that was more important. She walked out onto the deck with a beer and a box of tissues.

Sabrina was leaning on the deck railing. Sunglasses were hiding her blood shot eyes. She had not spoken much since they arrived back at the house. They had all changed into more comfortable clothes, then Kirsa ushered Ayden up- stairs to work. Now she sat on a porch chair drinking her beer. Neither had said much, Kirsa was giving Sabrina the room to think and put her thoughts together.

"Was this how you felt after Anton?" Sabrina asked sipping her beer and turning to look at Kirsa.

"Yes. It didn't matter how horrible he was I still loved him, or the person I thought he was." Kirsa replied. She got up and walked over to Sabrina.

"I curled up on Brian's couch last night. His girlfriend, Emily, forced him to go to the bar with friends. She rubbed my back and just let me cry. Then she made me a disgustingly fattening ice cream sundae."

"Emma came home early from her weekend with her boyfriend. And you drove down to DC. The two of you dragged me to the spa, and we gorged all weekend on take out." Kirsa reminded her.

Sabrina nodded swallowing back the tears. "I haven't even ended it but Kirs; I don't know what to do."

Kirsa put an arm around her. Sabrina rested her head on her shoulder.

"Have you talked about kids before?" Kirsa asked. Knowing Sabrina, the conversation had most likely been brought up. Sabrina would never get serious with a guy if they weren't at least interested in kids.

"Yes, he knew I wanted kids. He would laugh about being a dad at his age," Sabrina said wiping a tear away. "He never once said anything about not wanting kids."

Kirsa heard Zero come out on the deck. He walked up to Sabrina and leaned right up against her waist. Sabrina let a hand down on his head and scratched his ears.

"Can you give up being a mom?" Kirsa asked Sabrina.

"It's funny," Sabrina began. "I can give up my mortality. I am willing to watch the people I love die and I live. I am willing to go against my faith and become a creature of the night and risk eternal damnation. It's seems like such a small thing really in the scheme of things."

"It does," Kirsa agreed. "I think you and Lars need to sit down and have a conversation. Without screaming at each other, you need to talk about what you want.   If he's unwilling to be a dad or support you in adopting then you're going to be faced with a choice that is not easy."

"How did you know with Anton?" she asked Kirsa.

"Know what with Anton?"

"To end it?" Sabrina asked.

"Oh wow," Kirsa said thinking back to that night. "It had been in my head for a while. We weren't seeing a lot of each other because of school with me and his involvement with the church. I was starting to realize that I was having more fun when I wasn't with him then when I was. He kept pressuring me into going to one of his church meetings. He kept telling me that it was embarrassing how high up he was and I would not go to one."

"He was on our cases about never attending as well," Sabrina recalled.

Kirsa nodded and continued."Then one night he was visiting and we got in argument. He told me that his sin was loving me because of what I was and that each day he had to ask God for forgiveness."

"Oh my god, Kirsa you never told me that." Sabrina said. Kirsa rarely spoke about what happened the night she broke up with Anton.

"It was then I realized that he was not worth it. He was not worth the emotional strain, he simply wasn't worth it. If he had to ask for forgiveness for loving me then I did not want to be with him." Kirsa said.

"I had broken up with him before and he always man-aged to convince me to take him back," Kirsa continued. "But whenever he called, after that last time, and tried to convince me to take him back, I would just think how he felt it was a sin to love me. I realized that I didn't care if I lived the rest of my life alone; it was not worth being with a man who didn't appreciate me."

Sabrina stared at Kirsa. "You were strong enough to get over all that, so maybe I will be too."

"You will, Brie," Kirsa promised her.

They talked until late into the night. Sabrina past out at some point, Ayden had carried her to one of the guest rooms. Kirsa was glad that she was staying over, she didn't want her alone at the moment. Zero had curled up next to Sabrina on the bed resting his chin on her hip. He looked at Kirsa as if telling her it was okay, he had it all under control. Smiling Kirsa followed Ayden back to their room.

Ayden had started to move some of his things into the master bedroom. On the desk in there, were his notes on the case now mixed were hers. Kirsa walked over to them to see what he had written over the last few days.

"How's your research going?" she asked him. Ayden came up behind her, wrapping his arms around her.

"Nothing new has come up," he said. Kirsa turned and smiled up at him. "What's up?"

"Just realizing how amazingly lucky I am," she told him.

He smiled and kissed her lightly. Though the hunger was building, he was always afraid to lose control with her. He could hurt her severely if he ever did. She made the kiss deeper.

He pulled away. "Kirs, you make me want to forget about everything even caution."

"Good," she said. She stood up and pulled off her tank top. "I think I am going to take a nap."

As she walked to the bed she carefully removed her clothing. She laid down on the bed wearing nothing and watched Ayden. He was on the bed in a flash of the eye, kissing her. His control and hunger that he kept in check when around her began to fade. His mouth was on hers as his hands were rough as they explored.

"Ayden, I'm tougher then you think," she whispered in his ear as she began to stroke his length.

She was pinned under him in a second; her arms were yanked above her head as he lost control. Her eyes were wide as all new sensations began to arise as he assaulted her body with his mouth and hands.

He caught her breast in his mouth and tasted blood, he accidentally cut her. He pulled his mouth away and tried to get control back.

"Ayden, go ahead," she told him in barely a whisper.

That was all he needed for his last thread of control to snap. His mouth returned to her breast and he licked the blood away. He felt her body ride up as his fangs slid into her skin, felt her intake of breath as he began to feed. As he drank he pushed himself hard into her, he heard her scream as her orgasm ripped through her making her blood taste so much sweeter. When he kissed her on the lips she wrapped herself around him.

Ayden, oh my god Ayden I love you. He heard her voice whisper in his head.

I love you too. He thought back. He saw her eyes go wide as she heard his voice in hers.

He felt her body begin to rise again and this time when she let go he followed shortly after. Their bodies and minds completely joined.

They lay drained and still entwined. Her

felt her heart racing against his skin. He knew if he had one, his also would be. Ayden feared the aches she would be feeling. Kirsa nuzzled his shoulder with her nose and he heard her sigh of contentment as she began to curl around him.

He kissed her forehead then her nose and finally her lips. She smiled against them. Ayden pulled a blanket up over them as they nestled into the bed.

She looked up at him with dreary eyes. "All the little aches are so worth it."

"Did I hurt you at all?" he asked, concern showing in his eyes.

"I don't think you could ever hurt me," she assured him tracing his face with her finger. "I have not felt this good in I don't know how long."

Ayden pulled her closer so that she was draped over his chest. She traced her fingers around the muscles in his chest. She looked at him.

"How old are you actually?" she asked him.

"What do you mean?"

"I guess how old were you and I mean I know you're over 150?"

"I was 25 when I was attacked."

"You mean I'm three years older than you?" she said propping herself up.

"In that sense, yes you are older than me," he answered kissing her nose. "However I died in the year 1853."

"Oh, ok," she said kissing him again.

He smiled and kissed her nose again. Kirsa laid there for a moment. Hanging out with Sabrina and helping her out for a change, just being with Ayden. Reality would set in eventually but for now all was normal.

"I love you," she whispered kissing him lightly.

"I love you too," he answered pulling her close.

"Do you think that's why we can hear each other's thoughts?" she asked looking up at him.

"I think when I took your blood with absolute trust from you it opened a psychic link," he explained. It was rare but it did occur. "For now, let's keep this quiet. With all that is going on I do not know who to trust."

"Agreed," Kirsa said. What was one more secret at this point.

Chapter Twenty Six

Sara had realized shortly into her capture that the chains were silver. It would limit her ability to transform and would slowly poison her if she tried to break out of them. She tried not to cry for there was no one to hear her. But the traitor, the one who brought her here when she had the hood on. She knew who he was, she knew his smell, and when she got free she was going to rip him apart.

Sara studied her cell once again. The door stood four feet in front of her. The only light came from a dingy bulb that dangled from the hallway. She tried not to think of her husband and what he was going through. Her only solace was that Kirsa or someone would figure it out. They had too.

"Praying to God?" a voice asked from the doorway. "He won't hear you."

Looking down she saw him standing in the doorway. He was the biggest traitor of them all. He dyed his hair a light brown as oppose to the electric blue it had been, making his blue eyes even more pronounced. His accent was gone; he spoke with a completely neutral tone.

"Praying that they find out who you really are," Sara told him.

"Ahh, yes," he sighed, "They will of course but by that time it will be too late. My plan will be ultimately in place. Once that happens there will be no turning back for anyone."

He sat in a chair next to her, studying her face. "I hope I did not harm you and that Chris did not harm you in transporting you here," he said taking in the scratches   and faint scent of blood.

"Do they know what you are?" she asked.

He laughed. "Neither group knows the real me."

****

Kirsa heard the doorbell ring upstairs meaning the take out was here. She was in the basement where Lars had stayed. Whatever energy she picked up seem old and faded. Looking around one more time she went upstairs and walked into her office. She went to wake Zero so she could feed him but she saw the note lying on her desk. Kirsa picked it up closing her eyes before she read it. The vibes she felt were confusing and odd.

Hey Kid.

I know it's a bad time. With everything going on, you need as many people to lean on as possible.

I cannot be one of them. I have left. I'm sorry. The argument with Sabrina opened up places in me that I thought I had closed. There are things I need to do. I cannot promise that I will return; all I know is that I can no longer be there for you. I am sorry, you have become like the sister I lost during the plague. And yet like her, I am abandoning you when you need me most. Do not hate me for what I must do; I need to finish working on me before I can be a lover or father.

Please forgive me,

 Lars

Kirsa read the note three times before it

began to sink in. Ayden knocked on the door frame to tell her dinner was waiting. He saw the look of pain on her face, he quickly rushed to her. Before he could ask he knew it was not him that caused the pained look. She handed the letter without him asking for it. Ayden read it again and again. He closed his eyes and tried to control the rage that was surging through him. Kirsa could feel the energy spiking. She laid a hand on Ayden, he took a deep breath.

"Let's eat," she suggested. "Then we'll deal with this." Ayden kissed her forehead. "Agreed."

Despite the letter, they made the best of dinner. They sampled from each other's plates and talked about Europe and the places they had been. Kirsa told him of the countries and sites that she still wanted to see. The future was brought up.

"Would you stay with me if you could?" Ayden asked her playing with her hand.

She smiled. "Even if the disorder kills me, I want to be with you. I don't care if I have a week or years left."

He leaned in and kissed her. There was a scent of bitterness on her lips; he knew that it was not because of him. Ayden leaned back and looked at her.

"What are you thinking?" Ayden asked sipping his blood wine. It was half-blood half-red wine. He thought of it as a cocktail for vampires.

"That he's right I need him right now. I keep thinking about what did I do to have so many people I love leave me?"

Ayden brushed a tear away. "If I can help it, I will not leave you."

She smiled weakly. "Ayden, I know that. I have always known that you would always be there for me no matter what."

Kirsa sipped his wine. "He mentioned the plague, which means that he could be close to 600 hundred years old. That bothers me. He has always been so mysterious about his past. I mean, most vampires are not open with their past because it is painful. But I know more about Wyrm then Lars. Isn't that odd?"

"According to Shamus, Lars has always been like that," Ayden replied. "When Dietrich found him he was already a matured vampire. The joke amongst the Inner Council is there is a guaranteed spot on the Council if you can find out his past."

Kirsa rolled her shoulders; she could feel the stress creeping back in. "How much more am I supposed to handle?"

Ayden pulled her close and let her lean her head on his shoulder. They were like that when Tony knocked on the back door. Ayden motioned for him to enter.

"I don't mean to intrude,"Tony said. He picked up on the vibe in the room. "What's wrong?"

Ayden handed him the note. Tony took it not sure what to think. When he got done reading it he said a few curses under his breath and handed the note back to Ayden. Tony sat down in one of the chairs. Ayden motioned to the wine bottle and Tony nodded.

"Kirsa, I want you to stay with Donna and me. Ayden that goes for you as well," Tony told them.

"Tony I am not leaving." Kirsa replied. "Please don't make me make it an order, Kirs."

Ayden picked up on the stress. "What's wrong. Tony?" Tony ran a hand through his hair and sipped the wine.

"First,Sara was abducted. Then this afternoon a letter was left at Ryan's house. Thankfully his dad got to the note before Ryan did."

"Oh, God. Tony what did it say?" Kirsa asked, fear was bubbling in her belly. Ryan had down syndrome and to think that someone would target him because of this made her sick.

"A threat, about how he is helping the wicked. I have made arrangements to have Ryan and his family to be escorted to one of their family's home in Maryland. Jeff got a phone call today with wild laughing. Please Kirsa," Tony pleaded reaching for her hand across the table.

"I will make a deal with you," Kirsa started. "The second we get anything Zero, Ayden and I will be there are your doorsteps."

Tony nodded. He finished the wine then stood up. "Ayden can, I talk to you a minute outside?"

Ayden nodded. He squeezed Kirsa's hand and got up. He joined Tony outside on the deck.

"What's up?" he asked Tony.

"The only scent that was picked up was that of a vampire's," Tony informed him. "Phil thinks he knows or at least has picked up the scent before. There were also four sets of tire prints. Which, our expert thinks are all from the same car."

"Dietrich called me last night," Ayden told him taking a pull on his cigarette. "The spy is targeting the entire Inner Council, each have received threats."

"Damn. This is bad." Tony stared out onto the lake.

Chapter Twenty Seven

Louis sat on a bench watching the children play on the playground. Grabenberg was a quiet and peaceful town. He had often slipped through the town over the centuries. Yet it was different now, he had brought horror to this town. He was so close to his salvation, kill the girl and his soul would be free. The letter he had written Kirsa was to be a taunt. To let her know he knew who she truly was, that he had killed her ancestor. That he would kill her too.

Yet now he had begun to wonder since writing the letter if he had turned into the monster from fiction? It had been over a thousand years ago since he had killed Hagan Adulwulf.

That single act had plagued his sleep for

decades. He had sought out Hagan's widow for forgiveness in order to keep the nightmares away. It was in her forgiveness, in her kindness that he had been able to move on. But yet here he was killing again, slaughtering the young because they were like him. Their death would lead to his salvation. Kill Kirsa Heinrich and your soul shall be saved.

Kirsa, the name meant kindness and forgiveness to him. For it was her namesake, that walked with him and even invited him, a monster, into her home. Yet here he was ready to kill the heir to the sixth bloodline. He put his head in his hands and wanted to sob but no tears came. Taking a deep breath he knew he had two choices and he knew which one he should take.

****

Kirsa was in the fenced in part of the house that ran along the side playing with Zero when she picked up on a vibe. She stood up with the gnarled tennis ball in her hand; Zero was looking past her still as a statue. Kirsa turned and saw him standing at the gate, which was at the side of the house. She knew that this should mean death, but the vibe she got was peaceful.

"I did not come to kill you," he told her.

"I know," Kirsa replied. Zero came up and

leaned against her as if he was unsure what to make of their visitor.

"Your vampire is unsure if he should listen to you or not at the moment," Louis informed her. She looked up to where he pointed with his head and saw Ayden standing in the window.

"I told him you meant no harm," Kirsa assured him. "He is torn between protection and trusting me to handle myself."

"He loves you."

"I know," She walked toward the visitor. "I am Kirsa Heinrich."

He took her hand and shook. "I am called Louis now."   "Hello, Louis. Why don't we go to the deck where we can sit and talk, or would you rather go inside because of the sun?" Kirsa asked him.

He looked up at the window and the man nodded in silent agreement of truce. "If indoors is not a problem, I would prefer inside."

Kirsa patted Zero on the head and walked to the gate. Louis opened it for her. Zero walked up to him and sniffed at him, he smelled the offered hand then walked up the deck stairs and stood at the French doors.

"Did I past his test?" Louis asked, following Kirsa up the stairs.

"He knows you mean me no harm." Kirsa explained. She ushered him inside and then pulled the blinds down.

"Pardon the appearance; we have several paint samples on every wall of the house. We are in the middle of redecorating," Kirsa explained. She poured two glasses of lemonade and handed one to Louis. "We'll go into the living room; the wood blinds are always drawn in that room."

Louis followed her down the hallway and then into the library. Deep wood bookshelves lined the wall. There was a couch and two leather chairs, all in earth tones to match the gold tone painted walls. Kirsa sat in one of the chairs curl- ing her legs under her. Louis took in the room for a little bit, looking at the books on the shelves and the artwork on some of the walls. The room had a way of making a stranger feel welcomed, even if they weren't. He sat on the couch that was across from Kirsa, she slid him a coaster for his glass.

"I'm supposed to kill you," Louis told her.

"Yes, I know," Kirsa acknowledged. "Yet you are here to talk. Why?"

Louis sipped the lemonade realizing it was

homemade. He smiled and studied Kirsa. "You look very much like the woman you are named for."

Kirsa cocked her head. "You knew her?"

Louis leaned back into the couch. "I did. I watched her while I watched Hagan. Their marriage was not of convenience like so many were in those days. When you watched them together you could see and feel the love they had for each other. They also deeply loved their children. It is why his death haunted me for so long," Louis explained.

"I have been reading some of her journals that we have found. I've gotten up to right after his death. Why did you kill him? I know what she said but why?"

"I was angry," Louis sighed. He was so weary of the anger, of all the hate.

"Tell me," Kirsa said gently.

"I was the youngest of four sons," Louis recalled. It was odd to think of that after so long. "Being the youngest I was sent to a monastery. In exchange my parents got extra grain."

"There are many family's that did similar arrangements," Kirsa replied.

"When I was born the church was still new,"

Louis informed her. "It felt as if we had been chosen for something grand. They were arguing over what books to be put in the New Testament when I took my oath."

Kirsa stared at him for a moment as she realized how old he really was.

"I loved Jesus, I loved being a monk. Then it was stripped from me. I did not choose it, I had known some brothers who fell for a woman and left because of it but I did not. I did not crave the touch of another. I craved knowledge and God. Then a monster came and created me."

"Raymond," Kirsa said. "He berated your trust."

"He told us he knew how to destroy the vampires," Louis informed her. "That if we aided him we would help destroy the demons sent to curse our land."

Louis got up and walked to one of the book shelves. "Yet he turned you into what you hated," Kirsa said.

"Yes," Louis replied. "He left me in those ruins. On my own I learned to become my own being. Learned that if I drank from animals I did not have to feed from humans. I would be weaker than other vampires but it was fine."

"If you didn't have to kill, or harm another human you could live with what you had become," Kirsa realized. He nodded. "How did you learn of Hagan?"

"I traveled," Louis said simply. "I had all the time in the world. So I traveled and studied. I reached what is now Germany around the time your ancestor had already been lord for a few years. That there was a town where the unusual could be normal."

"You went to see if you could find your place?"

"Perhaps I could be a monk again," Louis admitted.

"What changed?"

"I went to the village, I heard the rumors of who the lord might be," Louis explained. "There was no fear from these people. They loved, he protected them all from the evils of the world. All he asked was they keep the secrets. At first I wanted to meet him because we were both vampires. Then I wondered, if he had come out of hiding during the war would I have been created. Would Raymond have been defeated sooner."

"You asked him?"

"I did and I did not like the answer I was given."

Kirsa, who had been sitting listening to the whole thing, spoke up. "So you killed him. He was there and for you it meant retribution."

"Yes," Louis said turning to look at her. "I thought I would be free, instead I was haunted by his death. I thought of his grieving widow, of his children and how I took their father from them. I traveled to the far east in hopes that the farther away I was the less I would be haunted."

"It didn't work did it?"

"No," Louis answered returning to the couch. He took a sip of lemonade before continuing. "I went back to your family's village a few decades later. I approached silently; she stood up and turned to where I stood. She recognized me, and still she approached me. She greeted me and asked why I returned, I told her. I asked for her forgiveness she smiled and laid a hand on my face and told me she had forgiven me a long time ago. She then invited me into her home where she fed me with food and ale and above all, kindness. We talked into the early hours of the morning. I promised her I would not harm any that came from her; I stayed true to my word."

Kirsa smiled. "You were amazed that she did not see you as a monster?"

"Yes, she told me that if we had no souls then how could she have loved one so deeply and had been loved so deeply in return? I could not answer her. She humbled me."

"You came here today to see if I was like her? If I would welcome you into my home or if I would see you as a monster?" Kirsa asked him.

He looked at her. "Do you see me as a monster?"

She smiled at him. "I see you as someone who has been used as a pawn over the centuries. All you want is salvation and to confess your sins but everyone has told you that in order for you to do that you have to go kill some people. The people who do that to you are humans and are the monsters," Kirsa explained.

"I have committed crimes, horrible crimes, I have murdered and mutilated," he confessed.

"You know I am an agent?" she asked him.

"Yes, Miss Adams was furious when she learned you had returned. Why?"

"Then here is the deal I am offering you. Turn yourself into me, I will be part of the interrogations," Kirsa explained. "I also happen to know a priest who will take confessions from vampires. I can arrange for him to talk with you."

Anger flashed in his eyes. "And if I agree you will set up a meeting with him after the trials?"

"No," Kirsa answered seeing surprise flash in his eyes. "I will call him before we leave and have him meet us at the Police Station where you can talk to him before beginning any questioning."

"Why?" he asked.

"Because instead of choosing to kill me you came to talk to me," Kirsa told him. "Plus I want to bring Veronica and the cult down. I think we both can use each other to get what we want."

"I will testify against them all," Louis told her. "Because you have been honest with me."

"Let me make the arrangements, I want to get you into the station house without anyone knowing," Kirsa told him. He got up when she stood up. "This could take a while."

"The head of the cult is in Grabenberg. He showed up last night at their hideout," he informed her as she made her way into her study.

Kirsa looked at him. "I will let Tony know."

He watched as she got on the phone, she did not close the French doors. He could hear the murmur of conversation.

"She is one of a kind," Louis said. Indicating that he knew Ayden was in the doorway.

"She is. Kirsa has grown up with vampires around her," Ayden explained walking into the room. "I'm Ayden."

"Louis," he replied shaking Ayden's hand. "You are her Shadow I take it?"

"Yes," Ayden answered. "I take it the Council spy told you?"

"Just that she had a Shadow. I was here one night and you detected me. I informed Veronica that there was a slim chance of getting past you."

Ayden nodded. "I have to ask, did you take our friend?"

Louis looked puzzled. "What do you mean? Another was taken?"

"A were-tiger who is a friend of Kirsa and works for the police was taken the other night," Ayden informed him.

"I was told none of this." Louis scratched his chin. "With Veronica in hiding I have not been in touch with anyone of the inner group."

Ayden nodded. "Why don't we go into the TV room, making these arrangements will take a while." He was not going to trust the other vampire, but if they sat in the same room he could get a better feel for him and be able to keep an eye on him.

****

Tony stood in the center of Chris Washington's den. He had men in each room tearing it apart for evidence. Chris's wife Cristina was currently filing a restraining order against her husband over at her neighbor's house. When they found what was hidden in his den she cried and was then escorted over to the neighbors. The last time he went to check on her she had been cursing out her husband. Her neighbor, Melissa, had given her brandy spiked tea in hopes to calm her down.

Tony put gloves on and walked around the office. The walls were done in a deep blue with dark wood accents. There was a poker table in one corner and a desk in the other. A flat screen TV hung up one of the walls with a small leather couch across from it on the other wall. There were three book shelves that turned out to be fake.

When they were opened they revealed a treasure trove of information: spy equipment, spy logs on Kirsa's movements upon her arrival in Grabenberg, an unregistered cell phone, three unregistered guns, and false id's. There were also pictures and notes on what became victims. It looked like Chris also spied for the cult.

Tony's phone rang. He saw Kirsa's home number and picked up.

"What's up Kiddo?"

"Hey," Kirsa said. "Where are you?"

"Chris Washington's house. I am going to want Ayden to come and see if he can pick up anything and you too for that matter," Tony told her as he nodded to an officer who had asked him a question.

"Well that might have to wait for a minute," she informed him.

"Why?"

"I need an unmarked car to come to the house and pick me and a guest up. I also need your relative to meet us at the station house," she told him.

Tony raised his eyebrows. "Should I ask why?"

"I would rather not say on the phone, but let's just say that currently in my possession is someone very closely involved in the Church of Light."

"Give me an hour to get everything in order."

****

Kirsa walked into the TV room where Ayden and Louis were watching baseball. It could have been a normal scene in any house, except for the tension that filled the room. The two men watched her as she entered. There was no sneaking up on a vampire.

"Tony said to give him an hour to get everything in order," Kirsa told them. They both nodded.

"He was busy?" Ayden asked as she sat next to him on the love seat.

"He was currently going through Chris Washington's things."

"Ah yes the blockhead," Louis replied with a chuckle. Kirsa and Ayden looked at him. "He, I believe, might be more warped then I am. He did not believe in any of the religious ideology of the church. All he agreed on was the killing of those deemed wicked."

"What did he do for the cult then? I'm pretty sure Veronica would not want a non-believer to be that involved?"

"He spied for us when we could not spare another person. He would also let her know how the investigation was going; from time to time he would transport people from place to place."

"You really have no issue talking to us about this?" Ayden asked him.

"I want to be able to live with myself, I have not been able to do that in a very long time," Louis answered simply.

Chapter Twenty Eight

Within the hour that Tony had promised, they were all in the station. Louis was in a room with Tony's uncle who was a priest. There was no tape recorder and no one listening in via the viewing room. The man was going to talk without a lawyer present and had already begun to talk. Tony had cleared out the station house, only the most trusted were there. Jeff Cliver was there, along with his partner, and chief of the Morris County Sheriff 's department. They had gone to college together. While Louis confessed his sins, Kirsa called her cousin.

"Hey Adam," she greeted when he picked up.

"Hey, what's going on?" he asked. His son was currently being chased by Erin and her little brother David.

"What's all the noise?"

"My son is being chased around the courtyard by one of our house guests," Adam explained.

"Ahhh, how is that going?" she wanted to know.

"Anne and I went on a date the other night and Wyrm did not have to baby-sit so   he got to go do librarian stuff."

"Good. I was wondering how it was going to work out."

Adam laughed. "It's been good for everyone," he assured her. "Erin has been spending some time with Wyrm talking to him about what she went through. He's been filling her in on the holes. Dietrich stopped by yesterday to meet them and see how everything else was going."

Adam withheld the information about the four guards and three Shadows that had been dropped off at the estate. Or the fact that Dietrich had three body guards with him. His cousin was going through enough without adding more to worry about. He knew about her friend being taken.

"Lars took off." Kirsa was not sure where that had come from.

"Wait, did you just say Lars is gone?" Adam asked. He saw Wyrm stop what he was doing.

"Yes, he left a note explaining that he needed to go find himself. He also made reference to the plague killing his sister," Kirsa told him.

"Isn't he a little old to be having a midlife crisis? Wait do vampires get midlife crises?" Adam asked to no one in particular. Wyrm raised an eyebrow as he leaned against the wall.

Kirsa laughed. "I found the note yesterday. Can you relay the information about his sister to Wyrm and see what he can dig up?"

"Yes, are you going to tell Dietrich about him leaving?" "Do I have a choice?" Kirsa asked her cousin.

She saw Louis and the priest leave the room. "I have to go Adam I will call you soon. Give my love to the cutie pies."

They hung up and Father Daniel walked

over to Kirsa and shook her hand. "We are all done," Daniel told her. "He has my card and permission to call me if he needs to talk."

"Thank you," she replied giving him a hug.

"For you my dear, anything," he walked over and shook hands with Ayden and hugged Tony goodbye.

Kirsa looked at her watch and saw it was close to eleven. She looked at Louis and everyone.

"I say we start tomorrow morning," Tony replied. "Louis, one of the were-lions is going to be taking you to their safe house. That way if the cult comes for you they have to get through a pack of were cats. He will bring you here around 9am."

"You do not want to start now?" Louis asked confused. "I thought once I met with the priest the interrogation would begin."

"What Tony is saying is that we are all tired and need some rest before we begin talking with you about every- thing," Kirsa told him. "In the morning when we are all refreshed and a little more awake we will start."

Louis nodded. "You all have offered more kindness to me than many have in the last few centuries. Thank you."

"You came to us, Louis, freely. We are

simply repaying you with kindness," Tony told him.

"Captain, Devon is here," Jeff replied entering the room. "He backed his SUV into the transport garage."

"Jeff you're ok doing this?" Tony asked him.

He nodded. "It keeps my mind occupied." Louis smelled the fear and hope. "Your wife is their friend who was taken?"

"Yes she is." Jeff told him.

"Captain White, do you by any chance have a map of the area that I can look over tonight?" Louis asked. "I do not know specific locations but I have overheard directions and landmarks."

"Jeff can you get him those?" Tony asked.

"Devon has a bunch of different types of maps of the area at the house. When we get him settled in we will get the maps to him. Come on Louis, before anyone sees you."

The two men walked off toward the back of the station. Tony walked over to Kirsa and hugged her.

"I mean it kiddo, anything out of the ordinary and you are at my house," Tony told her.

"Yes pops," Kirsa replied kissing his cheek.

Ayden promised Tony that once they got home they would be in for the night. They said there goodbyes then headed home. Tomorrow was going to be a long day.

****

Kirsa wore brown cargo pants and a white t-shirt, she wanted to be comfortable for the day. It was 8am and she was at the Grabenberg Police Station. Sabrina had called her at seven to tell her that she too had received a letter from Lars. Too her, he was taking the easy way out. After calming

Sabrina down, Kirsa left to do her job. Now, she was sitting in Tony's office with him and Al. She sipped her coffee while Tony talked to his wife on the phone. The DA, Tessa Morgan, knocked on the open door, walked in and sat down in the last empty chair. Her blonde hair was pulled back in a ponytail; she wore a cotton black dress with short sleeves and black sandals on her feet.

Tony hung up the phone and looked at his three visitors. He took a sip from his coffee.

"Good Morning, I wanted to let you all know that we have sent out three groups today to go look at the places on the map the FBI made for us," Tony explained. "They are posing as a real estate agent and an interested buyer. This way they have a reason to be exploring the grounds and buildings of some of the locations. Our witness has given us some areas that we should focus on."

Tessa nodded. "I went through the files that you and Al gave me. I can do the cases on a state level, but there is potential to be able to try the cases in the Federal Court. In that case I would not be able to be lead counsel because I do not have a special license for the occult laws," Tessa explained.

"We have enough evidence this time?" Tony asked. "Based on what you gave me: Veronica Adams and Chris Washington will be facing charges along with whoever else is involved. Since Louis is waving his right to counsel I had my boss look at the plea agreement. After we hear what he has to say I will go over it with him and explain it all to him."

"May I ask what it entails?" Kirsa asked.

"He will be a low threat inmate; I have talked to the prison already on some of this. They would allow him to be a faith leader there if he wants, he will be placed in with some of the other low threats, so he will have some time outside at night and not be in solitary confinement 24-7. Because he is a vampire, he will not be able to have a roommate. That's the basics for right now."

"Good," Kirsa replied. "I just don't want him to be treated like high threat when he is trying to amend for what he has done. Don't get me wrong, he's a murderer and should be in jail for the rest of his life. But he should not be treated the way they have to treat Anton."

There was a knock on the door, Jeff poked his head in. "Louis has arrived."

"Good. Bring Al and Kirsa to the room. I will be there shortly," Tony instructed. He waited until Kirsa and Al vanished from sight. "What's going on Tess?"

She pulled out three separate envelopes from her briefcase and laid them on Tony's desk.

"Sabrina Black dropped one off this morning. She wanted me to look over it and then give it to you. The other two were sent to the office of the DA."

Tony pulled out the letter addressed to Sabrina, he read through it and felt a shiver run through his spine. It threatened her life because of her association to Kirsa and because she had a vampire as a partner.

"Tony, did Sabrina and Lars break up?"

Tessa asked. "That's what confused me. Because if they have it's fairly recent and quiet so the fact that it is referenced is worrisome?"

"He left town the day after Sara was taken. Sabrina was going to call it off," Tony informed her. "It's been kept quiet, I only found out yesterday."

He went back to the other two notes that had been left for the DA. One dealt with turning over Kirsa at a certain time and location. The other was what would happen if Kirsa was not surrendered. Tony put them back in their envelopes and handed them to Tessa.

"Who knows about the letters?" he asked her walking to the door.

"Just you and me, and obviously Sabrina on the one letter that deals with her. Why?" she asked.

"Can we keep it that way for a day or two?" he asked her opening the door.

"Yes, I can."

They walked to the hallway that led to the interrogation room. He opened the door and led them into the viewing room. Louis had just been brought in. Kirsa told the officer not to handcuff him to the chair. Al was shuffling papers around.

Kirsa handed Louis a cup of tea and a bottle of water. She then placed a small digital voice recorder in the center of the table.

"Are you alright with us taping the conversation?" she asked.

"Yes, I am fine with it." Louis told her.

It took a few minutes to go through all the legal procedures before they start with the actual interrogation.

"We're going to start with when you first were contacted by the church," Kirsa told him.

"That would be about ten years ago," Louis told them. "They had just elected a new leader; I believe the one prior had died of mysterious circumstances."

"That would be correct," Al replied. "Rev. Arthur Carpath who had no medical problems died in his sleep at the old age of 43. Cause of death is still unknown; there was not a mark on the body either."

Louis nodded and sipped his tea. "I was in San Francisco at the time. I was working for a private detective who used me to do surveillance for him on some of his cases. I kept a low profile; no one knew what I was, or if they did they never said anything about it. I wanted to be as normal as possible. It had been twenty years since I had killed anyone at that point. I did not trust myself with blood from a blood bank. I feared I would crave human blood again so I relied on animals that I could find in the city. It worked for me."

"How did the church get in contact with you?" Kirsa asked.

"I was on my way back to my apartment from the laundry mat when this man appeared before me. He stood around 5'10 and had brown hair. I stopped because I would have plowed into him. I remember saying excuse me and he continued to stare. I kept walking and knew the man was following me. He finally spoke when I reached the entrance to my apartment building. He called me by my true name, Alois, which startled me. I had not gone by that name in a few hundred years by that point so I first thought he was talking about someone else."

"Why did you change names?" Al inquired, it was not all that uncommon for vampires to change names from time to time.

"It was easier to move about, to start over; I know some keep their names. It is easier now to do so, but for the first 1000 years of my existence it was safer to change name and location every few decades. I was going by Louis at this point, it was simple and common," Louis told them. "Alois was dead to me in a way; when the mad said my name I turned and looked at him. I first thought he must be a vampire, how else would he know who I am. Yet, all I got from him was this neutral vibe.

"He explained that he wanted to save my soul and undue what had been done to me. I believe I laughed at him and walked into my building, he followed. My doorman noticed my unease and escorted the man out. When I came down two hours later to go to my favorite bar, the man was waiting for me outside. This time I walked up and asked him what he wanted. He told me again that he wanted to save my soul. I will sum up the next month, every day he waited at my apartment and would say the same thing to me. I want to save your soul."

"You finally gave in and asked how?" Kirsa asked, "Anyone at that point would have done the same. I am surprised you lasted a month, I probably would have lasted a week before I punched him."

Louis laughed then drank more tea. "I agreed to meet him for lunch to hear what he had to tell me. We met in China Town; he picked a noisy restaurant so that no one would hear us. He said his name was Laurence, that he was aware I was a blood drinker and that I had come from the Vampire Wars. How he knew I do not know, but he did. He told me that he represented an organization whose goal was to rid the world of evil. I chuckled at that. He smiled and explained that if I became a member they would give me the chance to save my soul. Then he handed me a business card for the church and when their next meeting time was."

"Did you go to the meeting?" she asked him as she wrote the information down. She circled the name Laurence.

"I did, and the one after and so forth. I told myself it was all foolishness but I could not help myself. I kept returning, I thought maybe God would forgive me and that I could be saved. I thought my days as a monk were over; I wept for what had been taken from me. I know now they fed off of that. After two months, Laurence appeared at my apartment again. We went to same restaurant we first went too. He explained he was proud of me for going. He hoped I was finding peace of mind. I told him I was. Then he told me that the road to salvation   was up to me."

"What did he offer you?" Kirsa asked curious.

"My soul would be saved and sent to heaven," Louis replied. He sipped the water. "He had me at that. He told me that there was an inner part to the church, they were recruiting the most faithful and he felt that I belonged in this Inner Circle. He explained that the church was rebuilding and I would be called on from time to time to aid them in their crusade against evil. I agreed to it.

"My first assignment was to hunt out a meeting spot of a coven of witches. At this point we were not killing or physically harming anyone. We were using written threats, or anonymous messages to their place of work and family about what they really were. I thought it was all very petty but I gave my word to help and I did."

"When did they decide to start the killing?" Kirsa asked.

"About seven years ago our new leader, who only the Inner Circle got to meet, thought we needed to up the tactics. I later figured out that Laurence was our new Father. Anyway, for the first few years I was did not take part in the violence. I would hunt down the person and give the information and proof to Laurence, he would then hand it over to his 'disciples' as he called them. About a year later he asked if I was willing to inflict harm in order to rid the world of wickedness. I was so caught up in everything that I said yes. He wanted to know how to torture vampires, what worked what didn't and so forth. When I told him he then asked me about Were-animals. I told him that can be tricky because of all the species but was able to give him the general information such as silver weakening and hurting them."

"Did you ever suspect that Laurence might be something more then he said?" Kirsa asked. Al looked at her with a raised eyebrow.

"You are asking if I thought that Laurence was a vampire," Louis repeated. He thought for a moment before answering. "There were times when I would look at him and think he must be. Yet if he was I could detect nothing of it from him, no scent nothing. But it is a suspicion that always hung around in the back of my mind."

"When did Kirsa's family enter the picture?" Al asked. "Your family all of a sudden came into the viewing about

six years ago, which was odd. All of a sudden we knew a lot about the Heinrich's and their lineage and how your ancestors had been hunted. That was about the time Anton Black joined the Inner Circle. I used to think he was the one that provided the information. I was originally asked to kill your parents; I told Laurence that I could not kill regular mortals. He was not happy but handed it over to someone else."

"You didn't tell him about the promise you

made to my namesake?" Kirsa asked him finishing her coffee.

"Something in me told me not to tell him that. He was not happy but he accepted my decision and went to Anton for the information. Kirsa, I am sorry if this hurts you,"he laid a cold hand over hers. She shook her head and he continued. "I was told to watch you and photograph your movements and actions. At some point on your voyage around Europe I was told to come here to Grabenberg and begin scouting out targets."

"Is there where Officer Washington comes in," Al inquired. He was glad this was being recorded because of the amount of information they were getting.

"We had an inside man with Christopher but they wanted another. I agreed and came here. The first five murders I had nothing to do with. I did kill the were-cat in the corn field; I helped with the death of your friend and also the young Catholic girl."

"What of Isabella?" Kirsa asked him.

He shook his head. "That was not me," he answered. "I knew who she was and could not do that to her family. After she was dead, the mutilation was done so you would not recognize her. The young girl though, I did that. It was pure frustration and hatred with myself that led me to mutilate her like that."

Al glanced at his watch and saw it was noon. "Let's break for lunch then we will go through the murders."

They all nodded. Jeff came in this time and led Louis to a holding cell, Kirsa heard Jeff ask him what he wanted for lunch because they were all ordering out. Al studied Kirsa carefully.

"You ok kiddo?" Al asked her as Tony walked in.

"It's hard to separate it all, to keep the personal out of the professional," Kirsa explained. "I'm going to run home and take Zero out. I will be back."

"Take Jeff, with Ayden at Chris's I don't want you anywhere alone," Tony ordered. Kirsa went to argue but he silenced her with a look.

Chapter Twenty Nine

In silence, Jeff drove them two Kirsa's house. Kirsa needed the time to digest everything that Louis had told them. While Jeff dealt with Sara's abduction in his own way. For Kirsa, Louis was able to paint a clear picture of events. He gave them details on how the inner circle worked, on how they recruited. And that is what was bothering her. The unknown person that recruited Louis. She felt like the answer was right there but they were missing it.

When Jeff pulled into the driveway Kirsa felt a that something was out of place. Jeff notice her tense up, resting a hand on his gun they both got out of the car slowly. They heard the frantic barking coming from inside the house.

"That's not normal," Kirsa told Jeff. She

went to rush toward the house but Jeff caught her arm.

"Kirs, stay behind me," he instructed.

Nodding, she followed Jeff. She handed him her keys when they reached the back door. Once the door was unlocked, Zero bolted outside practically knocking them both over. He was trembling and there was blood on his snout.

Jeff radioed it in. Then instructed for Kirsa to stay behind him as they entered the house. He should have told her to stay outside, but not after Sara was taken from their own driveway was he going to that. They headed toward her study with Zero leaning against Kirsa as they walked.

Kirsa gasped as she walked into the room. Chaos was everywhere. Books had been ripped off the shelves, her lap top had been ripped into two, and her files that she had left out where thrown about the room. Kirsa went to pick a book up but Jeff stopped her, he handed her a pair of gloves. He called it into Tony as Kirsa just stared at the chaos.

It was then that they heard a large bang upstairs, Zero gave off a warning growl.

"Stay here," Jeff told her. "I'm locking you in with Zero."

"Jeff," Kirsa began to argue.

"I can't lose both of you," he answered as he shut the door.

Kirsa watched him head toward the stairs. Kneeling on the ground she pulled Zero close to her. He licked her face and just pressed his weight against her. She rested her head against his fur. In the distance she heard sirens heading toward them.

A gunshot had her tensing as she readied for anything. Moment's past then Jeff appeared. He unlocked the door."

"It looked like Lars, he as leaping out of the attic window as I rushed into the attic. He was covered head to toe. When I ran to the window he was already to the edge of the yard," Jeff looked around the library. "It's worst upstairs."

Kirsa went up the stairs with him; he led her into her bedroom. The furniture was overturned, some pieces broken. On the walls were massages written in blood. Her alter was strewn across the floor, her statues of   the goddess and god were smashed, it was all ruined. Each piece that she had carefully selected was now destroyed.

"Do you have a camera on you?" Kirsa asked Jeff.

He got out his cell phone and began taking

pictures with it of the messages on the wall and the room.

They heard the front door open, then Tony and Ayden were both calling for them. She yelled back that they were upstairs. Footsteps came up the stairs then she heard the intake of breath as the two men took in the scene.

"I saw Lars leaving from the attic window," Jeff told Tony.

"Shit," Ayden said running a hand through his hair. He then went to Kirsa and pulled her close.

"Both of you pack what you need and what Zero needs," Tony instructed. "Kirsa you are officially under police protection."

Kirsa nodded, not even arguing. "Alright."

She walked to the ornate trunk that had been her altar. Kneeling before it she pulled out the bottom drawer and inserted her hand and found the latch the opened the secret compartment. The three men watched as she pulled out a stack of folders and a flash drive.

"I take it that's what he was looking for?" Jeff asked her.

Kirsa nodded. "Do you want to finish taking pictures before I get some things?"

"Why don't you pack up somethings from the bathroom," Tony suggested.

Nodding, she walked into the bathroom and called Sabrina. Sabrina answered on the first ring, she was with Joe, one of her security guys.

"What's up?" Sabrina asked.

"We think Lars broke into my house and vandalized it." Kirsa knew there was no easy way of telling her.

"Someone tried to break into the old storm cellar," Sabrina told her. She knew that Kirsa understood what that meant; in the Black's old storm cellar was one of the vaults for the vampires. It contained copies of the most important material, that way if the other vaults were destroyed they would have backups.

"What?"

"The alarm system we installed went off, Joe sent one of the were's that works for me to check it out, he thought he smelled vampire."

"When?"

"About an hour ago, we're watching it on the video right now," Sabrina added.

"He must have come here afterwards." Kirsa began to put things in a duffle bag.

"Look I have a huge favor to ask you."

"Yes. You, Ayden and Zero can stay with me for as long as needed," Sabrina replied.

"Thanks."

"Your going to stay at Sabrina's," Tony asked from the doorway."

"I'm not running this time, Tony," Kirsa told him. "I'm not letting him force me from my home."

"You are too stubborn sometimes," Tony informed her. "You are still under protection."

"Fine," Kirsa agreed.

She packed up some essentials than Jeff poked his head in to let her know they could start packing some clothes that were still in drawers or the closets. Once the bags were packed, and Zero's essentials were boxed up, Ayden hefted up one of the boxes.

"I'll go load this into your car, Sabrina called on the way over," Ayden explained. "When they're done here they're going to head over there to look at the cellar."

Sh grabbed one of the bags while Tony grabbed the other. They headed downstairs followed by Zero, than loaded it all into the Durango.

"I have the team sweeping the house for prints and anything else. If it was Lars, do you know what he wanted?" Tony asked her.

"Yeah, he didn't get them." Kirsa ran a hand through her hair. "He wanted the files that deal with my ancestry."

Tony and Ayden looked at her as they took the news in. Tony looked off to where Lars was said to have taken off.

"Jeff and I are going to look and see if he left any traces when he escaped. Ayden take her to Sabrina's. I will meet you there then we need to talk." Tony motioned to Jeff and they walked to his car.

Ayden loaded the bags into the car and then opened the back hatch of the Durango so that Zero could jump in. Kirsa climbed into the passenger seat and Ayden got in the driver seat.

"Ayden they wrote on my walls and destroyed my things. My bedroom was ripped to shreds," she told him.

"He left a message?" Ayden asked stroking her hair. "One was weird, it said *we warned you long ago but you have not listened*," Kirsa told him turning to face him, she smelled fear coming off of him. "What is it Ayden?"

"Call Dietrich when we get to Sabrina's and

talk to him. He wants to know how you are doing and he is the one that should explain it all to you."

They drove the rest of the way in silence. Ayden pulled into the family drive of the Black Estate and followed it around to the back of the house. Sabrina was standing there with a surprising face. Collin Lyon was standing there next to her in a slate gray suit with navy blue dress shirt. His dirty blonde hair was wavy from the heat, and his green eyes were hidden behind sunglasses.

Kirsa got out of the car and ran up to him where he pulled her into a hug then swung here around in a circle. He put her down and shook hands with Ayden. Zero was already running around with Sabrina's three dogs.

"What are you doing here?" she asked him as they unloaded the car.

"I got a call from Tessa, the DA. She's needs a Paranormal Lawyer for the case, so I agreed to take the case with her as my assistant. When I called Sabrina to ask if she could pick me up from the airport she offered me a place to stay."

Kirsa just stared at him in disbelief. "I can't believe you're here."

They walked into the house. While Ayden and   Collin talked about what had been going on Sabrina brought Kirsa upstairs. They walked to one of the guest suites in the family wing.

"I figure you would like the one my grandparents stayed in. Collin is two doors down in Brian's old room, and I finally am in the master suite," Sabrina told her. Kirsa set the duffle bag down on the ottoman at the foot of the queen size bed. "Sabrina, thank you for this."

"You don't have. This is your home too. Take your time settling in then we'll figure out dinner. It's Mrs. Hanson's day off so no home cooked meal from her."

Kirsa looked at her, "You are going to warn her about the blood in the fridge so she doesn't faint when she comes in tomorrow?"

Sabrina laughed at the image. "I already talked to her so she knows and is fine with it. She wants Ayden to write down how he likes it when he wakes up so she can have it ready."

"Let him know and he'll write it all down," Kirsa told her.

Sabrina looked at her friend, "Alright let me see how the boys are getting along, why you don't lie down or take a shower?"

Kirsa nodded and waited until Sabrina left. She grabbed her cell and did not bother to calculate the time difference. She dialed Dietrich's private number as oppose to the house number.

"Hello Kirsa," his voice was heavy which was unusual for him. He sounded stressed and old.

"Ayden told me to call," she told him. "How are you holding up?"

"Has the cult ever threatened me before?" she asked, she was going to lead up to the question but decided against it.

"What do you mean by threaten you?" Dietrich asked in such a way that she knew he was withholding information.

"Don't placate me; have I ever been threatened by the cult?" she asked again. Her patience was running thin and she was tired of things being withheld from her for her own good.

There was silence as he debated on what to say and what not to say. Sometimes the truth was far worst then a lie. Yet sometimes the truth was the only answer.

"Yes, you were," Dietrich replied. "When?"

"The most serious of threats occurred about three days before your parent's death; Al intercepted the threat and told me about it."

Kirsa sat silent on the edge of the bed for a moment as her thoughts registered. "Did they threaten my parents?"

"Your father received one before you did. He did not want you to know about it," Dietrich informed her.

"Let me guess the warning said: The sins of your father have fallen on you."

"Roughly yes, how did you know?" Dietrich asked, he was rather confused that she would know what the threats had said. He also had fear coiling around his intestines.

"You know that the house was broken into today?" She asked.

"Yes, Ayden called to tell me. Why?" Dietrich asked.

"Lars was in my house and spray painted a bunch of things, along with the sins of the father, was they had warned me before and Thou shall not suffer a witch to live," Kirsa explained.

"Where are you now?" he asked.

"Sabrina's, he also tried to get into her storm cellar."

"Ayden is there with you correct?"

"Yes, along with Collin Lyon who is going

to prosecute the case."

There was silence from Dietrich. He was trying to swallow down the rage and the fear all at one time. Closing his eyes, he took several deep breaths, the glass of wine he was holding shattered.

"Kirsa, listen very carefully, we are under watch by the cult. I want you to stay at Sabrina's, you are only to leave the house if Ayden is with you. I will be there as soon as I can."

Kirsa heard the dial tone in her ear and closed the phone. She looked at Ayden. "I've never heard him that angry before."

Chapter Thirty

In was three pm in Germany. Dietrich walked through the family wing of the Adulwulf Manor. He was currently looking for Adam. Dietrich found him in the kitchen finalizing kitchen plans with the contractor. It always amazed Dietrich how much Adam and Kirsa looked alike. He waited for Adam and the contractor to finish their conversation.

"Are you settled in?" Adam asked Dietrich.

For the last week members of the Inner Council had been arriving in Geheimestadt. With the realization that there was a spy within the council and possibly in the Order of the Shadows, this was the safest place for them all.

"Yes, I cannot tell you how much we appreciate this," Dietrich told him again.

Adam looked at the man who was like a second father to him, "Honestly, Dietrich, we are thrilled you are all here and safe."

Dietrich nodded and the two men sat at the table, Adam brought over a note pad with the date and times of the carefully planned arrivals of Council members. Dietrich, Sebastian and his family, Shamus and his brood, and Dimitri with his two children had arrived two days ago. It had been all carefully organized and planned out. Since the four mentioned families had received direct threats from the cult, they were brought first.

Dimitri was the hardest, the Russian lines had a severe reaction to sun, their skin would begin to melt. Trying to get them from Russia safely to Northern Germany during the summer was difficult. The sun set well into the evening during the summer months.

"Amanda, one of the heads of the French sub lines, is coming tomorrow with some of her people," Adam told Dietrich. "One of the farmers is going to put them up, he has a small apartment above his barn. One of them is a newbie. The farmer has a safe room in the barn."

Adam was a bit relieved that a group

would be in a different spot. While the manor was large, much of it was still in midst of repair. The manor had 35 bedroom suites, however only about ten were usable. Thankfully the large kitchen was finished as well as what were deemed the public rooms: the ball room, parlor, library, smoking lounge which had been converted into a game room, and what was once the Council room.

It took a bit of arranging, Erin and her family would be staying with Wyrm in his cottage. Dietrich took over the smaller of the three guest suites in the family wing with Shamus and Sebastian's family taking the other two. Dimitri and his children were currently taking one of the guest suites in the guest wings.

"Some of the old servant's quarters were not completely ruined during the war or from water damage so if we have to we can put more there," Adam went on. "It won't be as comfortable but they will be safe with access to this part."

"Tomorrow night we are going to have the Irish Council members arriving since they were just targeted yesterday," Dietrich confirmed with Adam. "They are going to take one of the guest suites still available. I told Sebastian that his group could have a suite but apparently one of them is fresh, as he said, so he wants them somewhat secluded. So we might out his newbie with Amanda's."

"Will the farmer be safe?" Dietrich asked, even though the town had opened their arms to the Council coming he did not want his people to pray on the kindness of villagers,

"Klaus's son is a were-wolf; the apartment was his after he was attacked and became one. His son uses it when his pack finds a new were. So it is very indestructible, which is why he offered it to us when we were going over the town yesterday," Adam told him. He had asked for a town meeting to inform them what was going on. It was a unanimous vote to allow refuge for the vampires.

"What else went on during the meeting?" Dietrich asked.

"The mayor got approval to lock the gates at night," he answered. "A night watch list is being made so that walls can be watched for any newcomers and any threats."

"What of blood?" No one knew how long they would be here for.

"The the farmers will be storing all blood from the slaughters for you guys so that there is a fresh supply of blood. "

"This is most impressive," Dietrich stated. He was amazed in what Adam and the town had been able to do in a short time.

"Yea well apparently mine and Kirsa's ancestors had plans for things like this," Adam admitted. "So we dusted them off and updated them."

"Can you tell me where Erin is, I would like to talk to her?"

"She is in the nursery watching Adala. Anna had some clients at the diplomat school nearby so Erin offered to baby sit."

"Good I am going to go talk to her," Dietrich said. He walked out of the kitchen feeling like they were safe for the time being. Wyrm was coming down the hallway.

"Hello, sir," Wyrm said greeting Dietrich.

"Hello, I have two questions for you. Are you doing anything important at the moment Wyrm?" Dietrich asked.

"No I was just finalizing some plans with the wood worker, why?"

"I need to speak with Erin and I know she is comfortable with you. I would like you to come with me."

"Ok, she is in the nursery." Wyrm informed him. "What is the second question?"

"I am going to be leaving Sebastian, you

and Adam in charge; I will be leaving as soon as I can."

Wyrm did not need to ask where he would be going. He knew the answer already.

"Certainly, sir."

Dietrich nodded. They went up to the second floor and then turned into a room fit for a young princess. The walls of the sitting area were done in a soft ivory with gold crowns stenciled here and there. The walls of the interior bedroom were done in a soft pink, with a canopy crib trimmed in ivories, golds, yellows and pink fabrics. Erin sat reading a book in the sitting area with lullabies playing on the stereo softly for the sleeping baby. She looked up when the two men entered.

"Hello Wyrm, Mr. Nacht," Erin said closing the book.

Dietrich was happy to see that the haunted look that had once been in the young girls eyes had begun to vanish. She was more relaxed and at ease then she was when she was first brought here with her family. Dietrich had left after a day when he saw that she truly meant no harm.

"Hello, Erin. Please call me Dietrich," Dietrich told her. "Is it ok if I talked to you for a bit?"

"Sure, is Wyrm going to be here?" Erin asked. She no longer got nervous when she was going to be asked about her involvement with the cult.

"I thought it would be easier for you if he was here since you know him much better than me," Dietrich explained.

"That's fine," she told him.

"You know about the Council coming here for protection?" Wyrm asked her. She nodded yes. "The reason for that is the Church of Light is now targeting the Council. They somehow have managed to get the names of the members and their locations."

Erin nodded, her brain began to start thinking to try and put things together. "Are they still in Grabenberg with Kirsa and Ayden?"

Dietrich nodded, "Yes this new tactic has not deterred them from Grabenberg and their goal there."

"I know I'm young and all, but hasn't history shown that a two front war doesn't work?" Erin asked the two older men.

"Yes that is often true, however the person usually raging a two front war is after power," Dietrich told her.

"Gotcha. So what do you want to know?"

she asked them.

"Whatever you can tell us would be helpful. What people looked like, people you might not have liked and so forth," Dietrich told her. He had gone over Kirsa's timeline of events and they were both trouble with a pattern she had discovered. he hoped that Erin might shed some light.

She sat back in the chair getting more comfortable. "I guess I could start with the beginning. Wyrm knows some of this already."

"I find that is often a good place to start," Dietrich agreed. "How did you meet the cult?"

"A guy," Erin sighed. "It's so cliche. But I met a guy when I was at college in the midwest. I was finishing my freshman year when we were introduced at a party. When I had to go home for the summer we kept in touch."

"Were you dating?"

She shook her head. "Not then, but we started during sophomore year," Erin answered. "He was the perfect gentlemen, a few months into it he asked if I would go to church with him. I thought why not, what's the worst that could happen. I was uncomfortable the first few times I went."

"Why were you uncomfortable?" Dietrich

inquired.

"The church preached about the second coming, and ridding the world of evil. The people there creeped me out because they had these glazed looks on their faces," Erin replied. "It kind of reminded me of the horror movies where people get brainwashed than are led to their death."

"Why'd you keep going?" Dietrich asked.

Erin let out a little laugh. "Why do you think? It made the boyfriend happy."

Wyrm looked at Dietrich. "We've heard that before."

"At any of these meetings did any of the leader in the church come?" Dietrich asked Erin.

"One of the times we went they had a special speaker. I believe who we heard speak was the Father they all talked about it," Erin recalled. "It was weird because looking back I realize they never introduced him by name. I remember his words were hypnotic almost. I was a linguist major, I knew he was using all the methods to get a crowd to agree with him. The irony is that I fell for it. I was caught up in what he was saying. He never fully explained what the plans were, most of the people have no clue that the church is going around killing the innocent."

"If they did how do you think they would react?" Wyrm asked.

"Honestly, I think most would agree what they were doing was right," Erin told them. "Anyway I remember this guy because of how he spoke and how he held himself. You would have thought he was the tallest person in the room."

"Was he?" Wyrm asked her this time.

"He made a point to shake each of our hands at the end," Erin replied. "I think he was only about 5'8 maybe 5'10 because I'm 5'7 and he was not that much taller than me."

"Did you see him after the sermon he gave?"

"You know I kind of forgot about him, well not him but what he looked like until I saw him again which would been when I began working for the church," Erin said. "I had pretty much cut off all contact with my family and needed money. I could no longer afford college so I really needed a job. I began working for the East Coast office I guess about a year ago. They sent me to New York about seven months ago. Even when I was in Chicago where the old East Coast office, there was this guy who would come in from time to time. The way the higher ups would act made me start to think this guy was important. The weird thing is that it was hard to remember anything about him. I remember the height thing because it surprised me that he was not that tall."

"Erin, is it possible that he was in away making you not remember him so that if you saw him again you wouldn't know who he was?" Dietrich asked.

"Yes," she replied without hesitation. "I will say this when he entered the room you instantly felt calmer, not happier, just calmer. About three months before Veronica shot Kirsa and Ayden, he stopped in. This time I was determined to remember him, I could remember every face I saw, it's this talent I've always had. It was driving me crazy that I could not remember him anytime I saw him. So this time I focused without looking like I was trying to focus."

"What happened?" Dietrich asked. He was not going to get into the possibility of some type of photographic memory with her.

"Besides a migraine afterwards, I remember what he looked like. I was somewhat upset. I was hoping for this stunning dream guy like Brad Pitt or Orlando Bloom. He was cute, but very normal almost too normal. You know like he was trying to come across normal. He had brown hair that was really dry, like he died it often. Yet he had the most intense blue eyes I have ever seen."

"Erin if we gave you pictures to go through do you think you would be able to pick him out?" Dietrich asked.

"Holy shit you think the Father is your spy?" Erin asked as she realized what they weren't saying.

"We're not sure but anything is possible," Dietrich told her.

Chapter Thirty One

Kirsa, with the help of Mrs. Hansen, decided to have everyone over who was working on the case. They were close to burnout and they were all equally frustrated. Get together, eating, drinking, and relaxing for a few hours was something they all needed. And Mrs. Hansen was thrilled at the idea of cooking for more than just Sabrina or her brother.

She invited Jeff so that he was occupied and some of the pack that had been guarding him. Sabrina and her brother and his girlfriend were also there. Tony brought wife Donna and their two kids. Their son was running around with their dogs, while their teenage daughter batted her eyelashes at Collin.

Ayden was helping Mrs. Hanson because she would not let Kirsa or Sabrina help. Collin and Brian were playing catch and keep the ball away from Zero who was going crazy running back and forth between them. Kirsa, Sabrina and Emily sat at the picnic table drinking wine.

"It was nice of Mrs. Hanson to do this," Emily replied.

"She's excited to have multiple mouths to feed," Sabrina explained. "How is the moron by the way?"

Emily laughed. "He's good, worried about the two of you."

Sabrina laughed and caught the look that Kirsa gave her. "What?"

"Nothing. It's just good to see you laughing is all," Kirsa told her.

"Yeah well, I figure I gave that asshole about two days of me crying. Now I need to move on," Sabrina told them which caused them to clink their glasses with hers.

"That's good," Kirsa replied.

Sabrina raised an eyebrow, catching the look Emily got up with the excuse that she needed another beer.

"I don't want to talk about it now, after dinner. It's a theory I've been working on." Kirsa told her without Sabrina having to ask.

The dinner was needed; it was good to talk about things not dealing with the case. Mrs. Hanson brought out straw- berry shortcake for dessert and after that was done she had a tray with the makings for s'mores. Then she retired for the evening. Ayden went to the fire pit and started a fire there as they pulled chairs around it. Brian and Emily left after the cake; they felt that they did not need to take part in the discussion about the case. Tony's family followed them out.

Sabrina looked at Kirsa, "So it's later now, time for your theory."

"Yes. Ayden saw the start of this theory that I have come up with," Kirsa began. It started a few days ago, and then with what happened yesterday it started to put things into perspective for me. This was tough because there were a lot of emotional barriers that I had to move around."

"What did you learn?" Jeff asked.

"I know who our spy is and who is responsible for the murders here in Grabenberg," Kirsa said. She saw the mixed reaction filter through the faces.

"This is not going to be good," Sabrina whispered.

"Who Kirsa?" Tony asked.

Kirsa closed her eyes and took a deep breath. Ayden put his hand over hers to let her know he was there with her. "It's Lars."

There was silence; all that could be heard were the crickets in the background. Kirsa looked around and waited as what she said began to sink in.

"Kirsa that's crazy," Tony told her. He got up and walked over to the windows.

"I would like to hear this theory." Sabrina asked. Her voice was rough with emotion.

Kirsa looked at her and Sabrina nodded. "First, from the day that I arrived Lars has barely been at my side. He was always off doing something; I figured he was probably with Sabrina most of the time. She told me the other night that he wasn't with her on the times that he was gone."

"Second," Ayden began, "the night in the hospital a huge red flag went up for me. Tony was in the room when he got the call about Sara. He left for the scene. About 45 minutes later Lars showed up telling me that Tony had told him to go."

Jeff looked at Tony. "Lars wasn't there when Tony came to the house. He was there when I got there."

"He was there when myself, and three other pack members showed up," Phil told them. "We got there before Jeff because he was on the other side of town and wanted someone there ASAP. We never picked up another scent but for those who were there."

"Think about it this way also, Kirsa and Ayden were still in NYC. It wasn't like they were in Morristown or Denville where you could get there in 45 minutes. It took me over an hour and a half to get to the hospital," Sabrina told them.

"Another is that Lars and Laurence come from the same Latin route, Louis did the same thing when he moved away from using Alois," Ayden explained. "There are a lot of vampires that will use variations of their name throughout their life."

Tony held up a hand. "The question is why?"

Kirsa took a deep breath. This meant coming out with a secret that only Sabrina knew. She had hinted at it with Tony and Ayden.

"Lars suspects that I am the heir to the sixth

bloodline, which would put me in a position of great power in his mind. He wanted files pertaining to my family but did not know that I had them hidden. That's why he went to the storm cellar and then in desperation tried the house. By giving the church the theory it makes me their number one target. They begin to kill in hopes that I hear about it and either come to help or it will make me feel responsible for the deaths that I would turn myself in." Kirsa explained.

Collin looked at Tessa who nodded. "Ok, Jeff gave a description of who he saw to a sketch artist. The sketch resembles Lars. Second thing, how would one prove that Kirsa is the heir to the line?"

Ayden spoke up, "Each line has a signet ring. There is only one known image of what the six ring looks like, though it is known the elements that are carved in it. There have been a few forges in the past. But all missing one key element that only Wyrm knows."

"Ok so if someone had this ring it would signify that they are the heir. Would they need any other proof?"

"Some type of documentation about how they got the ring."

"For example, an inventory list for a hidden vault discovered in the oldest section of a castle in Germany?" Kirsa asked.

All eyes turned and looked at her. She cleared her throat and rolled out the map the FBI has created. Before they got way off topic, she was going to bring the conversation back to the case.

"I also think they are using the mines or the old mine houses," Kirsa told them. "I know the FBI doesn't even have them marked on the map as a possible location.There are still roads that lead to the mines, most of them are over grown but if you have a four wheel vehicle you could do it. Plus it would not be odd to see a car at any hour on Old Mine Road, most people that do use it, use it as a cut through from this side of town to the other side of town."

Tony grabbed his cell phone. "Hey Pete," he said into the phone. "I need a car to go to Old Mine Road. I want them to pay attention to the old roads that lead up to the mines. Have them mark down which one's looked like they have been used recently." He hung up the phone.

"So Lars took Sara you think?" Jeff asked his voice ice cold. "It makes sense. She wouldn't have been on guard if it was a familiar scent."

"He's not going to kill her," Kirsa said. "I'm

not just saying that to reassure you but he won't. She's bait."

"For what?" Tony asked.

"If we go with Lars being the spy, the cult would know that Sara and I are really close. The cult would also know that I would do anything to save a friend, even if that meant turning myself in, in exchange for her release."

"A note was sent to the station asking us to turn you over in three days' time in exchange for Sara," Tony informed them all. He gave them a look to know he was not done. "That gives us two days to find their hideout and come up with a plan that does not involve you going to them."

****

Lars leaned against the door frame of the back porch door. It was close to midnight and he was listening to the night sounds of the country. He was impress with how pre- pared the house was, Nick had done not only an amazing job but a thorough one as well.

He picked a house not only with a basement but an old storm cellar and worked on both of them to fit the cause. Lars was currently upset with Chris Washington, who was currently in one of the bedrooms freaking out about what might happen to him.

Weakness like that drove him up the wall. There had been no sign of his killer monk and that troubled him. He heard a noise behind him and he turned to see Nick coming down the back stairs.

"Good Evening Nick," Lars said. "Hello, Father."

"Is Miss Adams with Sara?" Lars asked as Nick joined him by the door.

"Yes, she wants to feel a part of this." Nick informed him. "I see, well I am glad that she wants to help. Nick are you alright?"

Nick stared up at the night sky and then at the man next to him. He had put all his faith behind this man. Helped him get rid of the old Father and yet now he began to wonder who was this man he helped.

"There are rumors about what happened between you and Arthur," Nick told him.

"Has it taken this long for them to start talking about the change of power?" Lars asked him.

"What with Anton being caught and rebuilding I think it got swallowed up until now. I only say this because some are saying he was murdered and that you were the one that did it."

"What else are they saying?" Lars heard the hesitation in Nick's voice.

"They say you are a monster one belonging to the night and not to God," Nick told him. "I've told them, how that cannot be true when you have led us so close to our goal. If you were truly one of the monsters we were hunting, wouldn't you be out there protecting them?"

Lars laid a hand on Nick's shoulder. "Perhaps I am a monster for not helping them and letting them know what is going on. I do love a good rumor, it livens things up."

With that Lars turned and walked inside leaving a confused Nick standing in the doorway.

Chapter Thirty Two

Ayden lay next to Kirsa watching her sleep. It had been late, well into the early morning hours before they both had finally fallen asleep. Ayden had set their alarm for ten in the morning. The clock was at nine. So he lay there watching her sleep, watching her breath. He had already fed Zero so that the dog would not make up Kirsa. Ayden was exhausted. While the sun did not effect as it did others, he used a lot of energy to walk around in it. And with this case, he was using up most of his stored energy.

He heard Zero's nails on the floor and he caught Zero as the dog launched himself onto the bed. Catching an 80 lb dog was nothing, trying to keep it from squirming without hurting it was a different story. Kirsa rolled over and opened her eyes. She laughed. Ayden sighed and let Zero go, which in response ran around in circles on the bed and stuck his wet nose in Kirsa's face.

"Good morning to you too, Zero," she said scratching his ears. She then focused on Ayden. "Good morning, Ayden."

"Good morning Kirsa," he responded kissing her nose. Zero settled down at the foot of the bed and was asleep in seconds.

Kirsa stretched and looked at the alarm clock. "You let me sleep this late?"

"The alarm is set for 10 actually, Tony said to sleep in and take your time getting over to the station house. There is no rush."

Kirsa yawned and stretched, "Let me take a shower and get ready then I will meet you downstairs.

She climbed out of bed and walked into the bathroom. Turning the shower on hot, she selected what she would be wearing today. Today was addressing all the different groups that would be coming together, which meant more formal than jeans and khakis. She stepped into the shower; the water pounded away all the stress she was feeling.

Her best friend from childhood was being held prisoner by the same group that was responsible for the death of her parents and aunt and uncle. How could she not take this personal? It was as if they had made it their mission to eliminate her line. But why? That was the nagging question, she was miss- ing something. She climbed out of the shower and changed while thinking about what she could have missed.

Ayden turned his head when he heard her come down the stairs; he had been talking to Mrs. Hanson about what had been going on. Kirsa put on a pair of light gray pants and a short sleeve purple top. On her feet was a pair of black heels with a hint of purple at the heel.

Mrs. Hanson handed her a mug of coffee, "It's been spiked with your dosage, and my darling dear Sabrina left a message for you."

Kirsa took the note and kissed the elderly lady on the cheek. It was note telling her that her items at the Jewelers' were ready and they could go at lunch time. Kirsa folded it and slid it into her back pocket. She sipped her coffee while she got out a travel mug. Opening the fridge she cracked up, large pitcher filled with red liquid labeled O+ juice. Kirsa missed the look exchanged between Ayden and Mrs. Hanson.

"I'm ready to head out," Kirsa informed Ayden.

"Don't you want me to make you anything?" Mrs. Han-son asked.

Kirsa shook her head no as she gathered up the shoulder bag that contained her notes and copies of files. "I'm good, but you can plan dinner."

"Um, Ayden do you eat?" Mrs. Hanson asked nervously. Lars had never stayed for meal times.

He smiled. "Don't make an entire portion for me. I would say we can sample food more than eat it. If we eat too much it can act like a poison and take us awhile to recover."

"I see, well then I will figure out what to make," she replied as she ushered the two out the back door.

They drove in silence for a few minutes; Ayden rested his hand on Kirsa's thigh and watched her drink from the travel mug.

"You sure you don't want me to stop and get you food?" he asked as he drove.

Kirsa looked away from the window and at him. She could see the worry in his eyes. The truth was she was los- ing her appetite for food, she had yet to face it herself so the thought of confiding at this point seemed harder.

"I'm not hungry. We'll be at the police station, trust me there will be food there when I do get hungry," Kirsa assured him.

Tony met them outside the station, he looked every bit of the police chief that he was. Kirsa walked over to him and he gave her a quick hug.

"Al's team is here, same with several FBI, SWAT and our guys are all here," he told as they entered the station house. "We are in the back room; it has been checked for any types of bugs. All cell phones and other devices including laptops not authorized have been taken."

Kirsa nodded as she heard Ayden talking in Gaelic on the phone, which meant he was talking to Shamus. He hung up the phone and joined them; Tony filled him in on the security look.

What's up? She asked him silently.

I'll tell you later. He assured her as they walked with Tony down the hall.

So far no one knew that they could communicate through their mind. It was a rare event when a human and vampire could, mostly because it required absolute trust between them.

Tony escorted them into the room, where everyone was met. Like her, everyone had their own coffee mugs in front of them. Many were catching up on what was going on. Collin and Tessa came in shortly after them. Tony nodded at Al. Tony stood before the podium and waited for the room to quiet down. It took only a few seconds for this to be done. By this time Al had a map of Grabenberg up on the power point so that the whole room could see it.

"I'm going to start with some basic introductions," Tony began. "We have three civilians that all of you might not know. The large bald man with the gold earring is Phil. Phil is the head of Sara's pride and is going to help with some of the were issues that might come up. Next are Ryan and Todd Clark. Ryan is also part of Sara's pride and came to our attention through Joe the farmer. He has some in- formation and has been picking up and identifying scents for us. Todd is lending us his house to use as surveillance. Agent Heinrich is going to explain what we are going to be doing."

Kirsa stared at Tony and wanted to curse.

Nothing like being prepared, she glared at him as she moved up to the podium. "I love having no warning about when I am going to be addressing a group. Thanks Tony," she said. They chuckled which broke some of the tension in the room.

"Ok so here's what going on. We have some key players of a large cult hiding out in our town. They are responsible for the murders that have been occurring over the last few months. One of their hit men actually turned himself in and has been giving us a lot of information that has gotten us to this point. We believe that they are holding Sara Cliver captive in the mining area that is highlighted on the map."

The mention of Sara's name caused everyone's attention to snap into focus. It did not matter anymore about what was wrong or right or what the cult had done. All the people in the room cared about was that the cult had taken one of their own. That was reason enough to go out and fight.

"The teams that Tony has set up, which I am assuming he set up already, will be at the Clark House," Kirsa stopped because several hands went up once.

She called on the guy closest to her. "Yes?"

"What do you mean we will be at the

Clark's house why won't we be in a perimeter around the area?" He asked.

"Because Chris Washington is with them meaning he has probably given them all of your procedures on what to do in a situation like this," Kirsa told him. Several curses were heard throughout the room.

She motioned to the next guy who stood up. "First question, what is going to be going on while we are bored out of our minds and second why do we have to listen to you?"

There was silence in the room as the others tried to look away from the guy who had spoken. Tony mouthed "new guy" to her.

"I'll answer your last question first," Kirsa said with a hint of ice to her voice. "With the exception of Director Moore, I out rank everyone in this room: I am not only a USA OPIA agent but I am also an International Agent as well, which means I can give the orders if I so feel to do so." She watched the guy's face sink.

"And finally your first question, while you will be bored out of your mind here at the station, everyone else is at the Clark's house. I will be turning myself over to the cult because they want me dead."

There was silence in the room. "Anyone

else feels like asking any personal questions?" she asked. No one said anything. "Good then I will tell you the plan."

An hour later Kirsa walked out of the room and into the other meeting room. The group was now broken down into their four person team and going over their duties. Kirsa walked in and saw Louis in the chair. Jeff sat across from him, they were playing solitaire. They both stopped when she walked in. She sat next to Jeff.

"Ok Louis, we figured out who the spy is. His name is Lars, he was my father's body guard and mine. He took off several days ago which is when pieces started to fall into place," she told him.

"What can I do?" Louis asked sitting straight in his chair, he folded his hands on the table.

"What can I expect when I turn myself over? We have two days to iron out the plans." she asked him.

The shock flashed in his eyes for a second then they went back to their bland stare. "They will not kill you right away. If anything they are going to show you all they have done, explain to you why. They will treat you like a guest and try to get your guard down. With you, you will not have the option to repent as others did. For they see your blood as pure evil with no hope of salvation" he told her.

"So they'll sweet talk me and then kill me?" she asked.

"After they torture you for a bit," Louis told her. "The Father likes torture; he believes it brings out true repentance for a person sins. Then they will kill you."

"Next part, the chains they use for the were's, I'm assuming silver?" Kirsa asked.

Louis looked confused for a second; then he understood. "They used pure silver in South Carolina when our numbers were high and we had the money."

"What do you use now?" Jeff asked.

"I don't know for sure but I believe silver alloy or something. I don't know the level of purity. I do know that the were's they imprisoned could not transform or break free of them."

Kirsa nodded. "Thank you Louis."

"Kirsa, one last thing," Louis said as she got up. "They will sweep you for bugs, tracking device and anything else that might let someone know where you are. You will be dead immediately if they find one on you. They also, or did, have a well extensive arsenal. I have given your captain the list of what I know they have."

Kirsa nodded and left the room. Phil waited for her in Tony's office along with Bryan. Tony had them sniff a shirt belonging to Lars to see if it matched what they had been picking up.

Kirsa walked into the office and shut the door. Bryan got up so that Kirsa could have his seat.

"What's the verdict?" she asked Tony.

Tony looked at Bryan. Bryan swallowed, he was around 20, around 5'9, had sandy blonde hair and green eyes. He had an athletic build too him that was deceiving because Kirsa bet there was killer muscle under his clothes.

"The smell from the shirt Tony gave me matches the scent that I have been picking up all over Joe's farm. I also picked up on it at Sara's house when we helped try to find her," Bryan told her.

Kirsa looked at Phil who smiled. "The kid has one of the best noses for tracking that I have known," Phil told her.

"Ok," Kirsa said. "Let's talk about silver." She relayed to them what Louis had said about the restraints.

Phil scratched his chin thinking. Ryan

watched his leader; he took the water bottle that Tony handed him.

"I know that when were's decided to pierce we use a silver based metal. My earring is gold plated silver so that the hole would not heal up," Phil told her. "Now it's just jewelry and I have broken my earring a few times from pulling on it too hard. But that's a thin piece of metal. How about the were's that were killed before? I know the one found on Joe's yard. She had only been a were for five years."

"What does that mean?" Tony asked.

Bryan answered. "A were-animal is stronger than most however the longer you are one, and I mean transforming, the stronger you become. The more you are able to change at will and also the more control you have over changing if caught in a bad situation."

"If it's a young were there is no way she would be able to transform with silver alloy anything," Phil filled in. "You're asking me if there is a possibility that Sara could break free?"

"There's a full moon tomorrow night, the most powerful night for you guys," Kirsa replied. "This is why we are doing this tomorrow at not today."

"If it is very diluted silver, then

theoretically she might be able to transform. If she is able to transform then there is a chance she could break free," Phil said he read the look in Kirsa's eyes. "But Kirs, don't count on her transforming for whatever you have up your sleeve."

Kirsa smiled and walked out of the room. She looked at her watch and saw it was one o 'clock. "Hey Tony can I run out real quick?"

Tony turned and looked at her, "As long as you bring Phil."

Kirsa nodded and went to where they had left Phil. He was talking to some of his guys, they stopped when Kirsa walked in.

"What's up kid?" Phil asked.

"I need to run an errand, Tony wants you to come with me," she informed him.

Phil nodded, "Let me finish here and I will meet you in the lobby in a minute."

Kirsa went to the break room and grabbed her pocket book. Ayden was on one of the computers; she walked over to him and leaned her chin on his head.

"What's up?" Ayden asked as he turned to face her in the chair.

"I'm running out," she smiled as his brows

bunched up. "I'm bringing Phil with me don't worry."

"Where you going?"

Kirsa took a deep breath before carefully wording her sentence. She knew he would read between the lines.

"I had the family jeweler resize a ring for me that has been in my family for a while. Because of the age of the gold it took a while and he wants me to take a look at it and then of the mold to duplicate the ring. He wants my approval before he starts work on it."

Awareness flooded his eyes, he kissed her forehead. He understood what she meant with the ring. "This doesn't change anything."

She kissed him quickly before she went to meet Phil in the lobby. He was there waiting so they headed to his Nissan Leaf.

"Where are we headed to?" Phil asked climbing into the driver seat.

"Olde Thyme Jeweler," Kirsa told him. They drove through town and parked in the community lot behind the main square.

Olde Thyme Jeweler was a third generation shop. It was located in the town square. Kirsa knew her mother had certain heirlooms reproduced by them. There was a "closed" sign on the door, Kirsa rang the bell and Eddie, the grandson of the original owner, unlocked the door and let them in. He was in his forties, his oldest son was apprenticing at the shop already.

"Allie, we'll be in the vault if I'm needed," he told his receptionist. He escorted them into the back vault.

He closed and locked the door then covered the cameras in the vault. The vault was a large room; the walls were lined with locked cabinets and drawers. In the center of the room were a large table and four leather chairs surrounding it. Kirsa and Phil took the seats at the table while Eddie walked to one of the locked drawers.

He unlocked one of the small drawers and took out two boxes. The first was the insignia ring, the gold was an old yellow gold, gems outlined the circle, and in the center of the ring was the image of a wolf with the moon behind it. The sides of the ring had carvings of five other animals on it.

Phil looked at the ring and let out a whistle. "Is that what I think it is?"

Kirsa looked at him, "Breathe a word and your furry hide will make a nice rug in front of my fireplace."

"My lips are sealed just never thought I would see it in my life time," Phil replied in awe.

"We placed a sizing band that goes across it; I want you to try it on before we affix it. Once we verify the size you can have it tomorrow," Eddie slid the ring on her right middle finger. "Ok good it fits."

"Is the other box the mold?" Kirsa asked trying to hide her nervousness.

"Yes, now we can do it in platinum with diamonds and sapphires outlining the circle. Which is what my expert thinks are in the original," he opened the box and the mold was perfect.

"Did you ask him the age of the ring?" Kirsa asked as she examined the mold.

"He puts it no later than 1000 C.E., but thinks it is definitely older than that. He was very upset when I told him no pictures or anything."

Kirsa looked up at Eddie. "Eddie, thank you for all of this, I really appreciate it."

"Your dad brought the ring in a few months before the accident, he wanted to make sure it was alright to be worn if need be," Eddie told her.

"I didn't know that," Kirsa whispered.

"My father didn't even know, can I ask what the ring is?" Eddie inquired. He had an idea already but wanted to see if he was right.

"It's the sixth ring," Kirsa told him. He knew the lore and legend around her family, it was hard not to when you worked for them.

"That's what I thought," he put the rings back in the box and locked them up again. He escorted them out.

"I will call you when the sizing is finished," Eddie told her.

No one paid attention to Allie who was texting someone on the phone with a nervous look on her face.

Kirsa and Phil left the store, he lit a cigar. Phil raised an eyebrow at her as they walked. He was picking up on her nervousness.

"I'm not ready for this," Kirsa said after a moment.

"I don't think anyone is when they are about to enter a world of power," Phil told her. "I wasn't ready when I became pack leader and then as elected voice for the east coast packs."

They walked in silence and noticed a

university tour heading their way. Grabenberg University liked to show perspective students around the town. Phil motioned for Kirsa to stand next to him as they stopped at one of the street lights. As the group past by them, two individuals with base- ball caps pulled down low approached them. They acted as if they were long lost friends of Kirsa.

"Don't move," Nick breathed into Kirsa ear as he put his arms around her tightly.

The other individual forced Phil to shake hands, where he pricked him in the hand with a silver pin. Phil went to say something but Nick quickly showed the gun under his sweatshirt.

"While Kirsa and I catch up, why don't you and Chris discuss some current affairs," Nick suggested as he walked away with Kirsa.

Anyone watching would have seen some friends who hadn't seen each other in a long time. What they didn't see was Chris slipping a syringe into Phil and then slid him down onto a bench. There wasn't enough silver to kill him just enough to make him immobile for long enough to get away. They didn't see Nick get Kirsa into a car and then give her a pill that would knock her out for the ride.

Chris rushed toward the car and climbed in the passenger seat. He helped Nick get Kirsa on the floor and fix the restraints so that she couldn't get away. Kirsa did not fight them; she let her body go limp to minimize injury. When the car started she closed her eyes and took a deep breath. She knew they had incapacitated Phil somehow, so that left her to let them know what was going on. Relaxing her mind, she focused on Ayden. On his scent, on his mind. Then it was like a switch turned on and she could hear a faint echo of him.

Ayden. She said, she wasn't sure if he would hear her; they had never tried this much of a distance to read each other's thoughts.

Where are you? Neither Phil nor you are answering your cells. He sounded worried.

Kirsa pictured him pacing Tony's office. *Look, I've been drugged. They did something to Phil. I am in a car and we are heading toward the mines from what the road feels like.*

Are you sure?

Kirsa could feel the drugs starting to take hold. *Really tired. Will let you know.*

Tony was watching Ayden as he paced his office. His face had been like a stone for the last few minutes. When Tony had asked him something there had been no response. Ayden slumped in a chair.

"They've done something to Phil and got

Kirsa," Ayden informed Tony.

Before Tony could ask how Ayden knew that, Jeff came rushing into the office, "Phil is on the phone."

Tony looked at Ayden, who nodded. "Let's just say Kirsa let us know."

Jeff went to say something but stopped. "Phil is being treated at the square, let's start there."

Chapter Thirty Three

Lars stood on the back porch of the rotting house. He was going to spend some time with his prisoner. The full moon was tomorrow he wanted to taunt her a little bit about it. Nick had radioed to him that all was quiet at the police station, and there was no sign of Louis. The loner probably found a safe hole to hide in until this all blew over.

Lars froze. He listened very carefully hearing each leaf and grass blade blow in the faint breeze. Underneath that he heard the low vibration of a car coming up the road.

Everyone that knew where the hide out was, was here. Moving slowly he entered the house. Veronica was currently watching the prisoner on the security cameras they had set up.

As he walked through the dilapidated kitchen he heard the car approaching. It was speeding but it was still in control. This made him think they had been successful in what they had been set out to do. They had agreed no radio contact after Nick and Chris had entered the station. Not even after they got back in the car.

The car pulled up to the house, Chris rolled down the passenger window. "Where do you want us to park?"

"Pull around back, I will meet you there," Lars said without any trace of an accent.

Lars followed the car around to the back of the house. Chris closed the driver's door quietly and walked around to the back passenger door to help Nick. Lars came over by them.

"I can see it went well," he replied. In the back of the car Kirsa laid unconscious.

"We couldn't have planned it better," Nick told him as he undid the restraints. "The drugs have hit her harder than I thought."

"Take her to the storm cellar, put her in the

extra cell," Lars instructed. "I will come down in a bit to watch her."

Nick nodded; Chris went with him to help open the cellar doors. Lars watched them then turned to walk into the house. Veronica met him in the kitchen. She was making herself a cup of coffee when he entered.

"I got some chicken in the oven downstairs," Veronica informed him as she stirred her coffee.

"You don't have to cook for us," Lars let her know.

"I heard the car," She stated. When he didn't respond she raised an eyebrow and took a sip from her mug. "I take it Kirsa is here?"

"Yes, and no you cannot go down there yet," Lars told her.

"Why not?" Veronica asked, not wanting to sound challenging. But she was feeling useless at this point.

"I would like to talk to her first before anyone gets a bat at her," he explained. "I also believe that if I were to send you down now you might take advantage of her unconscious state."

Veronica went to argue but decided against it. She let it drop, Chris came walking into the room.

"Good, coffee," he exclaimed. "She is all set in the cell. Nick's concerned we might have given her too much because she is still not waking up. He is checking her vitals now."

"Then I will go down and relieve him." Lars nodded to them both.

"Did I come in at a bad time?" Chris asked.

Veronica let out a breath, "He won't let me go down and see her just yet."

"That's why there was all that tension in the room when I came in," Chris realized.

****

Slowly awareness began to filter through; Kirsa began to be aware of dampness, noises and a hard surface under her. She felt very groggy. Very cautiously she opened her eyes until they adjusted to the dim light. Her head was pounding as if a metal band was performing inside. She saw that she was lying on a hard cement floor. Then she remembered the abduction and what   happened.

"Good afternoon," a deep neutral voice said from some- where in the darkness.

Kirsa looked in the direction the voice was

coming from and could make out a shape that looked to be Lars.

"Hello Lars," she replied.

"You're not surprised?" he asked.

He was a bit taken aback by her reaction. Lars had been expecting hurt, rage and more. He had been relishing in the fact that smelling all the emotions raging through her would have been worth everything so far. Now, all he felt was annoyance. He handed her a water bottle.

"I like how you can lose the accent," Kirsa observed. She took a slow sip of the water, trying to detect any odd taste in it.

He smiled slowly. "It is convenient," he answered sliding back into the accent.

"They don't know who you are, do they?" Kirsa asked.

"Honestly, neither do you," Lars responded. "But no, they don't know that they have been taking orders from a vampire."

Kirsa wasn't sure if he had realized what he had said. It was a subtle statement but enough of one that the last puzzle piece fell into place. She was impressed that she kept the shock from showing on her face. But he had just confirmed their theory. Lars ran the church.

"When you have gotten more rest we will talk," he told her. "Have a good night."

Kirsa leaned back against the cold damp floor. She closed her eyes and began to breathe deeply, using the technique she used for yoga.

Ayden, can you hear me? She figured it was worth a try.

What's going on? Ayden asked. She felt relief rush through him.

I am at the mines somewhere, we have a bigger problem.

What?

Lars confirmed he's the father.

There was silence for a moment before she felt Ayden's rage at what she had just told him. It was their worst fear recognized. She didn't hear what he said because her head began to swim and fogginess came back over her.

Chapter Thirty Four

Kirsa adjusted to the dim light after she came around the second time. The cellar had been carved out of the earth, with cement floors, and rough stone walls. Wires and pipes ran across the exposed ceiling. Bare bulbs hung from the ceiling giving an eerie flow to the place.

As far as Kirsa could make out, there were three cells in total. Sara was in the cell across from her. When Kirsa had fast woken up in her cell, Sara held a finger to her lips and with her eyes motioned to the ceiling. There was a camera mounted there watching their every move. They began to use a secret sign language they had created when they were younger. Through that, Kirsa learned that next to Sara was a young teen. They had brought the girl in two nights before Kirsa arrived.

As Kirsa began to move about her cell she noted a steel door at the end of one hallway. She asked Sara about it. Sara grimaced at the door. Then she signed to Kirsa that was where Lars took them to torture them. They stopped when they both heard the cellar door open.

Chris came walking down the stairs smoking a cigarette. He saw that Sara and Kirsa were both awake.

"Hello, kitty cat," he greeted Sara. "Has the cub woken up at all?"

Sara looked at the cell next to her, "She stirred once during the night."

He nodded. Chris then stared at Kirsa as he took the last drag from his cigarette. He still did not get why the Father was so threatened and in some way scared of her.

"The boss man wants to see you," he told her, snuffing out the cigarette with the sole of his shoe.

He took a ring of keys out of his pocket. After selecting the right one he opened her door then walked to where she had been shackled. Grabbing her by the arm, he yanked her up and handcuffed her.

Chris dragged her behind him as they made their way to the stairs. Kirsa had to shut her eyes when they emerge into the sunlit morning. Chris pulled her along with him as he walked to the house. Kirsa made mental notes about everything as they walked from the storm cellar to the house. She could tell that it had been painted a brown at one point, but the wood siding was so worn from the weather over the years that it had become badly faded. Knowing the layout of the old mining development she began to figure out where she was exactly.

When he pulled her into the house, she saw that the kitchen was completely destroyed from years of neglect. They went into a hallway that was filled with debris. Suddenly they came to a stop, Chris knocked on the wall and soon it opened up revealing Lars' office. Lars was sitting at a desk looking over something. He was wearing a polo shirt and glasses. Chris shoved Kirsa into the room and shut the door.

"It did not have to come this, you know," Lars said taking a sip from the coffee mug in front of him.

"Didn't have to come to what?" Kirsa asked, she detected a familiar scent in the air and realized that there was blood in the mug.

"You being here, me having to kill you myself," he told her.

"When was I supposed to have died?" Kirsa inquired.

Lars smiled over the mug as he took another sip. He licked the bit of blood that was left on his lips. "What would have been your wedding night," Lars told her. He smiled at the horror that came over her face."But then when you broke that off. So we agreed it would be done in South Carolina. I even gave Anton advance notice of your arrival."

"Anton was supposed to have killed me?" She expected there to be pain, but instead she was not surprise by that at all.

"I need to ask you a question before this goes any further," Lars replied sitting in his chair. She raised an eyebrow, "Has Ayden bitten you in passion?"

"Now there's a personal question," Kirsa was kind of stunned by the question

"I need to know."

"I know because the theory is that biting a mortal during a moment of passion can cause the minds to form a permanent link," Kirsa said before he could. "No he hasn't. I have trust issues and that's a trust that I'm not ready for."

"Then if I was to search you there would be no bite marks?" he asked.

She chuckled. "Lars, I have been bitten by four vampires in my line of work. None of which were in the heat of passion, and no signs of me wanting to do their bidding."

"Really? Four times?" Lars asked surprised.

"Yep, four. None were pleasant."

Lars sipped his blood. Even if she was lying about Ayden not biting her, he could not prove it if she had been bitten on four separate occasions. He drummed his fingers on the table next to him and studied her.

"I do not remember when I was turned, but I have heard it is an unpleasant experience for the person on the receiving end," Lars replied.

There was a moment of silence, where they watched each other. Lars was wondering how it was possible that she could figure out not only who he was but that he was also the spy.

"Why were you not surprised when you saw me standing outside the car?" Lars asked her.

Kirsa formulated her thoughts in order to not blow anything. "The other day I began making a time line of everything that has occurred since the first crime scene I was brought to," Kirsa explained. It wouldn't ruin anything if she told him. If anything it bought her time. "I listed everything: whom I was with, what was going on and so forth. I started noticing that you were missing more and more. Then when I walked in on the argument you and Ayden were having, things just began to click."

"Did you tell anyone your theory?"

Kirsa laughed. "Right, because anyone would believe me that my bodyguard and the bodyguard of my parents was really a bad guy?"

Lars leaned back in his chair and finished his mug. When he was done with it he set it down and stood up. Kirsa watched him carefully. He looked at the back window.

"I always admired how you were able to connect the dots, now I find it rather annoying," Lars told her. Kirsa chuckled. "May I ask what is so funny?"

"I was going to ask if it was hard keeping up this whole pompous ass charade. Then I thought, hey you know what, maybe this is the real him, maybe he really is just this big asshole," Kirsa replied.

Lars went to slap her but she caught his wrist before his hand connected. He stared in shock; no human could stop or even deflect a move from a vampire. Vampires moved too fast, a human wouldn't see the move until it was too late.

"What Lars? Surprised? Maybe if you stuck around more you might have realized some things," Kirsa said.

"But you're not a vampire?" he asked, he knew she wasn't. Her scent would change slightly if she had become a vampire.

"No I'm just dangling somewhere in-between human and vampire, it's really annoying actually," she answered.

She failed to tell him how her senses were getting better. How she could nearly see in the dark, she could smell emotions if they were extreme enough. These were things he did not need to know.

"How'd you come across this place?" Kirsa asked, filling up the silence.

"When Nick realized we would need a secure hide out and base of operations he came here and began modifications to house. I know from what you saw it looked like nothing had been touched. What we did was keep the main floor untouched; we completely redid the attic and the basement."

His attitude fit in with what Louis had told

her. Lars was in "Father" mode at the moment. This meant he was going to offer goodwill to the woman with evil blood and treat her like a guest instead of a prisoner.

Lars dwelled upon what she had said earlier and how he knew her. Kirsa could not lie; she was honest and could not keep a straight face when she lied. The one side of her mouth always went up when she tried to. When she had told him how she figured it out her face remained the same, no faint movements.

"Can I ask why you are doing all this?" Kirsa asked as he got himself situated.

"Why I'm doing what?" Lars raised his eyebrows as if to show he did not understand the question.

"This, the cult, the house, the killings, Sara, me, everything," she said more specifically. "I mean after around eight hundred years of existence you're doing all this?"

"Are you guessing my age?" Lars asked surprised that she almost had his age.

"In your letter you said something about losing your sister to the plague; I took a guess and figured she died during the Black Death which spread through Europe toward the end of the 1340's. Am I wrong?"

He laughed, her brain was always working. It usually picked up on the most subtle of statements.

"1348 was when my sister died from the Plague," Lars said after a moment of thought. "Helena was 8. By then I had buried both my parents, my younger brother and another sister before she died." He thought for a moment before continuing the rest. "I guess it wouldn't hurt to tell you the whole thing."

Lars returned to his chair and began his tale. "I was the oldest of eight children. When the plague hit my town in Norway, I was an apprentice for a metal smith at an armory. I had a loft above his workshop and lived there while I was trained. The plague took my parents, a brother and two sisters."

"I'm sorry," Kirsa said softly.

"When my parents died," Lars continued as if not hearing her or ignoring her. "The oldest of my sisters came and got me. I had her bring the healthy ones to my loft and I went to our cottage. I tried my best but there was nothing we could do, we had expelled or killed all our healers so I did my best. It was the death of Helena that did it. After her death I figured I would be next so I went to a tavern, one that was still open and drank away my misery."

"Lars, there nothing you could have done

to save them or yourself," Kirsa assured him. There was a part of her that wanted to grieve for the young man who lost his family to such horrors, who blamed himself for not stopping the impossible.

"Needless to say, when I left the bar I was barely aware of my surroundings and that was when I was attacked and awoke the next night as a vampire."

"Your maker?"

Lars snorted at that. "I have no clue who turned me," Lars said angrily. "They left me to rot as my body transformed into a monster. It took me months to learn how to feed for blood. Years to learn not to drain a human. The council, they make you think they are all great. But where were they for me?"

"When did you meet Dietrich?" Kirsa asked. It was subtle, the way she took over the conversation.

"I would say about three hundred years ago I was introduced to Dietrich," Lars recalled. "He could not quite make out how old I was because one of my gifts was that of concealing parts of who I am from others. When he asked what line I belonged too I told him I didn't know. My maker never told me his name nor did he bother to teach me the ways of a vampire. I had to learn on my own, teach myself how to survive. I told Dietrich where I was from and from there it was decided upon that I would be part of one of the Nacht Lines."

"How did you become a body guard?" Kirsa asked.

"Wyrm noticed my unique gift in which I can make people forget me or forget certain parts of me," Lars told her. "He passed word of this to the Inner Council. They thought this ability was good for a body guard. They began to train me in the 1800's to become one of their bodyguards."

"Never wanted to become a Shadow?" Kirsa was intrigued in finding out about Lars' history.

Lars took his time before answering. "I did, very much so, want to be a Shadow. Yet one cannot ask to be one, you have to be asked by an Inner Council member or nominated by the General Council."

"I find it hard to believe that your name never was brought up," Kirsa stated. Lars had always been named as one of the best. She also knew that if she kept pestering him he would tell her everything.

"It was Sebastian who voted against me each time. The vote needs to be unanimous."

It clicked when he said that. "Sebastian

vaguely remembered you didn't he? He could not remember you exactly but he knew you were older then you were telling everyone else, to him that meant you were hiding something."

"The Council makes all these rules about what we can and cannot do," Lars snapped. "What is considered humane or inhumane. Why should we care what humans think of us?" Lars asked her with such fierceness that she felt herself pull back in her seat.

"What rule did you break?" Kirsa inquired, she really didn't want to hear the answer.

"I returned to my village ten years after my death. I expected to find my family dead but three of my siblings survived," Lars told her. She could feel the dread coming over her. "I saw them living their lives. My brother had taken over my family's property and my two sisters married well. I was spotted by my brother, he knew what I had become and tried to kill me."

"You killed him," Kirsa whispered.

Lars laughed. "I killed all of them. I wiped them all out like the plague should have."

Kirsa gasped. She couldn't believe what he had just said. "When it was discovered what I had done, the original Council decided that death would be too easy for me; instead they forbade me from having any official position on the Council. It was then I realized that something had to be done about the Council."

Everything clicked into place. "Not only are you the current Father, but you created it as payback for what the Council did to you," Kirsa surmised.

"What was I supposed to do? Sit back and accept my punishment," he looked down at his watch. "You need to go back to your cell."

****

Ayden sat on the edge of the bed he and Kirsa shared, Zero was curled on it looking at him as if he knew some- thing was wrong. Ayden felt a faint tugging on his mind as if someone was trying to get through, which could be the case.

Kirsa. He thought in his mind.

I know his reason. Also Sara is in a storm cellar behind bars. Kirsa told him.

Ok. Where are you? He had a pen and was writing down what she was telling him.

In the cellar, also. It's the one closest to the mines.

Ayden jotted it all down; complete with all

the details she could give him. She sounded tired.

Babe, are you ok? He asked, the paramedics that were going to be on call wanted to know.

They are drugging my water. Someone is coming.

With that she was out of his head. He closed his eyes and clenched his fist so tight that blood formed where his fingers dug in. They were working on a plan, but with both of them in different locations it was going to be tricky.

Chapter Thirty Five

Lars was at his desk staring at a picture. It was an old painting of a young girl with deep brown hair and eyes. She was around eight at the time the picture had been painted. It was a small miniature. Wherever Lars had gone that picture had gone with him. When he heard the knock on the door he slid it into his drawer.

"Come in," he called, focusing on losing his accent.

Veronica came slowly into the room due to the crutches Nick had given her. He could not help but smile at her outfit; she was wearing oversized gym shorts and a t-shirt. Chris and Nick were lending her clothes, since all she was the ruined suit she wore when she escaped to the house. Lars got up and helped her get situated in a chair.

"How are you doing?" he asked her, pouring her some coffee from the coffee urn.

Veronica took a sip before she answered. "I'm doing alright. The crutches are more of pain then anything, but Nick yells when he catches me walking without them."

"I asked for you because I have a favor for you," he told her.

"Alright, and what is it?"

Lars sat on the edge of the desk with a folder in his hand, "Tomorrow night is the witnessing. I am busy with arranging how to get everyone here without alerting attention."

"I can imagine that would be quite difficult," Veronica said. From what Nick had told her, they were expecting at least fifty top church officials to come between now and to-morrow afternoon. To do that without anyone being seen would be complicated.

Lars looked at the file on his desk which happened to be Veronica's church file. Every member had one, no matter how low or high they were in the organization. "It says that you have been to two witnesses?"

Veronica seemed surprise for a moment that there was a file on her. She had them on the lower members of her area. Trying not to itch her wound, she thought of the question asked.

"Yes two," Veronica explained. "The first was when I was just an initiate. Anton Black had received permission to bring me to one."

"I remember the petition for you to attend one, it is not our usual practice to allow non-initiate's into a witnessing."

"It was an honor to be there, and strengthened my faith," Veronica assured him. "The second was two years ago."

"Correct me if I am mistaken, but both came to the church to repent?" Lars asked. The procedures varied depending on the type of witnessing. Those that came to the church to seek repentance for their sins stood a chance of surviving. Those who were found would die from the proceedings.

"Yes, both had come seeking salvation. They were both were-animals. I understand that the procedures are differ- ent."

"They are. With me trying to arrange for people to get here, I am not going to have time to interview Kirsa." Lars handed Veronica a clipboard with a packet clipped to it. "When we do a witnessing like this, we go over their crimes and what they are repenting for. In the packet are the questions that Kirsa needs to answer for tomorrow night. I would like you to go through them with her. Chris will have her set up in the interrogation room and Nick will help you get down there."

****

Kirsa sat in her cell leaning against the cold damp stone. Staying linked to Ayden was draining; she only pulled at his mind when she had something to tell him. Sara sat across from her in her cell. Sara was focused on the young girl who was curled up in the cell next to hers. They had spent the day signing in the language they created when they were children.

Sara was pretty certain the girl was a teenager and a were-animal. She didn't think it was a cat, she smelled ca- nine. It was difficult to be certain because of all the old smells that were mingled in the cellar. All Kirsa knew was that the girl had not moved much since Kirsa had arrived.

Sara and she heard the door open from above. Within a few seconds Chris came down the stairs. He unlocked Kirsa's cell door and brought her to her feet without saying anything. Grabbing her by the arm he pulled her behind him.

He brought her to the iron door. The three cells were completely open with the exception of the bars. But the room behind the iron door was made of cement walls. There was no window in the door or anything. Kirsa saw alarm flash in Sara's eyes as Chris pulled her into the room.

The room was eight by eight. A single bulb dangled from the ceiling. One wall was covered in shelves and metal cabinets. There was a large medical table in the center of the room. Pushed to the side were some chairs. Kirsa almost wanted to breathe a huge sigh of relief when Chris had her sit in one of the metal chairs. He took out some handcuffs, then proceeded to chain her arms and legs to the chair.

He stopped before he left the room, "Veronica will be in, in a moment."

Kirsa looked around the room and noticed two security cameras stationed in the corners across from the door. Out- side the door, she heard faint voices. Even with her excellent hearing, Kirsa could not make out what they were saying through the iron door. The door opened, Veronica hobbled in on crutches. She sneered when she saw Kirsa. Nick came in after her to help her get a chair for her. After Veronica was settled, Nick left the room shutting the door.

Veronica sat in her chair with hatred and murder shown in her eyes. Kirsa knew that she would not kill unless ordered by Lars. In one of her hands, Veronica held a clip board. She sat down on the metal chair next to the bed and propped her crutches against the wall.

"The Father is currently notifying the other heads of your capture. They will be coming for your witnessing tomorrow." Veronica explained.

"Witnessing me?" Kirsa asked.

A slow smile spread over Veronica's face. "Yes, witness. I will explain it all when we are done with the questions."

"Oh Goody," Kirsa replied under her breath.

Veronica glared at her and uncapped the pen. "I will be asking several questions pertaining to how you have lived your life. This will be used for the list of charges in your witnessing. The first one is what your classification is?"

Kirsa raised an eyebrow. "My classification?"

"Whether you are Were, Vamp, etc; we like to hear the person admit to what they are." Veronica explained.

"Oh well then human and witch," Kirsa replied. She got amusement out of the surprise in Veronica's face when she said witch. She usually went with pagan, but it was worth it to see Veronica eyes bulge out of her head.

"Are you purposely being difficult?" Veronica asked her. "We know you are not human."

"Well technically my DNA says I am, and since I have not been bitten in order to become a were and have yet to take the final Kiss to turn into a vampire. I am a just a human who practices paganism and witchcraft." Kirsa explained.

Veronica sighed and wrote down what she said. "You are not a regular human and we all know that."

"That's funny I think the same about you," Kirsa told her with a smile.

Ignoring her comment Veronica continued, "Next question. Do you believe that those protected under the Paranormal Laws deserve to live?"

Kirsa just stared at her. "I have a question for you. Do you know anything about your Father?"

"He is an amazing man who is truly touched by God," Veronica replied.

Kirsa could not help but laugh. "He's touched alright but not by God. Veronica, do you know where he came from, what his name is, how he came to power, why he prefers only working during the night, have you seen him eat any food?"

"SILENCE!" Veronica screamed. "You have no right to question him. He is fasting to prepare himself for the witnessing. He is a far better person then you ever will be. He punishes those deemed to be evil. He does not fear going up against the Vampire Council brats. If anything he has shown that he is far stronger than those demons."

"He did kill Ivan and Isabella," Kirsa mumbled. "Isn't it odd that a human could kill two vampires?"

Veronica laughed at the statement. "Our Father has killed more than two vampires. If only you knew how many he has hunted down with his bare hands."

Kirsa shook her head. For the first time she began to feel sorry for Veronica. "I'm so sorry Veronica."

"Sorry for what?"

"That you have fallen for all of his lies. Your Father, is not a man of God, he is not your savior. He is a vampire; he is using your faith to help him over take the Vampire Council."

Veronica stood, forgetting about her leg and

crutches. Her anger numbed the pain. "Those are lies. Horrible lies!"

"Really then why does he not go out in the sun? Have you seen what he drinks? Does he come across almost too human?"

Kirsa saw Veronica's hand move. She could have stopped it but chose not to. The slap caused her head to hit the wall. Veronica spat at her and then turned and stormed out of the room.

Nick came in and dragged her out of the chair and threw her into her cell. "You will pay for whatever you said to her."

When doors were sealed from above, Sara stared at Kirsa. Taking a deep breath Kirsa began to fill Sara in on what happened.

Chapter Thirty Six

Dietrich translated the encrypted message. It was close to six in the morning and he was almost ready to turn in for the day. However it was close to midnight in Grabenberg, Ayden just sent him an update on what was happening.

Dietrich had a feeling when he was done reading it he would not be turning in for the night. Dietrich printed the document and then ran all the security protocols to erase the message so it could not be traced. There was a knock on the door of his sitting room, he gave permission for the person to enter. Sebastian walked in.

"I saw your light on still," Sebastian responded entering Dietrich's suite of rooms.

"I got an update from Grabenberg," Dietrich told him showing him the paper.

Sebastian sat down and watched Dietrich read the document. He watched as his friend face became as still as marble, the eyes turned black, and his jaw was set hard. The news could not be great, however if it was horrible he knew that Dietrich would have reacted differently.

"Is all alright?" Sebastian asked when Dietrich put the paper down.

"I'm going to kill the girl, if she survives I swear I will kill her," Dietrich bellowed, slamming the paper on the desk.

Sebastian chuckled to himself, he often found himself saying that about his own children. It only meant that he was right, that the news involved Kirsa. Some murmured about how Dietrich had no children, but then they had never seen him with Kirsa. Especially in the last five years, the two had become what each other had lost: a father and a daughter to each other. Not many knew Dietrich's history; there was only Shamus and himself who knew about Dietrich's family.

He had a wife, Gretchen, and a daughter

named Liesle. They were vampires like he was; Gretchen had given birth to Liesle before she went through the final change. Liesle had just become a vampire when Gretchen and she were abducted and held hostage. Dietrich was about two hundred at the time and a member of the General Council.

The Inner Council did everything they could, but they had been lied to. When they handed over the ransom, and two prisoners, Dietrich was handed two charred corpses that belonged to his wife and daughter. Those responsible were found and dealt with. Dietrich had never remarried or had a long term relationship since then.

"What has Kirsa done?" Sebastian asked.

Dietrich looked up; he almost forgot that Sebastian was there. He looked and saw that the door was closed. "She went out to run errands with Phil, a were-lion, and was abducted. They managed to incapacitate Phil, and got her that way."

Sebastian thought he felt his eyes pop out of his head. He went to say something but Dietrich held his hand up. Dietrich continued. "I'm furious she would do that but at the same time she is able to relay key information."

"How?"Sebastian, after mumbling a few swears in French under his breath.

"Ayden and she can read each other's minds," Dietrich was not going to focus on the reason why they could, "So he is reading her every thought and has drawn out a map of the hideout. Through Kirsa, he has confirmed our worst fear. Lars is our spy and the current head of the Church of Light. She also has learned some information about him that I want to pass on to Wyrm and see if he can find out more. Sara has not been harmed much, which is a positive."

"Did Al say what she learned?" Sebastian asked.

Dietrich looked up at his friend. There had never been secrets between them. "That you were right, you knew him somehow and remembered him. Sebastian, he killed Bella."

Sebastian sat in silence for a moment. Knowing who killed her did not change the fact that she was still dead. Yet in a way he felt strangely at peace with the knowledge that it was Lars who killed her and not someone else. Because he knew that when this was done Lars would be punished in the most fitting way possible and that made Sebastian feel as if justice would prevail.

"I won't tell my wife, I'm not sure it would do her any good. Also, find a replacement for me for the trial; I would be a biased judge if I were to serve, which would defeat the purpose. I want to watch him pay for what he did to Bella and the others. I can't enjoy that from the judge's seat."

"I have left my orders in this folder," Dietrich told his friend handing him the folder.

"How are you leaving?"

"A good friend of mine is flying from Berlin into NYC on a very private plane. She has offered me a ride."

After a quick discussion with Adam, while his wife and him were feeding their kids, Adam agreed to take Dietrich to the airport. Knowing time was of the essence, no one waisted anytime. Ann packed up food for Adam to take in the car and gave Dietrich a travel mug of heated blood. Then they were both in one of the armored cars driving toward Berlin.

Adam drove the car to one of the back entrances to Berlin's airport. He showed his security pass and was told where to take the car. He then continued to one of the private hangers and pulled into it. Air Force One was there along with an array of security and cars. Adam got out and nodded to one of the Secret Service Agents that he knew. Walter came over and they shook hands. Walter signaled for the hanger door to be closed. While they waited they caught up on   their lives.

When they heard the loud bang signaling that it had closed Adam walked to the back of the car and knocked on the back passenger door. It opened and Dietrich got out of the car. He had worn a black suit with red dress shirt and red and black striped tie. He also wore a dark pair of sunglasses so that his pale eyes would not disturb those who were not use to them.

"Good morning sir," Walter said bowing to Dietrich.

"It is good to see you Mr. Smith. Your family is well?" Dietrich asked.

"Yes sir, they are good. Do you have any luggage?"

"Yes in the trunk," Dietrich told him. "May Adam walk with me to the plane?"

Walter nodded. Adam walked with Dietrich toward the plane. They stopped a few feet before the steps.

"In your desk I have left you an encrypted drive that contains everything the Council will need to know, also on it is my will and the most updated version of Kirsa's," Dietrich began. "If anything does happen to Kirsa and myself you are to get my estate and fortune, if to both of us then you are my sole beneficiary."

Adam went to say something but stopped. "Nothing is going to happen. You are going to get there and Kirsa will have saved the day."

Dietrich smiled and gave Adam a quick hug. He caught the faint scent of Chanel No 5 and looked up. In the door way of the plane was Nora Jensen, also known as Madame President. She was 37 years old, not only the first female president but the youngest one at that. Nora wore jeans, an Oxford University shirt and a Yankee baseball cap. Her red hair was pulled back in a ponytail, and her green eyes were sparkling.

"I thought I heard you out here," Nora said descending the steps with two secret service agents behind her. "Hello Adam."

"Hello Madame President," Adam said kissing her on the cheek. He had worked as press secretary for her when she was Governor of South Carolina. When she had won the Presidency she wanted to him to reprise that role but he couldn't because of his own security issues.

"How are Anne and the two munchkins?" She asked.

"Good, we were sorry that we couldn't meet up with you on your visit," he told her.

"Don't worry, there will be time for us to

get together and spend time with each other again. We should get going," she told them.

Adam nodded and saluted both of them before walking away to his car. Nora motioned Dietrich to join her in the plane. Orders had been given that only when the plane was completely sealed and all blinds drawn could the hanger doors be opened. She walked to her office with Dietrich following her.

She faced her two guards who took position on either side of the door and then she and Dietrich entered the office on Air Force One. It technically was one of the safest rooms for him to be on since there were no windows in it. When the door shut Nora hugged Dietrich, he wrapped his arms around her also. For a moment it did not matter who they each were. Then they parted and each took a seat.

"So to what do I owe this great honor?" Nora asked.

"Grabenberg, N.J." he told her. He saw understanding flash into her eyes.

"How does it pertain to you besides your people being killed?" she asked. She was aware of what was going on and that OPIA was handling the case.

"The cult, the Church of Light, infiltrated the Vampire General Council and also managed to get some information from the Inner Council," he explained.

How the hell did they do that?"

"Inside person. One who happened to be our most trusted bodyguard."

"Lars?" Nora gasped. She laid a hand on his. "How's Kirsa handling this?"

He smiled bitterly, "Well she was going to turn herself over but they took her at some point yesterday." He saw the shock and horror in her eyes and felt her hand squeeze his. "The irony is that before the ambush, plans had been made on how to take the cult down."

"I understand, but how are you so calm?" she asked. In his shoes, if it was one of her own children, she would drop everything to be there.

"Ayden can tune into her thoughts and vice versa," Dietrich replied. "Lars does not know."

"How?" Then awareness flashed into her eyes, she blushed for a moment. "I understand completely."

He stared at her for a moment and she just smiled at him with that coyness that drove him nuts sometimes. Dietrich shook his head and sipped the drink she had given him.

"How are Darin and Kayla?" Dietrich asked referring to her 13 year old son and 9 year old daughter.

"They were both mad that they couldn't come. But they are with my late husband's parents so they are being spoiled rotten," she told him.

Dietrich laughed. He knew Edward and Alice Jensen and they would spoil their only set of grandchildren.

"When do they start school?" he asked.

"In another month, they both opted to take German as an elective this year," she told him with a smile.

"Really?"

"They are hoping it will convince me to visit their Uncle Dietrich over the winter holiday," Nora told him.

Dietrich went still. "Nora," he pulled his hand from hers.

"Dietrich Nacht, don't start that argument with me again," she said in a warning tone. "I like to think of it as fostering a friendly relationship with our allies."

"That's a way of putting it," Dietrich replied dryly. Nora just laughed at him. This was going to be a long flight.

****

Jeff waited at a small private Sussex County airport for the two person plane to land. He was the only one that would not be noticed leaving Grabenberg and coming back. The press had descended on the town when word got out that Kirsa had been kidnapped. Currently, Ayden was sleeping and Tony was giving another press conference.

Al was heading the investigation publicly and so far there had been no leaks about any of the plans that had be made before the kidnapping. He watched the plane come into sight and then a few minutes later land. It pulled into the hanger that he was currently parked in.

Getting out of the car he watched as the engine was turned off and the propellers slow down. Both doors of the plane opened and two men got out. He smiled at the dignified man in the black suit and dark sunglasses. A guard threw a blanket over him to shield him from the sun as they walked him into the back of the hanger where Jeff waited with the car. Shrugging the blanket off, Dietrich shook hands with Jeff. They had met on several occasions.

"Any word?" Dietrich asked as he climbed

into the backseat of the car with his luggage.

"So far both women are holding up. We also now know there is a third girl being held with them," Jeff told him. "When I left, Tony was giving a press conference about how the search for the location is going."

"What about her?" Dietrich asked.

"Checked in about two hours ago, Ayden is currently catching a quick nap," Jeff told him pulling onto the road. "He is completely drained. Al got in a huge argument with him because he's been supplementing sleep with blood. Al had to tell him to sleep or he was off the case."

"Vampires, and I am sure you know with Sara, are very territorial of their partners," Dietrich told him. "They will stop at nothing."

"He is no use though if he is drained."

"That is true. Do we know what is going on, where she is?"

"Since we last talked to you, they are bringing some of the other regional leaders of the cult to the hideout. We'r not sure how they are going to be getting them into town without causing suspicion. They are going to be bearing witness of Kirsa. None of us know what that means," Jeff said catching him up. He saw Dietrich's face turn to stone.

"I will give a detailed explanation when we get there, but in short, it means a trial where they read a list of complaints and crimes against the person and then lay judgment," Dietrich explained.

"That's what we were thinking. Before you landed I got a call from Phil, who is the leader of Sara's pack, we believe three regional heads are there. One of our guys got a glimpse of three people at the house that were not there yesterday or earlier this morning."

Chapter Thirty Seven

"Searchers continue to look for heiress Kirsa Heinrich and Medical Examiner Dr. Sara Cliver," The news reporter was saying. "Ms. Heinrich was abducted in broad daylight. Her guards were poisoned during the attack. For the surrounding area this is a major blow to a town that has suffered much over the last few months."

Lars turned the television off as the police scanner went off in the background. He sat at his desk with his hands clasped trying to come up with his next move. He had not expected the news about Kirsa to get out so soon. But America loved their millionaires, closest thing they had to royalty.

Lars heard noise from outside his office and he realized that people might be arriving, looking at his watch; he saw that it was almost noon. They would start moving things into the mine at some point through the underground passage. The old mine boss had a tunnel connecting the house to his office in the mine. That way if the miners went on strike or there was a disaster in the mine he could get out. Today they would be using it to get people into the mines without others seeing.

There was a knock on his door and then it opened. One of the heads from South Carolina came in. He bowed his head at Lars. He was a stocky man, a banker, and very wealthy.

"Henry, have a seat," Lars greeted the middle age man. He motioned to a seat. "I was not expecting you so soon."

"There were a few of us that met in Virginia late last night and drove here," Henry explained. "Father, I must admit some of us are troubled."

Lars angled his head. He caught the scent of nervousness coming off of Henry. "Oh? What about?"

"How public the abduction of Miss. Heinrich was. The others were done so that no one knew, and this one was done out in the open with dozen of witnesses," Henry told him.

"I understand, however it was one of the rare times that she was out without either of her bodyguards," Lars sipped his drink. "I felt that it might be the only way to ensure that she made it here without the involvement of authorities."

"I understand that, but it once again is making us look bad. A liberal news agency has already made the connection to us," Henry countered back. "We were just putting South Carolina behind us, now with all this going public we have concerns."

"What do you mean all this?" Lars asked confused.

Henry studied the man's face. It was hard to interpret what he was thinking. "Did you not hear the press conference this morning?"

"I heard the one last night to confirm that Kirsa was abducted."

Henry let out a breath. He had to draw the short straw didn't he? "Well my grace, Chief White gave another this morning. In which the cult was implicated in the murders and the abduction, that they had a key witness and strong evidence. It has come to their attention that it seems as if the head of this church is the one issuing these orders."

Lars was out of the chair quicker than Henry could register. Before Henry realized, Lars was leaning over him. "When did this go on?"

Trembling, Henry tried to speak. "A few hours ago, around 9am."

Lars looked up as he broke Henry's neck in frustration. Since the body was there, he decided to drink fresh human blood. Something he had not done in a very long time, he'd deal with body later.

****

Kirsa stared at the ceiling above her wondering what would happen to her today. She wondered if what she said to Veronica had sunk in or in the very least raised some questions. Kirsa had no idea what her thoughts were when she left. For the first time since she had been taken she began to feel scared that she could die. Part of her though wondered what would happen if she was killed, would she rise? Or would she stay dead? She heard the storm door open and someone begin to make the trek down the stone stairs.

Lars came down with a tray that held two plates of toasts and two glasses of water. He unlocked Sara's cell door and brought the food in. Taking a key out, he unhooked her one hand from the shackles so she could eat. He closed the cell door and locked it, then went to Kirsa's and did the same.

"Did you sleep well?" he asked Kirsa leaning against the wall and watched the two girls eat.

Kirsa just looked at him and then went back to eating. She was not going to answer him unless it was needed.

Lars watched Kirsa eat and the second she finished her water he was in the cell again. He punched her in the face then crouched in front of her, with a finger he tilted her face up so he could see the bruising on her face. Her right was starting to swell close; he moved her face so that she was looking him in the eye. He held her there by the chin.

"Do you fear me?" he whispered.

"No," Kirsa told him.

He smiled slowly, "Oh you will."

Taking the keys from his back pocket he unlatched both the shackles and dragged her to her feet. Grabbing her hair he dragged her into the interrogation room.

Lars walked over to her and pushed her toward the metal table. He motioned for her to get on it and then to lie down. When she did he got out the restraints and tied her to the table. Her legs were tied up so they were spread apart and her arms were tied above her head. She felt the cold steel of the scissors as he began to cut her jeans off of her.

There was no sound except for her breathing and her heart beat. She could hear the scissors cut through the denim and then humid air hit her legs, with a tug Lars had removed her pants off the table. Then she watched him as he cut her t-shirt off so that the only thing she was wearing was her bra and underwear. Kirsa turned her head to the side and there in the corner was a security camera with a small microphone attached to it. If there was a camera, it meant someone was watching.

Lars discarded her clothes into the garbage can and then sat down on the stool with casters so that he could easily move around the room.

"Do you know what Tony did?" Lars shouted with a hint of accent. His façade was faltering. He paid no attention to cameras in the corner of the room.

Kirsa shook her head. She was unsure of what to say, what to deny or what to even think. There were so many things that could have happened while she was down here.

"He gave a press conference. Connecting the cult to the murders saying they had a star witness?" Lars told her. He was an inch from her face. "Who is it?"

"Well since there is no chance of you

getting to the person, Louis. Or should I say Alois," Kirsa replied.

He stared at her unsure of what to say. This time he was speechless. He felt betrayal. Lars had handpicked Alois to be his assassin. A monk turned killer who was seeking forgiveness, it seemed so perfect.

"How does it feel Lars, to be betrayed by your own kind?" Kirsa asked. "Even he saw flaws in your vision."

Lars took black leather gloves out from under the table and put them on. He then pulled his sleeves down over them. Carefully he picked up a black colored glass bottle that had an eyedropper for a cap. Kirsa felt the fear rise in her throat.He carefully unscrewed the top and made sure to pull a few drops of the clear liquid into the dropper.

"I hear this has some effect on you," he told her with a smile. "Should be fun to watch."

He positioned her so that she was on her side and then she felt the searing pain as he dropped the Holy Water onto her back. Because he could not see her face and neither could the camera, she squeezed her eyes shut and bit the inside of her lip. She could fill the metallic taste of blood in her mouth but it did nothing to the pain as she could smell her own skin burning. Somewhere in the background of the pain she could hear Lars laughing.

Lars screwed the top back on and set it aside for later use. The next thing he took out was silver, pure liquid silver. He put a syringe in the vial and keeping her on her side he drew a nice line of silver over her back. He watched as her muscles bunched, but she had yet to make a noise at all. As he watched her skin bubble he rolled her onto her back and was disappointed to see that she had yet to shed any tears.

"I'm surprised, you have lasted longer than the others without making a sound," he whispered in her ear. She turned her head away from him.

"Isabella began to scream as soon as I started to put the liquid silver on her face," he told Kirsa. "She was always a vain one."

Lars watched Kirsa on the table. She had yet to make a noise even with the Holy Water and liquid silver. It was obvious her body reacted to it, but not a sound from her. He leaned against the wall thinking of more ways to torture her.

"I wonder what Ayden will think of your back, now that it will be horribly scarred," Lars remarked.

At the mention of Ayden's name, she felt

her concentration wavier and knew he would feel the pain she was in. She focused back to blocking Ayden out of her head when she felt his rage.

"Did you model the cellar after a medieval dungeon?" Kirsa asked him. "You've had firsthand experience with them I bet."

Lars grabbed a metal chair and brought it down over her knee. Kirsa bit back the scream that was filling her body. Lars threw the dented chair into the corner, and climbed onto the table. He knew that Nick and Veronica were watching and if they began to wonder if he would kill Kirsa in the most painful process possible.

"You are becoming the monster you criticized from the media and books," she told him.

Lars wrapped his hand around her neck and began to choke her, when she almost passed out he stopped choking her and brought her head up.

"STOP!" He then dropped her head onto the table and she went under.

When she came too she was in her cell again. Her leg laid out an odd angle and her ribs hurt, she tried to ignore the pain of her back or the burning sensation in her lungs.

Everywhere hurt on her. Her clothes were now in tatters leaving her no defense against the chill. She closed her eyes and slumped against the stone wall.

****

Veronica left the small security room, she was shaking from what she had seen. No mortal could have moved the way the Father did. The violence toward Kirsa was unlike Veronica had ever seen. Kirsa had kept calling him 'Lars', the name that belonged to the her bodyg aurd. Hearing footsteps coming toward her she saw Nick.

"Could you help me clean up the Father's office," Nick asked her. "He want's it all perfect for the Wittnessing."

Veronica nodded. She followed him on her crutches as they headed to what had once been the living room. All the windows had been boarded up so that not a drop of sunlight could enter this room. The Father had explained that no one should be able to see into the rooms they would be using. But doubt was starting to creep into Veronica's mind.

Nick held the door open for her so that she could enter first. "He just wants any dishes to be picked up, anything that looks out of place to be straightened," Nick told her.

"Of course," Veronica said. "I'll take his desk."

"If you need help let me know," Nick replied as he began to pick up newspapers and crumpled paper up.

Veronica made her way over to the desk and began to pile up some of the dishes. There were a few coffee mugs left by his computer so she went to grab them. She bit back a gasp as she stared into one of the cups. There was the obvious tint of coffee around the interior of the cup. But around the bottom was a faint reddish brown color that resembled the color of dried blood.

"I'm going to bring the mugs to the kitchen," Veronica told Nick. "They are the easiest for me to carry."

"Sure," Nick agreed. "When I'm done here I'll bring the plates."

Veronica nodded in agreement then headed out of the office. She took the stairs to the basement where the kitchen was. Setting the mugs down next to the sink she leaned her crutches against the counter. Turning the water on hot, she got ready to wash the mugs.

"Ah, I see that Nick found you," the Father stated entering the kitchen.

"Yes, he is still tidying your office," Veronica

said hoping her voice was calm. "I was about to start washing the dishes from your office."

The father eyed the mugs that were sitting on the counter. "Why don't you start typing up the reports we will need and I'll wash my own mess?"

"Are you sure?" Veronica asked. "I really don't mind."

"You shouldn't be on your feet so much," the Father pointed out.

"Alright," Veronica said. She grabbed her crutches and headed away. Her mind filled with more questions than answered.

Chapter Thirty Eight

Dietrich was brought into the Clark's basement by Ellen Clark. Ayden was up and working on his morning blood when Dietrich came down. Ayden set the glass down and walked over Dietrich and they hugged each other. They moved apart and Dietrich greeted Al who had walked over to shake hands.

Dietrich walked to where Ayden sat. Ayden looked up, he had sensed him entering the room. He went to say some- thing but Dietrich held a finger.

"Do not blame yourself, someone told me once that keeping a person like Kirsa under constant guard would only make her try to break free," Dietrich told him. "There is some logic behind that. Do I hear correctly that you two can read each other's thoughts?"

Ayden was unsure how to handle that question. "Yes, since she's been abducted we have been able to communicate a few times. Enough to let us know what is going on and where they are going to be."

"I am not going to dwell on the how this came about, because it is benefiting us," Dietrich decided. "Now what is this about a witnessing?"

"Kirsa told me that they will be witnessing her tonight," Ayden told him.

"Wyrm and I have been working on them since you left," Dietrich told him. "Witnessing to them, means they have a sinner who would like to repent. All the leaders and congregation of the area are brought in. The sinner then explains their crimes and why they should be forgiven. It is voted on and the judgment is given."

"Yeah but Kirsa is not doing this willingly," Al replied.

"No she's not, and that when it begins to differ," Dietrich replied. "When they themselves capture a sinner they still have a witnessing but it changes slightly. Instead of the entire congregation being invited, just the leaders are brought in. Depending on who the person is, determines how many leaders are invited. The sinner is then brought before them; their sins are read before the leaders. The leaders then discuss and come up with a fitting judgment. Usually this leads to death."

"Well we have until sun down and then we move," Ayden told them. "From what Kirsa has been able to determine, sundown is when they are going to start it."

****

Nick had assembled them in the basement. So far there were twenty and roughly that many still had to show. Nick has been meeting them at a hiking trail and leading them to the house through the old mine shafts. Veronica was watch- ing the prisoners on the video, when he went to check on her she was silent and looked out of it. He had seen Lars quietly enter the house and knew that he had been with the prisoners.

Lars carefully cleaned up and changed clothes in his room. He touched up the stage makeup he wore so that he did not seem so pale. When he walked out of his office Nick was waiting for him to show him to their guests.

"Did she crack?" Nick asked him as they headed to the stairs.

"Not a sound from her," Lars said disgusted. He liked it when they screamed.

They descended the stairs and Lars walked into the room of his followers. He greeted all of them as he went to the head of the room. After a moment of silent prayer he opened the meeting.

"Brothers, today is a great day," Lars began. "Today we bear witness to the sins of Kirsa Heinrich. She is a member of the oldest vampire blood line, and with her death all from her line shall perish with her."

"How are we certain they will perish?" A leader from Alabama asked.

Lars held the man with a stare. "If they do not die because of her death it will lead the Council into civil war when they find out about her identity. As we know, Miss Heinrich suffers from a rare genetic disorder in which her blood is similar to that of vampires. Earlier this morning I tired getting information from her but she will not speak. We do know, from her earlier encounter with Miss Adams, that Holy Water affects her."

"Well then," a member form California spoke, "Why don't you introduce us to this young woman and we each take turns anointing her with Holy Water. We, after all, have to prepare her for tonight?"

Lars smiled slowly as the leaders all agreed with this. It was so simple to turn small minds into violent people.

****

Kirsa awoke again and still sat in the corner with her back against the cool stone walls. Ayden kept trying to get through to her but she would not allow him to see what had been done to her. When the right moment came she would remove the block she put up and let him see all. Kirsa flinched when she heard movement and then she saw Sara picking the lock on her cell. Sara came in and crouched next her.

"I blocked the security camera," Sara whispered to her. Kirsa stared at her dumbfounded. "Very diluted silver apparently can't hold me. How bad are you hurt?"

"A broken rib, sprained ankle, he busted my knee, I think while I was unconscious he injected some stuff into my lungs because they burn, and the list goes on," Kirsa told her, this was not the moment to focus on what happened.

"If you drink blood, will you heal faster?"

Sara asked her.

"Theoretically, yes. Why?"

Not answering, Sara reopened a wound on her arm courtesy of Lars with one of her teeth and held it too Kirsa. "Drink."

Kirsa stared at her friend not sure what to think or do. The young girl, who they found out was named Bridgette, was watching from her cell. Slowly the girl had started to open up them. Now she played look out while Kirsa drank. When Kirsa finished, Sara helped her lean back against the wall. She then relocked the cell and did the same with her own.

"My father died, which meant I had to go live with my mom and step-dad," Bridgette started filling the silence. "The problem is, I'm a were-wolf and my stepdad thinks we should be hunted. So I ran away to go live with my best friend up in Warwick, NY. I was taken from a bust stop."

"My pack, though filled with cats, has been known to adopt a were-wolf attending the university since the closest pack is two hours away," Sara replied making the girl smile for the first time in days. She wrapped the new wound up with some scraps of bandages.

"We should get some rest," Kirsa said as the fresh blood began to run through her system.

"We're going to need all the energy we have for tonight."

Chapter Thirty Nine

*E*veryone was assembled in the Clark's basement. The Clarks had arranged for sandwiches to there for the team to eat. They also had ziti, garlic, bread, and pies. Tony protested but Ellen Clark told him no one was going hungry while at her house. After that both him and Al chose not argue with her over the amount of food. The only things they all agreed on was no alcohol because at any moment they would be heading out.

So they ate and joked and talked about nothing. Tony talked with Dietrich about what had been going on in each other's lives since they last saw each other. When Al and Tony saw that people were finishing up they both nodded to each other. Tony stood up and whistled, which silenced the room.

"Hello," Tony said. "It's 4pm. We have about two hours before we have to start getting into position."

Al handed Tony the list of teams. "This is how the teams are going to break down," Tony informed them."There are going to be five teams. The leaders of each team are as follows: Tony, Phil, Dietrich, Ayden and I. We have gotten permission to use Phil since he is a registered tracker. Jeff will be on Phil's team and be the police leader for that team. Our Swat Team will be with Dietrich, OPIA's will be going in with Al. Ayden and I will be taking the other two teams of officers. Ayden's team will be entering from the back where the cellar is located. They are using it to hold Sara and Kirsa. My team will go in through the front."

Tony looked around the room. "Ok Al's going to explain what you guys are going up against and who all is there."

Al nodded and took the floor. "Our number one priority is Lars. For those of you who don't know him we are passing a picture around. He will not have his Norwegian accent, according to our info he has dropped it for his role. We would like him alive, but if he has to be killed then do so. I want silver bullets in the guns, silver harms vampires. You also will have steel containers of Holy water.

"As far as we know all the other members are normal humans. Take them alive. We want as many alive so we break this cult down once and for all. Do I have any questions?"

No one raised a hand. Tony took the floor again. "We will hand out the lists of the groups. I want them collected after you are all assembled into them. Each one is numbered so don't try anything. If you do your off the assignment. We have already pulled three off."

He and Al took the lists and began handing them out to everyone. He glanced at his watch; it was about 4:30. By the time they finished with this and got ready it would be closer to seven. He just hoped nothing happened between now and then.

****

Kirsa and Sara looked at each other through their cells when they heard the upper door open. Someone was coming down- stairs; when they got the third stair they saw that it was Chris.

"Hello monsters," he replied walking to Kirsa's cell. He spit into Sara's cell before he opened the door to Kirsa's cell.

Chris crouched to Kirsa's level; she was still in the corner of her cell. "You look banged up darling; did the old man have some fun with you?"

Before she could say anything he yanked her up, Kirsa's face grimaced with pain and Chris laughed at it. She still refused to scream.

"You know the Father likes it when they scream," Chris whispered in her ear. "It turns him on. But it's pissing him off that he can't get one sound out of you."

He let her fall back to the ground and then threw the red bundle on top of her.

"You need to change into this," he informed her. He then turned and walked out her cell and up the stairs.

After recovering from the jarring her already abused body had taken, she looked at the red thing in her lap. She picked it up and saw that it was a red dress, one size fits all, it had no sleeves, and a low neck. There was a red rope belt to tie it so it would fit. It went all the way to the floor. Kirsa touched and cringed. The thoughts that clung to it were dark and horrible. Taking a deep breath she pulled herself up onto the cot so that she could slip the dress on.

Chris was standing next to the storm doors smoking when Veronica hobbled over to him. She had two brown paper bags. He raised his eyebrow at the bags.

"Food," she told him as she awkwardly made her way down the stairs.

She saw Sara watch her cautiously, Veronica unlocked the cell door and placed the bag next to Sara on the cot. She then unchained her hand again.

"Sandwich, apple and juice," Veronica told her. She turned and walked out of the cell and locked it.

Veronica then walked to Kirsa's cell and shook her head when she saw Kirsa. To think she had been afraid of her once. She unlocked the door and set the bag next to Kirsa on the bench. Kirsa opened her eyes and looked at Veronica. They stared at each other for a second and then Veronica walked out of the cell locking it. She made her way back up stairs. It was about 4pm and they had plenty of work to do to finish getting ready for the witnessing.

Chris helped her out of the cellar. "When do I retrieve her?"

Veronica looked at her watch,"Give her fifteen minutes to eat then go get her. Nick and

I will be out to help you with her."

She went to go back to the house but stopped and faced him again. "Chris, no tormenting the prisoner,"

He grumbled. They never let him have any fun with any of the prisoners. Just because he wasn't committed to the whole religious thing, they kept him around for all the dumb shit. He crushed his cigarette under his foot and lit a second one.

Chris watched as the sky began to darken, it looked like a storm might be rolling in at some point. He finished his cigarette and figured his fifteen minutes were up. Kirsa heard Chris coming down the stairs and looked at Sara. Chris took the keys he had out and walked over to Sara's cell. He opened it up and then made sure to chain her free hand back up. Then he locked her cell again and went to Kirsa's, he unlocked and walked in.

"Alright whore, get up," he instructed her.

Kirsa tried but her leg gave out. Chris cursed under his breath and walked to her. He then scooped her up in his arms. He cautiously went up the steep steps. She closed her eyes against the sunlight. The sun was beginning its descent which meant two things. Night was coming and so was the full moon.

They moved at an awkward pace towards the house, this confused her. Nick opened the back door and moved aside so that Chris could enter. By this point Kirsa had passed out from pain. They walked to basement door and cautiously proceeded down the stairs.

"The leaders and the Father already made their way to the mines," Nick informed him. "The Father wasn't sure he could control them if they saw her brought down."

"He left us a flashlight for the tunnel, right?" Chris asked. There were no lights in the tunnel, and the last time he went in there the Father had forgotten a flashlight.

"I have one ready just in case he forgot," Nick assured. "Veronica was also brought there, two of the leaders carried her."

"So it's just us?" Chris asked. Nick nodded and opened the hidden door.

There were two flashlights hanging on the side of the wall, Nick grabbed one and turned it on. He motioned for Chris to follow. Slowly they made their way through the tunnel, Nick made sure to highlight any uneven terrain so that Chris would not trip.

Kirsa realized she would have to rely on her senses to let Ayden know where they were going. Lars changed his mind about the ceremony being in the clearing like she had over- heard. Kirsa was showing Ayden in her mind where they were going, she kept her eyes open just a bit.

They approached a set of stairs and soon they were ascending them. They came to an old wooden door, Nick knocked and the lock clicked and soon the door opened. It would be an easy door for Ayden to get through. She saw that they were in an old office and then she was being laid down on the old desk. Water was thrown on her face, causing her to wake up.

"Good, you're awake," Nick said.

Kirsa looked around and saw that Chris had left. "Where's the cop?"

"He went to tell the Father you are here," Nick told her. He paused then whispered in her ear. "You will pay for your sins."

"They are ready, and he wants her walking in. He feels if she was carried in they might feel sorry for her," Chris said with some sort of enjoyment in his voice.

Carefully Nick helped her to her feet and put a hand around her to steady her. She nodded that it was ok and he slowly let go. Slowly they made their way through the tunnel until they reached a large cavern.

In the center of a large cavern was a wooden platform with a pole sticking out of the middle. Under the platform was a pile of wood and paper. Nick stopped at the stairs allowing Chris to drag her up the three steps, Nick helped him prop her up against the pole.

Veronica came out of one of the side tunnels to steady her. The two men worked tying her securely to the pole. When Nick pulled up the dress to tie her legs, he saw her knee and sucked in a breath. Even though he hated her, the sight of her mangled knee was gut wrenching. After a few more minutes they had her firmly attached.

Before the platform were rows of benches and toward the side of it was a podium for someone to speak from. Chinese lanterns were strong from the rock ceilings, speakers were set up on stands.

Lars stepped out of a tunnel; he would not have to reapply the sunscreen since they were now having it in the caves. He had changed into a light weight gray suit, navy blue shirt and a striped tie. Lars walked toward the platform and smiled at the progress that had been made in such short amount of time. Scratching at his chin, Lars thought it would be a good idea to video tape the Witnessing; it could be useful in conversion. Stepping towards the platform he nodded at Veronica, Chris and Nick.

"It's about 5pm, why don't you three go into the old meal area and eat with the others that way we can begin when everyone is done eating," Lars ordered them. "I will stay here with her."

Chris and Veronica finished securing her to the pole and walked off the podium. Lars stopped Nick.

"When you come out again, bring the video camera. I want this recorded," Lars instructed him.

"Sure thing, boss," Nick replied and continued to the old rusted trailer at the far end of the chamber.

Lars watched them enter one of the tunnels before he walked onto the platform. He stood before Kirsa and looked at her. She had a black eye; there were bruises on her arm and scratches here and there.

"It's a shame really that we have come to this," he told her in his 'Father' voice. "I had such hope for you."

"Meaning?" Kirsa whispered. Her throat was still sore from when he was strangling her earlier.

"That Anton would have been able to bring you around a few years ago. There would have been a lot less killing had you come then."

"Bullshit," Kirsa replied. "You would have found other people to torture and kill."

He laughed a dry yet maniacal laugh. "True. I do have this annoying thirst for blood."

Kirsa shut her eyes and went silent again. Part of her feared that they would not show up in time and she would be burnt to death. She hoped that Ayden got the visions she sent him so that they knew there was a change of venue. Would she turn if they killed her? Even if she did change, a vampire could not survive fire. She heard movement and looked to see Nick coming out   of the tunnel with video recorder.

"Where do you want it to be set up?" Nick asked Lars.

"In the center of the aisle. Make sure that you get the platform and the podium in the viewfinder," Lars told him. "Are they done eating?"

"They are finishing up," Nick said as he set the camera up. "Most of them are asking Veronica what it was like to go up against two monsters."

Lars nodded. "And so they should."

The next ten minutes seemed to tick by forever. Ayden sent her an image of them on their way to the caves, there was another team surrounding the house so that if anyone was there they would be taken care of. Apparently he got her message.

Noise was heard from the tunnel, and soon thirty church leaders came out of the eating area with Chris and Veronica. Nick helped Veronica to a seat in the first row; a chair had been set up for her. He and Chris sat in the bench next to her. The others, after staring at Kirsa first, took their seats and waited for the talking to come to a hush.

Lars walked to the podium and nodded to them all. Soon they were all silent. Nick got up and hit the record button on the camera, when he was sure it was recording he sat back down in his seat.

"Welcome brothers and sisters," Lars said. "I welcome you to this glorious evening where we will bear witness to a great sinner. Not only has this creature lived with vampires, but is currently sleeping with one as well." This got a reaction from the crowds.

Lars continued. "She also is practitioner of a pagan religion, speaks out against our organization and protects those considered protected under the Paranormal Laws. She sees nothing wrong with how she has lived her life, and refuses to repent. I permit that we question the witness before a judgment is reached."

The audience agreed to this. Lars nodded in satisfaction. Kirsa shook her head slowly. For the fact that Lars was a vampire he had no clue what was coming towards them.

We will be there within minutes. Ayden told her. *Hang in there.*

Hurry.

Lars walked away from the podium and walked up the platform steps. He stood to the side of Kirsa so that she could still be seen by the audience.

"State your name," Lars instructed.

"Kirsa Heinrich," she told him.

"What is your profession?"

"I'm an agent with OPIA."

The next handfuls of questions were similar to this, general questions that meant nothing. But Kirsa saw that as he asked questions each member took out a vial of Holy Water. That wasn't good.

"Is it true you are a descendent of Hagan Adulwulf?" Lars asked.

Kirsa looked at him and would not answer. He took the vial he held in a gloved hand and threw it on her. She knew it was supposed to be holy water yet there was no reaction to it when it hit her skin. Then she saw the look in Veronica's eye and realized what had happened. But thankfully Lars had not.

"Is it true you are the descendent of one of the original six children?" Lars asked differently.

"Maybe, but then that would make me your leader. Wouldn't it Lars?" she asked.

This caused confusion amongst the members.He smacked her so hard she blacked out for a moment. In her mind she saw Ayden breaking down the office door. She couldn't help but start to laugh. If only they knew what would be coming out of the tunnel in a moment.

"Answer my question bitch," Lars snarled. He drew a silver knife out and with a glove hand held it to her throat.

"Yes," Kirsa whispered. He dug the edge of the knife into her neck. "Yes I am a descendent of Hagan Adulwulf, rumored to be one of the original six bloodlines."

She watched his face as joy came over it. He thought that he finally had her where he wanted her.

"See brothers and sisters, she has confessed," Lars started. He had walked away from her and was now on the edge of the platform.

"But how did you know?" Kirsa asked. "How did you know a secret that those of the Inner Council don't even know?"

Lars turned and looked at her not sure what to do. Someone from the audience yelled for an answer, another was outraged by her speaking to him in such a way.

"There are a few people who are aware of my identity, all of them interconnected with the Inner Council."

Whispers began to spread among the audience, Veronica slowly got up and walked to the podium. In her hand was a vial of holy water. She slowly made her way up and walked over to Kirsa. The whispers died down.

"Before we punish we should test her with the Holy Water," Veronica said. "I know it works on her for I have seen it with my own eyes."

Veronica threw the contents of her bottle onto Kirsa and watched with the rest as nothing happened. She turned to Lars who was unsure of what was going on.

"Maybe she is no longer a sinner?" Veronica asked the crowd.

Lars rushed forward and shoved Veronica to the side, however he did it with his full strength causing her to hit the stone wall ten feet from the podium. Lars rubbed a drop of the water on Kirsa between his fingers and nothing happened. He turned and looked   at Veronica.

"She is in league with this woman and with the devil," Lars screamed pointing at Veronica. "That was regular water thrown on our sinner."

The crowd was totally confused by what was going on. Lars was losing his control over them. There were too many for him to control their minds.

"This leader of yours, he's a vampire. He has fooled every one of you," Kirsa yelled over the murmurs. Lars turned and cut her from the pole.

"I will kill you myself," he whispered. He motioned for Nick.

Nick came up the stairs. "You are losing control, and scaring the audience."

Using persuasion, he began to calm them down. "Brothers and sisters I am sorry for the dramatics. It has come out that one of our own is in league with this sinner. Mr. Cullen will lead the witnessing of the traitor. I will handle Miss Heinrich on my own."

Everyone had taken their seats again and appeared calm. Lars smiled at Kirsa and scooped her up over his shoulder; he began to walk toward one of the tunnels. He paused for a moment when he heard a noise in the distant. He laughed silently to himself.

The tunnel he had chosen was unlit and was a mile long. It ended in a small chamber that had been created by a dynamite blast. It could not be finished because it was found that had they gone deeper the tunnels would have collapsed.

Lars whistled as he walked down the tunnel. This was turning out better then he thought it would have. In the distance he heard some noises and what would appear to be gunshots. Lars noticed that Kirsa did not react which meant she did not hear it. When they reached the chamber he threw her down on to the floor. He chuckled when he watched her face grimace.

"You really don't want to make a noise do you?" he asked her.

Kirsa looked up at him and spat blood at him; he wiped it from his shirt then licked it off his finger.

Chapter Forty

When the teams reached the cavern it turned out the church leaders were armed. Ayden reloaded his gun; Dietrich was at the foot of the cave still. He was not to enter until they were all rounded up. Ayden made his way through the mass of people. Tony was propped up against a wall; one of officer was tying a makeshift bandage around his leg.

"I don't see Lars or Kirsa?" Tony told him. "Go find them. I'll be here."

"Where's Al?" Ayden asked. He had not seen him since the shots had started.

"Up on the podium. Dietrich said the cellars were guarded. He was told to wait outside while they swarmed the cellars."

"Just take it easy," Ayden told Tony.

Ayden rushed to the podium so fast that it appeared as if he came out of thin air. Al looked startled at first then shook his head.

"They killed Miss Adams just before we made our entrance and shot Mr. Cullen for trying to save her. According to Mr. Cullen here she betrayed them by helping the sinner."

"Will Mr. Cullen tell me where Lars took Kirsa?" Ayden asked staring at Nick.

Nick swallowed hard, "He took her down that tunnel."

Ayden rushed toward the tunnel, a man tried to stop him but he snapped his neck without thinking. There were more important things to worry about.

"Lars, why?" Kirsa asked as he pulled off his coat. "Why? Because I should have had the power, but I show lack of moral judgment," he spat at the ground. "Imagine fucking vampires telling me I lack morals."

"What made them think this?" Kirsa asked.

Lars looked at her. He stared at the entrance to the tunnel for he thought he saw movement. He laughed. "They saw me and believed I was the devil coming to call. I was. I killed them all. I drank their blood, I reveled in it all."

Kirsa shook her head. Even among

vampires, feeding off your family was the ultimate crime. The only reason he probably survived after the council learned of his deeds was because he believed he was his family died from the plague. At the same time he would never be able to get into the higher ranks. Unless of course you wipe out the Council and start a revolution and wipe the slate clean.

"I craved their blood from the moment I had been reborn," Lars continued. "For decades after I killed them, I still craved their blood. But because I acted on that craving I cannot gain entry into the upper levels."

"Even if the Council was killed the histories would still be there," Kirsa told him. "No matter how hard you tried you never destroyed the vaults in any of the places you blew up."

Lars turned and looked at her. "When I began to realize who your family really was and that the morons had no clue, I began to think if I seduce the daughter I could maybe be forgiven. You never had eyes for me only Ayden, you also wanted to be in love." At that he began to laugh.

"It's such a stupid human emotion," he told her. "Yet it also a powerful weapon. See if I kill you it will destroy Dietrich, Tony and Ayden. It will weaken the Council because their leader will be weakened."

"You honestly think you would survive killing me?" Kirsa asked him.

He crouched down and looked into her eyes. "I trained Ayden; he could never harm me even if I took your life."

"Lars," a voice said from the tunnel behind him.

Lars turned and saw Ayden there, he smiled. "Ah the heroic lover comes to save his dear maiden." Lars stood up. "What makes you think I will surrender to you?"

"I don't," Ayden told him. "Dietrich is here. In case you did not realize."

Lars eyes went wide. "Impossible, he is in Austria."

Ayden smiled. "See, we figured out that you were involved and set a complicated system that would show you that all the Council members were where you thought they would be."

"Impossible, there was no flaw to my plan," Lars said in disbelief.

"Your ego was your flaw," Kirsa told him. Lars backhanded her causing her to hit her head against the stone wall.

Lars jumped at Ayden; Ayden caught him and threw him into the rock wall. Lars got up and sprang through the air taking Ayden down with him. Kirsa watched the blur of motions. When Ayden began to lose the upper hand, Kirsa showed him everything that had been done to her that day. Having Holy Water being dripped on her, the liquid silver, everything.

It was the last scene that she showed him that had him slamming Lars' head into the stone floor. When his body went limp, Ayden took the handcuffs out of his cargo pocket and cuffed him. He then walked over to Kirsa and knelt down to her. Pulling her into his arms, he held her as she wept.

****

In the main part of the cavern, Dietrich was now supervising the gathering up of the cult members. Veronica Adams body had been covered up; they were waiting for one of Sara's assistants to come help with them.

They were able to get the two women out of the cellars but not without some sacrifices. Tony had joined them in another ambulance much to his dismay. Dietrich threatened to carry the stubborn man to the ambulance if he didn't listen. Now Dietrich was helping Al round up everyone. Dietrich was paying close attention to one of the men, Nick Cullen. He was getting a sense of danger still coming off of Nick.

Nick did not think that anyone was paying attention to him. He did not notice that the older vampire was watching him. Slowly, Nick moved through the group of church leaders that were being handcuffed and processed by several officers. He knew these caves better than anyone, for he was the one that wired it with electricity and moved all the equipment into it. There was a large crack in one of the walls that a person could fit in and hide in. Before he could reach it he felt a cold hand on his shoulder when he looked around he saw it was the older vampire.

Dietrich slowly turned Nick around; he went to say something but saw Nick pull out a syringe. Dietrich grabbed the hand in a blur of motions and broke it causing Nick to release the syringe.

"You fucking blood sucker!" Nick howled and lunged at the vampire with a vial of holy water.

Dietrich caught him in midair and with a quick move broke Nick's hand. Dietrich looked at the onlookers, "Anyone else who tries something should reconsider."

Chapter Forty One

Morristown Memorial Hospital's
paranormal ward was filled with people. Sara,
Bridgette, and Kirsa were all rushed into
different operating rooms. Tony, refusing to
leave any of them, was also brought into one
while doctors from the regular ER came to help
with surgery. Finn was already there, waiting
for them and went with Kirsa. She had been
unconscious when she was brought in.

Ayden was ushered into a private waiting
area. Cops came in and out. Dietrich stayed
with Al to help with the paperwork. The doors

opened and Donna White walked in. Ayden got up and hugged her tightly.

"Where?" Donna asked Ayden. All she knew was that Tony had been shot.

"In the thigh," Ayden told her."He's been alert and barking out orders the whole time."

Ayden guided her over to the couch and sat down with her.

"Where's Jeff?" Donna asked. "He should be here with us."

Ayden closed his eyes for a moment. While the church had lost several members in the quick battle, they had also lost their own people.

"No," Donna gasped.

"There was a third prisoner with Sara and Kirsa," Ayden explained. "When his team went to the cellar there were guards there. Nick took a bullet that had been meant for the girl."

"Does Sara know?"

Ayden nodded. "She saw it."

The door opened and one of the nurses walked in with a clip board. She held her hand up before they could say anything.

"Mrs. White, your husband will be out of

surgery in another hour. The bullet missed an artery in the leg, but tore through the muscle," she directed towards Donna. "Mr. O'Brian, they are finishing up on Dr. Cliver as we speak. I was told to speak to you since her pack leader is still at the crime scene. Then she will be admitted into the hospital for a few nights as a precaution due to minor silver poisoning. Also the young girl that came in with you?"

"Bridgette?" Ayden asked.

The nurse nodded. "She is waiving the right for us to notify her parents. She has asked for you or Phil to come be with her."

"What of Kirsa?"

"At this point, all I can tell you is that she is alive," the nurse told Ayden and left.

Donna and Ayden tried to do their best at keeping each other optimistic but it was difficult. Ayden watched Donna be told Tony was out of surgery and being moved to a room upstairs. Jeff popped his head in to tell Ayden what room Sara and Bridgette would be in, Ayden wrote them down. When the door opened again he hoped it would be a doctor instead it was Dietrich, Phil, and Al Moore. Ayden sat back down.

"Sara and Bridgette?" Phil asked.

"The nurse has Bridgette's room number so

ask her and she will give it to you, the girls must of told her who to trust," Ayden said. "Sara is in recovery at the moment."

"Is it okay if I go?" Phil asked the men.

"Go be with them," Al told him. "You have done more than enough to help us tonight."

Phil nodded then headed through the doors. Dietrich handed Ayden an insulated thermos and took the chair next to him. Al took the seat on the other side.

"Any word?" Dietrich asked. Every time he had called the hospital he had been told there was no information.

Ayden shook his head as he chugged the contents of the thermos. He had forgotten to eat, and had not realized how hungry he was until he opened the thermos.

"I've talked to Tony," Al informed Ayden. "We are going to work here in the hospital until everyone is released from it. This way we can work on the case with all the key players."

"Tessa was on the phone with a federal prosecutor, Collin Lyon has officially been appointed chief prosecutor for the case," Dietrich took the thermos from Ayden and put it on a side table.

Once again the door opened, this time Dr.

Finn walked in. Knowing he would be talking to a vampire he had changed out of surgical scrubs.

"I'm giving you the condense version, I'll have her report faxed to your office with the details." Finn told Al.

They nodded in agreement; a nurse walked in and handed a tray of coffee mugs to the men. Al handed the two with blood to Dietrich and Ayden; he took one for himself   and handed the other to Finn.

"She's stable at the moment," Finn began. Both Ayden and Dietrich sighed with relief. "We'll start with her leg. The knee cap was shattered, and the shin bone is broken in two spots. I would say she needs surgery but her body has begun to heal itself. If the knee heals wrong we will have to operate to fix it. If it heals ok, then no surgery."

"Do you know why her leg healed so fast?" Dietrich inquired.

Finn sipped his coffee, "Her disorder is advancing in odd areas and in various ways. For some reason it seems the more severe the injury, the more her body focuses on that area causing it to heal faster than it should."

He waited to see if there were any more questions. When there wasn't he continued.

"Kirsa also had five fractured ribs. One pierced her lung, but that apparently healed before we got her here."

"But those aren't the worst," Ayden replied.

Finn took a deep breath. "As we did with Sara and Bridgette. We did do a rape test on Kirsa. I don't know the results on that end. But no the ribs and knee are not the worst."

"The most serious of her injuries comes from being injected in two separate locations with Holy Water," Finn informed them. "One in her arm, and the other punctured one of her lungs, actually the same one that her rib pierced. I want to give her body time to heal; there is the possibility that I will have to do future surgery on the lung to remove the scar tissue from the Holy Water. But right now it would cause more damage if I were to do it immediately. I am treating it as you would with vampires, by transfusion. That's all the serious injuries, there are more but they do not pose a serious threat to her. We have heavily medicated her to give her body a chance to heal faster, oh and blood of course." Finn leaned back in his chair when he was done.

Dietrich nodded and sat there letting the last bit of information sink in. "Where did he inject her with Holy Water?"

"In the arm and her left lung," Finn replied.

When he saw the look of rage in Ayden's eye he wanted to duck, but refrained from doing so. Instead he nodded to the men and left the room.

****

Kirsa awoke in a hospital room, there was an IV hooked up to her. The IV said it was an antibiotic. Blinking her eyes a few times so that things would come into focus, she saw Dietrich sitting in a chair with his eyes closed. She raised an eyebrow because he was wearing jeans and a short sleeve polo shirt. There was also a strand of gray hair out of place. Kirsa carefully scooted herself up in the bed, she ignored the mild sense of pain as she did this. There were flowers all over the place and balloons and stuffed animals.

"You have many admirers," Dietrich said causing Kirsa to jump. He got up out of the chair.

"Where do you go when you do the whole eyes closing thing?" she asked him.

"To a quiet place," he said bending down and kissing her forehead. "Ayden is at a press conference with Al and Tony. He is representing the Council at the moment."

"I see,"Kirsa looked around."How long have I been in here?"

"A little over three days," Dietrich told her. He chuckled at her surprise. "Sara is next door to you and is sharing a room with the young girl Bridgette."

"Are they ok?"

Dietrich paused. He was not sure if now was the time to tell Kirsa or not. But then death was something most were never ready for. "Kirsa, Jeff was killed while freeing both Bridgette and Sara."

"No," Kirsa whispered shaking her head.

"A guard pulled a gun and was going to shoot her with a silver bullet, Jeff stopped that from happening," Dietrich explained.

"How is Sara?"

"Focusing on the young girl you two seem to have adopted while captured," Dietrich said. "Phil is going to take her in."

` "What else happened?"

"While you were off in one of the tunnels, the church leaders pulled out guns and tried to take us down. It was unsuccessful. Four church leaders were killed, unfortunately. The members that survived and the evidence were all brought to the police station to be processed," Dietrich explained.

"Lars?" Kirsa asked.

"Is in a vampire proof cell," Dietrich told her. "He will await his trial by the Vampire Council. Officer Chris Washington is pleading the 5th and has requested counsel. The real shame is the church's lawyer has retired and refuses to take the case. So until they find a new one, they have a court appointed attorney."

"Veronica?"

"Miss Adams was killed by her own church members before we arrived, moments I believe."

"She had dumped all the Holy Water out and replaced it with regular water so that when Lars threw it on me it would have no effect," Kirsa explained.

"Then she died a hero," he watched Kirsa turn away from him. "You are not to feel guilty. She knew that if found out, she would be killed and yet she chose to help you. Feel honored that you were able to show someone the truth who had been brainwashed."

"It's kind of hard not to feel guilty about those that died," Kirsa told him. "I should've been dead instead of them."

"Yes by the way, I am curious to know how you're severely broken knee and leg and four ribs were partially healed?" Dietrich asked.

"That's all you want to know?" she asked him

"No, there is much I want to know," he kissed her forehead again. "It can wait until you are out of the hospital."

****

Kirsa was released two days later; they were keeping Sara another day. The silver poisoning was a little worse then they first thought.

"They're freeing you?" Sara asked.
"Yep, I bared fangs and growled at the night nurse who wanted to check my bandages for the third time last night," Kirsa told her. "I'm too much of a pain in the ass."

"I heard that rumors about who you are have been leaked to the press," Sara said.
"Tony and Al are trying to see if it happened on their end."

"What happened to Bridgette?" Kirsa asked.

"She is talking to a lawyer about the pact, mainly Phil, becoming legal guardians. Since she is eighteen it should be pretty easy. She is going to become an adoptee in our pack until we locate a wolf pack for her to meet with."

"What about the hearings?" Kirsa asked.

Lars and Chris' hearings were scheduled for next week. Both Kirsa and Sara had volunteered to give statements which had Tessa almost crying with joy.

"I will be there," Sara looked at Kirsa. "How are you doing? They did more to you in that one day then they did to me."

"Sara, you lost Jeff," Kirsa said.

"He saved Bridgette's life," Sara replied. That had become her mantra for when the grief became too much. His death ensured that Bridgette would get a second chance at life. "Now back to you."

"As Ayden says it's part of the healing process," Kirsa said. She heard a rap on the door and saw Ayden standing there with her overnight bag and a wheelchair. "I'm not going out in that, absolutely not."

Ayden raised an eyebrow. "Kirsa, get in the damn chair or I will pick you up and put you in it."

"You wouldn't dare," Kirsa said. The words had no sooner left her mouth then she was in his arms and then sitting in the chair with her leg raised up. "Damn vampire."

Sara was cracking up as Ayden waved

goodbye and pushed Kirsa down the hallway. Due to the mob outside of all the entrances, they were going out the way of the morgue. No one would think of a breathing patient going out that way. Ayden wheeled her into the back of the black van and belted her into the seat. He gave the wheelchair back to the nurse.

Kirsa watched as they pulled away from the hospital. She drifted off to sleep and missed the drive up the driveway to the guest house. Ayden woke her up with a kiss.

She looked out, "Ayden…" he kissed her again to silence her.

"While you were lying around in the hospital, I hired a paint team. Every room in your house has been primed. They are waiting to hear what colors to do, there are also some kitchen sketches and bathroom sketches for you to look at. As well as three blue prints the architect drew up for your parent's house," Ayden told her as he unbuckled her. "Sabrina said we can stay with her if it gets to smelly and loud here."

"Oh," Kirsa said as the door slid open.

Ayden helped her out of the car and she saw Donna and Sabrina standing on the porch with a very excited Zero. Sabrina had him on his leash so he could not bound and knock her down. Slowly with her crutches she made her way to the deck, Donna helped Ayden get her up the three steps. When she was balanced again, Donna hugged her and then just held on to her for a minute. She let go so Sabrina could have a turn.

Kirsa tried not to cry, but it was hard when your best friend was holding you. So she let the tears fall. Ayden laid a hand on her shoulder to let her know he was there. He knew right now she needed to be with women. He kissed the top of her head and walked into the house, Tony sat at the table with Adam. Adam had arrived earlier that morning; he escorted Erin and her mom here.

"How is she?" Adam asked.

"She's going to be ok," Ayden said. "She has a long road ahead of her but she'll work through it all."

"She'll survive," Tony said as he was getting used to his crutches.

Ayden shook his head, "No, she'll triumph."

They were quiet when Donna and Sabrina came in with Kirsa. They sat her down on the padded bench in the kitchen so that Zero could sniff her and rub up against her. He whined a bit as he sniffed Kirsa's enormous knee brace. She scratched his ears, and started to laugh when he began to lick it. Kirsa then looked across the table and stared dumbfounded at her cousin.

"Just noticed I was here?" Adam asked getting up and giving her a hug. He sat down on the edge of the bench.

"When? Why? How long?" She asked almost laughing with happiness.

"This morning, to escort Erin and her mom here and until the hearings are over," he raised a finger to silence her when she went to open her mouth. "Anne and I played rock paper scissors on who was coming out here, I won. We both decided that you needed one of us here. So don't argue."

"I love you, Adam." Kirsa leaned her head on his shoulder.

"Same here kiddo," he replied kissing her forehead.

Chapter Forty Two

Kirsa sat on the bench in front of the pond on her property. It had only been two days since she was back from the hospital. Parts of it seemed like it was all just a nightmare. Jeff's funeral was tomorrow. She was not allowed to go, a decree that had been made by her doctors and the Council. Sabrina promised to be there for both of them.

She had come to the pond to think and reflect. She had spent much of the day on a conference call with Tessa and Collin going over what happened. After going over all the evidence they decided that it would be a good idea to start Lars' criminal trial in a week. The Vampire Council had agreed that they wanted him tried and convicted quickly before he had the chance to manipulate others.

Earlier, she had called Veronica's parents; she wanted them to know how she died. They were relieved to know that her last actions were against the cult and that those actions allowed for another person to live. It still didn't make Kirsa feel better about it. She caught the whiff of someone approaching but did not recognize it right away.

"I was told you would be here," a voice said from behind her.

Kirsa turned and saw Collin standing there in brown dress pants and a white polo tie. His wavy blonde hair was slicked back; his green eyes were hidden by sunglasses.

"I figured you would still be at the house," Kirsa told him as he sat next to her.

"I left after my parents called." He studied Kirsa through his sunglasses.

"How are they?"

"Mom and Dad are going to be coming in another month," he told her. "They figure   I'm going to be out here for a while. They also figure you will be almost fully healed by then and in a better mood."

"I'm glad you are my lawyer, Collin, it was bad," she stared out into nothingness.

Collin slung an arm around her. For a while they sat there, watching the clouds float pass them. Collin looked at Kirsa.

"How you doing?" he asked her.

"Good, for the most part." Kirsa looked at him, "I have my moments but that's to be expected. Otherwise, I'm already fed-up with the crutches. I'm pissed I can't be there for Sara tomorrow."

"I know but the concerns are valid," Collin told her. She had a long road of recovery before her. "Your ribs aren't bothering you?"

"Um, they kind of were completely healed by the time I got home from the hospital."

Collin let out a whistle. "Brie, said that you were developing some nifty abilities."

Kirsa started laughing at that. "Did she really say 'nifty'?"

"She was trying to assure mom that you were fine," Kirsa raised an eyebrow. "She was in the room when they called. Anyway she told them that because of your disorder it was helping you heal faster than if you didn't have it."

Kirsa nodded, understanding how his mother would be worrying about her. "I take it everything is in order since we are moving quickly?"

"Just by the evidence alone, Lars is screwed. That's not including the affidavits from you, Sara, Bridgette, Erin, Chris and Louis."

"Part of me wants him staked then the other part wants him to rot away in prison," Kirsa admitted. It was bothering her that she could want someone, she had cared for like a brother, dead. But he killed Isabella, had plotted the deaths of her parents, aunt and uncle, as well as her.

Collin said nothing; instead he put his arm around her shoulder and pulled her toward him. He knew he didn't have to tell that it was okay to feel like that, with time she would be able to move on. Not only did she know but she had told someone else that numerous times in her career.

"She's single you know. Unless you're still with the brainless Barbie you were with last Christmas," Kirsa told him.

Collin chuckled. "No, Krista and I parted ways. I don't think she understood the word monogamy."

"Ouch, sorry."

"Don't worry about it, I wasn't in love."

He helped her get up. "We should get you inside, the last thing you need is a cold," Collin pointed out.

They headed to her porch, Collin keeping up with her slow pace. "Do you want help up them?" he asked when the stopped up the stairs.

"No but go before I lose my dignity in front of you," Kirsa told him.

Collin kissed her on the head before leaving her. Kirsa stood before the stairs contemplating the thought of climbing them. Between the crutches and the huge brace on her leg it was making it difficult to do stairs. Maybe they should move back to Sabrina's' since she had a first floor guest suite.

Before she could make a decision she was lifted up and found herself staring into Ayden's face. He sniffed her neck.

"You smell like the sun," he whispered in her ear as he began walking up the stairs with her in his arms.

"Probably because I was outside with Collin talking for like an hour," she replied kissing him.

"Ahh, I can see that he and Adam being here make you happy," Ayden told her.

"It's like having an actual family supporting me while I go through all this."

Ayden stopped when they got to the landing. "In which direction did you want to go?"

The master suite was currently a construction zone. The bedroom walls were being painted, new carpet was going to be laid, and the bathroom was being re-tiled as well.

"Our temporary room works for me," she told him.

Ayden smiled and walked to the room he used before they had become lovers. He thought it was fitting that the room they first made love in they were now using until they could return to the master suite. Ayden laid her gently down on the bed and sat down next to her.

"So how are you today?" he asked her.

It was a question he asked her once each day since she got home. It let him know how she was and what he could do for her. She was fine with it, as long as he only asked it once in a 24 hour period of time, that was her stipulation.

She smiled, "Today has been a good day pretty much from when I got up this morning."

Ayden had been reverting back to his normal hours. Sleeping for most of the morning and early afternoon and then being awake until dawn came. He lay down on his side and rested his head on his elbow.

"Tell me what you did while I slept?" he asked her.

"Adam and I were both up around 9am, we had breakfast together which involved throwing cheerios at each other and Zero eating what landed on the floor. I had my normal dos-age and then had a conference call with Collin and Tessa."

"What did you do there?" he inquired as he played with one of her curls.

"She outlined what we needed to do so we are prepared for next week. Dietrich wants us all to sit down and discuss the protocol of a vampire trial. Sara and Erin will both be there for that meeting, since they will both be at the trial." Kirsa told him. "Then we discussed the videos that were found."

Ayden studied her closely; the days where she talked about the case were usually her worst days. Yet here she was smiling and almost completely happy.

She laughed at him, "Ayden I'm fine. It's just in talking to Tessa and going over the videos I realized that I am lucky to be alive. And that I have two choices, I either waste this second chance or I take it and live my life. I've been lost before, I didn't like it. But this foundation that I have built in the last few years, I think is strong enough to help me through all of this."

Ayden reached up and pulled her head down to his where he kissed her. "I love you Kirsa Heinrich."

"I love you Ayden O'Brian," she whispered back. "Now when are you going to start seducing me?"

Chapter Forty Three

Kirsa was sitting in Al's new office in the brand-new OPIA buildings. The headquarters were now in the Ironbound district of Newark, NJ. The entire complex consisted of three buildings, only one was completed, the second was halfway done and the third would be started later in the year. The main building held the court rooms, holding cells, agent offices, interrogation rooms, conference rooms, forensic lab and a press conference room.

The second building held the cafeteria, a large athletic center and the training center and classrooms were done. The firing range, technology department, evidence lockers, and other similar spaces were almost finished. The third building was going to hold dorms, visitor suites, and a small cinema room.

It was Kirsa's first visit to the new complex. Collin and Tessa wanted to have the last few meetings at the headquarters so that everyone could see the vampire court room and what a vampire trial would entail.

The door to the office opened, Al walked in shutting the door behind him. He took a look at Kirsa in her black suit and shook his head. No one would know that a week ago her knee cap had been shattered to pieces, or that a rib had pierced her lung. Kirsa gave him a hug, he always smelled like lush green meadows.

"I see Irish has yet to figure me out," Al stated as he sat at his desk. "He sniffed the air a few times as I walked by him and   shook his head in frustration."

"It's driving him crazy," Kirsa laughed. "I don't help because I end up leaving the room laughing my head off."

"You can tell him," Al told her, breaking the vow she was bound to.

She shook her head, "Nah, I want him to figure it out so he can see the irony of it all."

"Look I wanted to meet with you before you head to the court library for a few reasons," Al began. "The first is how are you doing?"

Knowing she couldn't lie to him, she lifted her hand and tilted it side to side. "Some days are good some days are bad. I have Ayden and the rest of you to help me through the bad days."

"Good, the other reason is I need a favor from you."

"I'm not working a case right now," Kirsa warned.

"No, that's not it," Al assured her. "Next month is the big four meeting: head of the CIA, FBI, Interpol and me. It's of course in an undisclosed location. I want you to be the go-to person if anyone gets in trouble while I'm gone. You don't have to come into the office unless absolutely necessary; I can link your laptop to ours so that you can handle the problems from home."

"Sure," Kirsa agreed. "That I can handle."

"Good now I can tell the UN that I have someone to take care of the place while I'm gone, they have been breathing down my neck for months about this."

"That's what happens when you refuse to appoint an assistant director," Kirsa told him. "Anything else I need to know in advance?"

"I might need you again come winter," he decided to tell her.

"Why?" Kirsa asked then raised an eyebrow. "It's not time for the Summit is it?"

Every four years all the heads of houses in Fae meet to go over policies, any problems, and changes that needed to be made.

"No, there is a verdict on my brother so I might need to go in person to hear the court's decision," Al explained.

His was the middle child, his older brother Patrick should have been head of Al's house. However, Patrick was in a bad accident involving iron, which left him brain damaged. Since the death of Al's father five years ago, Al had been acting as the Head while the courts assessed the situation and made their decision. It was taking its toll on Al, his mother and younger sister.

"Anything you need Al," Kirsa promised. "When is the Summit?"

"Next winter I believe," Al replied. "Want to be my date?" He asked.

"Me in the world of Faery, you're funny Al," Kirsa said.

"You will go to a vampire ball but my family gatherings scare you?"

"I have tried to explain to you what us humans are taught about your kind, but you just don't believe me."

Al laughed as there was a knock on the door. Ayden popped his head in, "Collin and the rest are here."

"Go, out of my office you freak," Al joked.

"I could say something but it would spoil the fun," she warned as she left the office.

She nodded to Al's secretary, Betty, who was so proficient it was scary sometimes. They walked to the elevator and got in when the doors open.

"You know it's driving me crazy that I can't figure out what he is," Ayden told her.

"I know, which is what makes it all the funnier," Kirsa told him kissing him lightly on the lips. "When you figure it out, you will understand our laughter."

"That's just mean," he pouted. "So what did the man of mystery want?" Ayden asked changing the topic.

"The big four conference is in a month and the UN needed him to put someone in charge for the four days that he is gone, so he asked if I could run the ship from the house."

"What's the big four conference again?" Ayden asked.

"Every two years the heads of the FBI, CIA, OPIA and Interpol get together with other law agencies and they have a big conference on the Paranormal Laws. It's at an undisclosed location and the heads are cut off from their agencies unless in a state of emergency."

"Gotcha," Ayden said. The door opened letting them out of the "law floor" as it had been nicknamed.

It housed the Paranormal Law library, judge's chambers, four courtrooms, several meeting rooms, a waiting area, and a press room. Each courtroom was designed differently.

Court A was for humans being tried, court B was if a were-animal was involved, court C was for the Fae, and Court D was the vampire court. Because the Vampire Council had a court system in place, the Paranormal Laws adopted their system, allowing the Vampire Council to run with few alterations. The only thing the law changed was that along with four vampire judges and a vampire head judge, there would be four non-vampire judges. It was agreed upon, so the judges table in Court D fit nine judges and there was no jury box.

Ayden and Kirsa walked to the one of the

meeting rooms, they entered finding Tessa, Collin, Sabrina, and Erin. Sara and Bridgette were coming later after physical therapy. Ayden nodded to Collin who nodded back, he kissed Kirsa quickly then left the room to stand guard with the four other armed guards.

Collin opened a folder and handed out a packet to each of them, "Vampire court is different from any court you might have seen," he started. "I know Kirsa has been to a trial before but the rest of you haven't so you need to listen."

Taking a sip of water he began, "In regular court you swear on a Bible that you are telling the truth. In the vampire court you will sign an affidavit stating that you are who you say you are and that no one is controlling your mind, what you are saying is the truth and not lies. If someone is controlling your mind your testimony is null and void; if you are lying then you will be faced with federal charges."

"Then what do we do when we get up there?" Sabrina asked. Erin looked thrilled that she asked the question.

"The head judge, who will be seated in the middle with four judges on both sides of him, will announce your name, which side you are testifying for and what your part is," Collin answered. "This means that when you get up to the witness seat questions start right then and there. I don't have to ask who you are, why you are up there, because that has been told to the court already."

Tessa spoke up, "So don't be surprised if let's say Erin the first question you are asked is some specific question about the running of the church. Because the court is already going to know your name, the fact that you are testifying for the prosecution and that you were a member of the Church of Light and at one point worked in the office of the head of the East Coast."

"Good to know," Erin whispered nervously. Sabrina rubbed her arm getting the girl to smile.

"Now in Kirsa's case, she is testifying twice. Once as an expert witness and then once as a witness," Collin added. "The first time she will be called will be as an expert, the second time as a victim. For the expert they will just list her credentials, and for the second one just her name and how she is a victim."

"The other main thing you need to know is that the judges can ask questions directly to you if they feel that something needs to be cleared up, all questions will go through the head judge. The head judge can also challenge a lawyers question without the other lawyer raising an objection. Kirsa do you know who the head judge is? I know they were still arguing it."

"Why, I thought Dietrich was head judge because he's current head of the Council?" Sabrina asked confused.

"Both he and Sebastian have asked for substitutes be- cause of their connections to the case, they feel they would be biased in their decisions," Kirsa explained. "I know one of Sebastian's advisors is stepping in for him. That was approved a few days ago."

"Yes I knew that," Collin said. He didn't want to try to pronounce the French name.

Kirsa smiled slightly, "They appointed Wyrm as head this morning."

Both of Collins eyebrows shot up, he let out a low whistle, "Well then no one better be lying."

"Why? Not that they should," Tessa asked.

Collin motioned for Kirsa to answer, "Wyrm is the librarian for the vampires because he is able to be completely neutral. Not only that but he can also see a lie hidden within a story."

"That's a handy gift," Sabrina agreed.

"My mom would love that ability," Erin said.

"Speaking of your mother Erin," Collin remembered. "The Council approved her petition to be with you at all times, except of course when on the witness stand. They also added that if she can't then your father or brother would be allowed." He slid the document over to her.

Erin let out a huge sigh of relief, "Thank you."

The rest of the meeting was going over statements and any issues that the defense could potentially bring up. Tessa, Erin and Sabrina left the room. Collin motioned for Kirsa to stay back for a moment.

He waited for the door to close before he spoke, "I want to let you know that this defense attorney is slippery. He acts like a fool, pretends to be clueless and easily influenced, that way he can get his clients off on technicalities. This is his first vampire trial though, so it should be interesting."

"Collin, you didn't pull me aside to tell me about the lawyer," Kirsa replied. "What's up?"

"He petitioned to have Anton be brought in as an expert witness," Collin informed her. "I heavily objected, thankfully so did all eight of the judges. I have a feeling he is going to try and use Anton against you so be prepared."

"I will," Kirsa assured him. When she walked out of the room Sara and Bridgette were there talking to Ayden. Kirsa gave them each a quick hug then walked with Ayden to the awaiting car.

When they were settled in the car, Ayden looked at her. "What did Collin want?"

"The defense attorney petitioned for Anton to be called in as an expert witness. Their petition was denied," Kirsa explained.

"Collin just wanted to warn me the asshole is most likely going to play dirty."

"When this is over, we are barricading ourselves in the house here or in Germany and not doing a thing for a while," Ayden replied.

"Sounds good to me," Kirsa agreed.

Chapter Forty Four

The courtroom looked like any other courtroom a person would fine. The only differences was that the judges stand was a table raised off the floor and could seat nine judges. There was no jury box. The prosecution sat to the right of the Judges table, and the defense to the left. Next to the defense table was the other thing that was crucial for a paranormal courtroom.

It was a clear cylinder that fit a chair and some leg room. It had an iron from and was lined in silver. This was where the prisoner sat during trial. The only way into the cylinder was from an underground tunnel and a platform that rose to form the floor of it.

The double doors that led into the courtroom were guarded. The press had been placed in the press room with a court circuit TV that would only show them certain parts of the trial but not every moment. The attorneys were already at their desks.

Kirsa waited in an antechamber, twirling a ring around her right middle finger as she did. She had been torn about wearing the signet ring at all, but decided in case it got brought up she would have it. She had slipped it on when she got into the antechamber for she had yet to show it to Ayden. There was a knock on the door and three armed guards walked in to escort her to the court room. Due to the large protest by the Church of Light outside, protection had been ordered for all the witnesses. With Ayden acting as a Council member, Al appointed his best men to the task.

When she entered the courtroom all eyes turned on her, she made her way to the prosecution table where she would be sitting. Lars was already in the holding cell that had been raised up into the court room. He watched as Kirsa moved down the aisle, his smile was evil. Kirsa focused on Ayden. The judges table was empty; the judges would be brought in after they sat. Since Kirsa would be the first witness to be called she was to sit with the prosecution, for in vampire court opening statements were allowed to be no longer than five minutes. When they were seated, one of the OPIA agents opened the judge's door and the nine judges filed out.

"All rise," Wyrm instructed. "Tonight we will be hearing the opening statements and the first witness will be called."

Collin smiled at Kirsa and walked to the center of the courtroom, he stood in front of the podium that was located there. He put his notes on it and took a deep breath.

"Ladies and gentlemen of the court," he began. "This trial is simple. It is about murder, torture, kidnapping, betrayal and treason. We have several witnesses that will be able to show that defendant was responsible for the deaths of over fifteen people. Seven of which occurred in or around the town of Grabenberg, NJ. Amongst that number are five vampires, four were-animals, several witches and two innocents.

"He also imprisoned and tortured a were-tiger, a were- wolf, and a human. All three would have been murdered if the authorities had not intervened. He created a religious movement several hundred years ago as a guise for his murderous habits. His act of treason was his plan to kill a member of the Inner Vampire Council. We will be able to show and prove what this man has done and would continue to do so." Collin gathered his papers and nodded to show that he was done.

He always found it nerve wracking when going before vampires, because you could not read any emotion from them. From several of the other supernatural judges he saw curiosity and understanding. But from the vampires, nothing. Collin returned to his seat, Tessa gave him a pat on the back.

The defense attorney got up and went to the podium. He was a small and frail man probably in his mid-forties. His hair was thinning, and his suit looked disheveled. He had no notes to read from.

"You heard what the prosecution has said,"Thomas Allen began. "It is all lies, my client is innocent. They are using his beliefs to paint him as evil. We will show that his is innocent."

He was going to retreat when Wyrm pointed a finger at him. "On what grounds is he innocent?"

Thomas looked at Wyrm, "Religious persecution."

The judges stared at him and there was a murmur amongst the audience. Wyrm looked over at Lars who just stared back at him and then at the lawyer. Thomas had entered the plea earlier in the week and it had been denied because not enough evidence could be shown to support the claim.

Wyrm studied the defense attorney with a narrow gaze, two judges were whispering in his ear. "Mr. Allen we will allow you to enter the plea, however you are advised that you must prove that your client is innocent due to religious persecution, and that he did not violate anyone's rights while practicing his beliefs."

The lawyer nodded and returned to his seat. Collin looked at Kirsa and she stared back at him. She had hoped that opening statements would have been longer, but knew that the longer the speech the more annoyed vampires tend- ed to get.

"Ready, kid?" Collin asked her quietly. "Remember we are going to try and keep tonight's questions to you being an expert witness."

She nodded and watched him return to the podium he just left. Collin lay down a folder on the podium and opened it.

Wyrm took the piece of paper, "First

witness is an expert witness on the paranormal and religious cults, her name is Dr. Kirsa Heinrich. Make sure all questioning on both sides are relevant to her purpose here tonight and not for any other purpose."

The witness stand was across from the prosecution table, this limited eye contact from the defense. This also eliminated mind control from the vampire in the cell. Kirsa smoothed her pants suit and played with the ring on her finger.

"Dr. Heinrich, can you explain to the court how you got involved with the case?" Collin asked her.

"I was at my family's home in Germany when Director Moore called me," Kirsa began. "A case had come to his attention that he needed some advice on. It turned out that it involved my area of expertise, religion and cults. After a few questions it came out that it was happening where I had grown up. I asked if I could be on the case."

"Didn't you quit a few years prior?" Collin wondered. He knew the defense would ask so he figured better to get it established now.

"If one knew anything about OPIA you would know that one cannot quit. We can take a sabbatical for an unknown length of time, but it is a position we hold until death unless we are fired, its part of the oath we take as an agent," Kirsa explained.

"Please explain to the court why you needed to take some time off?"

"After the death of several family member, and a particularly horrific case, I decided that I needed to take a break. This is not uncommon amongst OPIA, we tend to see and witness things that are often beyond human comprehension."

"Thank you. Can you also tell the court what your degrees are in so we can establish your expertise?"

"I hold a Master's degree in Anthropology, Ancient History and Occult Studies. Then I hold a doctorate in Parapsychology and History with an emphasis on the evolution of religion and cults," Kirsa informed the court.

"So Director Moore called the right person when he called you," Collin suggested.

"Yes. The particular cult that he thought was occupying Grabenberg had been involved in a few papers that I have published. He knew that I would be able to decipher some of the evidence pertaining to the case," Kirsa explained further.

"At what point in the investigation did they bring you in?"

"Body number five, Kelly Abrams. She was a were-tiger," Kirsa remembered.

"Can you tell us how she died?"

Kirsa closed her eyes; the manner was painful and brought back her own memories of torture. She took a deep breath before answering.

"Yes, Kelly had been injected with liquid silver into the heart," Kirsa stated. She heard the appalled murmurs fill the room.

The prosecution finished after another hour of questioning. It was eleven at night when the defense began its round of questioning.

"How old are you Miss. Heinrich?" Thomas asked.

Kirsa raised an eyebrow, "I'm 29."

"Yet by the age of 25 you held two doctorates and three master degrees. Am I right?"

"Yes, why?" Kirsa wondered.

"Yes Mr. Allen, what exactly is your point?" Wyrm asked, startling the lawyer.

"Isn't it odd that you have so many degrees at a relatively young age?" Thomas inquired.

This was a line of questioning that Kirsa

had not thought would occur. "I graduated high school at 16 and was done with undergrad by 19. My first two masters were finished by the time I was twenty and a half years old. I finished my third while working on my first doctorate which was done by age 23 and my last one was completed at the age of 26, not 25."

Thomas just stared at her for a moment. He had been trying to poke holes in her character. "But you were working on your dissertation when your parents died?"

There was an intake of breath throughout the courtroom. Kirsa stared hard at him. "Why this is important I'm not sure, but I completed my dissertation around the time of their death. But that does not mean the degree is completed. One has to defend what they wrote, only after that can a degree be awarded. Because of their deaths, my defense was rescheduled."

"You stated, Miss. Heinrich that Director Moore called you because he thought a cult was involved. Why you? Why not ask another agent that wasn't taking a break?"

"You will have to ask Director Moore that question. I am not a mind reader," she replied. "However, I figure it is because I have worked cases that involved this particular cult and had presented and published several articles on them."

"You say you are not a mind reader, yet can't you read the mind of an Ayden O'Brian?" Thomas asked.

Kirsa looked at Lars who smirked at her. "In that particular case, yes. Ayden O'Brian and I can read each other's thoughts when we focus. But he is the only person I can do that with."

"And why is that?" Thomas asked figuring he was now on a roll.

"Withdraw the question," Wyrm warmed. "Her connection to Vampire O'Brian is not relevant to her expertise that is speaking on tonight."

Thomas swallowed as the next question came to him. "Miss. Heinrich, how did you learn about the Church of Light?"

"I first learned about them during research for a paper in one of my graduate classes," Kirsa explained. "I was doing a paper on religious sects that later became cults. I began researching the group and realized it had movements dating back to the medieval era. Yet it was not publicly known at that point."

"What were your thoughts on it at that time?" Thomas questioned.

"That it had the potential to be a cult. But at the time I was researching it, it was non-violent. It had at that time just started to publicly protest the Paranormal Laws," Kirsa answered.

"Did your view of it change?"

Kirsa knew where he was going with this. "Yes. A man I dated and was almost engaged too was a member of the church. In the beginning it was not an issue between us. But I could start seeing things that are common amongst cults. He was reciting what he was told; he was becoming more irrational about things. It was the main reason that I ended the relationship."

"Why? Why did religion end your relationship?"

"Religion didn't end it. Extremism ended it," Kirsa corrected him. "If you must know he told me that loving me was a sin because of my family's connection to vampires. That loving me was like loving Satan himself."

"I can see how that would put an end to a relationship," Thomas replied. "Did that make you biased towards the church? It would make sense for you to have a deep hatred for what ruined your relationship."

Kirsa smiled at him. She knew what he

wanted. "The break-up did have me looking deeper into the church, I wanted to understand if what he was saying was actually coming from the church or from him. Then I became involved in a set of serious crimes in South Carolina that were connected to the Church of Light. It was then I made my conclusion that we were dealing with a cult."

"Isn't it true the church is rumored to be responsible for your parent's death?"

"That bit of information did not come out until this case and was not made publicly known," Kirsa replied. "There was thought that they were involved but no proof until now."

"Ok. So you are an expert on cults, especially this one. Why pin it and other charges on one man, the defendant?"

"Simple. He admitted to me that he was the head of the group, that he formed it specifically to kill, that he wanted me dead, and that he killed numerous people in the guise of religion. That would be why." Kirsa took a sip of water and waited for   Thomas to be done.

"Am I allowed to question her about her supposed kidnap?" Thomas asked Wyrm.

"Dr. Heinrich is here tonight as an expert witness. She will return later in the week for those questions," Wyrm informed him. "I believe we told you that. If you are done then we are adjourned for tonight. Tomorrow night we will have Director Moore and Chief White testimonies."

With that court was over. Kirsa got up and was surprised she was not shaking. Collin took her arm and guided her out of the room and then into the counsel chambers. She picked up the closest book and threw it against the wall with such force a picture fell off. Collin and Tessa let her gain control of herself.

"You were wonderful up there," Collin told her. "He is trying to damage your character and yet you had a reasonable response to each question."

"I swear that some of those questions were coming from Lars," Kirsa said.

"The Council and judges are aware that there is a chance he might manipulate his lawyer," Tessa told her. "It is being looked at and monitored."

There was a knock on the door, Collin opened it. Dietrich and Ayden walked in and shut the door.

"Dietrich walked over and hugged her. "You answered each question brilliantly."

"Seriously, can we sum this up tomorrow? I

really just want to go home and curl up into bed," Kirsa told them all.

"I'll take you home if my duties are done here?" Ayden told her looking at Dietrich. He nodded. Ayden held the door open for her and ushered her out.

Dietrich waited until the door was shut. "Can we expect any more surprises from the defense when she goes back on the stand?"

Collin undid his tie and rolled his shoulders. "From what I have learned about him, Allen is a loose cannon. He is known for being reprimanded by judges, trying to rattle the witnesses, and even coaching the defense witnesses. I have a strong feeling he is going to ask her about her connection to the myth about her family. You should all be prepared; she will have to answer it truthfully. It will go public with what- ever answer she gives."

"And you know the answer? She has hinted at it but I do not think she wants to think about it."

"Dietrich, I can't tell you because of the client confidentiality. Just be prepared for either response," Collin told him. "Now I'm going home and going to bed."

****

It was one in the morning by the time

Collin got back to the Black estate. Mrs. Hanson had left the porch light and kitchen light on for him. When he pulled up the private drive he saw that a light was on in one of Sabrina's room. He set his briefcase on the entry table in the mudroom off the kitchen.

As he walked through the kitchen he noticed a note taped to one of the ovens. Mrs. Hanson had a small homemade chicken pot pie in the oven. The note gave him directions on how to heat up. He did what the note instructed, and then took the back stair cases up. He walked down the hallway and saw the light under Sabrina's door and knocked on the door. A few seconds later Sabrina opened the door. Her hair was pulled back; she wore no make-up and was in pajamas.

"I have pot pie warming in the oven; would you like to join me?" Collin asked her.

Sabrina nodded and followed him downstairs. She got out the wine she opened at dinner and poured both of them a glass. Collin got two forks out and placed them on the breakfast table.

"How was it?" Sabrina asked as she took a seat at the table.

Collin took a sip of his wine first, "Rough, in a way, and in another routine."

Sabrina watched as he took the pot pie out of the oven and got it situated on a plate. He walked over and sat next to her, placing the plate in between them.

"Tessa is going to do some more research into this defense attorney that he has, he can afford the best yet he picks least inexperienced person," Collin confided. "This guy took the paranormal bar a few years ago. Most of his cases since have focused on were-animals; this is his first vampire trial. All I have been able to learn is he is not one to follow the rules."

"That's an odd jump," Sabrina observed sipping her wine. "It's two totally different set of rules and protocol."

Collin nodded as he ate. "Tessa is looking into see if there is a reason for the jump."

"Lars never does anything without a reason," Sabrina told him. "If he hired this guy, he did so for a very specific reason."

She took the fork that was lying next to the plate and took a bite. She had quickly eaten than ran to the court house for opening statements, then had to be back because one of the horses were sick and she was on call. They ate in silence for a few moments.

"Laura Heller?" Collin asked. He knew she was Kirsa's cousin but was unsure of the history there. "She was on the list of family approved to be in court for Kirsa. Kirsa had been stunned when she saw Laura waiting for her outside the courtroom."

"Laura is the daughter of Bethany Heller, Kirsa's mom's sister," Sabrina informed him. Knowing she was going to have to give the brief sum up she sipped Collin's wine. "Okay quick family lesson, Ana was the middle of three children. She was still talking to her family when Hagan and she got married. It was after they got married that her father, aka "the dictator," found out about Hagan's dealings with vampires. He gave his daughter an ultimatum, divorce Hagan or be disowned and disinherited."

"Obviously she choice the later," Collin replied. "I take it he made everyone stop talking to her."

"Yes, Bethany resurfaces at the funeral. Apparently a few years prior to their deaths, Ana and she had started communicating again. At the funeral she met Kirsa for the first time and since then they talk frequently."

"She's stunning," Collin commented. He noticed Sabrina raise her eyebrow.

"You know how Kirsa can show her brains sometimes and we call it the brainiac zone?"

"Yeah, why?"

"Laura can make Kirsa look like she has a normal IQ at times," Sabrina told him as she took another sip of his wine. "It's one of the reasons they are particularly close, they both have insane IQ's."

****

Laura sat with Kirsa and Adam on the deck; Ayden was playing with Zero in the yard. A bottle of wine sat between them as they talked.

"How's the family?" Kirsa asked Laura.

"I have been officially written off by the dictator," Laura informed her.

"What did you do, help a were-wolf?" Adam asked. Laura laughed.

"I got into the advanced hematology program at NYU, and in order to pay for med school I deferred for a year so that I can do some modeling gigs in the city."

"You really have been cut off," Kirsa agreed. "Not only did you get into med school but you will be displaying your body for the world to see. Have you no shame?"

"He also cut my dad and brothers off because they yelled at him when he told me I was nothing more than a dumb blonde bimbo," Laura replied.

"I am so glad I have never met this man," Kirsa yawned. "Alright I think it is bed time.

"You sure you don't mind me staying here?" Laura asked for the third time.

"Laura stop it, go to bed and be prepared for a cold nose to wake you up when Zero realizes there is one more person to sleep on," Kirsa said.

Ayden walked to the deck with Zero, "Bedtime?"

"Yep," Kirsa said yawning again.

"Then I will walk up with you," Ayden said.

"Come on Zero you can bunk with me," Adam suggested to the dog.

Chapter Forty Five

Kirsa was walking the fields with one of the farmers. Now she was down to a brace which made moving around a bit easier. Pete, who was a member of the local pack, was a short stout guy. He also rented a parcel of land from her to grow crops on. They walked to where one of the old barns had stood.

"We are going to rebuild the main house," Kirsa told him. "Then the architect is going to meet with you and the others, he wants to construct buildings for each of your needs. He is going to build the barn that was here as historically accurate as he can and that is going to be the office and hub for the farm part."

"How much is this going to cost us?" Pete wanted to know, when the other two farmers and he learned she was going to be fixing up the farm they were concerned about how much the land was going to cost them.

Kirsa smiled at him and motioned for him to follow, "Nothing."

He looked at her startled, "Kirsa you can't be serious."

"My land, my project, my pocket," she told him as they climbed in the jeep.

In the back was fresh picked Jersey corn and tomatoes for the barbecue at Sara's house. "So who is next on the 'watch Kirsa list?"

Pete laughed. Ayden was in court for the day and evening, he was testifying along with Al and Tony tonight. There was also a huge conference with the Council before the court session began. Since Ayden was in court all day, Sara was throwing a huge   barbecue at her house.

"I'm to take you back to your place where I believe, Ryan will be there to hang out with Zero while you get ready for Sara's."

Kirsa smiled and shook her head, "Well I

am sure that Zero will enjoy the company. So any supplies need to be ordered?"

"I will go over what I have and shoot off an email to the other guys and let you know," Pete told her as he pulled into her driveway. "When does construction start?"

"On the house during the fall, then after the harvest they will begin on the farm," Kirsa assured him. She knew he was concerned that the construction might interfere with the harvest and crops.

"You do think of everything," Pete said as he waved goodbye.

"Hey Ryan," Kirsa greeted him. "When does college start up?"

Ryan was entering his sophomore year at the University, "Three more weeks. I just sent off my schedule yesterday to my advisor."

"How's Joe doing?" Kirsa asked as she opened the back door to let Zero out. She grabbed two water bottles and handed one to him.

"Things are returning to normal finally," he told her. "Shelley and her mom are feeling more comfortable at the house. Her older brother moved in for a few weeks just to help make them feel better."

"I don't blame them for being freaked out," Kirsa agreed. "If a murdered body was found on my property and I lived far out of town like them I'd be freaked too."

They watched Zero run laps around the yard. Kirsa looked at her watch, "Alright I will be inside getting ready."

"I will be here," Ryan said with a smile as he threw the ball for Zero to chase. "Oh Kirsa, other Ryan and his dad will be there also."

Kirsa smiled knowing he meant the kid who cleaned Tony's office. "That was nice of Sara."

****

Sara's block was barricaded off, for when they threw the big pack barbecue her whole street was invited. Kirsa and Ryan pulled into the driveway; they unloaded the produce and met Phil and Jeff Cliver at the path. Phil took Kirsa's bundle and gave her a kiss on the cheek.

"Any word from court?" he asked her as they walked into the house.

"Just that it started," Kirsa said.

Sara was talking with Sabrina, they stopped when Kirsa entered the kitchen, "Where are your cousins?" Sara demanded.

"Adam is at dinner with the President," Kirsa told her. "Laura's photo shoot was running late, but she'll be here when they are done."

"How'd the meeting go with the architect?" Sabrina asked.

"We break ground on the manor in the fall," Kirsa said with a small smile. "Tim is going to wait until after the har- vest to start on some of the farm projects."

"Brian said he also stopped over to our place to talk about some of the upgrades we need," Sabrina told her.

"It makes sense to just do everything at the same time," Kirsa reminded her.

"Which is what Brian, Tim and my parents both said," Sabrina sighed. "He's getting me an estimate by tomorrow."

She ushered everyone outside into the backyard. The pack, or pride, contained twenty actual were-cats. But once the families were included, there was close to sixty people present. Kirsa saw that Bridgette was talking to Tony's daughter Stephanie.

"She seems to be doing better," Kirsa said to Sara as they brought trays of food out.

Sara smiled. "She really is," Sara agreed.

"She's been helping me around her during the day when Phil is at work."

"How are you doing?" Kirsa asked.

"I'm selling my house to the pack once I'm back on my feet," Sara said. "I can't stay here and not think of Jeff. His brother helped go through his things and brought them to charity. The department is checking in on me. But Bridgette, she's been the best gift."

"How's the custody arrangement?" Kirsa asked.

"They signed off on the paper work yesterday," Sara said. "I still don't get how a mother can sign away her daughter to people she has never met. Anyway, Bridgette was sad at first because it was final. At the same time she wants to begin her new lease on life."

"I understand that," Kirsa replied.

Tony came over on his crutches, with Donna close behind him. Kirsa kissed him on the cheek, "How many more weeks?"

"Three more," he groaned. He was hating not working and being on crutches. "I got permission from the state that as long as I stay at my desk I can do desk work for the time being."

"If they didn't I was going to drive to the

commissioner's office and plead with him," Donna told her. "The man cannot be stuck at home."

Tony laughed at her, Phil came over and pointed to a chair. Tony went to refuse but decided against it when Phil let out a low growl.

"Phil where were you the first few weeks he was home?" Donna asked.

"Probably making sure that Sara was following doctor's orders," Tony joked.

It was good to do something normal that had nothing to do with the case or the trial. If it was brought up it was for an update then the conversation would change to another topic. Laura showed up as Phil and Jeff were finishing up with the grill. Phil saw Laura and the big guy was awe struck. He found Kirsa who was talking to Bridgette.

"Who's the woman that just came in?" Phil asked Kirsa.

"That would be my cousin Laura." Kirsa told him.

"She must be what like 19?"

Kirsa laughed, "She's 25. She is modeling to pay for medical school; she got into Columbia's hematology program."

Phil looked at Laura again then grabbed a beer and began to make his way through the crowd. Sara came over with a plate of food for Kirsa.

"Where'd Phil go?" Sara asked her.

"To flirt with my cousin, I think," Kirsa told her taking the plate.

They watched Phil and Laura while they ate their food. Kirsa went to say something but felt her phone vibrate. She put her plate down, and went in to the house to take the phone.

"Hey Irish," Kirsa said answering the phone.

"Hey beautiful," Ayden replied. "How's the barbecue?"

"Good, let Dietrich know I am surrounded by twenty were-cats, a few were-wolves, and several police officers. So I am well protected," Kirsa told him.

Ayden laughed. "He will be glad to hear it." "To what do I owe this phone call?"

Ayden let out a sigh knowing there was no fooling her. She'd pick it out of his head later. "Two things have come to light that I want you prepared for."

Kirsa sat on the edge of the couch, "Alright

hit me." "The first is, Lars' lawyer has leaked to the press that you claim to be the heir to the sixth line. Dietrich and the rest want to strangle him, but we can't or it will be a mistrial and it starts all over again."

Kirsa ran a hand over her face,"Any chance they ,meaning the Inner and you, could be at my house before the trial tomorrow?"

"Yeah, why?" Ayden asked. He knew what the reason was but wanted to be sure.

"To go over the claim," Kirsa said.

"You ready for this?" Ayden asked her. It was during the late hours of night, that she confided to him her fears about coming out as the heir. They were hoping to buy some more time but that would not be the case.

"I don't have a choice," Kirsa replied. "What's the second thing?"

She heard his low growl at the intake of breath and knew this was not going to be good, "Anton will be testifying tomorrow."

"WHAT!" Kirsa yelled, forgetting about how good vampire and were-animal hearing was. Phil came running in with a worried look. She held up a hand to him.

"I know. They had to approve it because douche bag argued that the prosecution could not bring up your relationship with him and his connection to the cult if he could not testify on his behalf," Ayden told her.

"Damn it," Kirsa said. "Seriously?"

"Right, because I would joke about it."

"I know you wouldn't. Well fuck," Kirsa said. Phil raised his eyebrow. He knew it couldn't be good because she just swore twice in a row. "Who handled it worse, you or Dietrich?"

He laughed at that, "It was tie according to Wyrm. Al is annoyed because some furniture needs to be replaced."

"You're only allowed to break furniture with me," she joked. He laughed again at that. "Alright well call me on your way back. Phil will be at the house with Laura and I when you get back."

She hung up the phone and took the beer that Phil gave her. She chugged half of it before she could talk.

"What's up?" he asked.

"The press got wind that I claim to the heir to sixth line."

"I take it that's not what all the cursing was about," Phil responded. He leaned against the door frame. "If you tell me I can get the rest of them to not pester you, well except for Sabrina and Tony, thought I could growl at them if they bring it up."

Kirsa smiled, "How are you still single with charm like that."

"I wonder about that also," Phil laughed. "Seriously Kirsa, what's up?"

"Anton is testifying tomorrow night," Kirsa told him. He almost choked on his beer. "The defense is correct. We can't use him in my testimony if he can't defend himself."

"I will be with you tomorrow night. I'll talk to Dietrich later when he drops Ayden off," Phil told her. "Come on let's rejoin the party before rumors start."

When they walked out onto the deck, Phil gave a low growl letting his people know not to pester her. He then stared at the rest to let them know it went for them as well. Kirsa walked down to where Laura and Sabrina were.

"He's handy to have a round," Laura replied sipping her wine.

"That he is," Kirsa agreed. "He's taking us home tonight."

"Ayden said we would have someone at

the house until he came home from court,"
Laura said. "No sweat. I just wish my
grandfather could see me hanging with a
bunch of were's."

"I can take a picture and we can send it to
him," Kirsa suggested.

Laura looked at her and smiled. "Let's take
a picture of us and I will send it to him with
my email."

Sara took a picture of them together, then
one with the whole group for their newsletter.
She promised Laura she would have the
picture emailed by tomorrow.

"How'd the shoot go?" Kirsa asked Laura
when they were done with pictures.

"Ugh. My first shoot was supposed to be
for designer it turned out to be an anti-were
campaign. So I walked off that shoot and called
my agent who was furious because he had
three other models that were booked for the
same shoot next week. He called my other
shoot, they were thrilled that I could be there
early and assured him it was legit. So I got paid
double then what I was expected for that
shoot."

Kirsa stared at her. "What did they say
when you walked off?"

"That I would hear from their lawyer, I told

them that was fine because my lawyer would tell them how they misrepresented their contract there by making the original contract invalid."

Kirsa just laughed at the thought of the photographers and crew staring at this beautiful blonde who also happened to have a brain.

It was close to midnight by the time they got back to the house, Kirsa showed Phil where everything was. Laura was talking to him when Kirsa said good night to them. Zero followed her upstairs as she made her way to the room that she and Ayden were using until renovations in the master bedroom were done. He curled up on his doggy bed with his favorite stuffed penguin; Kirsa changed into her pajama's and grabbed the journal she had been reading. She knew she would not sleep until Ayden was home.

****

I write these words yet still cannot believe that they are true. Hagan is dead. Killed by another like him. My two children are asleep in our bed for they are distraught over the loss of their father. How can I tell them to sleep in their own rooms, when I fear what it will be like to sleep alone? The Council of the vampire has called me to a meeting, for they too are in shock over his death.

I know I must be strong for the sake of my children and the village but it is hard when I feel as though I buried my heart with Hagan. I wear his ring in hopes that it will be as though a part of him is with me. When I look at our children, Adala and Alderic, I see Hagan in them. Our beautiful daughter and son, so young to lose their father but I must be strong for all of us.

****

Kirsa awoke to Ayden sitting next to her in the bed. She smiled as she sat up in the bed, he kissed her gently. He had taken his suit jacket and tie off, and his sleeves were rolled up.

"Long day?" she asked.

"I can't wait until I don't have to wear a suit every day," he told her. "How was the party?"

"A nice distraction."

"Phil and Laura were talking when I got here," Ayden told her. "What's up with that?"

"A ten year age difference," Kirsa told him with a smile. "I have no clue otherwise."

"Dietrich agreed that having him as an extra body guard for you tomorrow is a good idea," Ayden informed her. "I also will only be acting as your Shadow. And the Inner Council will be here around five tomorrow night."

Chapter Forty Six

Kirsa stood in one of the ante-chambers off the court room for when Anton testified on the stand. Because of such short notice of his testimony, he was going to be questioned in front of the judge's panel then brought back in after Kirsa's testimony. They had allowed for a television to show a live-feed to the room for Kirsa to watch.

No one was in the room with Kirsa. It was what she wanted, this solitude while watching her ex fiancée give statements before the court. Kirsa knew that her life would be changing after tonight, that once the media heard her testimony it would be headline news all over the world. The meeting with the Inner Council at her house was brief, she showed them the evidence and they were speechless. After they read the evidence and reviewed what they knew their conclusions matched with information that Wyrm had uncovered.

Knowing this, Kirsa dressed in a tailored black suit, with a silver colored silk blouse. She wore her mother's diamond earrings and her diamond pendant, and on her right middle finger was a gold signet ring that was over a thousand years old and was deemed priceless. After tonight it would go into a secured vault and she would wear the duplicate for official events.

She paced the room as the judges filed into the courtroom and the court proceedings got underway.

They wheeled Anton in strapped to an upright gurney. The lawyer wanted him to be able to walk in but that idea was quickly shot down. Sniper trained vampires and were's lined the room, waiting for Anton to make any move. The armed guards put him into position by the witness chair they took their positions behind him.

"Due to the lack of time we had to process his statement before tonight's session we will be asking him basic questions to legitimate his role as a rebuttal witness," Wyrm explained to the court room. "When the questions are done by the judges he will then be removed so that the first wit- ness of the night can take the stand. All questions from both lawyers are to wait until he takes the stand in the capacity of a witness. Understand?"

Both lawyers nodded to Wyrm in agreement. Wyrm looked at the judges on either side of him as they handed him the list of questions they had agreed upon to ask.

"Please state your name before the court," Wyrm asked. "Anton Sebastian Black," Anton replied in a neutral tone. "Current address?"

"Paranormal Prison, New York."

"Please state your crime before the court."

"I object, your honors," Thomas shouted standing up.

Wyrm looked at him with an annoyed look. "Mr. Allen we went over this before it is standard procedure that if a person giving testimony is in prison or even on parole they are to tell the court what their crimes were and their sentence. We are not making an exception here. Now Mr. Black please tell the court your conviction?"

"Life in prison for the killings of those protected under the Occult and Paranormal Laws that took place in Charleston, South Carolina."

"Thank you, now may you explain to the court: how you know Kirsa Heinrich, your knowledge of the Church of Light. We can get to the more detail items when you return to the stand later."

"I have known Kirsa since she was born, her family and mine have a long history together. We were engaged at one point in time but that fell through. My involvement with the church began in my twenties; I was a stock broker in New York City. One of my co-workers brought me to an event lead by the church. I believe in what they teach, the more I studied, the more events I went to showed promise to the leaders.

"When I became leader of the East Coast Branch I became aware of the church's interest in the Heinrich's. They were stunned to learn that I was dating the daughter. I told them about the family ties to vampires and a little bit about the blood disorder that only seemed to run in their family. They wanted to save her but she refused, I was being pressured by her and by the church. Eventually our engagement fell through and I repented my sins. I was then hand-picked by the Father himself for the tasks that were to come ahead."

Wyrm nodded, "Thank you. The witness me be removed. We will take a five minute recess."

Collin got up and left the court room. He entered the antechamber from another door so that Anton would not know where Kirsa was. Kirsa stood looking out the window, her shoulders were rigid and the way she was holding herself he knew she was furious.

"What do you want to do about the blood line question?" Collin asked her. "Wait for the defense?" They had left the decision up to her.

Kirsa turned from the window; she closed her eyes to refocus then looked at Collin, "I want you to bring it up so this way it will be clear."

He nodded, his phone beeped telling him it was clear to bring her in. Ayden and three armed guards and another Shadow appeared in the room. Ayden walked up to her and kissed her lightly, "After your meeting it was decided to increase security around you."

"As long as your part of it," she told him. She looked at the guards then back at Ayden. "Guess I have to get used to this."

Putting a hand on her back he guided her out of the room. Kirsa knew it was a gesture of love and at the same time he was marking her before the vampires and were's that were in the courtroom tonight. It was telling them that she was claimed and that he was her vampire. They moved through the hallway, silence fell as conversations stopped short when

Kirsa and her guards walked towards the courtroom. It felt as though the entire paranormal community was in the OPIA headquarters tonight. The doors to the court opened revealing the judges were already at their table, Collin stood at his, but all eyes were on her.

Instead of showing fear or nerves, she walked into the courtroom with grace and her chin held high. No one talked, as she made her way to the witness seat. Her guards took their positions on either side and behind her, having Ayden close would help.

Collin walked to the podium and opened the top folder. This moment was history in the making, "Good evening Kirsa."

"Good evening. Collin," Kirsa replied with a slight smile.

"Earlier in the week you gave testimony as an expert witness is that correct?"

"Yes."

"Unfortunately though, tonight you are here as a witness, not as an expert witness, but because you became a victim of the crimes committed by the defendant. Is this correct?"

"Yes."

"We are going to start with basic questions before heading into some of the deeper questions. Can you explain to the court how you knew the defendant?"

Kirsa nodded, she spotted Laura and Adam for the first time. She then saw that Phil was one of the snipers, she took a deep breath for the first time. "I have known Lars for pretty much my entire life. Because of my father's work with the supernatural community and the connection to the Vampire Council, he was assigned a body guard from time to time. Lars was usually the one sent."

"Aren't there other non-supernatural's that work with the Vampire Council?"

"Yes, there are."

"Are they all treated to assigned body guards?" Collin asked. He noticed that Thomas was shooting daggers at him with his looks.

"No."

"Do you know why your family was signaled out?" Collin inquired.

"There was always speculation and rumors about why we were important," Kirsa replied.

"And we know that rumors and speculation can't be used in the courtroom," Collin commented. "So I guess my question is, are there facts to as why your family was deemed special by the Vampire Council."

"It's a long story," Kirsa began.

"We have all night," Wyrm told her. Though he already knew what she was about to reveal.

"Around 1000 c.e. an ancestor, by the name of Hagan Adulwulf, was murdered by a vampire. I believe the vampire Louis explained parts of the tale in his testimony," Kirsa began. Collin nodded to confirm that he did. "After his death, the Vampire Council feared that Alois, as he was known then, would also go after Hagan's wife and two children. They invoked a blood oath, which is when a non-vampire is given an oath of protection by the Council."

"You can date your family back to the one thousands?" Collin asked amazed. "That is impressive. Do you know why the Vampire Council felt the need to protect a human family?"

"Objection," Tom started. "What does this line of questioning have to do with the case?"

Wyrm looked at Collin, even though he knew where it was going he needed Collin to explain. "If the court will allow a few more questions I will be able to show how this is connected to the case."

"A few more, Mr. Lyon," Wyrm warned.

Collin motioned for Kirsa to continue. She looked regal sitting there in the seat and when she spoke her voice was clear, "Hagan Adulwulf was a vampire and is the only known vampire to be able to sire two children with a mortal woman who was not in the mist of the change herself. They believed that his blood must be different, so the five lines agreed to the protection."

"At the time of this decision how many seats were filled?"

"There were and are six seats however ever since the FirstCouncil there are only five seats that are filled," Kirsa explained. "Which is how many were filled at   the time of the oath."

"And each seat comes from one of the original six blood- lines, so why only five filled seats?"

"Because the sixth blood line was hidden," Kirsa answered. She began to play with the ring on her finger. "The head of the sixth line did not turn people into vampires and very rarely drank human blood. It is believed that because of this lack of turning people his blood line would be the closest thing to first vampire."

"I see," Collin said. "Did the First Council

suspect that your ancestor was possibly of this sixth line?"

"They didn't suspect," Kirsa began without faltering a word. "They knew he was the head of the sixth line. Just as they knew his blood ran through his children."

Collin ignored the tension that had filled the room as everyone waited for the question to be asked. "Then that would that make you heir to the sixth line? If his blood ran through the veins of his children then wouldn't that lead to you?"

"Yes," Kirsa said simply.

The murmurs began to fill the room making it sound as though a swarm of bees had entered the room. Wyrm hit the gravel on the table to silence everyone.

"Growing up were you aware of this fact?" Collin asked.

"As I said the sixth line had been hidden, though it had always been rumored and even suspected that my family could be the sixth line. It was not confirmed until recently."

"How many knew about the rumors circulating around your family?"

Kirsa laughed, "I feel like everyone in a way knew that my family had some sort of ties to the vampire community that went farther than the blood oath."

"How about those close to you? Friends, lovers?"   "Friends became aware of the rumors. Vampires were mortal once and the need to gossip doesn't stop when they turn into creature of the night. So my friends heard the rumors and the gossips. Which meant I was the butt of some corny jokes growing up."

"Then would it be safe to say that Anton Black and even Lars would have heard these rumors about your family?"

"It is certain that Anton would know the rumors, I am best friend with his sister and we were together for a time. As for Lars, he definitely knew about the rumors, he would joke about it from time to time."

"Do you think that either one or perhaps both pass this information on to the cult?" Collin asked.

"I am certain that Lars did for he told me so while I was held prisoner," Kirsa confirmed. "He also informed me that Anton had told the church some things about me but had never delved farther than the blood oath link to my family."

"Since you brought up you captivity, can you explain what happened?"

"I was abducted in broad daylight, and brought to the hide out that the church was using at the time. I knew that Lars was connected to the church and that he had been the spy that was leaking information about the Council."

"Did you know he was the Father?"

"I suspected but it doesn't stop you from being shocked when your suspicions are proven correct," Kirsa explained. "It was in that first conversation at the hideout with him that he explained his motives and plan."

"What were those plans and motive?" Collin asked.

"Pay back to the Council for a punishment given to him long ago," Kirsa replied simply. "He had become a vampire during the plague in the 1340's. When he returned to his village some years later he saw his family survived, he was spotted by one of them. Instead of making his family forget about him, he killed and drained each one of them. The Council, instead of killing him, made it so that he would never be able to hold a position of power within or for the Council."

"You bitch!" Lars yelled from his holding cell next to the defense table.

"Mr. Allen, please keep your client under

control or he will be removed," Wyrm warned. "Ms. Heinrich please go on."

Kirsa continued, "He then explained that he began the cult shortly after his sentencing, and has managed to keep it going for over seven hundred years. He then explained that when he began to suspect the truth about my family he be- gan to realize that a mortal would sit on the Inner Council, when he, a vampire, would never be. He thought that was an injustice. When Anton told the church leaders that we were seeing each other he also told them information about my family. Lars used that to start a rumor that if you killed my family, all of us, then it will kill every vampire in the world."

Collin continued for another hour to question her. It was then the defense's turn.

Tom walked to the podium placing his notebook down and smiled at her. "So what does one call you now? Majesty, Lady?"

"How about Kirsa," she replied with a smile.

"So you claim to be the heir to the sixth line that is some tale. Is there any proof to this claim?"

Wyrm spoke before she did. "A file was handed to you before tonight's session outlining the validation that Miss. Heinrich is indeed the heir to the sixth line. Not only does her genealogy line up, there are numerous primary sources that support the claim, and if you notice on her right middle finger is the signet ring for the sixth line that has been in her families vault."

"Very well then," Tom said. "Mr. Black stated earlier that you were engaged at one point, can you elaborate."

"We dated for over three years", Kirsa began. "I was splitting my time between New York City and DC; we mostly saw each other on weekends."

"Was it a solid and good relationship?"

"No it wasn't, though I am sure he will disagree."

"Why do you say it was a bad relationship?" Tom asked.

"He was controlling, manipulative, and kept pressuring me to attend his church and follow his beliefs."

"Did he break it off because of the religion differences?"

"I broke it off due to the religious differences," Kirsa corrected him. "It was after the break-up that I learned how high up in the church he was."

"You claim that Mr. Black relayed information to the church, yet you never heard him say anything to them?"

"I never went to a meeting with him, but he did tell me at the end that he had told them about my family's connection to the vampire," Kirsa explained.

"Did he explain why he told them about you?"

"Yes," Kirsa said with a harsh smile. "He needed to repent for loving me."

Tom looked at her for a moment startled by what she said, "That must have been hard to hear. Hard enough that one could convince themselves that he was the mastermind behind your parents, Aunt and Uncle's murder, as well as South Carolina."

"It is hard, in general, when a person you trusted betrays you in such away. Lars confirmed my worst fear, when he told me that Anton had been involved in my parents' deaths."

"Lars certainly confided a lot in you, I wonder why?" "Because he was going to kill me and knew I wouldn't be able to tell anyone anything if I was dead," Kirsa supplied.

Collin couldn't help but smile a bit at her comment. He saw Ayden fighting off a grin as well.

"Now you claim that Lars did all these things to you but you seem perfectly fine now," Tom said deciding to move forward.

"I have a rare blood disorder that is found in my family; part of the symptoms is that my body heals itself quickly. Though, I might have to have corrective surgery on my knee and lung from the injuries incurred by Lars."

"Is it the same disorder that allows you to communicate with Mr. O'Brian?"

"No, that has nothing to do with the disorder," Kirsa told him.

"So what does allow this amazing ability?"

"Irrelevant, your honors," Collin objected. "Psychic links between vampires and a human with whom they are close with are known to happen."

"Counsel is correct, Mr. Allen please move on to next question," Wyrm agreed with Collin. No one needed to know how such a link was formed.

By the time Tom was done with Kirsa on the stand she felt emotionally drained. He had questioned over every detail of her relationship with Anton, the death of her family, her relationship with Lars. After Collin was done with his cross examination of her, she was dismissed. Wyrm declared another five minute recess so that she could be escorted to a secure location and Anton could be brought in.

This time they were taking her up to Al's office. None of the guards spoke, as they made their way up the elevator. When they arrived on the floor Al greeted them with a few of his own agents.

"You have two options," Al told her. "You can go in my office and watch what Anton has to say or while he is on the stand we can sneak you out of here and get you back to Grabenberg before anyone knows."

Kirsa looked at Ayden and the guards surrounding her, "You will let my family know?"

Al nodded, "I will tell them personally."

The group of ten followed Al to the elevator that was located on the back wall of the floor, he pressed in a series of code before laying his finger on the scanner. He talked to Ayden who nodded; Al gave Kirsa a quick hug then stood back as the group entered the elevator.

The doors closed and the elevator began to move, "This elevator goes right to the underground garage where there will be a car waiting for us," Ayden explained. "When we get to the house Al will call to give everyone instructions on what to do."

The ride to Grabenberg was quick because there was little traffic at one in the morning. When they pulled into the driveway the three cars parked, everyone got out of the car. When Kirsa unlocked the back door Zero came running to her, than investigated each of the guards. Ayden pulled Kirsa aside, "Why don't you go take a bath and relax, I will be up when this is sorted out."

She nodded patting her thigh Zero followed her up the stairs to the second floor Kirsa was still in the bath when Ayden walked into the bathroom; he had taken his tie and jacket off.

"The guards are spread throughout the property; the other Shadow, Eric, will stay here in the house with us. Everyone will be relieved at sun up with a new group of men."

"I'm sure Tony will add to it come morning," Kirsa replied. "Any word from court?"

"Adam called after I got off with Al, apparently Lars tried to glamour his lawyer, Anton and one of the non- supernatural judges. They removed him from the building and is now in a secure location, the judges will discuss to- morrow if they will allow him to take the stand or have a private meeting with him and then discuss a conviction and sentencing."

"I can't wait for it to be over," Kirsa sighed sinking lower into the bubbles.

Ayden watched her in the bath, "Why don't you dry off and meet me in the bedroom."

Kirsa smiled shyly, "Why don't I."

Chapter Forty Seven

The following day, Kirsa put a ban on all electronic devices and news. Sabrina came over with some paperwork and was laughing as Kirsa groaned when she heard one of the guards talking to another one about a report on the case.

"Oh come on like being in the gossip columns is new to either of us," Sabrina laughed.

Kirsa looked at her, "You should see some of the titles they are coming up for me. You would think they'd be more creative than Queen of the Bloodsuckers, or any of the other titles they have come up with."

Sabrina drank her ice tea. "Well the phone has been ringing off the hook with requests to hold Halloween parties at the ranch and farm land."

"Ugh," Kirsa replied resting her head on the table. "Halloween."

Ayden walked in the room and raised an eyebrow at Sabrina. Sabrina smiled, "Her highness is having an issue with her instant celebrity."

"Ah," Ayden replied kissing Kirsa on the back of the head. Ayden poured coffee into a mug then heated it in the microwave before adding his blood. When it was ready he leaned against the counter and took a sip. "So what's going on?"

"The phones have been ringing off the hook at the ranch, everyone wants to hold a Halloween party there because Kirsa is part owner," Sabrina replied.

"I see," Ayden replied. "How about instead, the ranch throws a town wide Halloween party this way no one is turned down and Kirsa and you can control the situation entirely."

Kirsa picked her head up and looked at Sabrina, "Ayden you're brilliant."

"It's what happens when one is over two hundred years old."

Sabrina laughed, "Alright I have to get back to work. I will talk to you later."

Ayden sat at the table after Sabrina left, "How's the morning been."

"My phones are all on silent," Kirsa replied. "We are up to thirty guards, the mayor issued a statement that anyone stepping on my property without permission will be thrown in prison, and if I am out in public I am not to be hunted by cameras and reported. Again punishment is jail."

"Impressive," Ayden replied. He took another sip, "Dietrich called."

"I was wondering why you were up," Kirsa replied. Ayden had not come back to bed until six in the morning when the next shift of guards had taken place.

"The judges are going to have a closed door meeting with Lars, any questions they might need you to answer they will call, after said meeting they will then discuss verdict and sentencing."

"So it could be over by tonight?" Kirsa asked.

"Yes," Ayden told her. "Their concern is that after last night, there could be a repeat at which point a mistrial would be declared. We were getting close to the end anyway, this way it is done and over with."

She relaxed in her seat and took a sip of her drink. "What are your plans after the case?"

"Once the Inner Council is back at their homes, they will hold a meeting where I will be officially made your permanent Shadow. Dietrich figures it's pointless for me to leave here just to return in a week or two, so I remain here with you. Unless you disagree?"

Kirsa smiled at him, "I think I can handle you being here."

"What are your plans?"

"Decompressing some, rebuild the manor, work on some cases, there is some talk about locals wanting me to open a parapsychology office, Tessa and Tony like the idea," Kirsa said. "So a lot of choices, and no deadlines for me to make decisions on."

"Do I fit into those plans?"

Kirsa got up and moved to sit in his lap, she put her arms around him. "As long as you're willing to be by my side and deal with the craziness that is my life, then I want you here by my side, in my life and bed."

He kissed her lightly, "Good plan."

"That it is," Kirsa agreed.

****

It was dark when Ayden found her at the pond; she was sitting on the dock with her feet dangling in the water. Zero lay curled up next to her, it was oddly reminiscence of another moment earlier in the summer only this time he brought the wine and glasses. He sat down next to her, setting the wine and glasses next to him.

"Hey," she said smiling. Kirsa looked at the wine and raised an eyebrow.

"Wyrm called, he wanted you to hear the verdict before they went to the press conference to release their statement," Ayden told her. "He was found guilty on all charges including a new one: attempt to assassinate an Inner Council member. His sentence is the rest of his life in solitary confinement in a paranormal prison in an undisclosed location. Where upon him entering his cell, the lock will be melted shut and the key melted down. He will be given enough blood to survive and the blood will be dispensed during the sunniest part of the day."

Kirsa let out a huge sigh of relief. "Do we know where this location is going to be?"

"Dimitri recommended the one in the Caribbean, it was a unanimous decision to send him to that one," Ayden told her.

He poured wine in to each glass, handed her one then took his own. He raised his glass, "To starting our lives together and facing whatever comes."

Kirsa clinked her glass with his and took a sip enjoying the peaceful night.

"One quick question," Ayden asked kissing her hair.

"Hmmm."

"He's a leprechaun isn't he?"

Kirsa smiled at him, "Finally figured it out did you?"

"Is that why Al thought it was hysterical that I had no clue what he was?"

"You have to admit it is funny that a person born and bred in Ireland can't spot a leprechaun," Kirsa admitted.

"It's not like one sees one everyday besides with all the other fae creatures on the island it's a challenge keeping them all straight," Ayden defended himself with a pout.

Kirsa kissed his pout and laughed. "This is one of the reasons that I love you."

Ayden went to kiss when her phone went off; she looked and saw it was Al. "So much for decompressing," Ayden said when she answered the phone.

ACKNOWLEDGEMENTS AND THANK YOU'S

First, to my husband for putting up with me. The poor guy would walk into my home office to have a conversation with me and would finally leave. I would then stumble out of the office two hours later only to learn he had tried to have a conversation with me. He also kept the wine and tea flowing.

Second to Christianne Mariano at bunburistedit.com. She is pretty much family and has to deal with all my crazy editing questions at random hours. If you don't have an editor, look her up, she's awesome and a true friend.

Adulwulf Series:

1. Shattered Past

2. Shattered Dream

3. Shattered Ghost

Upcoming: A novella dealing with events after Ghost and some up close and personal time with Ayden.

Other Books by Meg Castro:

Fallen Descent